The Lazarus Child

THE LAZARUS CHILD

Robert Mawson

BANTAM PRESS

LONDON · NEW YORK · TORONTO · SYDNEY · AUCKLAND

TRANSWORLD PUBLISHERS LTD
61–63 Uxbridge Road, London W5 5SA

TRANSWORLD PUBLISHERS (AUSTRALIA) PTY LTD
15–25 Helles Avenue, Moorebank, NSW 2170

TRANSWORLD PUBLISHERS (NZ) LTD
3 William Pickering Drive, Albany, Auckland

Published 1998 by Bantam Press
a division of Transworld Publishers Ltd

A catalogue record for this book is available
from the British Library.
ISBN 0593 043782

Typeset in 12½/14½pt Ehrhardt by Falcon Oast Graphic Art
Printed in Great Britain
by Mackays of Chatham plc, Chatham, Kent.

With heartfelt thanks to my family, children and friends for their encouragement, forbearance and love. Also to those vital wider acquaintances for their ongoing support over the years. To agent Christopher Little for plain talking, to editor Francesca Liversidge for extraordinary patience and sensitivity, and to Dr Paul Barnett for running an eye over the numbers. Finally to the Danel family and everyone at La Lussière for their wonderful kindness and hospitality.

RM

Anjou, France

For Juliette

Chapter 1

AT TWELVE YEARS OLD, BEN HEYWOOD DID NOT THINK IT FAIR
that he should have to witness the death of his younger sister at
such close quarters. Yet at the instant of its happening he also
knew that having to witness it was part of the punishment.

They left the house at the usual time, the air crisp and
sparkling, the early morning sun bright on their hastily wiped
faces.

'Sunnyday,' said Frankie from the porch, looking up as
brilliant white petals of cherry blossom drifted from above. It
was the last thing she said to him. Ben said nothing, but glanced
at her as she gazed upwards, taking in the zigzag parting down
the middle of her pigtailed brown hair, the telltale trace of
green felt pen on her chin, the gap formed by the collar of her
too large shirt where her incorrectly knotted school tie nestled
incongruously off centre, way below the base of her throat.
Fleetingly it occurred to him that he could reach out and
straighten it for her. If he felt like it.

'Come on,' he said morosely. 'We've got to go.'

They walked along the pavement in silence. Ben allowed her
to remain at his side as far as the gate of Isabelle's house. As usual
Frankie's best friend was already waiting, perched on top of the
gate, repeatedly tossing a scruffy rag doll high into the air above
her, its limbs spreadeagled ridiculously as it spun skywards.

'Hi Ben,' Isabelle called mischievously, as though there was some great mysterious secret going on that only she and Frankie knew about. But he ignored her, walking on without pausing, head down, hands thrust deeply into pockets, school-bag slung over one shoulder, irritated beyond measure. How he detested having to walk with the girls to school these days, it was so humiliating. He heard them fall into chattering step behind him, fussing and giggling idiotically.

It happened at the corner of Newmarket Road, where Goldhanger Crescent joins, on the bend right outside Mr Gupta's newsagent's shop. Ben glanced across the road at the shop, then back at the girls, by now thirty yards behind. Unhurriedly they ambled after him, arms linked, heads bent together, deep in conspiracy. If he was quick, he could run across, check if the latest Road Ranger pack was in, pick up a packet of peppermints and be back with the girls before they realized it.

The road was wide and busy with early morning commuter traffic. Timing a gap in the cars he darted to the middle, waited as a taxi sped by in the other direction then sprinted the last few yards and into the shop.

He emerged less than a minute later onto the pavement. The girls were half way across, clinging together in frozen terror as startled drivers from both directions swerved violently to avoid them. Ben gaped, Frankie's eyes found his, wide with fear and uncertainty, her lips working, mouthing his name. A driver sounded his horn in shock, then another. Ben lost sight of the two small figures for an instant as a lorry thundered by, the driver's voice a receding shout: 'For Christ's sake!' A motor-cyclist moving swiftly up the centre between the two traffic streams saw the girls too late, swerved into the oncoming stream and smashed into the side of a van before careening sideways into the gutter at Ben's feet. Suddenly the air was filled with the sound of car horns, screeching brakes, squealing tyres and a succession of splintering crashes as cars piled into the back of one another. Ben scarcely noticed it. Above the noise and confusion he could hear Isabelle. She was screaming, panicked and disoriented, struggling to run back, blindly, across the far stream to the pavement. Frankie turned, grabbing her friend, bending almost double as she dragged at Isabelle's arm to stop her. But Isabelle was unstoppable, wild-eyed and thrashing like an injured animal, desperately intent on achieving the far pavement as her only chance of salvation. Ben saw Frankie pulled one faltering step, then another, in slow motion like a tug-of-war. There was the blood-chilling sound of six heavy locked-up wheels sliding uncontrollably across the tarmac, a frantic drawn-out blast from the bus driver's horn. Then, with a sickening, muffled thud, the bus struck the girls.

They were in the air. A confusion of arms and legs, hair, clothes, school-bags, flying across the clean blue sky, limp and flapping and spreadeagled. Like tossed rag dolls.

Jack Heywood awoke with a start. He lay for a moment, blearily striving to force his mind into focus through a fog of drink and sleeplessness. Something important . . . He checked his watch, then remembered with a curse, and jerked upright. Throwing back the travel rug, he gasped, piercing pain shooting through his neck and upper back. He stiffened, straightening slowly from the couch, wincing as he rubbed his hand against the base of his neck.

It was ten to nine. Ten minutes. They'd be here in ten minutes! Precious seconds elapsed as he stared dumbfounded at his watch: the damn alarm must have failed. Or maybe he'd failed to set it. He licked his lips and looked around him. His head hurt, his mouth was dry, throat like sandpaper. Unkempt hair escaped his fingers as he brushed it back, gazing round the room in mounting horror. The executive lounge looked more like a student's apartment after an end-of-term party: overflowing ashtrays, half-empty takeaway containers, dirty plates and coffee mugs, empty bottles.

And the smell. Suddenly he was galvanized into action. Moving swiftly around the room he began clearing the wreckage, carrying all into the little kitchenette where he threw it into rubbish bags, tipped it into the sink or hid it in cupboards. At the same time he poured fresh water and a coffee pack into the machine and switched it on. Sniffing distastefully he returned to the lounge, pulled up the blinds and threw open the windows, gulping at the crisp spring air. Bright sunlight flooded in, the sound of larksong and the idle burbling of a Lycoming as one of the flying-club Cessnas warmed up. Away to the west, spectral spires were barely visible, the distant Cambridge skyline materializing through the early-morning mist. Glancing down, he took in the company's three polished silver and green executive turboprops neatly parked on the tarmac below. Then he turned once more for the room.

He stripped his bedding from the settee, plumped up the cushions and straightened the aviation magazines on the coffee table. Clearing the conference table and reorganizing the chairs he glanced up at the wall clock. Any minute! Where the hell was Bill? And Carol, for that matter. What the hell use is an executive air-charter business without a receptionist? He had told them nine. Hadn't he?

Five minutes later he emerged from the tiny bathroom clean-shaven, hair brushed and wearing a fresh white shirt under his slightly rumpled navy blue suit jacket. He checked the straightness of his tie nervously and looked around the now restored executive lounge with something approaching a flicker of pride. Its leather-upholstered furniture, its glass and chrome tables and chairs, its metal-framed photographs of liveried aircraft gliding gracefully across azure skyscapes. Carefully chosen to suggest respectability, reliability, professionalism. But the leather was beginning to wear thin, the chrome to tarnish, the brightly coloured photos fading like dreams.

There was a buzz at the door. They were here. He took a deep breath, subconsciously lifting his chin and straightening his shoulders as he went across the room. As he skirted Carol's desk the phone rang.

Outside the newsagent's, a quiet had descended. All traffic had stopped in both directions, dazed drivers were getting out of cars, passers-by were gathering at the kerbside. Mr Gupta emerged from his shop. 'What happened?' he asked. 'Is anyone hurt?' Beside him a dark-haired schoolboy stood rigid and motionless, an unopened packet of peppermints clutched in one fist.

'Call an ambulance quick!' somebody shouted from across the road. Mr Gupta hurried back into his shop. A knot of onlookers was gathering around two small, unmoving forms lying on the pavement. On the near side a leather-clad motor-cyclist groaned, struggling feebly to free himself from the tangled wreckage of his machine. A dazed van driver bent slowly to help him. 'Easy now mate. Easy does it.' Across the road a woman's voice rose from the growing crowd, like a lamentation, a wail of protest. 'Mary Mother of Jesus, they're just little girls! Little girls – Mary Mother of Jesus.'

'Doctor. Is there a doctor? Anywhere?' An elderly man with a small dog straightened up and looked around. 'Is there a doctor here?'

Suddenly there was the sound of heavy boots running hard along the pavement towards the crowd. Moments later a beat policeman arrived. 'How many hurt?' he said breathlessly.

'These two,' said the man with the dog. 'And a motorcyclist on the other side.'

'Right,' said the policeman, elbowing his way into the throng. He dropped to a crouch beside the body of a young girl dressed in school uniform. She was face down, her pigtailed hair awry and sticky with blood. 'Right,' he murmured again to himself, through gritted teeth. Cocking his head to the VHF radio on his shoulder, he reached out to feel the girl's neck.

'I believe she's dead,' said the man with the dog.

*

'How are the children taking it?'

Alison sighed, picking up an uneaten corner of toast from the breakfast table. 'Okay. I think,' she said doubtfully, tucking the telephone receiver under her chin as she munched. The circular table had been laid for three by one of the children. Ben, she suspected. But instead of spreading the three places evenly around the circle, he had deliberately left a fourth place bare. Jack's place. He'd even put a chair there, testament enough to his views on the matter. 'Well, actually I don't know. Frankie seems fine, doesn't really talk about it – you know Frankie. But Ben, well, I can tell he's not happy. He's very, well quiet. Withdrawn.'

'Oh darling, are you quite sure you're doing the right thing? Ben adores Jack, they both do.'

'Mum, he went to bed with the damn secretary!'

'Yes, but apart from that. I mean, have you asked yourself why?'

'Apart fr– Mother, I'd have thought that it was enough that he did it, don't you?'

There was silence on the line. 'Well, I suppose you know best,' her mother said eventually, although Alison knew from her tone that she clearly thought nothing of the sort. 'Where is he staying, living?'

'I don't know. Bill's, the damn secretary's – park bench for all I care. It's not my problem.' It *was* her problem. She looked up from the table. There was a meeting. He'd told her about it – today, was it? Shit or bust, he'd said. She tried to remember, staring through the kitchen window at the cherry tree outside, the blossom falling silently like snow. Recently every meeting had been shit or bust. 'I think he's been sleeping at the office,' she said quietly.

'What will you do?'

'Move, I suppose. Sell this place, get out of Cambridge, back to London, get the children into schools somewhere and put this whole sorry mess behind us as fast as possible.' It sounded simple enough when she said it like that. But every time she considered the prospect her head filled with worries and anxieties, so many unknowns, so many questions, so many doubts. God damn you, Jack Heywood.

'What if he hadn't, done it? You know, slept with the secretary.'

'Mum, that's like saying "Apart from that, Mrs Kennedy, how did you enjoy your drive around Dallas?". It happened. He did it. Now he must deal with the consequences.'

'Yes, but what if he hadn't?' she persisted.

Alison sighed again. 'It probably wouldn't make any difference.' She picked up a green felt-tip pen from the table, snapping the cap back on with her thumb. 'It's been going wrong for ages, years really, ever since we moved to Cambridge. The business, it's all to do with the bloody business.'

'Couldn't you talk to him about it? You know, explain your feelings?'

'He's never here. I'd have to make an appointment,' she snorted ruefully. 'Probably with the damn secretary.'

'What about counselling? Couldn't you see someone, make some enquiries?'

'Mum, for God's sake what about him? I'm the wronged party, he should be making the effort, but he doesn't do anything, not a–' The doorbell rang. Once, then immediately again. 'Hang on, Mum, somebody's at the door.'

There were two of them. A male and a female. Both uniformed. She remembered thinking how short the female was beside the man. And how young and petite the face, the roundness of the eyes beneath that ludicrous little hat. The black-and-white-checked neck scarf tied in a neat bow on the starched white shirt. The frumpy black uniform skirt, the heavy black tights, the solid flat-heeled shoes.

'Mrs Heywood? Mrs Alison Heywood?'

*

The young policeman straightened up from the body of the girl and exhaled slowly. She was gone, there was no doubt about it. He was no doctor but he had seen dead bodies before and he had been through the basic training like everyone else on the Force. Her eyes were open, fixed and staring, he could find no evidence of a pulse, she wasn't breathing and, well, just from the look of her, with her head twisted up and sideways at that unusual angle, the ugly dark purple bruise on her forehead, the congealed trickle of blood coming from one ear. He suspected her neck was broken.

He sat back on his heels, the pavement hard and cold beneath his knees. Around him the crowd looked on. It was awful, she could only have been six or seven. He picked up an old rag doll lying beside her and placed it on her chest. As he did so he saw that his hand was shaking, the child's face blurring as his eyes filled. Two little girls, for God's sake, just wiped out like that. Why? A moment later he heard the wail of a distant siren. At last, he thought, thank God.

He stood up quickly, brushed the dirt from his trousers, hastily wiping a sleeve across his nose. He started to move through the crowd, his boots crunching on shards of smashed headlight. This he could do, this was what he should be doing, getting things organized as best he could for the emergency services. As he gesticulated to drivers to clear a path he glanced across to the far side of the road. A shopkeeper had his arm around a man who was sitting on the pavement openly weeping. The bus driver, the policeman concluded. He made a mental note: there'd be a lot of statement-taking later. A few yards further along, a small group of onlookers had extricated the motorcyclist from the wreckage of his bike and propped him into a half-sitting, half-lying position against the shop wall. One of them was holding a bloodstained handkerchief to the motorcyclist's head.

Between them the policeman caught sight of a boy. He appeared to be unaccompanied, standing quite alone, completely still and holding something in his hand. His face was expressionless. Probably saw it happen, thought the policeman. Terrible shock for a young boy to have to witness something like this. He thought about going over to speak to him but a renewed burst from the approaching siren stopped him and he turned back into the road, waving and shouting to clear a path as the ambulance, blue lights flashing, picked its way slowly through the lines of unmoving traffic. A minute later it pulled up in front of him and two men jumped out.

'What have we got?' said the first. Both were wearing fluorescent silver and yellow jackets with the word 'paramedic' emblazoned in blue across the back. The second man immediately set off towards where the girls were lying.

'Two girls hit by a bus,' said the policeman, nodding towards them. 'Motorcyclist over there crashed avoiding them. He's conscious. A few cuts and bruises suffered by other drivers in shunts behind.'

'Right then. First we'll need to clear this lot so we can get out quickly. Can we leave that to you? There's two more units on the way from Addenbrooke's – they'll take care of the cuts and bruises. Meantime we'll have a look at these three.' He lifted his chin. 'Stan?' he called. The second paramedic stood up and shook his head with a grimace. 'Jesus,' murmured the first.

The older man closed the file and removed his spectacles. Conjuring a handkerchief he began to polish the lenses, his face thoughtful. The room was silent; outside they could hear the drone of a Cessna buzzing round the circuit, while on the far side of the field a Hercules was running up an engine. Jack forced himself to relax, lowered his gaze to the white knuckles of his tightly interlaced fingers on the glass tabletop and waited.

'Tell me, Jack, is Bill Knight coming?' the second man enquired politely. He was younger than his superior, lean, balding, always smiled when he spoke, rested a hand on your back at the door and never failed to ask after your loved ones. But behind the genial façade and the guileless blue eyes, Jack knew, lay a razor sharp mind and a brutal capacity for ruthlessness.

'Yes, yes he is. He called just before you arrived. He's been held up in traffic, accident or something, he'll be here as soon as he can.'

'Well I think we'll get on,' said the first man, reopening the file. 'If that's all right with you. Let me just say that you seem to have gone to a lot of trouble producing your new business plan, Jack, very thorough, very professional.' Jack nodded, smiling weakly. 'Now, let me see if we've got this straight. We're looking at a complete rescheduling of Heywood-Knight's existing debts plus an immediate injection of sixty thousand, which is basically to be financed out of a remortgage package on the three aircraft sitting outside. Is that correct?' Jack nodded again. That was it, in a nutshell. He surreptitiously tugged the side of his collar away from his neck, cursing inwardly. Where the hell was his so-called business partner? Bill was the bloody accountant for God's sake. 'And the extra cash to pay for this refinancing comes from the new business derived in part from our package. Just tell us again about that, Jack, in your own words, if you would be so kind.'

He drew a deep breath. 'We've got tenders in on two big air parcel-handling contracts already, a Cambridge–Amsterdam–Glasgow and a Heathrow–Madrid, both nightly,' he said, not looking them in the eye. The Heathrow–Madrid tender had been rejected two days ago. 'There are a number of other contracts coming up for renewal during the summer that we will be bidding for. In addition, we're looking into the possibility of setting up a daily Cambridge–Dublin scheduled passenger service. Finally we will be using part of the sixty thousand on an advertising and marketing campaign to promote the air-taxi side of the business.'

'What, heaven forbid Jack, but what if you don't get these two contracts? How would you meet the repayments over the short term?'

'Well, as I say, there are several other tenders coming up, in the er, pipeline, and what with the extra marketing on the air-taxi side, I – we are confident that the repayments can be met. As you can see from the projections in the business plan, at the bottom there . . .' He trailed off.

The room fell quiet once more. Eventually the second man sat back, the open file falling to the table in front of him. 'It's just . . .' he began slowly, wincing as though in excruciating pain, '. . . ever so slightly thin, though, wouldn't you say? Hmm Jack?'

'Thin?'

'Jack, whatever happened about that offer?' the older man interrupted. 'The takeover offer from that other air-charter company on the airfield – Myriad, is it? Did you ever have a serious look at that?'

Suddenly Jack felt the bile rising. He pushed back his chair, palms flat on the tabletop. 'Now look here,' he sputtered, 'I've spent six years building up this business. It has cost me dear, very dear, and if you think I'm simply going to roll over and give up or, worse still, sell out to those sharks at Myriad–'

There was a knock at the door. Carol's face appeared, worried, apologetic. 'Jack, excuse me, I'm so sorry but there's a message, on the answering machine. It– You'd better come right away.'

The ambulance braked hard, heeling as it sped into the bend, siren blaring. Instinctively the paramedic in the back braced himself on a hand grab before continuing as the vehicle straightened.

He worked quickly. Tearing open a fresh pack, he withdrew a nine-inch flexible plastic tube and, gently tilting the second girl's head back, eased it into her throat and the entrance to her trachea. Next, he clipped tubing onto the mouthpiece and opened the gas regulator valve. A black rubber ambubag connected to the tubing inflated with oxygen. 'Airway straight, open and unrestricted, air on,' he murmured to himself like a mantra, re-fastening the Velcro on the neck brace at the child's throat. 'Maintaining CPR.' Moving his hands swiftly back to her chest, he placed one palm above her sternum, the other resting on top of the first. Then with a series of brisk thrusts, he jerked the heels of both palms hard into her chest. 'One, two, three, four, five,' he hissed through clenched teeth with each push.

Without pausing he squeezed the bag once then immediately ran the cycle again. Five quick jerks to the heart, a steady squeeze of oxygen to the lungs, pause and check for life signs. 'Oh now come on sweetheart!' he scolded breathlessly, the stethoscope head moving swiftly over the pale skin of her chest. A bead of perspiration trickled down his cheek. 'Try a little harder please. I know you can do better than this.'

Stopping only to fling off his heavy jacket, he swivelled through a crouched hundred and eighty degrees to face the inert form of the other girl strapped onto the opposite stretcher. 'Right then, little Miss Blue Eyes, and what about you?' Immediately he repeated the resuscitation cycle. There would be bruised, possibly cracked ribs after much more of this, he knew, as he thrust vigorously downwards onto her chest. But this was no time for half-measures, and the clock was ticking.

'About five minutes to go,' called the other paramedic from the driver's seat. 'How are we doing?'

'Christ knows.' He straightened for a moment. 'Never saw a pair play harder to get.' He wiped perspiration from his brow with his arm. 'I'd say one's a no-no, the other a don't-know.' He looked down at them, their blank faces, the stained white blouses, striped uniform ties, little grey skirts, white socks, one missing shoe.

'But I'm buggered if I'm done with them yet,' he swallowed, leaning forward once more.

Alison leapt out of the car and sprinted through the hospital main entrance. 'Accident!' she said loudly, casting around frantically. 'Where's Accident and Emergency?'

'Wrong entrance, Miss,' said an orderly, pushing a wheel-chair. 'You'll have to drive right round the other side, follow the signs to the A and E car park.'

'Jesus, isn't there any other way?'

The orderly nodded at the floor. 'Just follow the red stripe,' he intoned. 'That'll get you there, eventually.'

Four minutes and three wrong turnings later, she was running breathlessly down an endless corridor when it opened suddenly into a large entrance lobby that looked exactly like the first. She was back where she'd started. 'For God's sake!' she cursed, half gasp, half sob. She stared around. On the far side of the lobby there were people, some sitting, some walking about. Some looked like doctors; others, with bandaged heads or arms in slings, were clearly patients. Then she saw the glass-fronted counter and the sign above it: Accident and Emergency Reception.

As she hurried across towards the counter, automatic entrance doors beside her swung open and a fluorescent-jacketed paramedic's back appeared followed by a stretcher. Beyond him she could see that an ambulance had backed right up to the entrance, its doors gaping wide. She froze. Something leaden turned over in her stomach. 'Frankie,' she whispered.

'Excuse me, madam,' said the paramedic brusquely, as he backed towards her. A second stretcher was being unloaded from the rear of the ambulance. 'Madam, please, the through-way must be kept clear at all times!'

Alison remained unmoving, heart pounding in her throat, eyes locked on the second stretcher as it was manoeuvred through the doors. Two medical staff dressed in short-sleeved green coveralls appeared beside the first paramedic. 'Two on board,' he reported, as they bent over the stretcher. 'Road-traffic accident, no vital signs at scene, been carrying out standard resusc since.'

'Uh-huh. How long?' asked one of the physicians, as the other moved quickly towards the second stretcher. Alison found herself following. Slowly, as though in a trance.

'Estimated forty minutes,' replied the paramedic.

It was Frankie. The second stretcher. Her face was ashen, deathly pale. But unmarked, her expression calm, almost serene. She looked as though she were sleeping peacefully. Like she did as a baby. With that plug in her mouth like her old dummy, her head turned slightly to one side, her eyes closed and the blanket tucked up to her chin. Just exactly as she had looked as a sleeping baby.

'Darling,' Alison murmured, watching from a great distance as they fussed around her. 'My darling, darling baby girl.'

'Suspect both DOA,' said the second doctor, straightening up, 'but get them into the emergency room and we'll have a look. Anyone know if the families have arrived yet?'

Within an hour the tarmac had been swept clean, the twisted wreckage of the motorcycle removed and the damaged vehicles towed away. The mid-morning traffic sailed swiftly by once more as if nothing had happened; the only evidence remaining was a set of telltale twelve-foot heavy black skidmarks from the bus and a small dark brown stain on the far pavement. Shoppers walked across it without a second thought.

Mr Gupta put down the telephone again. What a morning. His mother this time. It seemed all his friends and relatives had heard about the accident and wanted to know every detail. A minute later he accepted money from a lady buying sweets for a child in a pushchair, then moved swiftly round the counter to hold the door open for her. As she thanked him with a smile he noticed the boy outside. The boy with the dark hair who had been there during all the fuss.

'Hello there,' he said, stepping onto the pavement. 'You still here?' The boy said nothing, just stood there, his head slightly lowered, his hands at his sides. Mr Gupta looked around at the passing traffic. 'It was a terrible terrible thing and there's no doubt,' he said, shaking his head. 'And absolutely not nice to see I'm sure.' He looked down at the boy once more. 'But you know, sometimes things like this just happen. It's – it's a part of life, although that may sound silly to say that a tragedy like this is part of life but it is.' Still the boy said nothing. 'And nobody's really to blame you see. That's the whole point. These things just happen.'

He fell silent, worrying about the boy. Who was he? It was strange that he didn't recognize him. Shouldn't he be at school? Or with his family somewhere, or something? 'I'll tell you what,' he said, patting the boy's shoulder, 'why don't you come inside and have a Coke and we'll telephone somebody, eh?'

Ben turned from him and walked quickly away. As he went Mr Gupta saw something fall from his hand. It was a partially opened packet of peppermints, and as he watched the retreating boy's back, it rolled slowly down the pavement and into the gutter.

C h a p t e r 2

ALISON THREW THE DOOR OPEN RATHER WIDER THAN SHE intended. It slipped out of her grasp and hit the door-stop with a bang. 'Whoops!' she sang out cheerfully, crossing the room without a pause. 'Well good morning my darling. Phew, is it stuffy in here or what?' She dropped a heavy shoulder-bag onto a chair, swept aside the curtains on the single window, lifted the catches and pushed it open as far as it would go. 'That's better!' she continued briskly, sucking down lungfuls of air like an over-enthusiastic PE teacher. 'And may I say that it is indeed a good morning, a truly "sunnyday", you could say.'

She stood at the window, gathering herself. Brilliant white puffs of cumulus clouds drifted across the blue like sailing ships on an ocean. The scent of newly cut grass, damp with dew, rose with the smells of shops, cars and streets five storeys below. All around her were the sounds of the city as people flowed along its arteries, hurrying to start their day: the clink of a nearby milk float above the background murmur of traffic, further off the chime of a college clock puncturing the per-sistent clamour of a shop alarm, in the distance the rumble of jetprops as a military transport climbed steeply out from the airport.

Flexing her arms on the window-sill like a boxer in the ring, she allowed herself a few seconds more to focus her thoughts, then took a final deep breath, set her face in a bright smile and turned back into the room. 'Now then,' she began, rubbing her hands, 'we have got one busy morning ahead of us. First it's a wash and brush-up, then the dreaded physio. There's a stack of reading material for us to go through, then Dr Stanhope's coming and, oh yes, look, all your classmates have sent another card. Isn't that sweet of them? We'll have to write back straight away . . .'

As she dropped into a bedside chair, her non-stop commentary never faltering, Alison plucked a notebook from her bag, automatically scanning the readouts on the tabletop monitor beside it. Heart-rate sixty-eight, temperature thirty-six, blood pressure a hundred over seventy, respiration eighteen. No change, she knew them all by rote. She jotted them down and only then, in accordance with her strict routine, did she allow herself to look at her daughter.

Frankie lay motionless on the bed. Her eyes were not quite fully closed, thin slits of filmy grey visible between the long brown lashes. The corners of her mouth were pulled slightly downward in a vague grimace of distaste, a shiny snailtrack of dried saliva trailing from one corner. At her throat, bandaging covered the entrance point of the tracheotomy tube through which air was pumped to her lungs from the ventilator beneath the bed. Intravenous drips entering below her collarbone and in one arm fed fluids, nutrients and medication directly into her bloodstream; beneath the bedcovers catheters drained waste to disposable bags from her bladder. Electrodes measured her heart-rate and blood pressure, a rectal probe the temperature of her body.

'Oh and by the way, I bought the new CD by that all-girl pop group you're always going on about – what are they called, Storker? Well I really don't know Frankie, is that supposed to be rude or what? Oh yes, here it is, Stonker, that's better, I suppose. We'll have a listen later, shall we?' A nurse came into the room, frowned at the open window, smiled thinly at Alison and picked up the clipboard hanging at the end of the bed. 'Good morning Mrs Heywood, good morning Frances,' she chanted, shuffling past Alison's chair towards the monitors with exaggerated difficulty.

'Frankie,' corrected Alison. 'Good morning Emily. What time is the consultant coming?'

'Oh my goodness who knows? Could be any time, I should think,' replied the nurse unhelpfully. She scribbled on the sheet, returning the clipboard to the end of the bed. 'You know these consultants, law unto themselves eh? See you later.'

In the fourteen weeks since the accident, Frankie had shown no sign of regaining even partial consciousness. She occasionally moved, a sudden twitch of the head or shrug of the shoulder. Sometimes her eyes could be seen roving from side to side beneath the pale veined skin of her eyelids, and quite often the muscles of her face altered, so that her nose wrinkled or her mouth fell into a lopsided grin. But there was no pattern, no sense that she made the movements herself. 'Spontaneous and involuntary,' the doctors called them. Alison had reluctantly conceded they were probably right.

Physically Frankie had been fortunate to escape serious injury. X-rays at the time of the accident revealed a cracked pelvis and fractured left femur, both now almost completely healed. There were some deep lacerations down her left thigh, which had become infected but which eventually responded to antibiotics. It seemed she had been astonishingly lucky. But the Heywoods' initial relief that Frankie had evidently not suffered multiple life-threatening injuries had been quickly muted. Scans showed she had sustained a big blow to the back of the head, the brain was badly bruised, the first twenty-four hours would be critical, and thereafter the prognosis for a full re-covery was very guarded.

For forty-eight hours Jack and Alison had barely left Frankie's bedside in the intensive care unit. They exchanged few words: there was little to say. 'This is all my fault,' Jack murmured at one point.

Alison looked up at him across the bed, her eyes softening. 'You mustn't think like that.'

During that period, Frankie's brain swelled alarmingly, driving up her temperature and suppressing vital life functions. On two occasions her heart stalled into bradycardia, triggering the monitor alarms and bringing resuscitation teams at the sprint. Throughout, she remained unconscious and unmoving except for a single moment late during the first night when she raised her head suddenly.

Startled from an exhausted reverie, Alison had jerked forward. 'Frankie?' she whispered, squeezing her hand.

Cheeks flushed, Frankie swallowed, her eyes staring sightlessly ahead, her neck swaying with effort.

'Frankie darling, Mummy's here. Everything's going to be all right.' Alison looked around anxiously, but before she could do anything Frankie's head fell back onto the bed.

Isabelle was dead, her neck snapped by the impact of the bus. The Heywoods spent a nightmare hour and a half waiting with her parents in an airless little room off the Accident and Emergency waiting area, while doctors fought to save their daughters. All feared the worst, none dared voice it. They spoke little, punctuating long silences with the illogical expressions of incredulity of the profoundly shocked.

'I don't understand it, she was absolutely fine at breakfast.'

'She's got a birthday party to go to at five. What should we do?'

'I haven't brought any of her night things.'

When the news finally came, broken cruelly and inexplicably to all four of them at the same time, as though they were all part of the same family, an awkward embrace was all any of them could manage before they were separated and led along different corridors towards the living and dead bodies of their children.

One overcast afternoon about a week later Jack and Alison stood among rows of gravestones in a breezy churchyard and watched in silence as the half-sized coffin was lowered into the ground. Neither of them could entirely banish the unsolicited sense of guilty relief that it was not their daughter they were burying. Glancing up as he carefully placed the spring-flower wreath, Jack's eyes met the heartbroken and uncomprehending gaze of Isabelle's mother, sensing her unasked questions with a sudden chill. They did not stay long after the funeral, a barely perceptible tinge of unspoken recrimination was pervading the grief.

Alison looked up as the door opened. Jack appeared. 'Have they come yet?' She shook her head. He picked up the only other chair and sat down across the bed from his wife.

'Ben all right?' she asked.

'Fine. Just dropped him off. Your mother's picking him up later.'

'Good, thanks.' She waited, looking at him expectantly, eyebrows raised.

'Right, yes, um well now,' he stuttered, clearing his throat. 'Hi there, Frankie, it's very good to see you. Sorry I'm late, got hung up at the office.' He hesitated. 'As usual, yes I know. Um, Bill sends his love. And Carol too–' He stopped at the gaffe. Alison's head was down. He exhaled slowly as his gaze circled the walls – the cheerful lurid glare of the pop posters, the soft pastels of the framed watercolour from Frankie's bedroom, the busy coloured patchwork of well-wishers' cards. Finally his eyes returned to his daughter's face, pale and lifeless. 'Sorry,' he said eventually.

'Is that it?'

'Pardon?'

'Sorry I'm late and Bill sends his love. Is that it?' She was scowling at him, nodding towards Frankie.

He sighed. 'Oh er, yes Frankie, where was I?' he went on, speaking loudly and slowly as though to a dim-witted relative.

'By the way, had a meeting yesterday in Liverpool with an air-freight operator who is possibly interested in some kind of partnership tie-up or joint-venture thing, provided he can stump up the necessary, er, anyway that's by the way . . .'

Alison pushed back her chair. 'Oh for heaven's sake,' she breathed, walking to the window.

'Look, I'm just not very good at it, this talking-to-her thing, okay?'

'Well you seemed to manage it all right before the accident, didn't you?' she said, her back to him. 'What's the difference?'

'The diff– Christ, all the difference in the world. It's just, very hard for me that's all.'

She turned from the window. 'I know. Sorry. It's hard for all of us.' She nodded towards Frankie. 'I expect it isn't much fun for her either.'

'Alison,' he went on quietly, 'you know how much I want to believe, desperately want to hang on to the slightest hope that there's something, a chance, the faintest glimmer.' He looked at his daughter. 'But it has been more than three months and there's nothing, absolutely nothing at all. Not one single sign that she can hear, can feel, is in any way aware of anything. Don't you see that?'

'No I don't. I won't. She's still in there and she's going to come out. And I don't think you should bother coming here any more if that's how you feel.'

It was Jack who found Ben on the day of the accident. Hours later, in the middle of the afternoon. At first, they had been so wrapped up with Frankie and the crisis at the hospital that it simply didn't occur to them that he wasn't at school. But then, around noon, while Frankie was being wheeled away for X-rays, Jack slipped off to the telephone and discovered that he had never arrived. The head teacher, who had been notified of the accident by the police, had assumed that Ben was with them.

Jack set off immediately. He drove home first, calling Ben's name as he let himself in through the kitchen door. Nothing. He scribbled a note and left it amid the abandoned wreckage of the breakfast table then ran back to the car. He tried the park and the playground, places nearby that Ben was familiar with and liked to go. He drove on to the school where the head teacher immediately interrupted Ben's class to ask if anyone had seen him at all that day. Jack telephoned the police from the head teacher's office before setting off once more. He tried the shops, leaping out to run the length of the arcade, stopping breathlessly to cup his hands at windows – the toy shop, the modelling shop, the sweet shop, the supermarket.

Then he drove to the scene of the accident. The owner of the newsagent's confirmed the exact spot, pointed out the skid-marks, the little shards of headlight still left after the sweep-up, even the bloodstained pavement. And with a stomach-turning lurch Jack learnt that, yes, there certainly had been a young, dark-haired boy matching Ben's description there, he had watched the whole thing, stayed there while the ambulance took the little girls away, until long after everyone had gone in fact.

Finally Jack drove home again to check with the police and ring the hospital. Half-way through dialling, he replaced the receiver and doubled up the stairs.

He was in his room, lying on the bed. Facing the wall. Curled into a ball.

In the first few days afterwards, Ben remained quiet yet somehow composed. He didn't talk about the accident at all and Alison and Jack were advised not to ask him. He ate food that was put before him, watched television, looked at his books and magazines, and went to bed at the normal time, asking only that the light be left on. He slept deeply, and frequently took extra naps throughout the day. He never once asked about Frankie, although Alison reassured him that she was going to be fine, nor did he mention Isabelle, whom he was not told about. He said he did not want to see anyone apart from Jack, Alison and Grandma, nor did he want to go out of the house. At all.

And his hair turned white.

It happened over a period of days, about a fortnight after the accident. At about the same time as the first visit by the child psychologist, Heather Pritchard. She said that up until that time Ben had probably completely blocked the accident from his conscious and subconscious mind. It didn't exist, it didn't trouble him, even when he was asleep. It was a defence mechanism, she said, very effective, very valuable. The problem was that it could only ever be a temporary block. The effort of sustaining it was exhausting him and severely affecting his ability to function at other levels. Sooner or later, she cautioned, he would have to begin to allow aspects of the trauma to seep back into his awareness and then be taught how to manage this.

Ben was fearful of the sessions with the psychologist, hiding in his room or locking himself in the bathroom as the hour of a visit approached. But Heather was deft and patient, never pressing him, always relaxed and encouraging. In early sessions they would sit in the kitchen or living room, alone or with Alison and his grandmother, he could choose. She would try to draw him out gently on any subject at all – school, sport, computers, space travel, whatever he seemed interested in. Sometimes he was co-operative and talked a little, sometimes he remained monosyllabic or silent, slipping away quickly to his room again as soon as the session ended.

One afternoon, seven weeks after the accident, he told Heather about a holiday the family had taken together in France two summers previously. He spoke more volubly than on any previous occasion, recalling more details of the house, the village, the food, the people than Alison would have believed possible. Towards the end, and for the first time, he mentioned Frankie by name. She had been stung on the leg by a jellyfish and got a huge rash.

Heather nodded. 'Frankie had an accident. Did you know?' she said after a while, very softly.

'She's dead,' replied Ben immediately, staring at his hands.

'No, she isn't. She's in hospital. She had a bad bump on the head but she's okay. You could go and see her if you like.'

'She's dead!' he shouted suddenly, his eyes filling with tears. 'I know she is. They both are!'

That night and every night thereafter he woke up screaming.

The consultant and his entourage finally arrived at around noon. Jack was staring out of the window while Alison transcribed notes from a medical journal into an A4 folder. The rhythmic tinny twittering of pop music came from a pair of headphones covering Frankie's ears.

'Incredible!' exclaimed Alison, picking up the journal. 'Listen to this. There was this patient in Stockholm who lost nearly eighty per cent of his brain tissue in an accident yet he could hold a perfectly normal conversation with his doctors.'

'Hmm?' Jack looked round, glancing at his watch. 'Yes it is. Doesn't seem possible, does it?'

'Apparently it's all to do with the remaining, undamaged parts of the brain training themselves to carry out functions that the damaged bits used to do. It really is an astonishing organ. Listen to this.'

Jack looked across at her. She was wearing grubby old jeans and scuffed trainers, the same blouse she'd had on when he'd last visited three days ago, and a ghastly old knitted cardigan that looked like a leftover from the sixties. Her face was tired and pallid, her once meticulously groomed hair dragged back harshly into an elastic band. In the space of just a few weeks she had changed beyond recognition. She actually looked scruffy. She had never been scruffy, never. In all the years he'd known her. Casual yes, informal yes, relaxed certainly, but never, ever scruffy.

He watched her, hunched forward on her chair, biting hard

into a thumbnail, rocking back and forth as she pored over the journal on her knee. The woman he had married had been trim, neat, conscious of her own attractiveness, fastidious about her appearance. Not vain or anything, just particular, careful. He liked that. When they had met, she was an air hostess, always managed to look good, even when she had just finished a twelve-hour stint and was exhausted, grimy and jet-lagged. They first spoke on a Luton to Athens holiday charter. He was a co–pilot, newly converted on to 737s, she brought the flight-deck refreshments and leant over him to refill his coffee cup. She had smiling, mischievous brown eyes and shiny brown shoulder-length hair, and she smelt wonderful.

'Ever done the Acropolis?' he'd ventured with a shy grin.

'Never on the first date.' She'd winked, backing out of the flight deck. The captain looked out of the window, sniggering into his coffee.

Now she looked for all the world like a fagged-out student fallen on hard times. But then, that's exactly what she was, Jack mused. She carried her worldly goods around in a canvas shoulder–bag overloaded with medical textbooks and clinical study papers, neurological theses, magazine articles, anything she could lay her hands on that might have any possible bearing on Frankie and her condition. And why? He didn't understand why. Of course it was natural to be concerned. Of course they wanted the best possible care for Frankie. Of course they wanted to do the right thing for her. But what was the point of this obsessive scrabbling for knowledge? What good would it do? They weren't the doctors.

Discreetly he studied her as she rubbed exhaustion from one eye before continuing with her note-taking. She was here every day, all day if she could manage it. She neglected herself, she never ate properly, just snatching sandwiches and vending-machine snacks when the need arose. She neglected the house – it had looked like a complete tip the last time she'd let him through the door. He worried that she might be neglecting Ben too: he seemed to be spending more and more time being looked after by her mother.

And she neglected *them*. They both did. Every day the gulf between them widening a little more. If only they could talk, if only he could try to explain his feelings, and she hers. Everything.

'Ali,' he began gently. There was a tap on the door.

There were three of them. With Jack and Alison and then a ward sister, who appeared quietly at the last minute, the room was suddenly crowded. Jack retreated to the far wall to observe from behind. He was joined by the ward sister and a slight, pale young man in corduroys and a sports jacket who introduced himself as Colin Winstanley. 'P-p-postgraduate research,' he stammered nervously, by way of explanation, as he shook Jack's hand. 'Here to assist P-P-Professor Keach, t-t-take notes and generally g-get in the way.'

'Ah,' replied Jack, more mystified than ever.

One face he did recognize was Trevor Stanhope's, the consultant in charge of Frankie, a small balding man of fifty with a penchant for loud ties, unnerving good humour and a tendency towards condescension. He began proceedings by introducing Keach to everyone, including Frankie.

'He's a neurology professor, Frankie, come up all the way from London especially to see you. How's that eh?'

Alison, who had not budged from her bedside position, accepted Keach's proffered hand with a polite smile, noting at the same time that he did not say hello to Frankie.

It was a check-up, a progress report, a routine service. Stanhope began by cheerfully confirming that the latest set of scans continued to show the brain swelling to be completely reduced, which was very good, that there were still substantial areas of shadow indicating possible damage where blood had haemorrhaged into the brain cavity, which was less good, and that the last encephalogram set showed no change at all in Frankie's brainwave pattern, which was not really very good at all.

Jack shifted uncomfortably at the wall while they ran all the usual tests. At one point Keach, in a useless attempt to move Alison, suggested that perhaps it was a little crowded. Alison ignored him. Jack, who would have gratefully left the room, almost volunteered. But since nobody else did, he remained silent, his hands fisted behind his back.

Tight-lipped, he watched them prise open Frankie's eyelids and shine lights into her eyes, peer with otoscopes into her ears, scrape skin cells from deep inside her throat. Then they removed the bedcovers and pulled up her nightgown, exposing the awful pale thinness of her body, the wasting of her limbs, the concavity of her stomach. They drummed on her chest, pressed in her stomach, flexed her arms and elbows and turned her to examine her back. They fiddled with her catheters, palpated her internal organs and examined her genitals. They lifted one arm and dropped it again, they pricked her fingertips with a pin, they bent her leg up and hit the knee with a little rubber hammer and they scratched the soles of her feet with a wooden spatula. He'd seen it all before and it never failed to upset him. She was like a lump of meat to them, a specimen, an interesting conundrum. Not a person, his daughter, his Frankie. He wanted to scream, to stop them. To make them leave her alone.

Throughout it all Alison's attention never faltered, her expression remaining fixed and concentrated as she peered under their arms or around their backs to be sure not to miss anything. Occasionally she made notes in her book. They carried on working around her as though she were part of the furniture.

At last they replaced the covers and stepped back, apparently satisfied. Jack exhaled with relief, and to his surprise he heard the ward sister beside him do the same.

'Well, that all seems tickety-boo,' said Stanhope, beaming around the room. 'Professor Keach, and his young assistant, um, Colin here, are doing some work on, on patients with similar symptoms to Frankie's, and he and I will discuss things and write to one another in due course, which I'm sure will be helpful and, er, jolly useful. Don't we?'

'What about the breathing-tube test?' Alison said quietly, flicking through her notebook.

'I beg your pardon?'

'It's a well-known test, you said. Disconnect the breathing tube to see if she will breathe unaided. You mentioned it last time.'

'Did I? Ah, well yes, I may well have dear lady,' blustered Stanhope. 'But that was really only in passing. I didn't mean that we would necessarily be doing it today.'

'Why not? She's fit enough isn't she?'

'Fit? Why yes, fit as a fiddle!' Stanhope laughed nervously. 'All things considered, that is. No, it's just that we hadn't decided that now was necessarily the right time and we didn't want to put you, or Frankie, under any extra, ah, unnecessary pressure at this stage.'

'I'd like it done. Now. We both would.'

Jack's mouth opened, but he was unable to speak.

'May I say something?' It was Keach, speaking directly to Alison for the first time. 'The breathing test is not in itself a determinate indicator of awareness.'

'Maybe, but my understanding is that as an autonomous function, breathing is almost unique.' She quoted calmly and fluently, her eyes fixed on his. '"Although under the general control of the autonomic nervous system, respiration is largely but not completely an involuntary action. To breathe unaided requires some minimal conscious or subconscious input."'

'That is possible but it is not fully proven,' replied Keach. 'And there have been many examples of PVS patients breathing unaided, sometimes for several hours and then stopping.'

'Frankie is not vegetative,' said Alison coldly. 'That diagnosis cannot be made after fourteen weeks. Kindly never refer to my daughter as PVS.'

*

He lies on the bed, his arms held rigidly at his sides, blinking up as a piercing shaft of bright afternoon sunlight catches the camouflaged wings of a slowly turning plastic Spitfire hanging from the ceiling. After a while, his chest begins to feel a bit calmer, his breathing slower as the dream fades. The dream. The one with Frankie. She's calling, shouting, but he can't hear her. There's too much noise, like a kind of thundery wind, and things keep moving slowly between them. Big shapes like huge ships or buildings, getting in the way, blocking his view even though he moves his head to try to see past them. Every time she reappears she's smaller, further away. She's calling him, calling his name, trying to tell him something. He can see her mouth moving. It's important, he wants to hear, wants to go to her, but he's afraid and part of him wants to run away. Soon she's very small, very far away and even though he can see she's still calling, she gets smaller and smaller until she's practically gone and the part of him that is afraid is glad that she's gone. Then he wakes up and sometimes the bed is wet.

He turned onto his side and let his hand fall to the floor, fingertips brushing the carpet. Mum had asked if he wanted to have a go at going back to school again today. But he refused. He hated it. Everyone tried to be so nice and then they looked at him strangely. The doctor said it was normal and they'd soon get used to him being there again. Give it time. But it was terrible, he could feel them gawping at him, or sometimes not looking at him at all, on purpose, like he was invisible.

It was his hair. And the accident. Mr Rawlings, the head teacher, had been very nice that first morning he went back. He had a long talk with him in his office and gave him a toffee, explaining that he'd spoken to the whole school at assembly. That he'd talked to everyone about what had happened with the accident and everything, and about his hair and that everyone was to treat him exactly like before but not to pester him with questions. To carry on as normal.

But nobody spoke to him at all. Except the teachers, who were all friendly and that wasn't normal, and one or two of the sixth-form prefects, who must have been told to talk to him, which was even less normal because sixth-formers never bothered speaking to second-formers.

Even Kevin and Davey wouldn't speak to him. His two best friends in the world. That was most un-normal of all. Once he'd seen them in the distance, walking back together along the cinder track from gym. When they saw him they ran away. He'd told the lady doctor about it afterwards but she said they were just nervous and didn't know how to manage being friends with him again yet, or something. Give it time, she said, give it time. She was always saying it. But that day he came back from school and told Granny he wasn't going back. Shit or bust. Mum was furious and said she'd telephone the school in the morning to complain about Kevin and Davey. Dad said you couldn't blame children for being children and to leave it. Then they had an argument.

He rolled over to face the wall. A while later Granny called him for lunch.

Frankie's breathing-tube test was a disaster. After ten minutes of preparation, Stanhope and Keach were finally ready to proceed. Once again Keach tried to clear the room. 'This really would be best carried out with just myself and Dr Stanhope present,' he said, looking around. 'You might find it a little distressing.'

Once again nobody moved. 'Thanks, I'm fine,' clipped Alison, shooting Jack a glance. He closed his eyes and propped himself against the wall. He felt dizzy and nauseous.

'Very well then.'

Keach leant towards the breathing tube.

Alison's hand shot out to his arm. 'Just a moment, if you don't mind.' She raised herself from the chair and put her mouth directly beside Frankie's ear. 'Frankie, darling, we're here, Mummy, Daddy and Dr Stanhope. The professor's going to take out the tube in your throat and I want – we want – you to see if you can breathe without it, all right?' Her voice faltered. 'Don't be frightened, darling, and we know you'll try your best.' Swallowing, she sat down again slowly. Then she picked up her notebook and nodded at Stanhope.

The tube came out of its seating with a soft click. Jack gritted his teeth, eyes tight shut. What seemed like an eternity later he opened them. It was like a video on freeze frame. Everyone was motionless. Stanhope and Alison were staring down at Frankie, the disconnected tube ready in Stanhope's hand. On either side of him Jack could sense the rigid and unbreathing presence of Winstanley and the ward sister. Keach was studying the second hand on his watch. Frankie's chest was unmoving. Jack clenched his fists, closing his eyes again. The silence went on.

'Stop,' he whispered after an age. He could stand it no more. 'Please stop.'

'Doctor.' It was the sister, just a murmur but it was enough.

Stanhope stiffened. 'Well, I think that'll do us all for now,' he said briskly, and reconnected the tube. Frankie's chest resumed its regular rise and fall. 'Well done everybody, well done Frankie. I think that was splendid – for a first time, that is.'

Alison's head was bowed. 'When are you going to start doing something?' she said quietly.

'I beg your pardon?'

She looked up, her gaze red and exhausted, switching between Stanhope and Keach. 'When are you actually going to start doing something about getting her back?'

'Well, Alison, we are doing everything we can, believe me, but we must proceed with–'

'No you aren't!' She shot to her feet, pencils clattering to the floor. 'You feed her, change her tubes, mop the dribble from her mouth, pump stuff in and pump it out again. You make sure she's warm enough and gets turned enough and has her exercises and her scans and her EEGs and her ECGs, but you don't do anything about reaching her, about actually reaching in to get her. Not one single thing!'

'Mrs Heywood,' interjected Keach quietly, 'I have studied this condition quite extensively, attended many patients with the same or similar symptoms. What I have seen here today leaves me in very little doubt that your daughter has suffered extensive and irrevocable damage to significant areas of the brain dealing with higher cognitive functions. In my view, we must face up to the possibility that this impairment may be permanent.'

'No. I won't do that. I just won't do it.'

'Alison,' continued Stanhope, resting a hand on her arm, 'we all want to do what's best. It's just that we must be careful. Proceed cautiously. So much of this is uncharted territory. We simply don't know enough—'

She shrugged him off. 'Well if you don't know enough then who the hell does?' Tearfully, she picked up her belongings, stuffed them into her bag and walked out.

She took the lift to the ground floor, ignoring the stares as she fled, hand at mouth, across the lobby and into the street. Head down, she walked briskly, the tears flowing unchecked, blurring her feet as they carried her steadily away from the hospital. She turned at random, following no particular direction, but at last subdued residential avenues began to give way to the high-street bustle she sought. Soon she was among busy early-afternoon shoppers, office workers hurrying back from late lunches, college students pedalling towards tutorials. Humanity, hustle, activity, life. She slowed, inhaling the city's breath, reaching to feel for its pulse, immersing herself in its steady ebb and flow. Borne on a fleeting moment of release, she let go gratefully, drifting free, without direction or purpose, unfettered, anonymous and invisible.

Gradually her chest slackened, the pain receding as the storm subsided within her. Blowing her nose on a crumpled scrap of tissue pulled from her bag, she caught sight of herself in a shop window and stopped, arrested by her own appearance. She was a wreck, her eyes red-rimmed and darkly ringed, cheeks flushed and blotchy, hair lank and dishevelled. Beyond the glass, a young woman was lifting summer dresses from rails, holding them thoughtfully against her body, replacing them, choosing others. She was dark and pretty, taking her time, engrossed, quietly absorbed in her own private moment. Alison stared at her, mesmerized. In an hour or so this woman would go to meet her children from school, walk them home for tea, listen patiently while they bombarded her with minute accounts of their day's triumphs and tragedies. Later she'd bathe them and put them to bed, read to them until their father came home. They'd embrace, go downstairs, have a drink together, talking about their day while she prepared food for them. Afterwards she'd settle against his shoulder to watch television, or listen to music, or read. After a while they'd snuggle closer, exchange tiny secret signals. So she'd go up, and while he turned off lights and locked doors, she'd make ready, relaxed and warm with anticipation, for him to come to her.

With a start Alison realized the young woman was watching her through the window. Their eyes met, the other woman smiling self-consciously, a dress on a hanger in either hand. Alison smiled back, the soft longing in her eyes closing the space between them. The union held a moment longer then the woman broke away as a sales assistant appeared at her side. Alison's gaze fell. She turned from the window and walked back to the hospital.

As she opened the door to Frankie's room she saw her mother standing at the bedside, peering intently while a nurse adjusted the flow of fluid into a drip tube. Everyone else had gone.

'Right, there we are then. Can you see?' said the nurse cheerfully. 'Once the new bag's hooked up and clipped on, you just turn the little tap until you have the correct drip rate set and that's all there is to it.'

'Marvellous,' Janet Catchpole said doubtfully, lifting spectacles up and down in front of her eyes. 'Rather small though, if I may say so. Thank you, Donna, that was most interesting.' She sat down and picked up a children's book lying on Frankie's chest. Alison held open the door for the nurse, then walked slowly over to the window. Her mother glanced at her, then began to read out loud from the book, at high speed, her voice a quickfire accentless monotone.

Alison turned round. 'What on earth are you doing?' she said. 'Where's Ben?'

'Ben's absolutely fine,' said her mother reassuringly, turning the page of the book. 'He's downstairs having a poke around the hospital shop. I'm devising a speed-reading teaching method for Frankie.' Alison watched as her mother gabbled an entire paragraph of the story in a single unbroken breath, then immediately thrust the book in front of Frankie's nose. Seconds later she removed it again and repeated the process with the next paragraph.

Alison sighed, and slumped heavily into the chair opposite. Janet rattled off the next paragraph, glancing at her daughter over the top of her spectacles as she held the book in front of Frankie.

'I saw Jack,' she said quietly. 'He told me about the breathing-test thing. I'm so sorry.'

Alison lowered her head into her hands. 'It doesn't necessarily mean anything,' she said doggedly. 'In any case, they didn't try for long enough.'

'Of course.' Janet put down the book. 'Darling, he's terribly worried about you, you know. Jack is. We all are.'

'I know.'

'Won't you talk to him about it?'

'He doesn't believe. He hates it, it upsets him.'

'Yes, but he does care. Desperately.'

'I know he does.' She fell quiet. 'But then there's the whole other business. I can't pretend none of that happened just because of Ben and Frankie, can I?'

'Perhaps you could, sort of put it to one side for a while. He so wants to be allowed to help, to understand, to be allowed to participate, have a voice. Don't you see? Whatever he's done, he is still their father.'

Alison shook her head miserably, turning to look at Frankie. Her tongue was protruding slightly, parting the lips at one corner of her mouth. A lock of brown fringe had fallen across one eye, Alison brushed it back from the slack face. 'I just feel so, utterly alone with all this,' she said quietly. 'In his heart I know he believes it's hopeless, everyone does, but I can't–' She broke off, the tears starting again. She turned to her mother, face anguished. 'I just can't give up on her. I can't!'

'I know, darling.' Janet reached across the bed and squeezed her hand. 'I know.'

In the evening Jack came round to visit Ben.

'Hi there, how's it going?' he said cheerfully, closing the kitchen door. Ben was sitting at the table, idly leafing through a book. Jack flicked a glance towards Alison. She was at the sink, her back to him, a glass of wine at her side. She turned as he entered, smiled wanly.

'All right?' he asked pointedly, eyebrows arched.

'Fine, I'm fine, thanks. Sorry about the walk-out earlier. Stupid, I overreacted.'

'No, you were right,' said Jack. Ben stared sightlessly at his book, listening from the table. 'A good old-fashioned ear-bashing now and then doesn't do anybody any harm.'

'Christ, that bad was it? How was Stanhope?'

'Water off a duck's back, dear boy,' Jack mimicked. 'Absolutely understandable reaction from the little woman, poor dear delicate creature.' There was the smell of cooking coming from the oven. Jack swallowed, he'd eaten nothing since breakfast.

Alison nodded wryly. 'I didn't like the other one, Keach.'

'No, humourless bugger, wasn't he?' Jack dumped a plastic

carrier bag on the table. 'But he is supposed to know what he's talking about. Leader in the field, according to Stanhope.'

Immediately Alison turned back to the sink. Jack stared at her for a second, then pulled out a chair next to Ben. 'Anyway, look Ben, I've brought some stuff, thought you might be interested.' He began emptying the bag onto the table. It was strange: he felt perhaps he should ask permission first. No, not strange. Stupid, humiliating. To ask if he could sit at his table. In his kitchen. With his son. 'Here we go, couple of aeromodelling mags, another one here all about the space shuttle and an Airfix Superfortress – thought we might have a go at it together. What do you think?'

'Okay.' The voice was neutral, noncommittal.

'Don't be too long Ben, supper-time in a minute,' said Alison lightly from the sink.

'Don't stay too long Jack, I want you out of here,' was what she meant, he reflected. 'Great! So tell me, what have you been up to today?' But Jack knew exactly already. Up at the usual school-time but no school. A one-hour session at the therapist's in the morning, lunch with Alison's mother, then back for a nap in the afternoon before tea.

'Nothing much,' came the reply.

At least he was getting out and about a bit, Jack mused, as Ben opened the model box. But he still refused to see Frankie, still refused to go to school and still refused to talk about the accident. Even after more than three months. It wasn't right, wasn't working. It was as though he was slipping further away from them, not getting nearer. Jack studied him as Ben looked through the model's instructions. He too had changed. Thinner, slighter, smaller almost. As though he had actually grown shorter, although Jack knew this was impossible. Diminished, that was the word. And the hair, of course, even though they'd grown used to it now. The psychologist told Jack and Alison privately that it would almost certainly change back to its natural colour eventually. 'When the original shock begins to wear off and when he is able to find a way of resolving the crisis within himself.' She'd said to watch the roots for darkening. Jack peered closely as Ben leant over the box, but there was no sign. Looking up again, he saw Alison watching him, lips pursed. She took a sip from her wine-glass and turned back to the sink.

'Right then,' he went on. 'What have we got? Wings and undercarriage first, is it? Okay, I'll trim you stick.'

None of them knew exactly what had happened on the road that day. They only knew that Ben had been given the respons-ibility for walking the girls to school each morning and something had gone wrong. The police said that eye-witnesses had described the girls in the middle of the road, panicking, then trying to get back to one side or the other, then being hit by the bus. Although the statement details varied, sometimes wildly, in one respect they were all consistent. No one recalled a third child being involved.

It wasn't right, bottling it up like this, it couldn't be right. There must be something more they could do. He rested a hand lightly on Ben's shoulder. He'd speak to the therapist again in the morning, fix a meeting.

'I've been thinking,' he began, picking up a piece of fuselage, 'what about a holiday? You know, a bit of a break. Long week-end or something.'

At the sink Alison's head lifted. Ben turned, looking at him. 'What, you mean go away? All of us?'

'I don't see why not. Seaside or something. Would you like that?' Ben stared at him then nodded slowly.

'Ben, could you go and wash your hands now, darling? It's supper-time.'

'But, Mum–'

'Quick as you can please.' A moment later they were alone. She turned to him, cheeks flushed. 'Have you gone completely mad?'

Jack shrugged. 'It was just a suggestion. I thought it might be good for him, lift his spirits.'

'Jack, we are separated. I am trying to help Ben and Frankie come to terms with that.'

'Good God Alison, it's for Ben's sake. We don't have to do anything, be together or anything. We can get separate rooms, whatever you want.'

'Oh yes and maybe we can get a separate room for the bloody secretary too while we're at it! Wouldn't that be cosy?'

Jack shook his head wearily. 'Alison, listen to me just for a minute–'

'No, you listen Jack.' She jabbed a wooden spoon towards him accusingly. 'There is absolutely no question of us going away on holiday together.' She walked across the kitchen towards him, ticking off reasons on her fingers. 'First, I am not leaving Frankie, not even for a day, she needs me. Second, we don't take Ben anywhere without consulting with the doctor first.'

The telephone was ringing. 'Of course Alison, I understand that for God's sake.'

She continued past him towards the phone. 'And third we do not start sending the wrong signals to either of them by going off for weekends together. Is that quite clear?' She picked up the receiver, cupping one hand over the mouthpiece. 'It's bad enough, quite frankly, your coming round here every day, but I put up with it for Ben's sake. Hello?'

It was Colin Winstanley.

'Who?' she repeated irritably.

'C-C-Colin, Mrs Heywood. I was at the hospital this afternoon with Professor K-K-Keach.'

'Oh, yes, Colin.' She sighed. 'I blew up, I'm sorry, I shouldn't have done that, it wasn't your fault. How can I help you?'

'Well, I d-d-don't know if I should t-t-tell you this b-b-but . . .' His stammer was getting worse.

'Tell me what, Colin?'

'Well there's this p-place. It's in Virginia. It's called the P-P-Perlman Institute.'

C h a p t e r   3

AFTER NINE YEARS AT STANFORD UNIVERSITY, CALIFORNIA, right at the end of her residency, Elizabeth Chase MD fell in love while carrying out postgraduate research. Ultimately to prove an unhappy although educative experience, the relationship and its aftermath nevertheless provided the catalyst for a chance encounter that would alter the course of her life.

She was twenty-six, shy, pretty, highly intelligent, but dangerously inexperienced in the ways of the heart and sexually naïve. He was more than twenty years her senior, twice divorced, a father of two grown-up children and a serial seducer of young women. Although alert to the power of her intellect and appreciative of her fine features and the way her legs moved beneath her summer dress, it was, as usual, her innocence and vulnerability that were of principal attraction to him.

He was a professor of biochemistry at Stanford, she was his star protégé and he ensnared her the way he had ensnared many others before her. Inviting Elizabeth to stop by his office after a lecture one day, he told her that he had found her last paper very well researched and presented but potentially flawed. Unfortunately, he went on, peering at the pages of his diary over the rim of his designer spectacles, he didn't have time to go through the paper right then, but he did feel it important to do so. Therefore might he suggest they get together Wednesday afternoon for a one-to-one.

At the appointed hour he arrived slightly late, apologized, said his office was being used by a colleague and since it was such a fine afternoon proposed they spread themselves on the grass outside. They sat beneath the shade of an old cedar and he spoke non-stop for an hour. Kindly but firmly dissecting her paper, flattering her for the accuracy of her research, chiding her good-naturedly for non-existent weaknesses in her method-ology, complimenting her on the strength of her argument. As the afternoon wore on she found herself paying less attention to what he was saying and more to the charming manner in which he was saying it. Suddenly she realized that he had stopped talking and was simply smiling at her. He looked at his watch, concluded that in any case she was not to worry, it was an excellent paper in all respects, and the least he could do after all his hectoring was buy her a glass of wine before they called it a day.

At the second meeting, they worked for a while, discussing outline ideas for a new project she was planning, then they went for a walk. She learnt that he too was reluctant to talk about himself, was the solitary, studious type and found relationships, even friendships daunting. When she pressed him daringly on the issue, he paused in their walking and looked at her sadly. Then he admitted quietly that, having been badly hurt in the past, he had long since abandoned the search for a companion and had resigned himself to a bachelor lifestyle with his books, his record collection and his cat. By the third rendezvous she was nauseous with anticipation. It took place in a bar up in San Francisco. They drank a bottle of Napa Chardonnay, talked for two hours without mentioning biochemistry once and then, almost without realizing because it felt so natural, she found herself returning with him to see his apartment, listen to some of his music and meet his cat. While she wandered about his living room, admiring his lithographs and scanning the crammed shelves of his bookcases, he cooked seafood pasta, plying her with Chianti and Burt Bacharach.

'But don't you ever get lonely?' she asked an hour later, her head spinning as she gazed around at the ordered masculine clutter of the room. They were cross-legged on the floor, a third wine bottle now open between them, their candlelit shadows flickering across the ceiling. A gentle breeze lightly stirred the Indian-cotton curtain at the balcony window; beyond, the late-evening sky over the bay was soft and pale blue-orange.

'I suppose you learn to adapt.' He sighed and leant forward to kiss her. Within minutes they were in bed.

It lasted a month. She had never known such happiness, such passion, such depth of feeling. It was exhilarating, exciting and fulfilling. At last she had found a soulmate, somebody who understood her and was not in awe of her, could talk to her as an equal, could teach her new things about life, politics, culture and love. And sex, lots about sex. He was so generous, so giving, yet at the same time so experienced and bold. They met regularly at his apartment; he kept a key hidden behind a loose brick by the door so she could let herself in. One afternoon she let herself in and found him being experienced and bold with a first-year student from behavioural sciences. She turned and walked out without a word, returned to her room on campus, closed the door and remained there for three days.

The opening at Boston General Hospital was posted the following week. It was for an internship in the neurology department, a discipline she knew little about and had hitherto not considered as a possible specialty. In any case she was a research graduate, not a clinician. But the post had two immediate attractions. First, it was open to her right away, and second, it was on the far side of the continent, four time zones and a million miles from Stanford. She packed her bags, headed back east and became a neurologist.

At first she was surprised and frustrated by the slow pace of clinical development at the hospital. While respecting traditional mechanisms and values, her own work methodology tended towards empiricism, a *modus operandi* that had already brought her into occasional conflict with professorial staff at Stanford. She frequently rejected established conventions in favour of a fast-track intuitive approach that owed more to the processes of induction and experience than the much slower deduction and analysis. Lesser brains soon fall foul of such methodology as it requires enormous powers of retention. But from an early age it had always been clear that Elizabeth's was no ordinary brain.

Gradually she settled into the new culture. One evening, about four months after she had begun, during a routine tour of the department, she came across a new patient, recently moved to Boston from another hospital. A glance at his case notes told her that he was sixteen, he was on life support and that he had been unconscious for nearly two years. His name was Gary Perlman Junior. Sitting at his bedside in the private room were an elderly couple. They turned out to be Gary's paternal grandparents. They told her that he had suffered head injuries in a car crash in which both his parents had been killed, that there was no sign of his condition changing, let alone improving, and that they were beginning to wonder whether they should give in to mounting pressure to terminate his life support. When Elizabeth asked them what action doctors had taken to try actively to revive Gary, they just looked at each other and shrugged. Simply tending to his basic needs and keeping him alive, they replied.

Elizabeth was astonished. Later that evening, long after the old couple had left, she went back to Gary's room and sat down at his bedside. She remained there the whole night. In the morning, just as the first streaks of pink were suffusing the Massachusetts skyline through the window of his room, she left his side and walked down the hall towards the pay-phone.

*

From early on in her life it was clear to Elizabeth Chase's parents, Elliot and Mary, that in their firstborn they had created a prodigy. The revelation, first evidenced when Lizzie began to talk and read at the age of two, brought both delight and concern to the bright young psychologist and his linguist wife. Elliot knew well the downside of an unusually powerful intellect. As a boy his own father had driven him mercilessly, goading him to ever greater heights of academic attainment, at the same time denying him the simple pleasures of unpressured childhood. Long before Lizzie was born, Elliot had vowed that his children would never suffer similar deprivation.

Even so, Lizzie's capacity for learning progressed at an astonishing rate. By the time Mary walked her apprehensively into the little grade school near their Albany apartment for the first time, she was already reading fluently, had mastered fourth grade mathematics, and as well as eloquently articulating her native tongue, had picked up the basics of both French and German. Although the Chases were careful never to push their freckle-faced daughter, feeding her only as much as she wanted, she appeared insatiable. Like a newborn chick her mouth seemed permanently agape: the more her harassed parents strove to satisfy her, the more she demanded.

Soon Mary, quietly conceding the superiority of her off-spring's mental aptitude, gladly surrendered responsibility for its development to her husband. Father and daughter grew close, all of Elliot's spare time being given over to Lizzie. They visited zoos, art galleries and museums together, listened to classical music, read poetry or simply sat together at the kitchen table, working through math problems. He was always careful: rest and recreation periods were built into the schedule and he insisted she spend time with children of her own age, even when she protested they were dull and stupid. Also he strove to ensure that her intake was balanced: they watched Disney films together, he bought her pop and rock cassettes, they joined a little-league baseball team. And he gave her a sibling. Driving with her to hospital one day when she was seven, watching her closely as she was introduced to Daniel, her new baby brother. He needn't have worried, she was immediately entranced, sitting straight-backed at Mary's bedside for hours at a time, wide-eyed and motionless, while the tiny bundle in her arms yawned and blinked up at her.

After a while, the steady growth of his psychology practice prompted Elliot to relocate the family from their cramped upstate New York apartment to a small house in Connecticut. From there he could commute to service his expanding Manhattan patient-base and Lizzie had access to a better range of schools and colleges. As she grew into her teen years, she continued to excel, quickly developing the knack of grasping the fundamentals of a subject, retaining them, moving swiftly on to the next, then returning to the original, often months or even years later. She evolved a talent for constructing great leaping bridges of intuitive deduction, effortlessly spanning the confused seas and jumbled thought processes of lesser minds to link previously unconnected notions, ideas or concepts. To her it mattered not one jot whether it was a different topic, or a different subject altogether: if there was a possible connection between an algebraic formula she had learned two years previously and the writings of Plato, she would make that connection and pursue it relentlessly until either she convinced everyone else or disproved it to herself.

Socially, however, she was far less adept. With the onset of puberty, she found it progressively harder to make and sustain close friendships at school. Her intellect masked a debilitating shyness, which people often mistook for disdain. Her genuine eagerness to please was misinterpreted as gaucheness. Also, in truth, she had difficulty in sharing the eternal fascination with trivia that seemed so to obsess girls of her age, and despite her innate prettiness, she found that boys were nervous of her and stayed away. Although she continued to try to join in, it became a habit to keep herself to herself at school, focus inwardly and concentrate on her studies.

Her family was her life. Whenever his increasingly hectic schedule permitted, she continued to spend hours with her father. Catching a train into Manhattan after school, she'd wait in his office while he tidied up, stretching out on his couch, riffling through his medical journals and pestering him for stories about his patients. Then they'd walk down Fifth Avenue together and spend the evening at the theatre or at a jazz concert or a movie. Afterwards they'd go to Pizza on the Park or Benny's Grill or occasionally a swanky French restaurant.

Her relationship with her mother was more subdued. Mary was introspective and bookish by nature, disliked social over-contact, vastly preferring to stay in and read of an evening than dine out with Elliot's work colleagues or go to a show. Quietly she acknowledged the strength of the bond between Lizzie and her father, recognizing without rancour that it substituted in part for certain aspects of her own relationship with her husband. She and Lizzie enjoyed an easy closeness but they were not intimate. When Lizzie's periods began, it was Elliot she ran to tell first.

But above all Lizzie adored Daniel. Right from when he was a baby she fussed over and cosseted him as though he was her own. It was Lizzie who taught him to walk, taught him to read, taught him to ride a bicycle, taught him to swim. On summer evenings they spent hours together out in the backyard in Connecticut, playing catcher's mitt or shooting baskets. She assisted him with his schoolwork, gently encouraging and cajoling him to help himself towards solutions. She was patient and tolerant, well aware that his prowess was not on a par with hers, would never even get close. For his part Daniel, more than making up in enthusiasm what he lacked in mental agility, taught Lizzie the importance of having fun, the joy of not taking the world too seriously, a love of sport, the exhilaration of the occasional broken rule.

One day he taught her the meaning of life.

With the full consent and support of his grandparents, Elizabeth began work on Gary Perlman. Her intention, she told them, during that first early-morning phone call, was to embark upon a comprehensive regime of treatments and therapies, some of which they might find quite unusual, but all of which would be designed with a single objective in mind: to try to recover Gary from his persistent vegetative state. She told them that, having studied his notes in detail during the night, it was clear that up to now most of his medical care had been directed towards maintaining a stable condition, the prevention and treatment of physical ailments or infections, and the ongoing monitoring of his unconsciousness. Very little, apart from 'a few handclaps, pin-pricks and bright lights' had been done to try to jerk him out of it. All that, she explained, was about to change.

From that moment on her every spare minute was spent on Gary and his condition. She scoured libraries, devouring textbooks, scientific journals and research papers by the basket load. She buttonholed bio-neurologists, biochemists, bio-sensory physicists. She doorstepped homeopaths, acupuncturists, behaviouralists, hypnotherapists. She cold-called hospitals with other patients like Gary, cajoling them, begging them, or simply deceiving them into sending her copies of their case notes. She spoke to their doctors, their relatives, their friends, their hairdressers – anyone she believed might contribute to her rapidly expanding information base. She attended seminars, lectures and conferences, hanging around in corridors like an over-eager schoolgirl just to catch five or ten minutes with a neurology professor or a behavioural therapist or endocrinologist. Then at the end of it all she would return to her apartment near the hospital and work, late into every night, writing up her notes, recording her findings, storing everything away in her swiftly growing data bank.

And planning her attack. For three or four hours every evening, after completing her normal round of duties, she worked on Gary. She began slowly, methodically running a series of long and exhaustive tests on the teenager using ever more complex combinations of stimulating and monitoring equipment. Almost immediately she encountered a problem. It quickly became impossible for just one person to operate the growing elements of the equipment, and watch for responses at the same time. So she seduced a young computer programmer called Nathan Greenwater from the bioscience department to patch it all together. Nathan, a tall gum-chewing black from Atlanta, was reluctant at first. Working late for that scatty bitch from Neuro for no pay sounded like a poor deal. Elizabeth, looking him straight in the eye, said she'd need him to test everything on her. All the electronic hook-ups, senders, receptors and feeds would have to be attached, by him, to literally every part of her body. To the bare skin of every part of her body.

Nathan was aboard. Soon he was able to sequence innumerable combinations of different stimuli from the expanding piles of equipment, and monitor for reactions, all from a single computer screen. By the time the new equipment was ready to be moved into Gary's room, he knew everything there was to know about Elizabeth's anatomy and was completely hooked on the programme.

Elizabeth started each session by raising Gary's physical metabolism with intravenous stimulants – her 'wake-up call', as she termed it. Then she and Nathan would begin programming different combinations of stimuli, separately and together. Sounds, ranging from low-frequency hums to inaudible ultrasonic whistles, patterns of fixed and flashing lights across the full visual spectrum. Minute electrical stimulation of Gary's nervous system, small pulsed charges to his lips, earlobes, fingertips and toes. Then she would alter the combinations slightly and begin the sequences again.

It was painstaking, laborious work and throughout it all there was not a single reaction from Gary that repeated or could be attributed to anything but an involuntary response. Furthermore, after three months and with nothing apparently achieved, doubts were being raised as to the advisability of the programme. Questions were asked about some of the more extreme methods being used by this little-known intern; rumours of bizarre experiments, even abuses, were spreading through the department. Before long a 'Stop the Chase' whisper campaign was circulating the hospital corridors. Finally, the head of the neurology department called a case-study meeting and demanded to know, in detail, exactly what Elizabeth was doing. Others at the meeting expressed grave doubts, talked about Gary's 'dignity', said the experiment might be doing him more harm than good, that artificially stimulating Gary's heart and other organs could place him at risk. And how did Dr Chase know that Gary wasn't in discomfort or distress? Worse still, what if he were to suffer a collapse or die? The legal implications for the hospital could be disastrous. She was given two weeks to wind it up.

In the end she got him with intravenous epinephrine, a high-speed strobe and Motorhead at full volume. That, plus a highly complex sequence of circulating low-power electrical discharges, a slightly raised body temperature, direct stimulation of the vagus nerve, repeating short cycles of vigorous foot massage and a heartfelt final curse.

It was late on a Thursday night, half-way through the final week. Elizabeth had just reset the strobe for the fortieth time that evening, she was exhausted and irritable, nothing was working properly, the computer program had crashed repeatedly, Nathan was sullen and Gary as unresponsive as ever.

'Set?' Elizabeth ran her sleeve across her forehead wearily, then placed her hands on Gary's foot ready to massage. Nathan grunted, his eyes on the screen.

'I said, set Nathan?'

'Set man, Jesus.'

'Right then. Go!' Nathan clicked the mouse, the cycle began. Elizabeth drove her thumbs hard into the ball of Gary's foot, the strobe burst once for two seconds then stopped altogether. Elizabeth exploded. 'For fuck's sake Nathan get it together!'

Nathan rocked back, raising his hands. 'Hey, back off bitch, I never touched the mother!' He studied the screen. 'Something interrupted the sequence. Look, there it is again. It's – it's something on the receptor bank. It's one of the fucking receptors, man!'

Elizabeth dived to the screen. 'My God it is!' For ten agonizing seconds they stared in silence. 'Yes look, there, and it's repeating, there it is again. It's the tongue receptor. Oh my God, Nathan, he's trying to move his tongue!'

Every summer Elliot and Mary Chase took the children to a cabin in Vermont. It was peaceful and remote, set on the edge of a still, wide lake surrounded by dense pine forests. A scattering of other cabins dotted the lakeside around them; five miles away was a small town with a general store, a gas station, an ice-cream parlour and a bar. The roads were no more than bumpy tracks, the mailman came by boat and knew everyone by name, there was no television and no telephone. Sometimes the power went out, nobody minded, days passed in an endless, tranquil blur of fishing and swimming, sunbathing and sailing, evening cook-outs and nights under the stars. To Elliot and Mary it was a blessed haven from the manic hurly-burly of the city. To Lizzie and Daniel it was a magical wonderland.

As the children grew older the family began escaping to the cabin for a few days over Christmas. Elliot would clear his diary for a week, load up the car with suitcases of warm clothes and boxes of provisions, snow chains and shovels. They'd lash a Christmas tree to the roof, clamber aboard and set off on the long drive northwards.

In winter the lake was transformed, the sparkling clear water solidified to sugar-dusted granite, the summertime buzz of motorboats and resonating children's laughter banished by a thick, snow-muffled silence, the heady tang of warm evergreen forest and barbecue replaced by resinous woodsmoke from the log fire. Although it was never designed for winter occupation, the cabin was thick-walled and sturdy. They moved camp beds into the front room, lit a big fire in the grate and settled down around it to read books or talk, play box games or pore over giant jigsaw puzzles, Christmas carols sounding from the cassette recorder in the background.

It was Christmas Eve morning. Lizzie sat by the window, feet curled up beneath her, flexing her cocooned toes within a pair of Daniel's thick hockey socks. On her lap was her diary, its pages filled with tiny meticulous handwriting. She'd always kept one, since she was seven, nearly ten years. Faithfully and accurately recording in microscopic detail her innermost thoughts, anxieties, hopes and dreams. She flicked back rapidly through the pages, eyes subconsciously speed-reading through the months in just a few seconds. Another week and it would be time to start a new year, a fresh volume. It lay waiting for her, wrapped in shiny silver paper beneath the Christmas tree, one of her presents from Dad as always. As the pages flashed before her she was unsurprised to detect a sea change in her dis-closures over the year. Boys increasingly dominated her preoccupations. One boy in particular seemed to have accrued a statistically disproportionate number of entries.

She looked out of the window, hugging her knees. Her parents would be back soon: they'd driven into town for some last-minute provisions at the general store, to pick up any mail and, most importantly, phone through to the answering-service in Connecticut for messages. She stared out at the solid expanse of the lake. Daniel was there as usual, endlessly circling the same carefully swept patch of ice on his skates for hours every day. She watched as he looped around the back of the two goalposts he'd set up, deftly flicking the puck from side to side as he doubled round, completed the figure-of-eight, turned and

fired the puck with relentless accuracy between the posts before
circling back, arms raised triumphantly, to collect it and begin
the manoeuvre once again. He must have done it dozens of
times already, she mused, her thoughts returning to her parents
and the answering-service. Happy Christmas Lizzie, have a
great vacation, looking forward to seeing you next semester,
yours, Tom Ryder. And who might Tom Ryder be? Dad would
demand, eyebrows raised in mock disapproval. Just a friend,
she would reply mysteriously.

'Idiot,' she muttered, picking up the diary. 'New year's
resolution number seven . . .' she jotted briskly, at the back of
her mind an image, watching her father as a little girl, he, lost
in work at his carpentry bench in the garage at Albany, carefully
scoring glass for a cabinet he was making. '. . . give up useless
fantasizing,' she wrote, scribbling the figure fifty-six in the
margin.

It happened incredibly quickly. There was a high-pitched
muffled shout from outside. She looked up. Daniel was gone.
Two precious seconds were lost as she gaped in disbelief across
the suddenly deserted lake. Then she was diving through the
door, down the snow-covered foreshore, skidding out onto the
ice. Her shoeless feet lost grip and she fell heavily, the ice catching the back of her head a stunning blow. Dazed and
disoriented she scrambled back to her feet. Behind her a car was
pulling up outside the cabin. 'Danny!' she screamed, running
on towards the goal posts. As she drew nearer she saw him, just
his head and shoulders, one hand still grasping the hockey
stick, fingers scrabbling at the edge of a pitch-black gash in the
white.

She slowed, the ice undulating beneath her feet as she drew
nearer to the breach. Instinctively she sank to her knees,
crawling towards him on all fours while the ice made sickening
splitting sounds, new cracks fanning out all around them.
Behind her on the shore her father shouted in alarm for her to
wait. But she crawled on, sinking lower and lower onto the

heaving ice as she drew near, until finally she was flat out on her stomach. Suddenly, when she was within a few feet of him, the ice beneath her dipped forward, a wavelet of jet black water rolling slowly up towards her chin as the edge of the floe tilted into the lake. She stopped, gasping with shock as freezing water soaked through her clothes to the skin of her stomach and thighs. The ice tilted down further, then steadied. At its edge, six feet away from her outstretched arms, Daniel struggled weakly, arms and elbows slipping uselessly as he fought to lever himself from the water.

'Danny, the stick!' she called, inching forward. Immediately the ice ahead of her started to dip again. To one side, horribly near, there was a crack like a rifle shot as a new fissure opened. She ignored it, turning slightly onto her side to stretch one hand towards him. 'Don't struggle, reach out to me with the hockey stick! Come on Danny, reach out to me now. Dad's coming.'

'Lizzie.' He shuddered, eyes wide with panic.

'Now, Danny. Reach out to me with the stick!' She could hear his breathing, low and hollow as the freezing water sucked the heat from his body. 'The stick, Daniel, now!' Slowly he responded, one arm reaching ponderously towards her, the hockey stick gripped between colourless fingers. She stretched for it, but it was still too far. She inched forward a little more. The ice tipped precariously downward, her chin and upper torso were awash with icy water. Still she crawled on, flat out, head sideways, one hand stretching into the space ahead of her. Finally her fingers brushed the stick. 'That's it Danny! Reach out just a little more.' A moment later she had it. 'I've got it!' She lifted her head to look at him. 'I've got you. Don't try and pull, just hang on. Dad's coming. He'll be here any minute.'

He managed another two. All the while Lizzie talked to him non-stop, encouraging him, berating him, begging him to hang on. Without pausing from talking, she turned her head, peering past her outstretched body to the distant shore. People had arrived – she could see more vehicles, men with coils of rope and ladders setting out onto the ice. She turned back. 'Look, they're coming!'

Her stomach lurched. He was quite still, gazing at her, just his head and one arm showing above the surface. His lips were blue, cheeks ashen, but the panic had gone, his eyes were calm and steady. 'Can't any more. Sorry.'

'You must! They're coming, they'll be here any minute! Danny, you must hold on, you must!'

'It's okay, Lizzie.' His voice was no more than a whisper. 'It's okay.' His eyes held hers, mouth moving, the ghost of a smile touching the corners of his lips. 'Don't cry.'

'No!' she wailed, hauling desperately on the curved blade of the hockey stick. She felt it give suddenly, staring in horror as together they watched his mittened fingers sliding from the handle. His eyes found hers again. A moment later his head slipped silently beneath the slate black surface.

As word of Gary Perlman's 'Return from the Abyss', as one newspaper headlined it, flashed around the country, Elizabeth found herself caught up in a spiralling whirlwind of media attention. Newspapers, television stations, documentary film-makers, even movie companies wanted to talk to her. There were endless interviews with TV and radio commentators, magazine editors and newspaper journalists. Endless photo sessions – Dr Chase outside the hospital, Dr Chase at work, Dr Chase at Gary's bedside. Always the same repeating rounds of banal questions, the same bemused smiles as she attempted to explain, the same lack of serious interest or even superficial understanding. It was fun at first but quickly wearying.

Inevitably others cashed in, scrabbling anxiously lest the spotlight of attention should pass them by. The head of Elizabeth's neurology department wrote an article for the *Boston Globe* and took part in a radio phone-in about the trail-blazing work being undertaken 'under his guidance' by his talented team. The corporate communications director at Boston General, never one to miss a media opportunity, also made best use of the story: 'Boston Leads World in Coma Recovery Treatment' heralded one of his press releases. Boston's mayor went on live television, talked about the pioneering New England spirit being alive and well. Even Nathan was briefly fêted by the press for what Elizabeth described as his 'priceless and patient assistance'.

At the same time, beneath the surface hubbub, an underlying debate began to circulate like a current through the medical profession. How had the breakthrough been achieved? Was it just luck? Had anything been published? Who was she? Who had she trained under? Scientific and medical journals wanted to publish Elizabeth's case notes, she was in demand to speak at seminars, offers from other institutions began to appear in her mail.

And then there were the requests to treat other patients. Initially it was just the odd tentative enquiry from another neurology department, or a low-key request for a second opinion from a consultant on a particular case. But one day, about three weeks after the breakthrough with Gary, she received a telephone call from an attorney in Portland.

'I represent the family of Dana Konakowsi,' he said, by way of introduction. The name meant nothing to her. 'Following a horse-riding accident nearly three years ago, Dana has been in hospital here in Oregon, in what doctors diagnose as a persistent vegetative state—'

'I don't believe in the term,' interrupted Elizabeth.

'Er, no, indeed, if you say so. Anyway, Dana's family have approved, and their medical insurers have underwritten, a provisional referral to your facility for a preliminary treatment period of up to six months.'

Elizabeth was stunned. Within a week four other families were asking for transfers. She didn't know what to say. Her work with Gary had been a one-off. She wasn't running a department, or even a ward. Strictly speaking, she didn't even have use of Gary's room any more. The 'facility' consisted of a tangled mess of mostly borrowed equipment that didn't work very well. That was it. She didn't have the people, the equipment, the computers, the beds, nothing. She didn't have the time, she didn't have the authority. Her 'facility' didn't exist.

That evening as usual she went to see Gary. His grandparents were there, as they were most evenings. They rose as she entered, hugged her warmly. 'Look at this!' said Mr Perlman, proudly holding up a little notepad. 'He says he feels absolutely fine, says it's too damn hot in here and that he wants a beer.' Elizabeth glanced at the pad, three words, HEAT FINE BUD. It could mean anything, she realized, but it was still enormous progress.

Gary was propped into a half-lying, half-sitting position, his head resting to one side. His gaze was fixed and staring, however tests showed that his vision was improving and had not suffered irrevocable impairment. He was still on the ventilator much of the time but as his chest musculature reaccustomed itself to the work of breathing unaided, he had begun coming off it for increasing periods each day. His left leg seemed to be showing signs of returning voluntary movement, and although he was as yet unable to generate sound, it was clear that he could hear perfectly and that his mind was alert and eager to communicate.

Elizabeth sat down on the bed. 'Hello, you,' she said softly, taking his hand in hers. A thin plastic tube ran from the corner of Gary's mouth to a little box the size of a paperback book which sat on his lap. Flexing the muscles of his tongue and jaw caused a buzzer to sound on the box, thus he could signal a simple one for yes or two for no. In the last few days he had begun the laborious business of spelling out short words by buzzing through the alphabet. Nathan was working on a mouth-actuated voice-synthesis programme designed for quadriplegics and hoped to have it ready for Gary to try out in a week or two.

'There's something you should know,' she went on quietly, 'all of you.' She smiled at Gary, scratching lightly at the tip of his nose. Along the corridor a telephone buzzed; in another room someone was watching television. 'Getting Gary back was, kind of an experiment, as I explained. But the thing is, I don't know, nobody knows, what happens from here on, how far it can go. It's up to Gary now.' She looked at him again, her blue eyes searching his face. 'But I'd like to thank you, all, for giving me the chance, for having the confidence to let me try.' She broke off, head falling.

'That's not necessary,' said Rose Perlman, patting her hand. 'It's us that wants to thank you.' Silence fell again. Rose sniffed and fumbled for a handkerchief. Suddenly Gary's buzzer went once and they all laughed.

'In fact,' said Mr Perlman, clearing his throat gruffly, 'we wanted to talk to you about a little gift. A donation. Something to help your research, something that might enable you to help others like Gary.'

It was an endowment for two million dollars.

Daniel was dead. A diver pulled his ten-year-old body from beneath the ice thirty minutes after Lizzie had been dragged screaming to the shore. A waiting helicopter ambulance air-lifted him and Elliot directly to the hospital at Montpelier, seventy miles away; en route attempts were made to revive him. He was given CPR, force-fed pure oxygen, injected with stimulants and repeatedly jolted by shocks from the air ambulance's portable heart defibrilator.

By the time they touched down on the hospital rooftop forty-five minutes later, a thin pulse had been re-established. But even before Mary pulled up in the car outside the hospital that evening, a stunned and heavily sedated Lizzie sitting in the back, it was already becoming clear to Elliot and the emergency room team that the damage sustained to Daniel's brain by half an hour's oxygen starvation was catastrophic.

Two weeks later he was flown back to Connecticut on life support and installed in a private room at a clinic in Hartford. There he remained for six further weeks while his condition was monitored and Elliot called in every expert on the Eastern seaboard to examine him and put forward a prognosis.

They were all the same. Danny was a vegetable and there was no hope. One evening, two months after the accident, a week before her seventeenth birthday, Elliot sat down in the kitchen with Lizzie and explained that they were going to switch off Danny's life support and let him go peacefully. At first she said nothing, staring silently into her lap while tears rolled down her nose and dropped onto the table. Eventually she looked up at her father, her eyes searching his. 'You can't!' she sobbed, collapsing onto his chest. 'There must be something more we can do?'

After a while, he replied quietly. 'Nothing. There's nothing more anyone can do.'

'But how do you know? How can you be sure?'

Elliot sighed, stroking her hair. 'The human brain needs a constant supply of oxygen to function, Lizzie, you know that. Danny's brain was denied oxygen for over half an hour, it suffered terrible damage, all the tests show it is not working any more, and never will again.'

'But it might, one day. I read about fish and frogs frozen in lakes for weeks, months sometimes, then recovering.'

'I know,' he said softly. 'But these are different metabolisms, different processes, different organisms. It's not the same.'

'But–'

'Elizabeth,' he interrupted, gently holding her away. Her face was pinched, eyes red and lifeless, her skin pallid. She'd lost weight, having barely eaten, barely slept since the accident. Elliot had consulted privately with colleagues. They had all confirmed what he already suspected. Prolonging Daniel's inanimate existence was only prolonging her suffering. 'We have to let him go now. We have to. We were right to try, right to do everything we could. But we can do no more, so keeping his body going now is wrong, simply wrong.'

He was buried ten days later. Within a few weeks Elliot realized his instincts and the advice of his colleagues had been right. But almost simultaneously he had also to concede that they were wrong. Yes, Elizabeth seemed to begin managing the crisis within herself, subconsciously at least, Elliot revisiting the trauma with her in the privacy of his consulting room, a deeply painful ordeal for them both. Yes, she began to eat, to sleep, to exercise. Gradually she appeared to regain her composure, her equilibrium, a measure of self-confidence. She returned to school, continued her studies, even socialized a little with classmates.

But she was changed. Their relationship was changed. A chasm had opened between them. She no longer sought him out at every opportunity, she stopped taking the train into Manhattan in the evenings. She spent more time with her mother, or in her room or, when the spring sunshine came to Connecticut, simply out walking. Although he tried gently to draw her out on the subject, she would not talk about Danny's death, carrying the burden of it inside her like a private injury. Gradually Elliot was forced to admit that far from losing one child under the ice that Christmas, in effect he had lost them both.

In May she graduated, passing out way top of her year as predicted. They didn't go to Vermont for summer vacation. Elliot booked a month-long tour of Europe for the three of them instead, springing it on Lizzie as a surprise graduation present. She thanked him warmly but said she had been invited to spend the summer with a girlfriend's family in Toronto and if it was okay she'd like to do that. Earlier they finalized arrangements for her entry into college, deferred following Daniel's death. A number of offers were being held open for her. Elliot favoured one of the east-coast colleges, MIT or Harvard. But at the last moment Lizzie quietly explained that she probably wanted to carry out research when she graduated, genetics or biochemistry perhaps. Having re-studied the prospectuses, Stanford seemed to offer excellent opportunities for her in that direction and so, if it was all right, she wanted to study in California.

When the time came he drove her to La Guardia for the flight to San Francisco. They were silent in the car, Lizzie staring through the window as Connecticut's leafy green gradually gave way to the graffiti-covered concrete and grid-locked tarmac of the city.

They checked in, then he carried her bag to the barrier. 'I love you,' he said simply, hugging her slight body to him. 'Please keep in touch.'

'I will,' she promised. They clung together for a moment longer, then she broke away and picked up her bag.

'And y'all come back real soon now!' he joked, his stomach like lead.

It was ten years before she did.

C h a p t e r   4

AT NINE O'CLOCK ALISON AND BEN WERE USHERED INTO A waiting room outside the psychologist's office. Jack was already there, hands thrust deep in pockets, pacing nervously. He stopped as soon as the door opened, smiled brightly at Ben. 'Well hi there folks, how are we doing?' he said, bending to kiss his son. Ben went immediately and sat on a plastic chair in the corner, swinging his legs and looking out of the window. His usual place, Jack guessed, raising his eyebrows at Alison. 'Okay?' he mouthed, tilting his head at Ben. She pulled a quick grimace, fluttering the fingers of one hand uncertainly. Today was The Day.

'Well, now then, Ben,' began Heather Pritchard, a little later. 'How have you been getting on these past few days?'

'Okay,' he said quietly. He was very tense, Jack could tell. Hardly surprising, sandwiched between them on that ridiculous little sofa. It probably felt strange having them there at all: normally Ben saw the doctor alone.

'Okay, fine. Last time, Ben, as you'll remember, and the time before, we talked about the idea of going upstairs to see Frankie, do you remember?'

The shock of silver white hair nodded fractionally, but Ben's gaze stayed fixed on the floor in front of him.

'We talked about the possibility of doing that today,

didn't we? How do you feel about that idea?'

Rag dolls flying through the air, arms and legs splayed.

'All right.'

'Ben tells me there is the possibility of a holiday,' Heather went on, deftly shifting topic from the contentious to the rewarding.

Alison stiffened. 'Well, it was just an idea, nothing definite, it may be too soon.'

'I wanted to ask about that, Doctor,' Jack broke in. 'What's your opinion of the idea?'

'Oh, I think it's an excellent idea. A change of scenery would be of enormous benefit. To Ben, and probably to you too.' She smiled at Ben. 'Provided he'd like to go that is.' He nodded slowly.

They talked for a while longer then Heather led Ben back into the waiting room. When she returned, she closed the door. 'I wanted a quick word with you both before we go upstairs. Ben is progressing, quite well, but there are one or two things that are giving me cause for concern. Tell me, how do you both find him at home at the moment?'

'All right,' replied Alison thoughtfully. 'Much the same as he has been. As you see him now. Quiet, the same.'

The psychologist glanced through her notes. There was the sound of birdsong outside; further off a road drill hammered into distant concrete.

'I don't,' Jack said quietly.

Heather looked up. 'I'm sorry?'

'I don't find him all right. Not at all.'

'In what way?'

'Every time I come round to see him he's more and more distant, remote. Not necessarily so much with me, but with himself, kind of detached, I can't explain it.'

'Every time?'

'Hmm?'

'You said every time you come round to see him.'

He felt Alison move on the sofa beside him. 'My husband and I are separated,' she said quickly.

'Oh, I see.' The psychologist fell silent, frowning at her file. 'I didn't know that. Is this a recent development, if I may ask?'

'Shortly before the accident. Um, perhaps we hadn't made it completely clear, properly.'

Jack took a breath. 'Is it, significant – would you say, detrimental to Ben. You know, harming his recovery?'

'Well, the break-up of a family is always significant to a child, Mr Heywood, no matter what the circumstances. And, well yes, in Ben's case it could be interfering with the normal course of his recovery. It's bound to be an added preoccupation, an extra worry. It's difficult to say but certainly it might explain some aspects of his behaviour.'

'How do you mean?' They stared at her, anxious and attentive, like two otherwise model school-children inexplicably caught playing with matches.

She had become increasingly concerned, Heather explained. Something was impeding Ben's progress, if not blocking it altogether. He appeared to be fighting something. Something other than his feelings about Frankie and the accident, something that ran very deep. 'Now, I can't say for sure what it is yet,' she went on, switching her gaze from one to the other, 'but I'm sure you don't need me to tell you it might be connected with your domestic situation.'

There was a long silence. Jack sagged forward on the sofa, his face in his hands, elbows on knees. Alison stared at the tired curve of his back, the rumpled creases in his jacket, the unironed collar of his shirt. He looked exhausted, had lost weight. She suspected he was not eating properly. And she knew he was still sleeping at the office. She'd checked.

They all went up in the lift together. When the doors opened onto the fifth floor, Ben stayed at the back of the lift, head lowered.

'We don't have to do this today if you don't want to,' Heather said kindly. Ben didn't move. Jack bent to him, Alison holding the doors. 'Listen, it's okay to be scared,' he said quietly. 'I was, first time. Still am in fact.' He held out his hand. Slowly Ben reached out and took it. Alison took the other, smiling encouragingly.

The room was small and stuffy, the walls covered in get-well-soon cards, posters of pop stars and paintings by children from school. There was a bad smell, disinfectant and dead flowers and something else, like diarrhoea. Frankie was lying on the bed, which was cranked up a bit so that her head was slightly raised. It was turned to one side and rested on her chest like a sleeping pigeon. Her hair had grown. Her eyes were open, or at least one was; the other was only half open. They were red and watery and sort of staring but also flickering, jerking from side to side. A small bubble of snot was coming from her nose; one corner of her mouth was hanging down and she was dribbling. There was an electric machine under the bed. A black rubber bellows rose up, then stopped, then with a hiss pushed back down. A pipe from the machine led to Frankie's throat. When the bellows pushed down, the pipe jerked a bit and Frankie's chest moved up, not smoothly like normal breathing but rather suddenly, lifting her chin up a bit, like a puppet's. When the machine clicked and let the air out, her chest went down and her head sank once more. There was a tube in her neck and another in her arm that led to a bag of clear liquid hanging on a metal stand. Wires came from her chest to a machine next to the bed with spiky green lines going across a screen. A nurse was standing by the bed, disconnecting a plastic bag of yellow-brown liquid from another tube coming from under the bedclothes. She put a clip on the tube before attaching a new bag.

'We've got a bit of a cold today,' said the nurse, wiping Frankie's nose. 'Goodness knows where we got that from but we'll have to keep an eye on it. We don't want it going to our chest.' She finished tucking in the bed, picked up a tray of instruments and the bag of yellow-brown liquid and left the room.

'Frankie, look who's here to see you,' said Alison, moving into her bedside chair. 'It's Ben.'

He stayed back, near the door, the psychologist observing from the wall opposite the bed. Jack went and leant against the window, feigning nonchalance, watching him closely.

'Do you want to come and sit with me next to her by the bed?' continued Alison.

Ben took a step back, shook his head. 'What's the matter with her?'

'She's, well, she's unconscious, as we explained.'

'Then why are her eyes open? And moving about like that.'

'That's because, being unconscious, the conscious part of her mind is not controlling her eyes just at the moment, and other parts of her body. So sometimes her eyes are open, and sometimes she moves a bit, or makes a face. They're called involuntary movements.'

She shouldn't be here, she doesn't belong. 'Can she see?'

Alison took a deep breath. 'Some people think so.' She flicked a glance at Jack: his arms were folded, his lips compressed. 'Some people don't. Because Frankie's unconscious she may not be quite aware of what she sees. In her mind. But that doesn't mean that she can't see and can't feel, and hear, maybe in another part of her mind. I believe she does. That's why we talk to her, and play pop music to her. You could talk to her, if you like. It might help her. Would you like to?'

He said nothing, staring at the foot of the bed.

'Isn't there anything you'd like to say to her, Ben?'

He hung his head. 'Sorry,' he whispered. Immediately his face crumpled.

'No, Ben! I didn't mean that, I didn't mean apologize, I meant anything, you know, news from school, silly things, Ben please.' But suddenly he was on his knees, folding onto the floor like a collapsing paper bag, a distant cat-like wail coming from deep within him. Alison and the doctor started towards him but Jack was already moving. Cutting them off in one stride, he plucked the stricken boy from the floor and up into his arms in a single movement. 'It's okay, it's okay, shush now, it's okay.'

'I wish I could die!' he cried out desperately from Jack's arms, crushing tears from tightly squeezed eyes. 'I do! I wish I could, I wish I could die!'

Jack dumped the briefcase on the carpet by his desk and picked up the morning post together with a sheaf of faxes liberally garnished with sticky yellow notes. A moment later the intercom warbled on his desk.

'Hello there. Bill's doing the banks this morning, be here after lunch,' said Carol's voice. 'Desmond phoned from Engineering, small hydraulic leak on Charlie Echo's brakes, says it ought to be fixed but it means the aircraft will be down until tomorrow, needs to know what you want to do.'

'Uh-huh, what else?' Jack tucked the receiver under his chin, flicking through the mail as she ran through the list.

'Shell wants last month's fuel bill paid. Today. Marshall's want to know what happened to the office rent, LAC have picked up a spare Brussels–Gatwick this afternoon, four passengers, need to know right away if we want it, if not they'll pass it to Myriad.'

'Yes we do! Bob Burgess can do it in Charlie Delta when he gets back from Glasgow.'

'And Bob Burgess is holding on the other line from Glasgow. Charlie Delta's autopilot is down again and he's not happy.'

'Isn't he? Poor lamb.' Jack dropped the heap back onto his desk. 'Right, tell Desmond to go ahead and fix the brakes, tell LAC we'll definitely take the Brussels–Gatwick, and ask Bob Burgess if it isn't too much trouble perhaps he could fly Charlie Delta back here the old-fashioned way, using his hands and feet. Shell can hang on a bit longer and I'll speak to Marshall's about the rent.'

'Got it. Coffee?'

'Great, and thanks, Carol, for holding the fort.'

'That's okay. How did it go?'

He pinched the bridge of his nose between forefinger and thumb. Outside, someone was running an engine up to full throttle, the noise building to a rumbling crescendo, rattling the glass in his windows. 'Not good,' he said, the floor vibrating beneath his feet. 'Not good at all.'

At noon he rang Alison. 'How is he?'

'He's asleep now, finally went off half an hour ago.'

'Thank God. What a nightmare.' He paused: she sounded very down. 'You all right?'

'Sick.' She sighed. 'I can't believe I said it. It was so crass, so absolutely bloody stupid. I just didn't mean it to come out like that.'

'Of course not, you mustn't blame yourself. He was very wound up, we all were.' He hesitated. 'Look, Alison, I really think we need to talk, alone, away from the hospital.'

'About us? Not sure I'm really up for that right now, Jack.'

'Not just about us. About the children, about everything. About this Perlman place, for instance. I know you're very hot on the idea but we haven't talked about it at all.'

'Did you check their web site?'

He glanced guiltily at his computer screen. 'Not yet,' he confessed. 'But I will, today, soon as I can.'

'Doesn't matter, I've already got most of the information.'

'Right,' he said flatly, pursing his lips. Of course she had. 'So how about it?'

'Mum promised to take Ben to the cinema this evening. Supposed to be a treat for going to see Frankie.' She hesitated. 'Okay, come round about seven. We should have the place to ourselves.'

In the afternoon, his partner Bill Knight appeared at Jack's door, his face drawn. 'How did it go?' Jack asked immediately, putting down the telephone.

Bill slumped onto a chair in front of the desk, running stubby fingers through his hair. 'Well, we've managed to talk them into another temporary stay of execution. Extended line of credit for a month, maybe two tops.' He wrenched his tie loose, unbuttoning his shirt collar with a relieved gasp. 'But the refinancing package is still on hold. They refuse to go ahead with it at the moment, not without firm deals.'

'But we have firm deals. There's plenty happening, lots in the pipeline.'

Bill shrugged. 'They want hard evidence, not warm words.'

'Like what kind of hard evidence?'

'Like customers' signatures at the bottom of bits of paper for a start.'

'But that's ridiculous! This business doesn't work like that.'

Bill shot him a warning glance. 'I know that, Jack,' he enunciated slowly. 'I did explain, again. But, as you may have noticed, they're not in a terribly listening mood these days.'

'Sorry, yes of course.' They fell quiet, lost in thought. Bill picked up a desktop model of one of their aeroplanes and began to fiddle with it.

'Little bit nip-and-tuck right now, wouldn't you say?' he said, avoiding Jack's eye.

Jack looked at him. 'What are you saying Bill?' he asked. 'Are you saying we should sell out?'

'Not necessarily. But maybe we should have another look at Myriad's offer. Just in case.'

'But it's a terrible offer. That vulture Gateskill only made it because he knows we're in difficulties. In any case Bill, we don't need it. We can work through this patch, I'm sure we can.'

Bill said nothing, idly spinning the model's propellers.

Jack's gaze fell to the confused jumble of notes, names, columns of figures and telephone numbers scribbled on the blotter before him. Air charter agents, aviation marketing consultants and freelance co-pilots mixed up with child psychologists, medical-insurance brokers and special-needs providers. Beyond the blotter, next to the telephone, folding framed photographs of Alison, Ben and Frankie. Smiling, happy, unconcerned, normal. All completely different people now, he mused. Changed, altered. Gone from him. He looked up at Bill. 'You're saying you want out.'

He was walking through a garden. It was warm and sunny, he had just a pair of shorts on, his old school plimsolls and the wide-brimmed straw hat Dad had bought him in France. His top was bare but he wasn't cold: there was a gentle breeze, warm and comfortable as it caressed his back and shoulders. The garden was huge, wandering but tidy, with long tunnels of twisted vines leading to little hidden corners with wooden seats, rose-covered arches opening suddenly onto patterned flower-beds, wide green lawns edged with box circling playing fountains. He had been walking a long time but he wasn't tired. Loping easily down a slight slope he followed a neatly trimmed lawn path, which meandered between beds of marigolds and pansies, turned beneath a tall privet archway and found himself at one end of a long, wide, tree-lined avenue. It was cool and shaded, occasional piercing arrowshafts of sunlight splitting the shadows thrown by tall beech trees along either side of its length. At the far end of the avenue, where the shadows converged, he could see a distant bright arch of sunlight. He began to walk towards it, the smell of warm soil and moist leaves filling his nostrils, the sound of birdsong and the hissing of beech leaves to either side. Moving closer towards the light, he could see that beyond lay a field of gently swaying grass and in the far distance beyond that the tiny speck of a figure walking towards him. As he neared the end of the avenue there was a wooden gate. It opened onto a wide meadow of long grass dotted with blood-red poppies, the grass swaying and swirling as the air wandered lazily through it like fish in a lake. The smell was of drying hay and cornflowers. He stopped at the gate. A girl was moving easily through the knee-high grass towards him. She was young, about his age. She was wearing a simple patterned swimsuit under small white shorts, and a straw hat the same as his. She had long hair the colour of corn and laughing green eyes beneath the hat, which splintered the sunshine on her face, dappling the tiny freckles on her cheeks. Her legs were long and bare beneath the shorts, the skin smooth and brown. He could see tiny golden hairs on the bare skin of her arm as she reached out a hand towards him. 'Come on.' She smiled, soft swellings showing beneath the swimsuit where her new breasts grew. In the distance he could hear the sound of other people, other children, where the meadow dissolved into far-off hills, beyond that, snow-capped mountains. 'Come on,' she said again, her face melting.

Janet Catchpole upended her handbag onto the hall table for the third time. 'For God's sake, where the bloody hell are they?' she fretted, rummaging through the scattered heap once more. 'Ben, come on!' she shouted in the general direction of the stairs. 'We'll be late! And have you seen my car keys anywhere?'

Alison appeared. 'In the kitchen,' she said, dangling them. She looked at the table. 'Mother, is that a packet of condoms? It is! What on earth are you doing with condoms in your hand-bag?'

'Good gracious, Alison, don't be such a prude. Shouldn't I be allowed to carry condoms if I want to? Ben! For God's sake, come on!'

'Well no, I mean, yes,' Alison blustered. 'But what are they for?'

'What kind of a question is that? What the hell do you think they're for? Honestly, Alison, I sometimes wonder whether you inhabit the same planet as the rest of us.' There was the rumble of Ben's feet on the stairs.

'Well, it's just that I hadn't – well, I hadn't ever imagined . . .'

'Hadn't imagined that a dried-up old prune like your wid-owed mother might still be entitled to a sex life. Alison, do try to see things from other people's perspectives occasionally, will you?' She straightened, looking her daughter critically up and down. 'Jack's, for example. Oh and couldn't you change into a skirt or something, make a bit of an effort? You look like an underfed scarecrow. Ah, Ben darling, there you are. Run and get your coat on, there's a good boy, it's coming on to rain, and your baseball cap is on the hook if you want it.' She turned to Alison, looping her handbag over one arm. 'And you can stop gawping like that,' she said, lowering her voice. 'They were giving them away outside the supermarket, Aids Awareness Week or something. I gave them some money and they gave me a leaflet and a packet of condoms. "Safe sex is for everyone," the girl said. I was rather flattered.'

Alison's face fell. 'Sorry. It's just that it was a bit of a surprise, that's all.'

Janet tugged the frayed collar of Alison's shirt straight above the faded sweatshirt. 'You know, having a quickie with someone doesn't necessarily mean the world has to end,' she said. 'It's not the sex that's important, it's what it signifies. Could just be a desperate need for companionship, or a brief release from loneliness, or a cry for help.' She was stretching her fingers into a pair of calfskin gloves. 'Think about that, will you?' Ben appeared at her side, his hair concealed beneath a large baseball cap pulled low over his ears. 'Ready are we? Excellent. Right, don't wait up, Mummy, I expect we'll be doing a drive-in burger or a McGin-and-tonic or something after the pictures. Have a good evening, see you later.' She pecked Alison on the cheek. 'Ribbed, they are,' she murmured, rolling her eyes. 'For heightened sensitivity.'

Fifteen minutes later Jack arrived, his shoulders spotted with raindrops. He was carrying a bottle of wine and a potted chrysanthemum. 'What's this all about?' she asked as he closed the door.

'Hearts and minds. Confucius or something, woman at the shop told me. One dilates, the other lubricates.'

'God, don't you start.'

'Sorry?'

'Mother – she, oh, never mind. Where shall we go?'

He followed her, mesmerized by a wafted tang of freshly washed hair, into the front room, where he found himself staring around surreptitiously as he uncorked the bottle between his knees. It was the first time he had been allowed there, invited in there, for weeks, months, since her eviction order. It felt strange, unfamiliar, even though it hadn't changed at all. The same faded floral three-piece suite, the mahogany coffee table, Frankie's upright piano, her music still perched on its stand, family photographs crowding the mock-Georgian fireplace. Although tinged with mustiness from disuse, it even had the same smell. Furniture polish, wood ash from the grate and a faint lingering hint of Alison's favourite scent.

They sat opposite each other in front of the unlit fireplace and talked polite generalities for a while, like two strangers introduced at a cocktail party. She asked him about business, he said everything was going fine thanks, then enquired after her sister Rosemary, who lived in Paris, and complimented her on the tidiness of the garden. Outside, the evening sky was grey and heavy, raindrops spattering against the windows in a fitful wind. Eventually she put down her glass on the coffee table between them and sat back. 'So, where do you want to begin?'

'Somewhere around two years ago?' he ventured, with a shy smile. Her face remained expressionless, he ploughed on. 'I even had some lines prepared.' He patted his pockets, pulling out a folded sheet of paper. 'Nervous, I suppose.' He dropped the paper on the table. 'Don't think I'll use them now, though. Doesn't feel quite right.'

'Jack, let's just try and keep this simple, shall we? The fact is, if it wasn't for the children's situation we would not be sitting here having this conversation.'

'Yes, I know, Alison. But I would just like to say, that what happened, what I did, with Carol, and all the crap you had to put up with before, it was unforgivable. I know that and I understand how you feel and I can't blame you for doing what you've done–'

'But what happened to Frankie and what is happening to Ben is bigger than that,' she interrupted, 'and you feel we should be working on it together, not constantly at each other's throats.'

Jack stared at her. 'Yes. Well yes I do.'

'I agree.'

'You do? Well, that's, good. Very good.' He picked up his glass, stealing a glance at her over the rim. She'd changed clothes since this morning, was actually wearing a skirt, a crisp white blouse beneath the yellow cashmere cardigan he'd bought her three Christmases ago. There was the palest hint of gloss on her lips. He swallowed wine, trying not to stare at the stockinged skin of her legs above her knees. How long had it been? Five months, six? Suddenly the penny dropped. 'Why?'

'You saw the doctor's reaction today. She clearly thinks it's a bad idea us going through separation and divorce right at this moment. It's bad for the children.'

'And?'

'And if we're going to get Frankie to Virginia, it would be much easier if we worked on it together.'

Jack sighed. 'I knew it.' His head sank back, his gaze lifting to flaking paint on the plaster cornicing of the ceiling. That's what this was all about. The ready agreement, the clean skirt, the touch of makeup. Frankie and the blasted clinic. 'Alison,' he began again quietly, 'I've been trying to say I'm sorry. For weeks, months now. I bitterly regret what I did to you and the children. But this has nothing to do with Frankie and some pie-in-the-sky magic clinic in America. This is about you and me and our future.'

'Presumably our future, as you put it, didn't feature so very strongly when you were busy fucking your secretary!'

'It was once, a one-off. That's why I told you about it straight away. I regretted it the moment it happened.'

'No, you didn't, you felt guilty and panicked. Do you love her?'

'No of course not.'

'Did you enjoy it?'

'I barely remember it, to be honest. I was drunk.'

'Doesn't say much for me and the children then, does it?' She drained her glass and sat back, folding her arms. The room was growing dark, their expressions fading into shadow. Through the window Jack could see rain falling steadily past the sodium glow of the streetlight on the pavement outside. The same streetlight they used to make love by sometimes, in the bedroom above their heads. Boldly leaving the curtains open, unhurriedly caressing each other's naked bodies, bathed in yellow glow, lying close together on top of the covers.

He blew out slowly. 'No, it doesn't.'

'Sorry,' she said after a pause. 'That was uncalled for.'

'No, you're right,' he said flatly. 'I'd feel the same in your shoes. Worse probably, male insecurity and all that. I'm sure I wouldn't be able to deal with it at all if you had, you know . . .'

'Had sex with Carol? I should hope not.'

He lifted his head, smiled gratefully. But her face was lost in shadow.

'Tell me,' she said at length. 'I need to know.'

He drew a deep breath. 'Well, it wasn't for the sex, Ali, believe me. That's the first point. Not like an affair or anything. But somewhere along the line, you and me, we stopped. Stopped talking, stopped communicating, stopped being a team. I felt you didn't want to know any more, about the business, about my feelings, worries. Carol was just, there. She knows the business intimately, she's a part of it, she cares about it. I just, desperately needed to feel that someone, somewhere gave a damn.'

'Go on.' Her voice was very small.

He sighed. 'Well, it was just as I told you. That Friday you went to Rosemary's with the children. End of a particularly shitty week, everything hanging in the balance, few too many drinks with Bill and Carol at the airport bar and I just couldn't face coming back here to an empty house. Carol offered to cook me something, we went back to her place and it just, happened. It just happened.' He trailed off.

She was crying. Softly, almost silently. At first he thought she was just lost in thought, hunched forward on the chair like that, studying her feet. But then he saw the dim outline of her shoulders shaking, heard sharp intakes of breath, the catch in her throat. Instinctively he got to his feet. 'Jesus, Alison, I'm so sorry.' He took a step towards her, but she sat up, raising her hand to stop him.

'It's okay, I'll be okay.' She sniffed, fumbling for a handkerchief. He stood back hesitantly. 'You didn't seem to care about us any more. Just gave up.' She sobbed miserably. 'You were never here. It was just business, business, business. We didn't exist for you, the children and me, I didn't exist. We weren't important.' She blew her nose noisily.

'Christ,' he whispered, slumping back into the chair. In the street heavy footsteps splashed by quickly as someone ran for cover.

'You never back me up,' she went on after a while, her voice thick but steady.

'Hmm?'

'Like this morning. With Ben's doctor. *I* had to explain we were separated. You didn't back me up, didn't say anything. I had to do it. It makes me feel I'm the guilty party, it's not fair.'

'I suppose it's because I don't want it to be true,' he said glumly.

'Then with Ben, in Frankie's room. I had to do everything, say everything. You didn't do anything, just stood there.'

'I was scared.'

'But I'm scared too!' she pleaded, her voice rising in the darkness. 'And it's the same with Frankie's doctors. You never say anything, never do anything. It's always me that has to push them, ask questions, demand things, get things done. I have to do it all, deal with everything.' She blew again. 'It's just not fair.'

'I know, but that's different,' he said. 'That's because I'm not sure I agree.'

Her head came up. 'Agree with what?'

'With what we're doing. With Frankie. Keeping her body going, all the talk about this clinic in America, everything. I just don't feel completely sure that it's the right thing to do, for her and for Ben.'

Alison stared at him in the darkness. 'But we have to do it. We absolutely have to.'

'No, we don't have to. What if I feel it's wrong? Suppose I don't think it's in her best interests. Or Ben's.'

'But that's impossible, Jack. It must be in her best interests. Ben's too.'

'But what if it isn't?'

He was in the flying-club bar. The bar was packed, but familiar and convivial, full of his own kind. After leaving Alison he had driven slowly back to the airport, let himself into the darkened offices, sat at his desk and booted up his computer. He worked for a while, then lay down on the couch in the executive lounge and tried to sleep. But his head was filled, he was exhausted but couldn't sleep, and there was a growing racket coming from the bar. He threw back the blanket and stepped into his shoes once more.

Raising his beer glass to his lips he looked around. Flying instructors deftly milking free drinks from wide-eyed students in return for endless stories of airborne daring. A visiting German Lear Jet crew on stopover from Düsseldorf becoming progressively more raucous on pints of Guinness. Engineers and mechanics from the maintenance hangars chatting up aerodynamics students from the aeronautical college. In one corner, two would-be commercial pilots, working their hours up the hard way flying the parachute-club Islander for no pay, told horror stories of failed parachutes and crumpled corpses to a group of office girls up from London for a sponsored charity jump.

'Thing is, Bill,' he went on doggedly, 'she's got it into her damn head that going to America is the only way out, as if it's the Holy bloody Grail or something. She's totally obsessed.' His partner nodded absently, attention faltering as he tried to attract the barman with a waved five-pound note. They were sitting on stools, wedged tightly into a corner.

'And what do you think?'

'I suspect a lot of it is to do with guilt, partly. She feels guilty.' On the far side of the smoke-filled room he caught sight of Carol, black hair spilling onto the shoulders of her blouse, smiling modestly as a tall, darkly suited man with his back to him spoke earnestly into her ear. 'We both do, about what happened, and somehow she's convinced herself that this American clinic holds the key to unlocking that guilt.'

'But for Christ's sake man, you're not to blame, neither of you. It was an accident.'

'It was three weeks after she threw me out Bill,' said Jack quietly. 'I used to drop the kids at school, remember? Every single day on the way to work. If I was still there, living at home, none of this would have happened, none of it. Believe me, there's guilt all right.' He stared into his beer. It was Gateskill, Myriad's boss, talking to Carol. Near them, arms linked and glasses raised, the Germans were breaking into song.

Bill reached out and patted Jack's shoulder. 'And what about this clinic?' he asked, above the growing clamour. 'Can they do anything do you think?'

Jack shrugged. 'God knows.' He picked up his glass. 'Sometimes I look at her, you know, I look at Frankie and I think it's hopeless, totally hopeless, there's nothing there. She's just a vegetable on a bunch of machinery and we should just switch it off and let her go. But then, maybe there is something,

something deep inside, a spark of something. But who knows, how do you tell?'

'What do they do, the clinic?'

He drained his glass, he was starting to feel dizzy. 'They charge around ten thousand dollars a month, that's what they do. And therefore it is out of the question, totally out of the fucking question.' He slipped off the bar stool and made for the door.

Outside the rain had stopped, the sky cleared; a faint scattering of milky stars was visible above the harsh glow of the apron floodlights. The airport lay still, flat and wide, silent save for the low grumble of a lone turboprop taxiing to its tie-down point, its red anti-collision beacon ricocheting off the puddled tarmac and wet metal flanks of the empty aircraft parked around it. As he watched, the pilot pulled the cut-off, the engine died and silence fell once more. He sat down on a wooden spectators' bench, inhaling the cool night air, the familiar acrodrome smell of jet fuel, wet tarmac and mown grass. Behind him a crescendo of laughter and music as the bar door opened then closed again. A moment later he felt a hand on his shoulder.

'Don't you miss it?' Carol said, looking out over the rows of deserted aeroplanes. 'Flying?'

He had thought he wouldn't. He had thought that being a big wheel in his own aviation business would be better than being a very small cog in someone else's. That being a mover and a shaker rather than a simple driver was a step upwards. That leaving the pilot's seat for a boardroom chair was an act of maturity, exchanging transitory self-fulfilment for a secure future for him and his family. But somehow it hadn't worked out quite like that. And he did miss it, being the organic orchestrator of a delicate but elegantly simple balance of man-made machinery and natural dynamic forces. The mix of high technology and simple boyhood wonderment. The fun.

'Do you know?' he began, patting the bench beside him.

Carol sat, the respectful gap between them an unbridgeable canyon. 'This business, Heywood-Knight, despite everything, all the problems, all the aggravation, everything, I still love it. It's ours, we created it.'

'I know,' she said simply. 'Jack, David Gateskill has offered me a job, at Myriad. Opening up an aircraft-leasing division.'

'Ah.' He looked out across the apron. 'Good package, I'd imagine.'

'Terrific.' She hesitated. 'I turned him down.'

They fell silent. 'I'm sorry,' he offered. 'These past few months must have been shitty for you.'

'Well, they can't have been exactly a ball of fun for you either,' she replied softly. 'How is everyone?'

He sighed. 'Frankie, no change, exactly the same. Ben, not good. Alison, well, she's trying to cope with an awful situation single-handed – at least, she believes single-handed.'

'And you?'

Angry, guilty, excluded, resentful, fearful, uncomprehending, isolated. 'I'm okay,' he said. 'Carol, what happened, that night, between us at your place?'

'Please don't say you regret it, Jack. I know it was wrong, I know it shouldn't have happened, and I know it can never happen again but I couldn't bear to hear you say you regretted it, even if it's true.'

'No, I don't,' he lied. 'It was a kind, generous, spontaneous gesture of friendship at a time when I was feeling very alone. But the point is it had a price tag attached and I knew that. It was my doing, my call, my responsibility. And now I'm paying. We all are, all of us.'

They sat in silence. After a while she began to shiver. 'Come on,' he took her arm gently, 'I'll take you back inside.'

'What will you do?' she said. In the distance a siren wailed as a police car sped across town.

'I don't know yet.' He reached for the door of the bar. 'But I am going to find out.'

*

For a long time Alison sat in the darkened room listening to the gentle ticking of the carriage clock on the mantelpiece and the dying of the wind outside. After a while her eyes fell on the faint white gleam on the coffee table. His notes. Reaching forward she picked them up, rose stiffly from the armchair and walked to the window. It was a single sheet of paper, heavily folded, badly crumpled. She smoothed it open, tilting it towards the glow from the streetlight.

'Notes for Meeting' he'd written in neat capitals at the top. Beneath, alone in the middle of the page, just two entries.

1) Sorry.
2) I love you.

C h a p t e r   5

ELIZABETH LOWERED HERSELF ONTO THE ONLY SPARE CHAIR IN the cramped and dimly lit room and buried her face in her hands. The room was quiet, the soft rustle of the night breeze among the pine trees outside drifting through the small window. Around her the only sounds were the rhythmic click, suck and blow of the ventilator, the soft hum of electronic monitoring equipment and the slackening breathlessness of three of the four other people present.

The fourth lay on the bed, his boy's body slight and pale and still. He was uncovered and completely naked, his head shaved. Above it, a twisted loom of electronic wiring as thick as a wrist curled from a socket in the wall like a giant umbilical cord, snaked onto the bed at his side then erupted into a myriad-coloured tangle of hundreds of individual wire fibres feeding a dense rash of electrodes completely covering his body. There were electrodes all over the smooth dome of his head, attached to his face, his lips, mouth, eyelids and earlobes. His chest, his arms and hands, his fingertips, his thighs, legs and toes, even his penis and scrotum. Dozens more curled towards unseen destinations beneath his limp body. It was as if he was completely sheathed in a dense haze of coloured wiring. A black visor covered his eyes, sticking plaster secured pill-like headphones to his ears.

For a long time nobody spoke. Then a nurse coughed softly. 'Dr Chase?'

She pulled up her head from her hands slowly, resting her chin on steepled fingers. Beside the boy's bed a computer console stood on a table, an operator seated before its screen. A nurse stood behind the operator, a second waited on the opposite side. Around them, wheeled trolleys carried resuscitation equipment, oxygen cylinders and trays of instruments. At their feet an untidy litter of hastily opened medipacks, thrown-off lab coats and discarded equipment. They waited, watching her, expressions taut.

'I'm sorry,' she said finally. 'He's gone.'

Instinctively they all looked at the boy, the regular rise and fall of the chest as the ventilator pumped oxygen through the breathing tube at his throat, the slack face beneath the electrodes, the glint of a single tear escaping the corner of one eyelid beneath the visor. 'It doesn't seem possible,' whispered one of the nurses. 'He was so close.'

Elizabeth straightened: footsteps were approaching in the corridor outside. Lewis, no doubt. Wanting an update. 'I know. But you did your best.' She stood up wearily. 'We all did. Thank you. You can begin unhooking him now.' She checked her watch, lifting her chin to a microphone hanging from the ceiling. 'That's it, Nathan. Time of death two thirty-five.' It had been a long night.

At that moment the door opened. Two figures appeared from the shadows beyond, a man and a woman. Then a third joined them from behind. It was Lewis.

'Lizzie, sorry,' he began, 'but they insisted. I–'

He was cut short by a stifled scream from the woman, who clapped one hand to her mouth, the other grabbing at her husband's sleeve. She was staring in wide-eyed horror at the motionless form of her son. It lay in its cage of wires and electrodes connected to banks of machinery surrounded by white-coated technicians like some obscene laboratory animal experiment.

'Lewis, please.' Elizabeth moved swiftly round the foot of the bed to cut them off, but she was too late.

'Good God Almighty,' gasped the man, staring at the bed. He was smartly dressed in a business suit, well groomed, in his fifties, a big man, accustomed to his own importance.

'Congressman, please, this is not the time. Please wait in the lobby and I'll be down in a little while.' Elizabeth reached up, put a hand to his shoulder, trying to turn him gently back towards the door.

'Good God,' the Congressman repeated loudly, shrugging her off. 'What have you done? What the hell have you done to my son?'

Elizabeth sighed. 'Everything, everything possible. Now please, Lewis, will you please escort Congressman Willis and Mrs Willis back to the waiting salon.'

Nearly a year after her breakthrough with Gary Perlman, Elizabeth Chase's fledgling coma-reversal clinic was in danger of stalling before it ever took flight. It consisted of little more than a name, an endowment, a few hastily jotted ideas and a steadily growing list of possible patients. But that was all. Her work at Boston General went on, she was still interned to the neurology department where her caseload was high. She was worked off her feet, with little time to pursue her own projects. In any case the hospital management had made it clear they strongly disapproved of staff engaging in personal commercial ventures while under contract.

She and Nathan still met occasionally, chatting through ideas over a coffee in the canteen or a beer after work. But it was just talk, they both knew it. He was back down in Bioscience full time, had been given a promotion, was busier than ever. Also, as he frequently reminded Elizabeth, he was a computer pro-grammer not a businessman. 'What the shit do I know about running clinics man?' he complained one day. 'I couldn't run a goddamn dime store.'

She was forced to agree. She was an academic, a scientist, not a businesswoman. Hers was a God-given talent, a natural intuitive gift. It was what she was born for, had studied and trained for all her life. Her future belonged in the laboratory, not the boardroom.

Yet there were the patients, so many of them, and each week brought more. She was assailed by their doctors, harassed by their lawyers, pestered by their insurers and besieged by their families. All single-mindedly intent on persuading her to attend their unconscious patient, client or loved one. And although she tried, for Elizabeth it was impossible to refuse, seeing in every visit the same anxious incomprehension in the faces of the families, the same uncompromising faith, the same desperate hope.

Using her own vacation time and weekends, she flew to Tucson, Chicago, Miami, Salt Lake City. She took the train to Akron and Indianapolis. She drove her battered Volkswagen Rabbit hundreds of miles to Rhode Island, across into Ohio and up into Maine. On one occasion, a holiday weekend, the VW in the garage again and all the airlines booked solid, she took the overnight Greyhound down to Washington just to keep a promised appointment. She travelled stand-by or economy, she slept in cheap motels, or in medical-student accommodation, even empty hospital beds. She ate airline meals, hospital food and cafeteria sandwiches. She used her own money, overspending on her credit cards, running up debts on her bank account, losing receipts and forgetting to file expense claims.

And throughout it all, frequently, too frequently, the visits were wasted. There was far too wide a range of patient-types and conditions. Pensioners with multiple organ failure, middle-aged stroke victims, teenage drug addicts, incurably diseased children, congenitally damaged babies. All unconscious. Most, she knew, irrecoverably so. Again and again she arrived at a bedside, tired and hungry, carried out a detailed examination under the hopeful gaze of the victim's family, expended precious hours studying case notes and consulting with physicians, yet all the time knowing it was hopeless.

Finally, one weekend she travelled to Philadelphia to see a heart–attack victim. It was against all her instincts. She knew precious little about the man except what she had gleaned from details faxed by his attorney, but she could guess the rest. Late fifties, overweight, probably a smoker, high–pressure lifestyle, bad diet, not enough exercise. Worked hard all his life, finally made it, wealthy and successful. But at a price. Felled in the street by a monster coronary which dropped him like an elephant on a game shoot. The crash teams at Philly got him going again, more or less, but he hadn't come round. Three months.

It was all wrong. She knew before leaving Boston that he wasn't suitable, instantly regretting her consent to attend the moment she gave it. But the patient's lawyer had been un-believably persistent. Badgering away on the phone at her like a second–hand car salesman. Fast-talking, adamant, persuasive, refusing to take no for an answer. In the end she caved in just to get him off her back. But no more, she vowed, trudging to the train station. It had to stop. This was the last.

When she finally arrived in Philadelphia the lawyer was wait-ing for her at the hospital reception desk. 'Lewis Kern,' he said, extending a well-manicured hand. He was young, short and dark with predatory lawyer's eyes, his thick black hair cut sharp and close, like his suit. 'You're rather late,' he went on, looking her up and down with his artificial courtroom smile. She was wearing the old grey suit she'd bought in Stanford for attend-ing interviews and giving dissertations. It was the only one she had, was badly worn. Tired and crumpled, like her, from the journey.

'Sorry,' she apologized wearily. 'Train got delayed leaving New York.' Over her shoulder she carried a tote bag with a change of clothes, in her hand a battered briefcase.

'You came on the train?' he said, gaping at her in

astonishment. He relieved her of the bag. 'From Boston?'

After the consultation they adjourned to the hospital cafeteria.

'I'm sorry,' she began, pushing spectacles up her nose. 'There's nothing I can do for him.' She started writing up her notes in silence. Kern said nothing, sat back and studied her, plucking a stray lint thread from the expensive blue wool of his suit trousers, one leg resting casually across the other. Eventually she looked up at him. 'Sorry,' she said again.

He shrugged. 'That's okay, no need to apologize. It's what we expected.'

'I beg your pardon?'

'Client. He's already six feet under, we both know that.'

'Excuse me, but we don't know that.'

'Sure we do – at least I do, from a professional legal standpoint, that is.'

She took off her spectacles. 'Then why, if that is your "professional legal standpoint", did you insist on dragging me all the way down here to see him?'

Kern sat forward. 'Come on Doc, you know the way it works. His life-insurance company is not going to allow his medical-insurance company to pull the plug on him until his medical-insurance company's attorneys can drum up a solid enough body of professional medical evidence to put before a Supreme Court judge who will then overrule the life-insurance company's attorneys' counter argument and approve a life-support withdrawal order to give to the hospital's attorneys so they can allow the doctors to pull the plug on him.' He grinned at her, raising the palms of both hands. 'You're an essential, credible and highly influential part of that process.'

'And what part of the process are you?' she said incredulously.

'Oh, I'm on his side of course.'

'But you want to have his life terminated!'

'Precisely.' He winked at her and drained his coffee, pulling a grimace. 'God, that is absolutely disgusting. Look, what say I buy you lunch, Doctor? You look like you could do with it.'

Elizabeth ignored him, staring down at her notes. 'In effect, then,' she went on quietly, 'I'm only here to help you see him dead.'

He leant forward slowly. 'You mean you didn't realize that?' She said nothing, her face thoughtful. 'My God, you didn't, did you?'

She let him buy her lunch. They took a cab across town to a tiny downtown Japanese restaurant called Hashomoto's. 'May not look like much,' said Kern, pulling a scuffed plastic stool out for her at the bar, 'but the sake is great and Hashi here is the best sushi mechanic in town.' Without waiting, he ordered Japanese beers and a selection for two from the menu. Elizabeth climbed onto the stool, burying her face gratefully into a hot towel that materialized beside her.

'So, what have you got?' Lewis said a while later, placing his chopsticks down on a porcelain rest. He reached into his jacket pocket and produced a hand-tooled leather notepad with matching gold ballpoint.

'Well, I've got the endowment.'

'Uh-huh, two million you say, not a heck of a lot but enough to get started. What else?'

'Um, well, there's Nathan. He's on the team of course, and we've started talking to one or two others, and accumulating some equipment.'

Lewis looked at her. 'Is that it? One oddball software genius and some secondhand hi-fi?'

She stifled a yawn. The sake was working magic with the knots in her neck, but she was beginning to feel the effects of months of accumulated fatigue. 'Well yes, I suppose it is for the moment.'

He stared at his notepad, absently thumbing a staccato burst of machine-gun fire from the ballpoint. 'Well that's pitiful, Elizabeth, if you don't mind me saying so. Utterly pitiful.'

He made an airline reservation for her from the restaurant then took a cab with her to the airport.

'But listen, Elizabeth, please,' he said, as the cab crawled through the mid-afternoon traffic. Outside the sky over Philadelphia was grey and lifeless. 'Start doing yourself some favours, if not for you then for me and my poor conscience.'

'Lawyers don't have consciences,' she replied.

'Sure they do. I keep mine in a box in the den.' He counted off on his fingers. 'First off, don't go anywhere on the train, or in your own car, or on the goddamn Greyhound bus, for Christ's sake. You're a big cheese now, you're doing all these people a huge favour. Your input could save someone's life or, more to the point, save someone else millions of dollars, okay? When they ask you to come, you get them to make the arrangements. Business-class air travel only, a meet at the airport by car – not a cab, a limo. Got that? And good-quality hotel accommodation only – Marriott, Sheraton or better. You charge twenty-five hundred a day minimum, and no charge of less than a day. And if it's inconvenient, or there's an airline strike, or you just don't feel like it, don't go. Cancel.'

'But I feel compelled to go, that they're depending on me. The families, the patients.'

'The patients are out of it, Elizabeth! They're in Never Never Land, and not going anywhere so they won't mind hanging on a bit. The families have probably been waiting for months, years, some of them. They'll wait a few days longer.'

'Lawyers,' she murmured, staring through the window. 'So, what about the clinic?' she went on. 'What do I need?'

He blew out. 'Well, technically it's a standard nursing home set-up, I guess. Some premises for a start. Got any ideas?' She shook her head. 'An appropriately licensed complement of medical and nursing staff. Then there's all the hospital furniture, office furnishings, medical equipment. There's communications, telephone, fax, e-mail, reception staff. You need corporate registration, a letterhead. You need a name–'

'Perlman,' she interrupted. 'The Perlman Institute.'

'Perlman Institute, fine. You need FDA licences, permits to practise, permits to store and use medications, permits to provide residential medical treatment and care, permits to wipe someone's nose. Insurance. You need tons and tons of insurance. You need professional marketing, accountancy, payroll and administrative management support.' He sat back, pausing for breath. 'Christ, you know it's endless, a legislative minefield.' He looked at her. 'Are you quite sure you really want to do it? Absolutely sure?'

It was insanity. A wonderful but impossible dream. She gazed through the window, the cab crawling past a school. Drab grey brickwork daubed with graffiti, reinforced frosted glass windows covered in chicken wire. Twelve-foot chain-link fencing, topped with coiled barbed wire. It wasn't a school, it was a fortress, stony-faced teachers patrolling the playground like sentries. Yet above the inner-city grime, the eternal smog-laden rumble of passing traffic, the grey oppressiveness of it all, clattering skywards like coveys of startled doves, rose the irrepressible clamour of children at play. A line of chanting girls skipping in perfect symmetry between two twirling ropes. A swarm of six-year-olds squealing in delight while ardent kiss-chasers pursued them like barracuda after mackerel. Sixth-graders shooting a basketball into a bent and battered hoop on the wall. To one side a small boy, ten or twelve, lost in concentration as he pushed a home-made hockey puck around a pair of makeshift goalposts.

She closed her eyes. 'Yes,' she said, pressing her forehead against the glass. 'Yes, I'm sure.'

'Okay. So what else do you need?'

'I think I need a business partner.'

Elizabeth folded her spectacles into her lab-coat pocket, leant back against the wall and blew a long, misted sigh into the still Virginia night sky. She allowed her head to sink slowly back against the brickwork, her eyes taking in the curved panhandle of the Plough as it rose over the firs surrounding the complex. It was a beautiful night, still and warm, the air filled with the scent of lilac tinged with pine, the sound of cicadas and the distant hooting of an owl. And she had lost Robert Willis on such a night. And now she had to explain to Robert Willis's parents how. And why. She shivered, hugging her shoulders. Two minutes more.

Something was going wrong, something she couldn't explain, couldn't define. She desperately needed time. Time to research it, analyse it, pursue every possible avenue of enquiry until she tracked it down. She needed time to think. But there was no time, there never was any more. They were waiting. Dozens of them, hundreds, with their anxious eyes, blank stares and silent expressions. It was a scene she played a lot, knew well, too well. Oh, the faces changed, sometimes the location, and maybe the lines varied a little. But it was the same scene, rewound and run again, on and on like an endless film loop. Pushing stray turns of blonde hair into the loose heap on top of her head, she took a final deep breath and turned the corner back to the entrance.

Mrs Willis was sitting in an armchair in the little waiting room. The Congressman stood at the window, his back to the door. Lewis was slumped into another chair, head bowed, one hand pinching his eyes closed, apparently asleep.

'Congressman, Mrs Willis. I'm sorry it has been so long,' she began gently, closing the door. 'I'm terribly sorry but I'm afraid I have some bad news for you.'

Immediately Mrs Willis broke down, body shaking as she fumbled for a handkerchief. The Congressman turned slowly from the window to stand next to his wife. His face was expressionless, his eyes fixed on Elizabeth's. 'What happened?' he said, his voice like ice.

Elizabeth lowered herself into the chair next to Lewis. 'Bobby suffered a heart-attack about four hours ago, as you know,' she said, drawing a deep breath. 'We called you straight away. In fact, his heart stopped for quite a while. We managed to get it to restart, only we couldn't get it to stabilize and eventually it gave out again.' There was a silence, broken only by Mrs Willis's muted sobs. 'I'm very sorry.'

'Why?' said the Congressman, departing from the script. His eyes were still locked on Elizabeth's.

'Excuse me?'

'Why? Why the heart-attack? Why now? What caused it?'

She considered. 'Well, that's very hard to say at this stage, we'll be able to tell much more after the autopsy, of course. But there are certainly any number of possible factors.' She began to list them. 'Bobby has been unconscious for a very long time. That has been known to weaken the walls of the heart chambers and, indeed, the vessels supplying blood to and from the heart itself. Then there is his medical history prior to his unconsciousness. Also, there is the possibility that some of the medication regimes used during retrieval may, as I'm sure was explained to you, place unusual demands on the cardiovascular system. Similarly–'

She heard an intake of breath, Lewis stiffening beside her. 'Look, Congressman, Mrs Willis,' he interrupted quickly. 'This is a highly difficult time for you both and I'm sure we're all very tired. Perhaps it would be better if we left it for now and went into it in greater detail in due course. In the meantime, the Perlman Institute would like to offer its deepest condolences and–'

'You keep out of this!' snapped Willis, his face contorted. He turned back to Elizabeth. 'I want to know what you mean by unusual demands? Does that mean you killed him with your medication regimes and – and–' he waved his hand at the ceiling '– electrical stimulation stuff?'

'No, it does not.' Elizabeth struggled to control her voice. 'Congressman, before he became unconscious your son had a long history of drug abuse. That alone could have damaged his heart irreparably.'

'Are you saying this is our fault, goddammit?' He was shouting now, shaking with fury, cheeks flushed. He looked down at his wife. 'She's saying this is our fault!'

'No, I'm not. Of course I'm not.'

'You killed him! You killed our Bobby and now you're going to pay for it. What the hell were you doing to him up there, anyway?'

Lewis rose, hands outstretched. 'Listen, folks, Lizzie, this isn't going to help—'

'I told you to shut the hell up,' spat the Congressman, jabbing a finger towards Lewis before turning to Elizabeth again. He took a step towards her, his voice suddenly low and menacing. 'Now, I want to know what the hell you were doing to him up there, trussed up like some laboratory rat like that. You even had his balls wired up, for God's sake!'

'We were trying to save him!' Elizabeth stood up tearfully. 'We were just trying everything we could to reach him – can't you see that? And we nearly had him, we so nearly had him back.'

As soon as the Philadelphia flight touched down at Boston's Logan airport, Elizabeth took a cab home, let herself into her apartment, threw her bags onto a chair and picked up the telephone. First she called Lewis Kern, leaving a message on his answering-machine offering him a partnership and the post of administrative director at the Perlman Institute. She then called Nathan and told him they were going ahead right away, it was now or never and, by the way, he was technical director. Then she called the three other hospital contacts she had been gently sounding out and offered them positions. Finally she called the Perlmans, apologized for her recent inertia and re-assured them that the project was right back on track.

The following morning she tendered her resignation at

Boston General, requesting at the same time that they waive her notice period. It was with a certain amount of relief, she detected, that they agreed to let her go at the end of the week. Within hours the word was spreading through the hospital. She began to get messages, her pager going off every few minutes it seemed, as friends, colleagues and sometimes complete strangers, called to offer support, wish her well and, in more than one case, ask for jobs.

Lewis called her during the afternoon and told her he already had a line on three possible properties. One in particular sounded promising, a small abortion clinic recently hounded out of business by human-rights activists. Set deep in a secluded and forested corner of the Virginia–West Virginia border, it was modern, well equipped, quiet but well located and easily accessible. There was the final eight years of a forty-year lease option on it, crazy cheap price, he said. They agreed to press ahead with it right away. 'Kind of ironic, wouldn't you say?' he quipped. 'Like opening a vegetarian diner in an old abattoir.'

'Do you think they'll come?' she asked him at one point during that first hectic week.

'Don't ever doubt it,' he replied. 'Like wasps to a goddamn picnic.' Within two months they had moved into the new complex. While he immediately immersed himself in organizing practicalities and coping with administration, Elizabeth began preparing for patients.

Her months spent travelling the length and breadth of the continent visiting them had not been wasted. Apart from greatly increasing her knowledge and understanding of their conditions, above all else it had taught her the need to be ruthlessly selective. First, it was agreed at the inaugural staff meeting, held over beer and pizza on the floor of the unfurnished lobby, the Perlman was a children's clinic. During the preceding months Elizabeth had increasingly and instinctively sensed that her work lay with young people. Gary was sixteen, his grandparents wanted the money used to help people like him, and there was no shortage waiting to be helped. Also Elizabeth knew well that the young, particularly the pre-pubescent, made the best subjects. They were stronger, fitter, their recuperative powers, neural pathways, bodily self-repair processes operating more vigorously, and far faster, than those of middle-aged or elderly patients. Second, applicants were to be carefully screened for acceptance onto the programme. The dangerously weak, the chronically ill, the terminally diseased could not, regrettably, be taken on. Third, as clinical director, the final decision on who was and who was not to be accepted rested with Elizabeth. 'I am absolutely not going to be rail-roaded by any more fast-talking attorneys,' she said pointedly. Lewis munched his pizza, nodding gravely.

While she concentrated on the patients and clinical staff, and Lewis buried himself in an apparently bottomless pit of paper-work, Nathan was in charge of assembling the technical equipment. With his small team of assistants, he converted the clinic's surgical theatre into an operations hub, fitting a large glass panel into one wall and adapting the storeroom next door into a control centre. Quickly it filled up: in no time it was floor-to-ceiling with banks of computer-controlled equipment, which arrived daily by the truckload.

Before they knew it, the permits were in place, the equip-ment assembled and ready, the rooms furnished, the staff prepared. Finally, one evening just seven weeks after moving in, Elizabeth called everyone together into Lewis's office. It smelt of fresh paint and new furniture. On the walls were Lewis's law and business school diplomas, a poster of Groucho Marx and a huge cork noticeboard with a single Polaroid of Gary Perlman in its centre.

'Tomorrow morning a nine-year-old girl from South Dakota called Becky Poulston will be arriving here in an ambulance,' she began, accepting a paper cup of wine from Lewis. Ranged in a semicircle around her, eight people squatted on the floor, perched on the edge of tables or leant against the wall, watching her intently. 'Over the next few days, five more children will be arriving. Waiting their turn are more than sixty others. They can't speak to us, they can't tell us of their feelings, their pain, their needs, their hopes, their fears. They can't tell us of their isolation. But we can listen to them. With respect and dignity, and with our hearts as well as our minds and with every means at our disposal. And, if we listen hard enough and diligently enough and long enough, I believe we will hear them. Our role, our one purpose, our sole aim, is to listen, and to hear. And in hearing, to lead these lost children back from the dark places they have gone.'

She put down her cup. There was silence. A moment later they all jumped as the telephone rang on Lewis's desk. 'Whoa, here we go!' he joked, reaching for the phone. 'Becky's changed her mind.'

One of the younger nurses was quietly dabbing her nose, another got up and took Elizabeth's hand. 'That was lovely, Lizzie, thank you.' Nathan grinned at her from the floor, one hand raised, thumb and middle finger in a perfect circle.

'Party by the name of Van Winkle,' said Lewis, handing her the phone. 'Wants a word about somebody called Rip.'

'Hello?' she said, smiling as one of Nathan's assistants shook her hand.

'Hello, sweetheart,' said her father.

She took it in her office. 'Just called to wish you the very best of luck,' he went on. 'Everything set?'

'I think so.'

'Great. Customers beating a path to the door yet?'

'Arriving tomorrow,' she replied quietly, her heart sinking. 'You don't approve.'

'Lizzie! Of course I approve,' he insisted. 'It's vital, pioneering work. Cutting edge. If it's really what you want, and it's for the right reasons, then why the hell not? Go on, get out there and blaze some trails.' There was silence on the line, the sound of laughter floating through the wall as the party moved into full swing. 'Anyway,' he chided gently, 'since when did my approval count for anything?'

'You think this is about Danny, don't you?'

'Is it?'

She put down the phone, sinking slowly into her new office chair like a deflating balloon. For a while she remained, alone in the darkened office, her head in her hands. Eventually she rose and went back to the party.

Lewis got up, stretched his back painfully and padded in his socks across the carpet to the coffee maker. He refilled his cup, lifting the jug up towards Elizabeth. She shook her head. 'It's nothing,' he repeated, returning to his desk. 'An aberration, a temporary glitch, a dip in the statistics. It will all come right, you'll see.'

'I'm not so sure,' Elizabeth said pensively. She was sitting on his office easy chair, feet tucked up beneath her. It was an hour after Congressman and Mrs Willis had driven off. She was still in shock, listless yet tense in the aftermath of his onslaught, sickened by the heat of his accusations, appalled by his threats of retribution. 'Lewis, do you ever stop to think about what we're doing?'

'Have you seen the state of my in-tray lately?' He waved his coffee cup at his desk. 'Sadly I don't have time to ponder the meaning of life just at the moment.' He was trying to cheer her up, jolly her along. Lewis knew well enough that the Congressman's anger was largely a tirade against his own failings as a father. His threats would come to nothing. Probably. He glanced at his filing cabinet. On the other hand . . . She mustn't lose it, not now.

'Whether it might be, you know, wrong?'

'Wrong?'

'Morally.'

'Ah, morally. Sorry, I'm a lawyer, we don't do morally, remember? For morally I think you need a rabbi, or an electrician or something.'

'Lewis, please.'

He lifted his eyes to the ceiling. Beyond his office window the first tentative touch of grey was diluting the pitch black sky. Further away, deep in the forest, a lone nightingale called forlornly, out of time. He lowered his gaze to study her. She was still in her lab coat, curled onto his chair like a tired-out schoolgirl. She looked barely older than some of her patients, her cornflower blue eyes clouded with doubt, her mouth small and compressed beneath the slight lift of her softly freckled nose. 'Do you mean do I ever think about it, or do I ever think about it being morally wrong?'

Their eyes met. 'Both.'

'Not much and not at all.' Her eyes fell again, but he held up his hand. 'Lizzie, listen, don't ask me to sit here and trot out a pack of lies to you about how I just want to save all these poor children. We know each other better than that. I willingly agreed to pass up the chance of fame and fortune in one of the east coast's most prestigious law firms and throw in my lot to come and live in the jungle here with a bunch of socially inept longhairs for just one reason. Maybe two.' He paused, head cocked. 'Right from the beginning, I could see that what you were doing, what you had already achieved and might yet go on to achieve, was ground-breaking stuff. That's all. High profile yes, high pressure certainly, high risk without a doubt. But the stuff of international recognition, Nobel prizes and coffee at the White House. The stuff of massive government funding, overseas investment, unlimited sponsorship from industrial conglomerates. The stuff, therefore, of very serious money indeed. I saw that, and I made a business judgement based on that, and that's all.'

'Really?' she asked quietly, her eyes searching his. 'For you, it's just about money?'

'Absolutely.' He tapped his wristwatch. 'That, and the nice regular hours.'

'I can't believe that.' She fell quiet again. 'Do you know,' she went on eventually, 'the further we go on with this, the more our knowledge grows and our techniques improve, the less comfortable I feel with what we find. Bobby Willis, tonight, in the middle of the evening he was right back, right here. Nathan had him, absolutely had him. Bobby was responding, signalling, better than we'd ever had him before. But then suddenly it was almost as if he pulled back, deliberately pulled away. Minutes later he was gone.'

Lewis ground the heels of his palms into his eyes. 'Elizabeth, look around you,' he said wearily, gesturing at the walls. There were dozens of framed photographs of patients, smiling families at their sides. Artful displays of newspaper clippings and magazine articles obscured his diplomas. His pinboard hung invisibly behind a wallpapering of thank-you letters. 'In a little over three years, you have helped thirty-seven kids back from the brink. Now you've hit a bad patch. But you'll get over it. That's all there is to it.'

C h a p t e r   6

ALISON CAME INTO THE KITCHEN JUST BEFORE ELEVEN. 'I'M going up now,' she said, rinsing her coffee mug. 'Will you do the lights and lock up?'

He looked up from the piles of papers scattered about the table. 'Sure. Do you want me to look in on Ben?'

'It's okay, I'll do it.' She glanced at the table. 'How's it going?'

He regarded the confusion of documents spread before him. 'Bit of a nightmare, actually.' He forced a smile. 'Now I remember why Bill was in charge of accounts!'

'Anything I can do?'

'Thanks, but I think it's under control.'

'Right, then, good luck. See you in the morning?'

'Uh-huh, sleep well.' He returned to the papers, forcing his mind to focus on cash-flow projections and balance sheets, while, without his consent, his ears followed her as she moved about above his head. Slowly up the stairs, lights and curtains in the bedroom, into the bathroom, undress and shower. Back across the bedroom, barefoot now, softer footfall. Over the landing to the airing cupboard, thence to Ben's room. He closed his eyes, waiting for the dénouement. Finally he heard her bedroom door close, a moment later the faintest of creaks as she peeled back the covers and slid carefully between the sheets. Exhaling, he opened his eyes once more, immersing himself in the figures.

Half an hour later the telephone rang. He listened, then replaced the receiver, gnawing a fingernail pensively. He glanced at the ceiling, checked his watch, then went up.

He knocked gently, opened without a sound, whispered an apology into the darkness. She stirred, it was okay, she said sleepily, she was awake. 'Come in.'

'Sorry,' he whispered again. 'Thought you'd want to know. Just had Colin Whatsisname on the phone.'

'Who?'

'C-C-C-Colin.'

'Oh, yes?' She turned over towards him. He was standing at the foot of her bed, a tall, faceless silhouette, one hand in a pocket, the other hugging his shoulder, the light behind flinging his shadow across her bedclothes. 'What did he want?'

'There's some young American girl, former patient of the clinic's – you know, the Perlman place. She's over here with her parents. He's been examining her, doing tests and so on. He thought we might be interested to go and meet her, talk to the family.'

'God, yes.' She sat up, sweeping hair back from the shadows of her face, a razor slash of pink from a deviant streetlamp chink bisecting the white swell of her T-shirt. 'Could be incredibly useful. For all of us. Ben too maybe. What do you think?'

'Yes, definitely. Only problem is they've gone to the coast for a couple of days' holiday, then they're leaving for the States at the weekend. So it'll have to be tomorrow.'

She pondered. 'Fine. That's fine by me. But what about you? You've got that presentation thing, the courier contract, in the afternoon.'

It was crucial, a major opportunity, final selection stage. He hesitated briefly. 'No problem, I'll call it off.'

'Sure?'

'Sure. We must go. I want to do this.'

They left late the next morning. Jack telephoned the Americans and fixed a rendezvous. 'All arranged, meet them at six. They're going out for the day, won't be back until then. They leave for the airport first thing tomorrow.'

Alison's mother helped organize, badgering them into booking a hotel for the night. 'You can't possibly traipse all the way back here tonight,' she nagged, pursuing Alison upstairs. 'Have a proper break. Suffolk coast, it's an absolutely delightful spot.' She glanced into Ben's room, he was on the bed listening to his Walkman. 'I'd come too, except I'd only be a bloody gooseberry.'

'Mother, don't start all that again,' Alison chided, opening her wardrobe. 'You could come if you want.'

'No, I can't. Got some old fart from the golf club taking me out to dinner tomorrow night. Anyway, I'm on two-day Frankie patrol, aren't I?'

Alison smiled with relief. 'Sure you don't mind?'

'Not a bit. I'm in the middle of telling her my life story.'

'Enough to put anyone in a coma,' muttered Alison from the wardrobe.

'I heard that. Actually we're just getting to the discovering-all-about-sex part. That should get her attention.'

Alison straightened from the wardrobe, narrowing her eyes. 'Just remember she's only seven years old.'

They arrived in time for a late lunch at the hotel, a small Victorian-style guest-house with a view overlooking the sea. Afterwards they went shopping in the high street, then strolled along the sea front. It was a mild afternoon, a gentle on-shore breeze wafting the warm tang of salt air and fresh fish across the steeply shingled beach. They bought sprats and whiting from tarred wooden fishermen's huts perched on the beach's edge. Jack bought Ben a model sailing boat. He and Alison sat by a children's boating pond eating ice-cream and watching him, lost in concentration as he plied it to and fro across the water.

'You were right,' she said after a while, pushing sunglasses onto the top of her head. She lifted her face towards the sky, eyes closed.

'Hmm?' Jack sat forward, elbows on knees, sucking his ice-cream. Ben trimmed the sails of the boat, then released it, immediately setting off at a trot around the pond to catch it on the other side. The baseball cap looked incongruous, tufts of white clearly showing at his ears, sunlight bouncing off the silver locks at the back of his head as he ran. There were other children playing at the pond. Nobody noticed. For once, for the first time in months, Ben seemed oblivious, utterly engrossed.

'Your infamous holiday suggestion,' she went on. 'You were right, it was a good idea.'

He nodded, watching Ben. 'Good to see him unwind, just for a few minutes.'

'Not just him.' Suddenly the touch of her hand on his back, a jolt leaping through his body like lightning. He froze, ice-cream mid-way to his lips. The hand rested, lightly, one second, two, then it was gone. Hesitantly he turned to look at her. Her eyes were still closed.

The Americans were staying with friends in a large house on the outskirts of town. 'Sam Corning,' introduced the father with a wide smile as they arrived at the door. 'Come on in. The MacNamaras won't be back for a while yet, so we've got the place to ourselves.' He was tall and broad-shouldered, with close-cropped fair hair. Lieutenant colonel in the US Air Force, he explained, leading them into a sun-filled conservatory. It was packed with plants, tall, glossy-leaved tropicals, exotically petalled orchids, giant fuchsias. 'Spent two years stationed down the road at Woodbridge air base some time back. Two of the happiest years of our lives, like to get back here often as we can to visit.' He sat them down then disappeared to the kitchen for drinks. 'Girls'll join us just as soon as they finish freshening up.'

'We're so sorry to just drop in on you like this,' Alison said, when he returned. 'It's a terrible imposition.'

'Not at all, glad to help out.'

'How is your daughter? Susie, isn't it? How is Susie enjoying England?'

'Loves it, just loves it. Having a whale of a time and getting into whole heaps of trouble.' He winked at Alison. 'You know kids.' Jack sensed a vague uneasiness in the pit of his stomach. There was tension beneath this jocularity, long-borne pain like an old war wound.

Ben accepted his Coke with a shy thanks, turning on the window-seat to stare out at neatly manicured rosebeds, a wide green lawn edged with box, in its centre a small playing fountain. A moment later his eye detected reflected movement in the glass, his head swivelled back to the room. Instantly his gaze dropped to his feet, face expressionless.

'Ah, here they are, my girls. And just where have you two been hiding? Been getting up to no good, I'll bet.'

She was in a wheelchair. Secured by a lap-strap in a half-sitting, half-lying position, knees bent up beneath a tartan blanket. Her head was turned ninety degrees to the right and moved in non-stop circular or figure-of-eight nodding patterns. Her arms were bare, white and stick thin beneath an embroidered summer blouse, yet they too moved constantly as though performing an obscure oriental hand dance, bending and turning at the wrists, long skeletal fingers stretching and waving slowly like anemones. Her eyes were wide open but unfocused, roving around in their sockets like a pair of restless animals. Hunting, searching, always moving, first ceilingwards, then sideways, then floorwards, then back up to the sky . . .

'. . . is my lovely wife Linda and this here is our Susie girl.'

They ate dinner in the hotel, late, after putting Ben to bed in Alison's room. The dining room was half empty, just four other couples seated at little tables with starched pink cloths and electric table-lights shaped like candlesticks. They followed a waitress in black skirt and white apron to a table next to the window. It looked directly out onto the sea front, ten yards away lay the beach. A young couple strolled by, arms linked. They stopped to look out at the sea, glassy grey in the gathering dusk. 'All right?' Jack asked, studying Alison as they sat. She nodded without meeting his eyes, her face pale and drawn in the glow of the table-lamp.

Susie Corning had been knocked off her bicycle by a drunk driver when she was nine. Fortuitously the man then drove home and shot himself, her father recounted, casually adding that he'd have gladly assisted with the task himself. Doctors advised the Cornings that their daughter had sustained extensive brain damage, was deeply unconscious and unlikely ever to recover. After eighteen months without change, Sam Corning, having apparently pestered every neurologist in the south-west, finally heard about the Perlman Institute and immediately set about securing a referral.

'That Dr Chase,' he went on enthusiastically, 'she's one hell of a tough nut, let me tell you. Wouldn't take Susie on at first, would she, Linda?' His wife nodded from beside her daughter's wheelchair, her face neutral. At the window Ben watched Susie closely, his eyes following the endless ballet of her eyes, arms and hands. 'But Cornings never quit, as my daddy always said. He flew two full tours of duty in 'forty-three, Jack, did I tell you? B17s from right here in Suffolk. Anyway, I just kept on and on at her, and finally she caved in. Three months later . . .' He gestured proudly at his daughter.

'How long ago was her treatment at the clinic?' Jack enquired.

'Coming up to two years.'

'And what is the extent now of her regained self-awareness, her cognitive autonomy, functional independence?' Alison asked.

'Come again, ma'am?'

'Communicating, managing for herself, self-expression, that sort of thing.'

'Hell, she can hear good, she can even talk some, kind of. In fact she can do pretty much anything she wants, ain't that right honey?' Sam leant forward conspiratorially. 'She and Linda communicate just great. They have this kind of secret understanding thing, girl talk I call it. That way I don't know what the hell they get up to sometimes, ain't that right Linda?'

'Sure.' She had one hand resting on the handle of the wheelchair. Susie was turned towards Ben, her head balancing, wobbling as though insecurely attached to her neck. Her eyes were piercing green, her long hair the colour of corn. He looked at her, his gaze calm and steady beneath the rim of the baseball cap. Fleetingly their eyes met, her head still for an instant as the softest hint of a smile crossed his lips.

'It must be, very difficult, for you sometimes,' Alison said quietly to Susie's mother, willing her into the conversation. Linda's face softened, but she said nothing.

Throughout the meal Alison was subdued. They ordered potted shrimps and fresh locally caught sole, drank a bottle of Chablis. Afterwards Jack chose apple pie from the sweet trolley, Alison declining with a polite smile.

'Do you know what she said? Susie's mother, as we were leaving?'

Jack picked up his glass. He and Ben had gone on ahead, Sam insisting on showing them the Mercedes he'd rented, Alison and Linda following a few paces behind.

'She said they shouldn't have done it.'

He said nothing. His eyes turned to the darkened window, travelled through his own reflection, down the beach, past the thin white line of the gently lapping breakers and on, far out across the sea to the slow-moving lights of a distant ferry. Above it, a brilliant white three-quarter moon was rising over the oil black water. There were lights dotting the darkly pebbled beach. Anglers settling onto the shingle behind green canvas windbreaks, carefully baiting hooks by the glow of their paraffin lamps. He turned back to her. 'What about a stroll?'

'I'll just look in on Ben and fetch my coat.'

He was walking along the middle of a high street. It was night, the road deserted, and he walked the full length of it without pausing, without seeing anyone, invisibly passing darkened shop windows, shuttered doors, drawn curtains. The night was pitch black and starry but he could see quite well enough by the light of the old-fashioned streetlamps. He wasn't at all cold, with his boat tucked comfortably under one arm; the sea air felt mild on his skin, the tarmac beneath his naked feet still warm and slightly soft from the day's heat. To his right, through gaps in the shops and houses, he caught glimpses of the moon keeping pace with him as he steadily traversed the length of the street. At the end he turned left, away from the sea and up a steep hill, which led him past a dark, brooding church. Opposite the church, he turned left again and entered a dimly lit close, with big houses framed by tall trees set back behind carefully trimmed lawns. He walked on steadily, confidently, past the third house, the fourth, until he found it, recognized the front door, saw the car. Without hesitation he turned in, sailing between tall brick pillars and into the drive, hard gravel crunching between his toes. Reaching the house he followed a narrow paved path along one wall around to the side, past a high-windowed room with lights on and the sounds of grown-ups laughing, then turned again at the end of the wall back into the darkness, the soles of his feet caressed suddenly by the cool softness of damp grass. At the end he could see the big glass room sticking out from the back of the house. Dim lights threw green shadows from all the plants and leaves inside it. As he drew near, it was as if the whole room glowed green. She was there, waiting for him patiently, sitting in her chair among the plants, her head tilted back, her face upturned, eyes ceaselessly travelling the star-filled canopy beyond the glass roof. She saw him immediately as he approached. He came right up to the window, pressing his face to the glass, his hair the colour of moonlight, his nude body slim and pale. He smiled as her arms rose in greeting, her hands twisting and turning, dancing silently through the soft shadows towards him, her green eyes alight and laughing.

He stayed, bound by the intimate ballet of her body, the ceaseless silent leap and swoop of her hands and eyes. And then, after a while, he stepped back from the window. Lifting the boat high above his head with both hands like a trophy, he smiled, his body motionless, naked, bathed in moonlight before her. Their eyes met once more, their faces lifting slowly to the stars one final time.

Then he was gone.

'He's not there!' Alison's eyes were wide, uncomprehending.

'What? Are you sure?'

'Yes! He's not in the room, I'm certain. Or yours, or the bathroom.'

'Christ!' They stared at each other in disbelief, precious seconds elapsing. A moment later they were running up the stairs to check again, searching the cupboard, under the bed, the room adjacent. They knocked on doors, soon other guests were joining in, then the hotel staff. The manager went up to check on the roof, the chef searched the kitchens, a barman went into the garden with a torch.

'I'm going outside,' said Jack, gripping her arms. 'If he's definitely not anywhere here you'd better call the police. I'll start looking around the town. Try not to panic, it'll be all right, he can't have gone far.' She nodded, swallowing, eyes fearful.

He ran outside, searching left and right along the deserted sea front. Doubling back, he clattered through a narrow passageway that opened onto the high street. Away at one end a group of people were spilling out of a restaurant and into a waiting taxi. From the other direction a car cruised by: he waved at it but it didn't stop. He hunted left and right, there was nothing, no one. He set off at a run.

Ten minutes later he staggered to a halt, bent double, gasping for air. Hands on knees, he stared around him, panting, struggling to remember. But he'd checked everywhere, he was sure. The sea front, the shops, the ice-cream stand, the grass where they'd sat beside it. The car park, the town hall, the war memorial, the public lavatories, the boating pond. Suddenly, a flicker of movement caught his eye. The pond. It was a hundred yards away, over by the town hall. Something had moved on it. 'Ben?' He ran back towards it, an icy rivulet of sweat trickling down his back. 'Ben!'

It was the model sailboat, the one he'd bought him earlier that day. He slowed to a walk, as he drew near, heart thudding, mesmerized with fear. But the pond was empty, the yacht bobbing gently on the clear water. Ben had been here, he must have been. Jack jumped up onto the pond's brick surround, his eyes travelling back along the promenade, across to the car park, over to the beach, down towards the sea.

'Oh, Jesus.' The sea. A tiny speck of white, way out beyond the gently lapping surf. A gull? A floating paper cup? He leapt from the brickwork, kicking off shoes and flinging his jacket aside as he gathered momentum down the steeply sloping shingle. He hit the water flat out, flinging himself full length into the breakers. He went deep, the freezing water shocking the breath from him, choking his nose and mouth and filling his head with the muffled suck and shift of breaking waves. A moment later he surfaced, kicking hard, thrusting the water back past him in a fast rhythm, his body ploughing a straight white furrow across the smooth black surface.

Half-way he paused, gasping, searching around, checking his bearing. He couldn't see him. 'Ben!' Looking back he could see that a wide black gulf had already opened up between him and the shore. Lights strung along the beachfront were receding to a tiny twinkling necklace; a car raced soundlessly along the distant promenade like a child's toy. Treading water, he twisted and turned, searching frantically, sensing the bottomless cold depths beneath his kicking feet with mounting panic. 'Ben!' he called desperately, his teeth chattering with cold.

Suddenly there was a concussive crack, high over his head. An instant later the sea all around was flooded with brilliant white liquid light. Immediately he saw him, dead ahead, twenty yards, perhaps thirty, still moving steadily seawards, the shock of silver gleaming wet like burnished steel in the harsh glare of the flare. 'Ben!' He lunged forward again, gauging the distance, counting the strokes. Twenty seconds later he reached him.

He was still paddling. Slowly but purposefully, his chin up, his small shoulders rocking gently from side to side, swimming calmly and steadily towards the distant horizon. And he was humming. Droning quietly and tunelessly to himself like a bee at a flowerhead. The instant Jack reached him, one arm quickly circling the bare skin of his waist, the humming ceased and he stopped swimming, his body suddenly limp, face slack in the flickering light of the dying flare. As though he was asleep. Jack gathered him into his arms. Seconds later the flare exploded onto the sea nearby with a savage hiss, and impenetrable darkness engulfed them.

Jack sat at his desk, staring out of the window. His legs were stretched out straight before him, his arms were folded, his face devoid of expression. The airport was busy. Three trainers buzzed around the circuit like endlessly circling wasps. A commuter from Rotterdam had just touched down and was disgorging passengers onto the apron. One of Heywood-Knight's own King Airs was inbound from Dublin, due in any minute. A massive wide-bodied Lockheed L1011, just converted from passenger use into a huge military flying fuel tanker was taxiing ponderously out to the holding point prior to a first test flight. Normally he'd have found it impossible to resist such activity, pulled magnetically from his chair several times in an afternoon to watch the comings and goings. But today he just stared, listlessly watching the slow passage of fluffy white fair-weather cumulus clouds across his line of vision.

The intercom rang on his desk. It was Carol: DDL Air Couriers were on the line wanting clarification on a final couple of points regarding his contract bid.

'Oh, um could you take it, Carol? Or tell them I'll call them back later or something.' He put down the phone and resumed his vigil.

It was four days since their disastrous visit to the seaside. Within ten minutes of Jack reaching Ben, they were pulled from the water by the crew of a high-speed inshore inflatable lifeboat. They spent the night in a hospital in Ipswich where doctors pronounced both of them physically undamaged although suffering some effects of hypothermia and probably shock. The next day the three of them drove back to Cambridge where Ben was put to bed and examined again by his GP. He seemed exactly the same as before, as if nothing had happened. Quiet, preoccupied, but apparently untraumatized by the drama.

Not Jack. He felt spiritless, unmotivated and lethargic. He couldn't sleep, tossing and turning in the spare-room bed, haunted by the recurring image of his twelve-year-old son paddling his way steadily out to sea. When he did sleep he was plagued by nightmares, thrashing across storm-tossed oceans or running blindly among darkened streets in a desperate blind panic, searching, always searching.

'There's something I feel obligated to say to you both,' the GP had said downstairs in the kitchen after examining Ben. He was their family doctor, he knew them well. They trusted him. 'I'm not a specialist, as you know,' he said, accepting a tiny glass of sherry from Alison's mother, 'but I try to deal in the holistic too. I look at the whole body, the whole family, the whole picture. I just wondered whether you have considered the possibility that Ben's behaviour, his condition in fact, is connected in some way to his sister's.'

'Well yes, of course,' said Alison, her face mystified. 'We understand that the shock of Frankie's accident, and probably his repressed guilt associated with that . . .'

The doctor stopped her, raising his hand. 'That's not what I meant,' he said. 'Have you ever considered the possibility that prolonging her existence is just prolonging, possibly compounding, his difficulties?' He drained his glass, handed Jack a prescription for sleeping tablets and turned for the door.

He and Alison had not really spoken about the visit to the Cornings, the whole episode so eclipsed by the horror of Ben's subsequent actions. But Jack knew she was devastated by the experience, bitterly disappointed. And he felt angry that they hadn't been better prepared. He called Colin Winstanley from the office.

'I'm s–s–so terribly sorry if I gave you the wrong impression,' he stammered. 'But from our point of view she is a very significant c–c–case. To recover this level of c–c–cognitive function after such widespread damage to the brain is little short of m–m–m–miraculous.'

'But is that really the – the best we can expect?' Jack floundered. 'The best we can hope for? For Frankie?'

'G–g–good gracious, I'm afraid that is quite impossible to say.'

Then Linda Corning had called Alison, late one night shortly after their return to Fort Worth. 'Don't take too much notice of me,' she began quietly. 'I was just tired out that day. Sam can be so exhausting, and Susie's a lot of work. We probably just did too much.'

'How is she?'

'Oh, fine, fine,' Linda said, brightening. 'In fact, perked up quite a bit these last few days since we saw you, even what with the travelling and all. Very chirpy, very – what's the word? – animated.'

Fumbling awkwardly, Alison tried to ask about Linda's feelings for Susie, whether she felt there was real awareness, whether Susie even knew her.

'Truth is, I just don't know,' she replied. 'Sometimes I think there's something, that she knows me, that she's coming on, you know, improving. Then again, sometimes I just feel for sure that there's nothing.' The line went quiet. 'Don't misunderstand me, Mrs Heywood,' she continued eventually, 'I love my daughter. But bringing her back has destroyed our lives, destroyed my life. She needs constant care. Twenty-four hours, around the clock. She is my life now.'

Jack picked up a ballpoint from the blotter, clicking it absentmindedly. A moment later the phone rang again. He jerked forward, snatching it up. 'Carol, I . . .' It was Dr Pritchard, Carol said, Ben's psychologist. Returning his call.

She'd been to see Ben twice since the swimming incident, talking both Alison and Jack through the possible implications, possible explanations, about what it might signify, about whether something similar might happen again.

Jack took the call. They talked about Ben for a short while, covering some of the same ground. 'Was there something specific you wanted to ask?' Heather probed cautiously, after a few minutes.

'Yes, yes there is in fact,' said Jack, rubbing his forehead. 'I just wanted to ask you, we've never really discussed the subject, and I don't want to, to upset my wife, any more, unduly, which is why I asked you to call me here. She's very anxious about all this, of course, we all are, but something the GP said, and I just want to know for my own peace of mind, well, clarity of mind if you like . . .'

'Go on, Mr Heywood,' she said gently. 'In your own time.'

He drew a deep breath, screwing his eyes shut. 'Would it be

better for Ben if Frankie died?' His heart was thumping, pounding in his throat.

'Yes, it is possible,' Heather said straight away. 'I have to confess the same thought has occurred to me several times lately. As I think I said before, something is impeding Ben's recovery. Under normal circumstances, had Frankie been killed outright, for example, or died subsequently, Ben could have been expected to go through a fairly typical grieving process. One that includes many phases and emotions; shock, anger, denial, resentment, guilt, sorrow and so on, but which follows a progression, so that in the end a cycle is completed and slowly but steadily his life could be expected to return to normal. However, with Frankie in her present state . . .'

'Limbo,' Jack put in sombrely.

'If you like. Then Ben is not able to go through and complete this process. It's as though he doesn't know whether she's dead or alive and so his mind doesn't know what to do, how to cope. Therefore it isn't.'

Jack breathed out, head sinking onto the back of his chair. 'What, er, what are the processes, the procedures involved?' He stared sightlessly at the ceiling. 'Should we decide to look into this option, situation.'

'You mean of withdrawing Frankie's life support?'

'Yes.'

'I'm afraid you must take proper professional advice about that, Mr Heywood, I can't advise you. The hospital management and its legal advisers, Frankie's doctors, your own solicitor, they'll all be able to help. I believe it can be a very lengthy process.'

'Yes, of course.'

'Is there something else?'

'How sure can we be? I mean, what if we're wrong, about Ben? What if allowing Frankie to die doesn't make him better?'

'We can never be certain. It's a terrible prospect, I know, but you have to accept the possibility that it won't.'

*

He told Carol he had to go and see a client urgently and to contact him on the office mobile phone if she needed him. 'It'll probably drag on late,' he said, avoiding her eye, 'so I'll see you in the morning.'

'I spoke to DDL,' she said quickly, searching his face. 'They're very happy with our bid. By the sound of things I'd say we've won it.'

'Oh, fine,' he said quietly, turning for the door.

'Jack?' She picked up the mobile phone from her desk.

He grimaced, slipping it into his pocket. 'Thanks.'

He drove out to Grantchester and went for a walk along the riverbank. It was a pleasant afternoon, busy at first, children playing, couples walking dogs, mothers wheeling babies in pushchairs. He strode on purposefully, anxious to be alone, incongruous in his office suit and polished shoes. After a while the pathway grew quieter, just an occasional passing rambler or lone sedentary angler. He began to feel hot and slung his jacket over his shoulder as he marched, loosening his tie and rolling up his shirt-sleeves.

On he walked, the footpath growing narrower, more over-grown with the passing miles. He clambered over stiles, traversed cow fields, jumped ditches. His shoes became muddy from puddles, his trousers below the knees damp and plastered in grass seeds. Finally he paused, panting for breath, head buzzing, staring around him as though waking abruptly from a dream. He was quite alone. Aloft, high above him, a single sky-lark twittered noisily: nearby a field of sheep munched the rich meadow grass, oblivious to his sudden appearance. In the far distance a tractor coursed back and forth, ploughing dark new furrows into the pale soil.

He sat down by the riverbank, watching the green water slide sluggishly beneath overhanging trees, weedstrewn branches trailing in the current. Lazy, plopping swirls on the surface marked the rise of feeding fish. Suddenly a kingfisher appeared in a flashing shimmer of iridescent blue. He followed as it raced past inches above the glassy surface until it vanished from sight beyond the reeds.

He picked up his jacket and folded it under his head, stretching out on the long grass. For a while he stared up into the bottomless blue of the late-afternoon sky, listening to the call of a solitary moorhen and the gentle rustle of leaves in the trees. Soon he felt exhaustion creeping through his limbs like lead, moments later his eyes fluttered shut. With his breathing deepening to the heavy scent of warm watermeadow and poppies, he felt himself sink gratefully into the void.

When he awoke it was dark. He was cold, his neck was stiff and his shirt damp with dew. For a few minutes he lay still, head clearing slowly, blinking up at the gathering night sky while his thoughts assembled. Then he rose, brushed the grass from his clothes and began the long walk back to the car.

The hospital was quiet, the night receptionist glancing up only cursorily from his newspaper as Jack crossed the lobby towards the lifts. As he emerged onto the fifth floor all was peaceful, the lighting subdued. The nurses' station was deserted, but he could hear voices coming from the store cupboard behind it. He slipped quickly past the desk and along the corridor, letting himself into the darkened room without a sound then listening, teeth gritted, while he clicked the door closed.

She was on her side, her face to the window, half in shadow, half dimly lit by the glow of the low-power night-light on the wall above her head. He sat down next to her, reaching beneath the covers for her hand. He held it gently, limp and lifeless, missing its warm answering squeeze, mourning the lost pleasure of it sneaking instinctively into his as they walked down to the swings, or to the shops. Or to school.

When she was born, and in what he used jokingly to refer to as an inexplicable attack of sentimental feeble-mindedness, he told Alison that he would take care of Frankie's night feeds. Ben was still a toddler and highly demanding. With a new baby to cope with as well, Alison's days were packed from dawn to dusk. By nightfall she was exhausted, it was the least he could do.

At first it was a chaotic stumbling nightmare. Frankie went off like a ship's bell every half-hour it seemed, dragging him from his bed, tousle-haired and groggy from sleeplessness. Blearily he would gather up the disordered contents of the cot and carry it downstairs at arm's length, depositing it in an untidy protesting bundle on the kitchen table. There it lay, squawking furiously and kicking at its blankets while he stumbled noisily about in preparation. Fumbling with inaccurately measured scoops of milk powder, contaminating the meticulously sterilized but inexplicably numerous components of the feeding bottle. Cursing at tiny buttons and poppers as she, purple and enraged, and he, slit-eyed and gasping, joined battle over the hated and unspeakable horror of the nappy change.

Finally she was in his arms and plugged in, calm descending briefly. She sucked vigorously, tugging at the bottle in his hand in a greedy pumping rhythm, staring up at him, her Delft blue eyes searching his face suspiciously while she fed. Towards the end of the bottle she would begin to tire, the pump slowing, eyes drooping until the teat slipped from her lips with a plop. He would carry her limp body back upstairs, drop it into the cot and fall exhaustedly into bed. Minutes later, it seemed, it all began again.

But after a couple of weeks they began to develop a routine. He made up the bottles before he went to bed. He asserted some order into the regime, establishing a natural feeding cycle that suited them both. Their body clocks fell into synchrony: often he awoke just before her, was at her side before her protestations had a chance to gather momentum. As soon as he picked her up they subsided, she flopping contentedly into the familiar ridge of his shoulder like a natural appendage, comfortable with anticipation.

On arrival in the kitchen he'd light candles, flick on Alison's portable television for the night-time soaps or drop the Eagles' greatest hits into the cassette player. The nappy change became slick and painless, she learnt that the sooner it was over, the sooner the teat was in her mouth, watching him demurely as he carefully ministered to her with the wipes, lotions and powders. He learnt the importance of pacing her feeding, exerting some control over the rate at which she sucked, winding her properly, ensuring she stayed awake for the last crucial ounce.

Afterwards they'd spend ten minutes playing, he humming the Eagles to her tunelessly, while she plucked at a button on his pyjamas or gnawed gummily at his knuckle. Alone, together and content. Engrossed in their own private congress while throughout the silent house and beyond in the darkened streets, an oblivious world slept. He never told Alison, but when Frankie began to sleep through and the night feeds ended, he missed them.

His hand reached out, brushed the hair from her face, caressed the warmth of her cheek, wiped a dried tear track with his thumb. 'You can't hide your lying eyes,' he whispered softly, tracing the outline of her face with his fingertips. The smooth curve of her forehead, the lift of her nose, the delicate cleft above her lips, her face melting as his eyes filled. 'And your smi-le's a thin disguise . . .' On, crossing the soft pout of her mouth and down the rise and drop of her chin. He closed his eyes. On, following the curve of her throat and down the shallow valley of her neck. On until, head bowed, shoulders shaking, he found the uncompromising corrugated plastic of the breathing tube. There was a soft warbling coming from his pocket. '. . . thought by now you'd realize . . .' The phone. It was the mobile phone! At that moment he heard footsteps in the corridor. He started, fumbling at his jacket, the ringing tone louder as he yanked the phone from his jacket, desperately thumbing at the buttons. The door opened, a nurse's head appeared, her face shocked. 'What are you–'

'Hello?' A tinny voice from the phone. 'Hello, Jack, is that you?'

'Good heavens, Mr Heywood,' said the nurse, recognizing him. 'What on earth are you doing here at this time of night?' She opened the door wider, a sudden dazzling flicker as she switched on the overhead light.

'Jack, can you hear me?' Her voice was strained, anxious.

'Mr Heywood, is that a mobile telephone? Heavens above, you of all people should know better than that.'

'Yes, um yes, Alison, I can hear you, what is it?' he stammered, hurriedly wiping a sleeve across his eyes.

'It's Susie Corning.'

'Who? Susie, oh yes, Susie Corning.' The nurse was still in the doorway, frowning at him suspiciously, eyes travelling the room, the monitors, the bed, Frankie. 'Susie, yes Alison, what about her?'

'She's dead.'

C h a p t e r   7

LEWIS HUNG UP THE TELEPHONE WITH A SIGH AND REACHED for his coffee cup, watching through his window as a laundry van pulled up in front of the main entrance. Behind it he could see the short tree-lined gravel driveway leading down to the main road, and beyond that, the dense deep green of the pine forests fringing a heavy grey sky. Ironic, he ruminated glumly, draining his cup. He'd originally placed his desk in front of the window so that he could enjoy the view. Increasingly, these days it seemed, it was so that he could mount guard.

The afternoon was hot, humid and airless. He loosened the top button of his shirt, eased the knot of his tie away from his neck and picked up the four-day-old newspaper again. Congressman Willis had kept his word. In the space of less than three weeks he had begun legal proceedings against the Perlman, law suits had been filed against the clinic and against Elizabeth personally. He had also been busy talking to the press. The *West Virginian* was hardly the *Washington Post*, but it carried the story on the front page and Lewis knew it was only a matter of time before others picked it up.

'Congressman Files Against Maverick Coma Clinic' ran the headline, then went on:

> Republican Congressman John K. Willis Jr today
> filed aggravated assault and culpable homicide com-
> plaints against the Perlman Institute – the Dalmatia
> County coma clinic – following the death of his son
> Robert (16) during treatment. County Police invest-
> igators are studying the complaints pending a
> decision whether to refer the case to District
> Attorney William J. Warner and press charges against
> the clinic and its controversial founder Elizabeth Ann
> Chase MD. In a separate action Congressman Willis
> has filed a private damages suit and is pressing for an
> injunction to close the clinic for human rights abuses.

'Asshole,' Kern muttered, tossing the paper aside. He
watched as the laundry van disappeared down the drive, a thin
cloud of dust drifting in its wake. Something was going wrong
and he didn't understand what. Lizzie said it was something to
do with people's unrealistic expectations. He suspected it was
more to do with patients dying. Robert Willis was the fourth in
a year and the press could smell a witch-hunt brewing. Never
mind the triumphs and successes, never mind the bringing back
of another kid from beyond the grave, that was old hat, old
news. The only thing that brought the press running quicker
than a pack of salivating hyenas these days was when another
one died. Or regressed, or went loopy . . .

Nor was Willis's the only law suit. Tucked safely out of sight
in his filing cabinet against the wall, multiplying steadily like
bacteria in a Petri dish, was a growing pile of dossiers. The
Antonetti girl had been first, Lewis recalled. Maria. Wealthy
New Jersey Italian family. Sicilian connections, he'd suspected
at the time, but hey, so what? Just so long as they paid. She
freefalls into a coma during a routine tonsillectomy operation,
allergic reaction to the anaesthetic or something. Anyway, she's
gone and gone good. Eighteen months later she's still completely out of it so they fly her by private jet to the Perlman and

in just six weeks Lizzie gets her. Fucking miracle. But she's blind and has fits and impaired hearing. All to do with damage sustained during the original reaction to the anaesthetic, Lizzie explains to the Antonettis. They nod, settle the bill, leave a ten-thousand-dollar tip and jet off back to Atlantic City. Everybody happy but what do you know: 'Perlman Girl Left Blind, Deaf and Dumb' trumpet the headlines. Next thing there's a visit from two men in dark suits. Mr Antonetti's attorneys, they say. Mr Antonetti is unhappy about what happened to his daughter, they say. He has 'lost face', they say. See you in court, they say.

Soon others began jumping on the bandwagon and now it was open season on the Perlman. Willis was just the latest in a growing line. But he was different. He was high-profile, he had connections, knew people high up in Washington, could bring a lot of pressure to bear. If he said he was going to close the place down, then there was a real possibility he might do just that. And, well, culpable homicide, Jesus, wasn't the press just loving that?

As if on cue his telephone buzzed again. 'Mr Kern? Bob Royce, Channel Three TV news.'

One floor above, Elizabeth stood behind the desk in the darkened control room staring pensively at the two bodies lying beyond the glass. Their beds were side by side but arranged head to toe. Beside each, a computer console stood on a table, an operator seated before each screen, a nurse behind each operator. The patients, a young girl and an older, dark-skinned boy were both naked, their heads shaven. Their bodies were sheathed in their electrode nets, the tangled wiring converging into thick bundles plugged into the control-room wall. On the other side of the wall Nathan sat at the master control console. Beside him, eyes switching swiftly from side to side, Elizabeth scanned his screen, two miniature blue reflections scrolling rapidly up the lenses of her spectacles.

It was hot and close in the windowless control room, the air stale and foetid. Sweat and chewing gum mingled with the smell of overheating electrical equipment. The whine of the equipment's multiple cooling fans surrounded them, all but drowning the asthmatic rattle of an overworked air-conditioning unit mounted in the ceiling over their heads. The equipment completely filled the back and side walls of the room from floor to ceiling. Batteries of flush-mounted boxes and panels cabled together into interconnected units. A mesmer-izing display of flowing oscilloscope traces, TV monitors, blinking status lights, liquid crystal arrays and switch panels. The home-entertainment centre from hell, Nathan called it. Arms folded, he watched her patiently while she studied the screen.

Finally, she stood back, lifted her headphones over her ears, adjusted the microphone in front of her lips and rested a hand on his shoulder. 'Again,' she said quietly. 'But let's go carefully.'

'Okay. Sally, Gardner, we go again. Can we have a medcheck first, please?' Nathan released his microphone button and sat back, watching through the glass as the two nurses bent to their screens. After a while first one, then the other stood up.

'Annie's fine, ready to go.'

'Raoul's fine, slightly elevated diastolic but within limits.'

Nathan leant forward again. 'All right then folks, we're all set. On my mark, three, two, one, go.'

Within seconds an alarm sounded in one of the control panels behind them, then another.

'What is it?' Elizabeth called anxiously over the headphones.

'System overload, same as before, but I can't figure it. There is no damn overload.'

'Can you override it?'

Nathan shrugged. 'Maybe, but it'll take a while and we may end up smoking the whole array.'

'Heart-rate up seventy-eight Raoul,' called a nurse.

'Got rapid eye movement Annie.'

'We have about fifteen seconds before the whole lot trips out again,' warned Nathan.

'Hold it together Nate!' said Elizabeth. 'Sally, what have you got?' She stared through the glass as one of the operators studied her screen before looking up at her. 'Bits and pieces, Lizzie,' she said, raising her hands in bewilderment. 'The odd receptor flash and multiple sporadic sender pulses too. But it's just bits and pieces, I can't figure it.'

'Gardner?'

'Same thing. It's garbage, but very fast garbage, there must be a sequencer error.'

'Lizzie . . .' Nathan muttered grimly.

'Not yet!'

'Heart-rate eighty-four Raoul.'

'Yep, Annie's way up now, blood pressure too.'

Another alarm tripped in the control room behind them, a shutdown warning flashing on the screen in front of Nathan.

'Lizzie!'

'Okay, stop, stop, do it.'

Instantly Nathan cancelled the sequence with a click, his fingers rattling over the keypad of his terminal. Soon, calm began to descend in the control room again as he powered down the equipment arrays and reset the alarms.

'See?' he said eventually, pulling a stick of gum from a pack with his teeth.

'Yes, I see,' Elizabeth replied thoughtfully. She pressed her microphone button. 'How are they?'

'Raoul's fine, dropping back, same as before.'

'Yep, same with Annie, heart now normal, everything looks good.'

'Thanks, we'll stop there for now, but leave them hooked up. I think we'll continue close monitoring for a while.' She released the button, turning her back to the glass to lean on Nathan's desk. 'And it's not the sequencer.'

'Nope. Sequencer's running great, ran diagnostics on it all morning without a single murmur.'

'So what is it? Why does everything keep going haywire? Why all the alarms?'

'Search me.' He lobbed the gum-wrapper into a waste-bin. 'But if it ain't the gear, then it's gotta be the kids.'

She looked at him. 'What do you mean?'

'You're the damn genius,' he grinned, raising his hands. 'You figure it out. I can only tell you that there is one hell of a data exchange going on out there and it's overloading everything.'

'You mean there's interactivity. They're – they're interacting in some way.'

Nathan shrugged, swivelling to his screen. She took off her spectacles, turning to gaze through the glass. There was a buzz on the intercom. 'Lizzie, it's Lewis. Have you got a few minutes?'

'Be right down.' She began gathering up her notes. 'Nate, listen, could you print it all out for me please? Everything, the whole sequence, from start to finish. Leave it on my desk and I'll have a search through it tonight.'

'Rather you than me, babe,' Nathan drawled, as the door closed. He swung back to his screen. 'That little bundle will run to about two hundred pages.'

Lewis was in front of the window, hands clasped behind his back. She went to his water-chiller, carrying the paper cup to stand next to him. An ominous dark grey-brown haze was suffusing the sky, the air heavy and still; the leaves on the trees lining the driveway hanging limp and motionless.

'What a day.' She sighed, glancing at him. She sipped water. 'The new VR suite just isn't working, Nathan's tried everything but it's hopeless. It'll have to go back. Intertech sent all the wrong connectors for the cochleal implants.' She hesitated. 'And something very strange just happened in the control room with Annie and Raoul.'

Lewis continued to stare out of the window. 'How's the Broderick kid?' he asked. A single giant raindrop plopped heavily onto the glass in front of him.

'Hmm?' Something was wrong, his voice sounded flat, distant.

'Broderick. You mentioned a couple of days ago that he was in and out or something.'

'Oh, yes.' Something was definitely wrong. Lewis rarely if ever showed interest in the well-being of individual patients, only the well-being of their individual bank balances. 'He's out at the moment. I can't understand it. Everything was going so well. We had him fine, making steady progress, but then he seemed to pull back. We haven't been able to get to him for two days now.' She studied him, the sag of the shoulders, the pressed lips, the faraway look. 'Why do you ask?'

Lewis shrugged. 'Oh, you know, just wondered if there might be any possibility of just the tiniest tad of good news for a change. Stupid of me, I know.'

She put down the cup. 'Lewis, what is it?' She reached up to rest a hand lightly on his shoulder.

He tensed at her touch, a spattering of raindrops appearing on the window. 'Nothing.'

She moved behind him, tugging the back of his collar away from his neck. 'My God, you're like a ball of wire down here,' she said, starting to massage.

He closed his eyes. 'Don't do that.' She turned her head, resting it against his back, her thumbs moving in slow circles at the base of his neck. 'Please.' A moment later he broke away. 'Don't!' he glared at her.

'Lewis, please, what is the matter?'

'Nothing!' he retorted. 'Nothing at all.' He strode over to his desk. 'Apart from the minor fact that we're flat broke, we're getting sued from here to hell and back, and our customers seem to be dying on us rather a lot, everything is just dandy.'

'They're not dying "rather a lot", Lewis, please don't say that. It's just a bad patch. You said so yourself, we'll get through it.'

'Bad patch? Lizzie, you don't seem to get it.' He reached over his desk and picked up the newspaper. 'Have you seen this?' He waved it at her. 'Willis is pressing homicide charges for God's sake. They're going to shut us down, then they'll throw the fucking book at us. We could end up in prison.' He smacked down the newspaper. 'The DA's office is sending an invest-igator here. Tomorrow!' He jabbed a finger at his notepad. 'Ask a few questions and have a little look around, Mr Kern, nothing to worry about Mr Kern, just routine.'

Elizabeth picked up the notepad, her face falling. 'Well per-haps, if he says there's nothing to worry about, then perhaps he's right.'

'Are you kidding?' Lewis snorted. They fell silent. Beyond the window heavy rain fell from the leaden sky.

'What's this?' she said eventually. He glanced up. She was looking through the notepad.

He sighed. 'I don't know. Some woman, insistent as hell, keeps calling from England. Hayworth? Heywood. Got a seven-year-old she wants to bring over.'

'England? What did you tell her?'

'Forget it. We had the usual little chat about the small matter of the ten thousand a month, she said they don't have it, I said sorry, no pay no way, and that was about the end of that.'

'What did she say?'

'She said she'll call back.' He watched torrents of rainwater cascading down the window. 'They're taking him back to Idaho,' he said quietly.

'What? Taking who back to Idaho?'

'Broderick. The family attorney faxed a letter this morning. They say they've taken advice and don't feel it's in his best interests to continue treatment. So they're shipping him home.'

He arrived the following morning at precisely ten thirty as arranged. The receptionist offered him coffee, which he declined, requesting instead that he be shown immediately to Mr Kern's office where he spent the morning questioning Lewis, checking through permits and insurance certificates and carrying out an audit of administrative procedures. Lewis offered him lunch, which he also declined, preferring instead to read through some of the patient case files while eating his own sandwiches. At two Lewis tapped on Elizabeth's door and showed him into her office. 'This is Investigator John Boyd,' he said solicitously, holding the door for him. As he passed, Lewis pulled a wide-eyed grimace at her, simultaneously sliding a finger across his throat. 'From the District Attorney's office. John, this is Dr Elizabeth Chase, our clinical director.'

She rose from behind the desk, smiling stiffly as he shook her hand. She was wearing one of the hated business suits that Lewis bullied her into wearing occasionally 'to distract and impress the hell out of customers, TV journalists and law-enforcement officers'. It was a navy blue two-piece, the silk-lined skirt cut close and worryingly short, rustling un-familiarly against her stockinged legs as she moved. Studying herself in the washroom mirror a few minutes earlier, her face made up, her thick fair hair brushed down about her shoulders for once, she had felt self-conscious and foolish. As soon as she was back in her office she grabbed her lab coat from the back of the door and pulled it on over the suit.

Boyd looked at her briefly then sat in the chair across from her desk. Lewis began to pull up a second chair but Boyd stopped him. 'Thank you, Mr Kern, but I'll be talking to Dr Chase on her own.'

Lewis froze, half-way into his seat. 'Fine. Fine. That's fine,' he said lightly, glancing anxiously at Elizabeth. 'I'll leave you two to it then. Be right along the corridor, if you need me, for anything.'

For several minutes Boyd said nothing. Pulling papers from his briefcase, flicking through a thick file of documents and jot-ting notes on a yellow legal pad. Elizabeth sat back and waited, her eyes falling on Nathan's computer printout lying to one side of her desk. Immediately her mind began crunching sub-consciously through the figures again, her gaze drifting to the window as Boyd leafed through his file and jotted on his pad. His car was outside, an ancient Chevrolet with faded green paintwork and whitewall tyres, a police light sitting on the paper-strewn dashboard. She turned back to the room, studying him while he unhurriedly continued his preparations. He looked like an almost-made-it FBI recruit. Clean-cut, suit and tie, earnest and serious. Younger than she had imagined, mid thirties, well built, with light-brown, tidily cropped hair above grey-blue eyes and a small, firm mouth. But something was not right. The smile was warm and polite but forced, the eyes clear and soft but solemn, tinged with sadness. And his appearance was not quite up to the mark somehow. The tie was silk but wrong, like he'd just pulled it from the drawer without looking, the shirt was clean but inexpertly pressed, the suit of good quality but dated. As though appearance was a bygone priority. Still he said nothing. She exhaled quietly, folding her arms. And the jacket didn't fit properly. With a jolt she realized there was a bulge beneath one arm. When he bent over to his briefcase again she glimpsed the dull gleam of holstered gunmetal.

'Excuse me,' she began indignantly, almost without realizing it, 'but why on earth would anyone want to bring a gun into a medical facility?'

'I beg your pardon, ma'am?' he said politely, looking up at her from the briefcase.

'The gun,' she repeated, waving at his shoulder.

'It's, well, it's a precaution, ma'am.'

'A precaution against what for God's sake? This is a clinic full of unconscious children!'

'I know that, ma'am,' he said, calmly. 'But when I get through here I have to drive over to Everdene to take statements from a man who we believe may have murdered his entire family. I was advised a precaution was recommended and we're not allowed to leave them in the car. Would you like me to take it off?'

'Oh, no.' She flushed in embarrassment. 'No, leave it, of course. I'm sorry.' She looked away. 'Sorry, I meant no offence.'

'None taken. Could you possibly describe in your own words the medical aims and objectives of the Perlman Institute?'

He was looking at her expectantly, pen poised.

'Yes, er yes, of course.' She pulled in her chair. 'Our stated mission objective is to recover persistently unconscious people to a stable conscious state.'

'How?'

'Using extensive ranges and combinations of methods, systems, techniques and technologies.'

'I see. And do you draw a line at how extensive these, er, methods, systems and so on might be?'

'In principle, no. Ours is a developmental science. As long as they fall within our strictly laid-down guideline values, any technique or technology might be considered.'

'What might these guideline values be?'

'Dignity, respect, freedom from unnecessary suffering.'

'And how would you define "unnecessary", ma'am?'

She blew out, looking at the ceiling. 'Well, these are very deeply unconscious young people. They are not going to just wake up if someone snaps their fingers or shines a flashlight in their eyes. We have to make a judgement – *I* have to make a judgement – each case being taken on its own merits, as to just how, rigorous, and extensive, treatments may need to be to effect the recovery to consciousness.'

'In other words, you decide.'

She nodded. Something felt wrong.

'You say that yours is a, yes, a "developmental science". What do you mean by that?'

'There are few if any procedural precedents. So by necessity we must experiment as we go.'

'Experiment.'

'That's right.'

'Let me get this straight, ma'am. Are you telling me that what you do here is conduct experiments on unconscious patients?'

'No – well, yes, to an extent,' she stammered, her cheeks reddening. 'But it's really not like that, not at all what you think. As I said, there are no precedents, no textbooks, no established procedures. Nobody has ever done anything like this before. We have to feel our way as we go to a certain extent, have to. But everything is under incredibly tight control.'

He wrote copiously. Eventually he looked up again. 'It has been said that you apply electric shocks to patients. Is that true?'

'Low-powered ones, yes.'

'It's alleged that you use strong lights, and high-volume music and other powerful aural and visual effects.'

'Yes, we do.'

'It is alleged you use unrecognized and alternative therapies such as hypnosis and acupuncture.'

'That's also correct.' She folded her arms, lips together. This was all wrong.

'It is alleged that you use hallucinogenic drugs, intravenous stimulants and notified medications including some banned substances?'

'Under licence yes, but–'

'It's alleged you use virtual-reality visors relaying graphic imagery, some of which might be considered pornographic. It's been alleged that you attach electrodes to these young people's genitalia. Is that correct?'

'It's just a route, a conduit, a way in. One of many dozens,' she pleaded, staring at him. He returned her gaze, face blank. Eventually her eyes dropped in defeat, falling to her elegantly stockinged knees with a sudden pang of disgust. This wasn't right. This wasn't how it was. This wasn't her. 'Do you have any idea,' she went on doggedly, 'any idea at all, just how receptive a seventeen-year-old boy can be to sexual stimulation?'

'No, ma'am, I'm just trying to establish the facts.'

'Are you,' she said flatly, tugging the lab coat across her legs.

'Dr Chase,' he began again, 'some very serious allegations have been made against you and your clinic. I have a duty to find out if there is any truth in these allegations.'

'What's the point? You've already made up your mind.'

'Excuse me, ma'am, but that I have not,' he said, an edge to his voice. 'I'm here, as I said, to establish the facts.' He looked down at his notes. 'And what you have confirmed to me so far is that you conduct an apparently open-ended list of highly unusual experiments on unconscious patients who, correct me if I'm wrong, are unable to tell you if they are suffering pain or discomfort, nor are they able to ask you to stop. And I'm sure I don't have to remind you that a young boy died here recently while undergoing such treatment. That, therefore, since you ask, is the point.'

After he'd gone, she sat for a long time in the gathering gloom of her office. At last Lewis appeared round the door, demanding a blow-by-blow account.

'What's up Doc?' he joked, seeing her face.

'Sorry, Lewis.' She sighed. 'I blew it.' He asked her what had happened. 'Not now, Lew. Would you mind if I was left alone for a bit?' He smiled, of course not, told her not to worry, 'We ain't done yet,' and disappeared back to his office. She sat for a while longer in the descending twilight, then hauled herself wearily from the chair and walked slowly to the wall above her bookshelves. A gilt-framed family group smiled back at her, Gary Perlman and his grandparents, a Christmas present from last year. Rose had written a greeting at the bottom. 'Dearest Lizzie, the pattern of all patience, Merry Christmas, with love from us all.' She studied the faces, the meticulous looping handwriting, the carefully chosen words. Then she stopped.

She went back to the desk and leant across it towards the intercom, her eyes fixed on the thick sheaf of computer print-out Nathan had left for her. 'Who's on with Raoul and Annie at the moment?' she asked, thumbing the button.

'It's me, Lizzie.' A voice came back. 'Sally. I came back on at six.'

'Are they still hooked up?'

'Uh-huh, but only at level two close monitoring.'

'How are they doing?'

'Both fine. Raoul very quiet, minimal activity, same as usual. Annie, well, she's more or less the same. Perhaps a bit more active, there's the odd burst, some spikes popping up on the traces, then it all goes quiet again.'

'Right, I think Raoul can go back down to level one. Can you get him completely unhooked please, Sally. We'll leave Annie to brew a little longer. Bleep me if anything happens. I'm going out.'

She took the clinic's Jeep, kicking mud up onto its smart white flanks as she crashed it through the previous day's puddles, propelling it urgently along winding tunnels of motionless dark forest. The Jeep was too big for her, she could barely see over the wheel, peering ahead while its lights pierced silken mist layers hanging low above the road. 'Infinitely more credible than a BMW,' Lewis had insisted when they bought it, proudly polishing the Perlman logo on its door with his sleeve. 'Like we're part of a United Nations peace-keeping force or something.'

Within thirty minutes she reached Everdene. Searching ahead through the windshield she passed a disused flour mill with collapsed brick out-buildings and rusting grain towers, bumped over a railroad crossing and turned onto a single main street. She passed a deserted shopping mall, a row of convenience stores, a K-Mart, a 7-Eleven, a couple of fast-food restaurants. Then, before she knew it, the street ended. She slowed to a crawl and wound down the window. Across the street a pink neon sign proclaimed that all she could eat would cost her only $4.99, the flashing arrow reflecting gaudily from the gleaming metal sides of the diner behind it.

Ten minutes later she parked up behind Boyd's Chevrolet and switched off the engine. For a moment she sat still, looking uncertainly around and listening to the wind sigh through the trees. The house was directly ahead, fifty yards away at the end of a narrow, wooded driveway. It was large, well built, timber-framed and solid. Set half a mile back from the road, it was so well concealed that she had nearly missed it. She stepped down from the Jeep and waited, her breath misting the night air around her. A single dim light burned in a downstairs window. A few minutes later another light came on, the front door opened, a figure appeared in the doorway and strode briskly towards her.

'Dr Chase,' Boyd said flatly, drawing near. His face was set like stone. 'I don't know why, but somehow this does not surprise me. However, I do not recommend we stand about here and in any case I could do with a drink. There is a bar a couple of miles up the road, if you'd care to follow me. We can discuss whatever it is you have on your mind there.' He walked straight past her, got into his car, started the engine and reversed along the drive.

'Sorry about that,' he apologized a little later, as she locked the door of the Jeep. 'I don't like that house and I don't like that man. They both give me the creeps.'

'Oh, um, did he do it?'

'Stamitz? No question.' They were walking towards the bar. 'Well, it's hard to say for sure, but I believe so. The worst kind, jackass mad but cooler than a mint julep. Shoots his wife, his parents and his brother-in-law while they're asleep one night, smashes a couple of windows, puts a bullet through his own leg then calls the police and swears they were attacked by intruders.' He shuddered, pulling the door open. 'Only problem is, we've just got to prove it, that's all.'

'Let me see if I have this straight,' he said a while later, waving an empty beer bottle at the bartender. 'You walked into Ross's Diner in Everdene and asked for directions to the mass murderer's place?'

'Something like that,' she said, stifling a smile. A middle-aged woman in heavy makeup and an overtight dress was staring at her from a table in the corner. 'In fact, I said I was a doctor and had an urgent appointment there. The truth, as it happens, more or less.'

'What did they say?' A short line of elderly men on stools wearing faded denim dungarees and John Deere baseball hats stole glances at them in the mirror across the back of the bar. Three youths in jeans and cowboy hats had looked up briefly from the pool table when they entered, winking at each other as they checked out the good-looking little blonde in the smart city suit.

'They said I was too late, they were all dead.' Two more bottles of beer appeared on the table at their sides; she was still barely half-way into her first. 'Then they laughed a bit and told me where to go.'

'I bet they did.' Boyd dropped a banknote onto the bartender's tray. He looked completely different she noticed. Less stiff, less formal. And nor was he calling her ma'am.

'I had to come,' she began quietly. 'After this afternoon. I just had to.'

'I thought you might.' He glanced around at the nicotine-stained walls. 'But to be honest I was expecting a call in the office in the morning.'

'It couldn't wait. You've got completely the wrong opinion.'

'Whoa, just a minute.' He held up his hand. 'I don't have any opinions, remember? Just establishing facts, that's all.'

'Well, impression, then. It's not your fault, it's me. I'm very bad at kind of explaining things to other people. I just gloss over detail, rush ahead without stopping. I suppose it's to do with the way I work, the way I study. Bad habit, I've always had it. I'd like the chance to explain properly.'

'Listen,' he sat back, spreading his hands, 'I'm no Arnold Einstein, but I made the finals of third-grade spelling bee. You go right ahead.'

'Arnold?' She looked at him doubtfully.

'Joke?'

'Ah.' She smiled shyly, their eyes meeting. Then she broke away, her face clouding in concentration. 'The first thing is about the caring. It comes top of the list, before everything. I wanted to talk about that, explain how fundamental it is. This isn't just some cold-blooded laboratory experiment, although I understand it may sometimes look a bit like that to – to outsiders. But it isn't. I really care about these people, all the medical staff do, it's part of our ethos, our culture.'

'I know,' he said simply.

She looked at him in surprise. 'You do?'

'Yes.' He reached for his bottle. 'You never refer to them as patients, or clients, or room numbers. You always refer to them as people, or by their names. It struck me right away.'

She nodded slowly before continuing. 'Well, then, there's the matter of unnecessary suffering. I didn't explain that very well either. First, we never, ever try out anything that hasn't first been tested by us, on us. Second, our monitoring equipment is incredibly sensitive. As well as watching their normal life signs, it tells us an enormous amount about what these children are going through, what they're feeling. We're constantly looking for the slightest signs of distress or discomfort.'

He nodded again, his face serious. 'Sex, drugs, rock and roll? Dirty movies?'

She sighed. 'These are just kids, young people locked into a dark place and unable to find their way out. We study them, learn everything we can about them. We look into their past histories, their school records, their hobbies and interests, their likes and dislikes, their habits, bad ones as well as good. What we're searching for are ways in, ways to reach in and let them know that they're not alone.' She picked up her glass. Over its rim she could see he was still studying her, his face impassive. 'Suppose I've got a sixteen-year-old boy who was known to have a liking for hard rock, loud clubs, soft drugs and girlie magazines. I'm sure you'll agree that it doesn't take Arnold Einstein . . .' she hesitated '. . . to see that focusing on some or all of these elements might just hold the key to establishing a line of contact to his subconscious.'

'Does it work?'

'I beg your pardon?'

'Are you getting results?'

'Well, statistically speaking, calculated using an arithmetical model we constructed to compare data on our systems with data gathered on other, mostly passive treatment systems, and a set of independently supplied control data, we believe we can consistently demonstrate a better than standard deviation from both the passive and the control data.' Her pager went off suddenly. Heads turned at the bar.

'Is that a yes?'

'I believe so.' She was fumbling at the waistband of her skirt. 'Uh-oh,' she went on, peering down at the pager. She pushed back her chair. 'Sorry, I've got to go.' She rose to her feet. 'You can come too, if you like. You might want to see this.'

'Wouldn't miss it for the world,' he murmured, following her to the door. 'Whatever it is.'

She put Boyd in the darkened control room with Nathan, who broke off briefly from his keyboard to hand the investigator a pair of headphones and gesture to the chair next to him. Through the glass, he could see Elizabeth, who was already at the bedside of a young girl, twelve or thirteen he guessed, her naked body encased in wiring, bathed in glare from overhead spotlights. As soon as he put on the headphones, his head was filled with background electronic ringing tones, together with the sound of several different voices. Among them Elizabeth's.

'Right, Sally, go. What have you got?'

'Okay, started twenty-five minutes ago with a single non-specific receptor alarm. We've had several bursts since then, lots of different spikes, but nothing we've been able to pin down yet.'

'Repeating?'

'Varying intervals but getting shorter. Every few minutes.'

'Nate?'

'Yeah, working on that right now, get back to you.'

'Okay, bed down a little lower, please. Life signs?'

'Nominal. Everything looks good.' Another man's voice. Boyd found him, a red-headed youth with a ponytail sitting in front of a monitor set back from the bed.

'Let's have the numbers, please.'

'One ten over seventy, temperature up to thirty-seven, heart level at seventy-six from seventy-three.'

'Thank you, Fulton, keep them coming, anything, any change at all.' She bent over the girl, gently rolling up each eyelid in turn. 'Folks, Annie, this is Mr Boyd,' she said quietly, without looking up. 'He's come along to see what we do here. Mr Boyd this is Annie Dean. Annie had a bad dose of meningococcal meningitis a year ago and she's been away from us for a while.' Boyd watched her through the glass as she bent to the girl, moving round her body, feeling her neck, stretching her fingers back, flexing her wrists, rotating her ankles. She stepped away from the bed, peeled off her suit jacket and threw it into a corner before leaning in once more. 'Annie's a star performer,' she went on, tugging up the sleeves of her blouse. 'Isn't that right, sweetheart? She doesn't need any assistance breathing. And she's been doing great work helping us with our research, she and her friend Raoul.'

'Here it comes again, Lizzie.' Sally's voice. 'Multiple spikes popping up everywhere.'

'Nathan?'

'Uh-huh, I've got it too but I can't say where exactly. It's, like, right sub-cortex so we could be at extremities, left-hand side. But it's weird man, all over the place.'

'Lights down please, thirty per cent.' Elizabeth went on circling the girl, her hands constantly touching her, caressing and squeezing as she went, her voice soft and melodious, talking non-stop. 'But she's a sly one, our Annie,' she continued, with a smile, 'never said a word, never gave us an inkling, did you, sweetheart? Our pattern of all patience.'

'The hell's she on about now?' hissed Nathan to himself, fingers racing over his keyboard.

'It's Shakespeare, I believe,' murmured Boyd.

'Uh-huh that's right,' came her voice over the headphones. '"I will be the pattern of all patience, I will say nothing." That sly old King Lear, eh Annie? And you never did, not to us. But then, what was it he also said? "Come, let's away to prison, we two alone will sing like birds in the cage."' She moved to the foot of the bed. 'Nate, run the code on yesterday's session with Annie and Raoul.' She stared at the girl's face. 'Somewhere around page sixty. It's in there somewhere, our two little singing birds in the cage.'

'Heart's up seventy-eight. Temperature thirty-eight.'

'Annie? Can you hear me?'

'It's everywhere now!' called Sally. 'She's, like, just surfacing, all over.'

'It's me, it's Lizzie. Come on now sweetheart, we all need your help, we need you here now.' She glanced at the glass. 'Nate!'

'Okay, getting it. Extremities, left-hand side.'

She moved swiftly round the bed. 'It's okay Annie, you're quite safe, it's time to come back now.'

'Left hand, it's the left hand.'

'Trembler switch, middle finger left hand, quickly now!'

'Fuck me, it's here, it's right here.' Nathan was staring at his screen.

'Annie, come on up now girl. It's hard but you must, it's time.'

'It was here all the time, there never was anything wrong with the goddamn sequence.'

'Heart eighty-one, still climbing.'

'Come on baby, it's quite safe, big try for Lizzie.'

'Sweet Jesus.' Boyd was rising to his feet, leaning closer to the glass. Elizabeth was clasping the girl's left hand, stretching across her, one leg up on the bed, practically lying across her body, her face right up against Annie's, her mouth inches from her ear, her free hand cupped across the wired dome of the girl's head. There were tears in her eyes.

'Come on, sweetheart. It's time now, please Annie, you have to do this, for me, please try, come on now . . .'

Suddenly an alarm went off through his headphones. 'Blood pressure one forty!'

'Multiple spiking, getting it all over.'

'Come on girl, do it! You can do it, please Annie–' She stopped abruptly, staring down at the hand in hers.

Nathan looked up from the screen. 'They were talking to each other.'

The room fell silent, everyone watching her. She was motionless, her free hand held up for quiet. She leant slowly to the girl once more, spoke softly into her ear. 'Yes I know, I know, sweetpea, it's tough but I'm so proud of you, you really are doing so well. I just want you to give it to me one more time, all right? I'll go first then I want you to give me your very biggest and best squeeze okay, then you can nap all you want, I promise, okay? We'll do it together, here we go.' She stood back again, holding the hand tightly in hers. Then she released it slowly, so that it lay in her palm like a new-born animal. As they stared, those nearest her saw it, behind her Sally saw it, the nurse at the monitor saw it, in the control room even Nathan could see it. Boyd, standing, face pressed right up against the glass, saw it.

The ghost of a smile was spreading across Elizabeth's lips. She looked up, gazing at him through the glass. Her blouse was unbuttoned, her skirt askew, her feet shoeless. Her eyes were wide, her cheeks flushed and tear-stained. She was breathless, sweating and dishevelled.

'Phone the family,' she panted quietly. 'Annie's back.'

Chapter 8

ALISON PULLED OUT HER NOTEBOOK AND BEGAN THUMBING slowly through. It was badly creased now, scuffed with over-use, dog-eared pages filled to overflowing with her dense handwriting, heavily underscored, with additional notes squashed into corners or scrawled up the sides. Her war diary, she called it.

She stopped, arrested by a familiar lone entry. 'Susie Corning died' she read, her heart sinking. The writing was small and neat, barely recognizable. Beneath, she'd added the date and time of death. That was all. The rest of the page was blank.

She lowered the book. There seemed to be nothing else to say. Seeing Susie, fastened, imprisoned in her chair like that, it had been almost as shocking as hearing that she had died. What kind of life could it have been? Did her existence have any meaning for her, some positive quality? Was there anything, any tiny, subliminal awareness of being that brought her a flicker of happiness? Or was there just nothing? Or worse still, was there pain and misery, an awareness of her own incarcer-ation, an endless living hell from which she simply yearned for release? And what if it was Frankie? How would they feel? What would they do? How could they live with it? What if, what if, what if. 'We shouldn't have done it,' Linda had said, the strain etched deep in her eyes. 'We shouldn't have done it.'

She snapped the book shut, looking up. Trevor Stanhope smiled at her, slipped on a pair of gold-rimmed half-moon spectacles and opened the file in front of him. His jacket was off, he was wearing a customarily loud shirt, broad blue and white stripes, bright yellow braces supported his suit trousers, a red and yellow polka-dotted bow-tie nestled gaudily at his neck. He beamed around the room and cleared his throat. 'Yes, David, I'd be happy to begin by giving us all an update.'

Jack hauled his gaze from the sky beyond the window, returning his attention to the people seated at the table. Alison was next to him amid the disgorged contents of her canvas bag. Opposite them sat the hospital's chief executive, David Barclay, flanked on one side by a dark-suited man called Lister, introduced as the hospital's legal adviser, and on the other by the eternally resplendent Stanhope. Monochrome at God's left hand, mused Jack, glorious technicolour at his right. In one corner of the room a grey-haired secretary discreetly transcribed proceedings into a shorthand pad.

'Briefly, I'm absolutely delighted to report that Frankie has made really super progress during the last week,' Stanhope went on. 'The chest infection she picked up is now responding extremely well to antibiotics. The little touch of jaundice associated with that has also cleared up, her temperature is just about back to normal and her lungs are almost completely clear again. There are the usual one or two areas of skin inflammation on her shoulders and lower back, which are always difficult to avoid, but we hope to keep those under control with more frequent turning and the usual anti-inflammatory preparations. And, finally, we're just going to keep an eye on her blood sugars, which fluctuated somewhat during the fever but which we anticipate will soon settle down to normal again.'

'Thank you, Trevor,' said the chief executive tactfully. 'And the underlying condition?'

'Oh yes, well, the underlying condition remains unchanged,' said Stanhope quickly. 'Obviously we continue to monitor it very closely, the last set of scans, plus the latest EEG results have just come back from the diagnostic unit at UCH where we sent them for analysis.' He pulled a letter from the file. 'They confirm our view that the unconsciousness is persisting and that the prognosis therefore is as before.'

Jack sat forward. 'What is that, exactly?' he asked quietly.

'I beg your pardon?' Stanhope looked up from the file, peering at him over his spectacles.

'The prognosis. What is it? Over the past few months there seems to have been a lot of talk about possible scenarios and speculative conjectures and hypothetical, um, presuppositions. But I don't think I've heard, we've heard, your, the hospital's, bottom line view. Your specific prognosis.'

Alison nodded minutely, rigid beside him. The chief executive inclined his head towards Stanhope. The legal adviser pursed his lips, studying the fingers of his interlocked hands on the table before him. The secretary waited, pencil poised.

Stanhope put down the file. 'I'm sorry,' he said, looking confused. 'I was under the impression the purpose of this meeting was to discuss the implications of the fact that your daughter's condition is unlikely to change.'

'But we would obviously first like to have that confirmed, or otherwise, by you. That this is the hospital's view,' said Alison.

'Official view,' added Jack, glancing at the secretary.

Stanhope looked quickly at his chief executive. 'Well, as of this moment, and taking into consideration last week's UCH analysis, and the earlier report from Professor Keach, then, at this time, that is my view. Official or otherwise.' He looked from one to the other. 'I'm terribly sorry, I thought I'd made that clear.'

Jack's gaze returned to the window. Beside him Alison was motionless, her pencil lying on the blank page before her. Stanhope, his lines delivered, retreated gratefully into his file. The lawyer sat patiently in the wings, awaiting his cue.

The chief executive sat back. 'Mr Heywood, Mrs Heywood,'

he said gently, spreading his palms, 'clearly, there is absolutely no need, no necessity at all, for you or anyone even to begin thinking about the longer term. About decisions. That's not why we are here. And let me also just reassure you that everything, positively everything possible, will continue to be done for your daughter. There is no question of that, you have my word. But I thought it might be helpful to ask our legal representative Jonathan Lister here to come along and talk to us, in very general terms, about any implied legalities. I think we'd all find it useful to understand these and the way they may affect any future decision-making process. If and when a time comes for that.' He paused, eyebrows raised. They looked back at him blankly. 'Jonathan,' he ploughed on, 'perhaps you could explain to us the precise legal position.'

Beside him Lister stirred at last. 'Yes, David, indeed, but I only wish I could,' he began, in a mellifluous you'll-never-believe-this tone. 'Astonishingly, there are no hard and fast rules on the matter. The law is not at all precise nor, you will be unsurprised to hear, is it formulated to help guide us. Since therefore there are no formally laid-down guidelines, we have literally to form our own, or perhaps more logically to adopt some that have already been used by other hospitals in similar circumstances.'

'You might like to know,' interrupted the chief executive helpfully, 'we're in touch with two other acute units in the southern region who have formulated and enacted policies of this sort recently. They are sending us copies of their procedural documentation.' He gestured at Lister. 'Sorry Jonathan, please go on.'

'One thing is quite clear however, and that is this. The law, as it stands, draws the line at actively assisting someone else to die. That is manslaughter.' He glanced around the table. 'Be in no doubt, there are many examples of prosecutions against hospitals and their clinical and administrative staff, general practitioners and patients' relatives who have, in the eyes of the law, crossed this line. What is less clear, unfortunately, is defining precisely where this line lies – in other words defining what constitutes active assistance. In the hospital context it is generally accepted that withdrawing medication or sustenance might be considered passive and therefore acceptable, whereas switching off a ventilator, for example, or increasing sedation levels would be considered active and therefore unacceptable.'

Jack sat forward again, raising his hand like a child in class. 'You mean, if we were to decide to – to go ahead with this, then the only way it could be done would be to stop feeding her, or, or stop giving her medication if she got ill again? Is that what you mean?' The lawyer glanced towards the chief executive before he nodded, his eyes on the table. 'So that, in effect, either she starved to death or – or was killed slowly by an illness or an infection that went untreated?'

The room was silent.

'But that's grotesque,' said Alison eventually. 'It's inhuman.'

'It's the law.'

The woman studied her notes for several seconds, absentmindedly wiggling the ballpoint pen between her fingers as she read through them one more time. Finally she looked up at him, her eyes narrowing, examining him thoughtfully. 'So if I understand you correctly Mr, er, Heywood is it? Yes, if I understand you correctly, you want to know what your, er, friend's legal position might be, given this set of circumstances. Is that correct?'

'Hypothetically, yes,' replied Jack, shifting uncomfortably in his chair.

'Well, I don't think I can tell you.'

'Sorry?'

'Not right away. I'd have to look into it, do some checking. Perhaps I could drop you a line, in a week or so.'

'No, um, I'm not sure that would be possible. He, er, lives abroad at the moment, just wanted me to telephone him with a rough idea.'

'A rough idea?'

'Yes. Couldn't you just give me your gut feelings, as it were, your initial thoughts on the subject? Obviously I – we wouldn't hold you to them. It's just sort of preliminary research.' He could feel his heart thudding in his chest, the back of his shirt pressing damply against his skin.

She exhaled. 'Well, at first sight, it's an incredibly complicated matter, and coupled to that I've never come across anything remotely similar. I must be honest, I'm more familiar with the legalities of rather more routine medical issues, fraudulent medical-insurance claims, malpractice suits, institutional liability, that sort of thing. I really wouldn't want to speculate on something like this without first having a chance to research it properly.'

'Please?'

He was staring directly at her, his eyes locked onto hers, hanging onto her disconcertingly, like an animal at feeding time. 'Well,' she sighed, breaking his gaze to pick up her notes, 'I suppose, hypothetically then, what we have is a patient who may or may not be terminally ill but who is not able to communicate or act for themselves, is that right?' He nodded. 'Furthermore, the next of kin are unable to agree on a proper course of action, options for which seem to be, one, do nothing and see what happens, two, withdraw treatment altogether thus probably allowing the patient to die, or, three, pursue other, developmental treatment options overseas. Oh, and medical opinion is completely divided down the middle so they can't depend on that to help them come to a decision. Is that more or less the case?'

'Yes, and it's a child.'

'A child?' She looked up at him in surprise. 'And the parents are unable to agree?' He swallowed, nodding once more.

'Well, a child is rather different, then again perhaps not. In short however, it is unlikely that either parent could go ahead and pursue a course of action unless the other is in agreement.

If they remained in opposition and unable to come to an agreement, what might happen is that solicitors representing the two parents could make an application to the high court for a ruling. The high court would have to look into the whole case, investigate all the options, take the best medical advice, and come up with an adjudication.'

'I see. And what if the parents still failed to agree, or maybe refused to abide by the ruling?'

'The court will always put the interests of the child first. If the parents failed to abide by the ruling, the child could be made a ward of the court. In effect, the court then takes over responsibility for its care, irrespective of either parent's wishes.'

'Mrs Heywood, do forgive me, I was held up at a staff review meeting, I do hope you haven't been waiting too long.' The woman strode into the office, extended her hand to Alison and sat down behind her desk. In her late forties, she was dressed in a bright pink wool business suit above a cream silk blouse. There was a string of pearls at her neck, her face was made up, hair cut in a neat grey bob. Conscious suddenly of her own appearance, Alison tugged the front of her cardigan straight, tucking hair behind her ear, as the woman removed files from a man's leather briefcase.

'Right then, here it is,' she continued brightly. Slipping off her wristwatch, she set it on the desk to one side of her. 'Now, I'm Madeleine Rutherford. I am the director of contracts and purchasing for Cambridgeshire Health Authority. I understand you wanted to speak to someone about your daughter, er Frances.'

'That's right.' Alison withdrew the file from her shoulder-bag. 'As you know, I requested that she be sent to a clinic in the United States specializing in the treatment of children with her condition.'

The woman was studying her file. 'Yes, indeed,' she agreed,

folding back a page. She glanced at Alison. 'I see that Social Services have requested an inter-agency meeting to review the care options being considered for your daughter.'

'I am aware of that. Anyway, the point is, my request for a referral has been turned down and I wanted to find out why.'

'Well, it would appear from the correspondence,' replied the woman, reading from a letter, 'that the consultant believes there is little to be gained from sending her there. In fact, he seems quite strongly opposed to the idea.'

'He may well be opposed to the idea of the clinic, but "little to be gained" is not quite what his letter says, if you'll excuse me.' Alison read from her copy. '"It cannot be said with any degree of certainty whether the patient would benefit from attendance at the clinic or not."' She looked up. 'In other words, he doesn't know.'

'Doesn't it come to the same thing?'

'I don't think so. Saying he doesn't know is not the same as saying there's little to be gained.'

The woman lowered the file. 'Mrs Heywood, let's be frank about this. At the end of the day this is about money. My job is to manage the budget with which this health authority buys all the health care needed for the entire population of Cambridgeshire. It is a fixed budget – no, in fact it is a diminishing budget in real terms year on year, but that's beside the point. From that budget I make contracts with health-care providers, such as hospitals, nursing homes, community and mental health services and so on, to ensure that the fullest possible range of good-quality NHS health services is available to all the people of this county.'

'What about ECRs?' Alison rubbed one eye tiredly.

The woman nodded. 'Indeed, I was just coming to that. Within that budget is a small, very small, provision for us to go out and buy services, on a strictly one-off basis, from providers other than those we normally use. These are the Extra Contractual Referrals you speak of and cover the purchase of unusual or specialist services that may not be available here.'

'Like those provided by the Perlman Institute for patients like Frankie.'

'Possibly, although nearly all ECRs take place in this country. It is very, very unusual to buy services abroad. But, in any case, before we can approve the spending of money on any ECRs, we have to be sure, as sure as possible, that the money will be well spent. In other words, that there is a strong probability that the patient will benefit from the treatment and therefore justify the cost. Now, we don't make that determination, it's based on clinical judgement. We rely on the patient's doctors to advise us whether, in their opinion, there is likely to be a benefit.' She picked up Frankie's file again. 'Unfortunately, we don't feel that the clinical determination made by your daughter's consultants is strong enough to warrant sending her to a very expensive and, let's be honest, highly experimental clinic in America.'

'What if I obtain second, third opinions? From other neurologists, other experts. What if I can get a body of professional opinion to support the case for Frankie to be sent there?'

Mrs Rutherford took a deep breath. 'Well, we'd obviously look at it again. But, to be perfectly honest, there's a good chance we'd still turn it down.'

Alison snorted. 'In other words, despite what you say, you would make the determination regardless of clinical recommendation.'

'Mrs Heywood. We live in a wonderful world of fantastic technical and scientific advances. Just pick up the newspapers – every day we read about miraculous new treatments and procedures popping up all over the world for Aids, cancers, infertility, organ failure. The list is endless. Naturally patients want access to all these treatments but it just isn't possible, not under the NHS. Many of them are developmental, some turn out to be of limited or no benefit, and all, almost without exception, are enormously costly. I'm sorry, really I am, and I do understand how you feel.'

'No, Mrs Rutherford, excuse me but you don't.' Alison began packing up her bag.

The woman shook her head wearily. 'The National Health Service just isn't structured, isn't organized to send patients all over the world for treatment. It never was. There just simply isn't the money.'

Alison's mother tiptoed across the landing, lowered the laundry basket silently to the floor, and peered through the crack in Ben's door. He was lying on his side, his back to her, on the floor, which was covered in toys. Dozens of little plastic soldiers, his model ships and aeroplanes. Circling columns of cars, lorries and buses. The entire contents of his toybox, everything he owned, scattered about in confusion, Ben lying amid them. She moved her head from side to side, squinting through her slotted arc of vision, then stopped. There were some of Frankie's things too. Rows of those little wooden troll-like family dolls she'd been collecting, her favourite stuffed rabbit, her plastic farm-animal set. She lifted her hand, poised to knock, when movement caught her eye. His arm, his elbow, pulling rapidly, oscillating mechanically like the piston of a motor. Janet stared, eye wide at the crack, while his unseen hand jerked swiftly inside his jeans. Then she looked away, exhaling softly. Within seconds it was over, the motor faltering erratically then slowing to a stop. She waited another half-minute, stepped silently back and picked up the laundry basket.

'Ben?' she sang out cheerfully, walking forward once more. She knocked briskly and opened the door wide. 'Ah, there you are darling.' She surveyed the room, feigning surprise. 'Goodness, what a mess.' He turned his head towards her, eyes watchful. 'Are you all right then darling? I'm just going to do a spot of ironing. Do you need anything? What about a drink?' He shook his head. 'Very well then I'll be just across the landing in the spare room if you need me.' He said nothing, turning back into the room. She pulled the door to, carefully leaving the last six inches ajar. Across the landing she opened the spare-room door, wrinkling her nose absently at the smell, toothpaste and men's toiletries. A pile of Jack's clothes was heaped on one chair, stacks of papers covered a table in the corner. On the bed his pyjamas lay on the pillow. She threw open the window. Carefully positioning it in front of the gaping doorway, she unfolded the ironing board.

All the people and all the animals and all the machines moved in concentric and orderly circles about him, journeying slowly across the wide plain in a great majestic sweeping procession. From his hilltop vantage-point he could survey all, keeping watch on his entire kingdom and all his subjects. From the elephants and giraffes below him in the nearby lush lowlands, the hordes of steadily passing travellers with their vehicles and animals beyond in the dusty plain, to the tiny distant soldiers slowly picking their way through the foothills beneath the far-off mountains. Silver bombers droned by overhead, warships and sailing boats plied the rivers and canals criss-crossing the endless panorama.

While he watched, shielding his eyes from the hot desert glare with one hand, the smell of dry grass and drifting plain dust filling his nostrils, the people and the animals and the machines greeted him as he guided them safely through the wilderness and into deliverance. Waving their arms, bending their heads, lifting their trunks and paws. Cars sounded their horns, aeroplanes dipped their wings, ships' funnels vanished in clouds of steam, sirens blaring, in grateful salutation.

And he waved back. Stretching his arm slowly skywards in greeting, his hand looping, twisting and darting, fingers opening and closing like petals on a flower, dancing higher and higher into the blistering azure sky while the power built in him once more, growing, unfolding inside him like a giant awakening animal.

Jack sat patiently in an armchair, slowly swirling the little puddle of golden liquid around the bottom of his tumbler. He looked about the room, his eyes falling on the silent mahogany case of the piano, the music book still open on its dusty metal stand, clowns and circus animals decorating the staves on the page. After a while Alison came in. 'Ready?' she said, gingerly stretching fingers into elbow-length white lace gloves.

'Uh-huh.' He drained his glass.

She looked down at herself doubtfully. 'Is it all right?' She was wearing a pale yellow chiffon dress. It was sleeveless, gathered below the waist with a silk bow at her hip, and extended to well below her knees. Beneath it she wore white stockings and flat-heeled cream shoes with round toes and buckled straps. A long string of costume pearls, looped twice about her neck, hung in a knot at her cleavage. A large yellow feather curled back across her pinned-up hair from a bejewelled strap encircling her head. Completing the ensemble, her mother's white fox stole lay loosely about her shoulders.

'Great,' he said. 'Spot on.'

'Okay, we're all set then. Taxi's here.' She glanced at him quickly. 'I suppose this is a good idea. Isn't it?'

Jack blew out. 'I can't say I'm exactly raring to go. But, on the other hand, as your mother said, it would probably do us good to get out. Even just for an evening. You know, change of scene, see a few people, rejoin the human race for a couple of hours.'

'Yes, yes she's right,' she said dubiously. She picked up a little satin handbag and turned for the door. 'I'm sure she is. Anyway, we should at least give it a try.'

Jack reached for his straw boater. 'Right then,' he grunted wearily, hauling himself from the chair. 'Party time.'

In the taxi they were quiet, watching through their respective windows as the city's residential avenues and crescents gave way to winding country lanes, the soft evening sunlight warming wide fields of ripening corn, slanting through ancient elder trees surrounding sleepy village greens.

'How was your day?' she asked at one point. The taxi-driver was watching them in the mirror, the man in his gaudily striped blazer and white flannels, she fiddling absently with the pearls at her neck, each sitting apart, turned slightly away, like strangers on a train in an old film.

'Fine, fine thanks.' He thought back. The taut little setpiece in the hospital chief executive's office, the nightmare charade with the medical lawyer, the phone call from their health insurers – no, Mr Heywood, we're quite sure, cover definitely does not extend to include treatment abroad. 'Yours?'

As well as the health authority, she'd spoken to Ben's psychologist again, and to another child psychologist recommended by their GP. And she'd made another call to Virginia. 'So-so.'

'I know!' the driver called out suddenly, tilting his head back towards them. '*Bonnie and Clyde*. No, no, wait a minute, that film, you know the one with Robert Redford in it. *Gatsby*! That's it, *The Great Gatsby*.' They smiled at him politely.

Twenty minutes later, they swung past tall wrought-iron gates into a tree-lined driveway. An imposing Georgian rectory rose at the far end of the drive, a huge striped marquee erected on the lawn beside it. 'Don't know about you,' Jack murmured, 'but I think I'll be getting plastered tonight.'

He sat back on his heels, waiting patiently, hands on thighs, hawking and spitting while his head swam and the cold dew seeped through the knees of his cricket trousers. Soon he began to shiver again, a chill sweat breaking on his forehead. A moment later his body convulsed and he jerked forward once more, vomiting drily onto the woodchips beneath the neatly trimmed privet hedge. On and on it went, a fist at his stomach, a steel belt at his chest, the image of Isabelle's mother a watery blur before him.

Finally the spasm passed. He raised his head, drawing moist night air deep into his lungs. Around him the gardens were quiet; further off he could see figures sitting at candlelit tables down by the lake. In the distance the sound of animated shouting and raucous laughter spilled from the tent above the rhythmic twang of the ragtime band. Gradually his breathing steadied and his head cleared. He got to his feet, brushed dirt from his knees and sat down on a nearby bench. He pulled a handkerchief from the pocket of his blazer and blew his nose, then rinsed his mouth from the water bottle snatched off a table as he'd fled outside.

'You're looking well,' Isabelle's mother had said, from behind a mask of heavy makeup. Reproach or compliment. She too was dressed in part, feather boa, gilt bracelets, pearl choker and all the rest of it. She was smoking a black cigarette in a telescopic holder, ruby lips pouting a greasy ring onto the gold stem, her drug-dulled eyes studying him closely. It was a shock. It had never occurred to him that Isabelle's parents might be here, yet there was no reason why they shouldn't. It was a big party, they lived in the same part of town, moved in the same circles, had many friends in common. He'd already bumped into several people from the school. How *are* you, and how *is* Ben, how *is* Frankie? The furrowed brows, the sad nods, the over-solicitous concern, all the while their eyes flicking past his, darting around the room, hunting for escape.

'You too,' he lied, holding out his glass to a passing waitress. She'd aged, dreadfully, the face sunken and haggard, the lines etched deep around her nose and mouth. And her eyes . . . He thought back, remembering those surreal hours in the hospital waiting room, the shock and disbelief at the doctors' pronouncement, the mute expressions on the faces at the graveside. What could he say? There was nothing then and there was nothing now. What is it like? Is it worse for you than for us? Have you started getting over it yet? Has your life begun to move on again, or is it suspended, on hold like mine, postponed indefinitely like the final weathered-off fixture of the season? He sensed that other guests were watching them. Isn't that the mother of the little girl who was . . . ? Wasn't he the father of the boy who was walking them . . . ?

Across the marquee, Alison stood at the buffet, an untouched plate in her hand, head turned, half listening while a man in a white dinner suit talked earnestly at her, strain showing in the tell-tale corners of her smile. He felt a sudden pang: she looked so young, so vulnerable. He'd have liked to go over and rescue her, smiling courteously at the man in the white suit, taking her gently by the arm and leading her to a table for two in the corner. But they'd hardly spoken all evening.

'We're going to sue,' the woman slurred dully, watching his eyes. He felt the colour drain from his face, the half-smile lingering ludicrously on his lips. 'It's absolutely nothing personal, of course. An insurance thing, negligence or something, Kevin's looking into all the details.' He swallowed blankly, tasting bile. 'I expect you'll get a letter from the solicitor or something.' She touched his arm. 'Please don't take it personally, we don't blame you. Really we don't.' He turned, hand on mouth, and fled for the night.

Draining the water bottle, he got up from the bench and walked slowly down the moonlit grass towards the lake. Around it small knots of people had gathered, the still air punctuated with the echo of laughter on water, the scent of wafted perfume and cigar smoke. Near the edge, a couple were stretched out side by side on a blanket, arms entwined, apparently asleep. He skirted around them, passing wide of the other groups, until he found an empty table beside the trailing fronds of a huge weeping willow. As he neared it he saw a figure in yellow striding towards him from the direction of the tent.

'There is just no fucking escape from it, is there,' Alison said, dropping into a chair.

He breathed out slowly. 'No.'

She picked up a discarded bottle from the table, poured some wine into a glass. Out in the centre of the lake a splash as a trout rose. 'Did you manage it?'

'Hmm?'

'Getting plastered. Seems like a bloody good idea.'

'Bloody bad idea, believe me.' He hesitated. 'I wanted to say, earlier, that you looked great, you know, tonight, better than any of the others. But I didn't. Thought it might sound trite.'

'Thank you,' she said quietly.

'Do you want to go?'

'In a minute.' She stared out over the lake. A pale mist, gossamer thin, was floating like a veil two feet above the water near the centre. She got up, stepped to the water's edge, looked out, hugging herself. 'We're completely alone with this.' She turned to him. 'Aren't we?'

'Yes.' He nodded simply.

Suddenly she stooped to the buckles of her shoes, kicked them off. Lifting the hem of her dress to her thighs, she bent, fumbled to unhook her stockings, rolled them quickly down in a single movement and dropped them onto the grass behind her. A second later he heard a sharp intake of breath and the gentle swirling at her legs as she waded, dress bunched to her hips, thigh deep into the chill water.

'Hurry,' she whispered urgently, a few minutes later. They were beneath the willow, completely hidden by the encircling curtain of fronds. One of her hands was already on him, palm rubbing hard at the front of his cricket trousers, the other at his neck, pulling his mouth onto hers. She kissed him furiously, a low guttural moan lodged deep in her throat, tongue hunting his mouth, fingers tugging impatiently at the unfamiliar fly-buttons, dragging him down on top of her. A moment later their teeth collided, heads jarring as they fell onto the moist grass. He dropped onto her heavily, his hand sliding immediately up the icy wet skin of her legs under the dress, cupping her mound, kneading her buttocks through the splashed cotton of her pants. Gathering the fabric in his fist he wrenched it away and down. She gasped, lifting her bottom, wriggling her thighs anxiously to be rid of it. He broke away, sitting back quickly to unfasten the buttons of his fly, his eyes on her as he fumbled, a faceless shadow beneath him. 'For God's sake!' A splitting sound as he wrenched them apart furiously. A moment later he was free, his hands on her hips again. 'No, wait!' She writhed beneath him, rolling over onto her stomach then scrambling quickly onto her knees. He bent her forward, hands slipping up the back of her thighs to feel for her buttocks again. Throwing the dress up onto her back, his fingers slid down into the cleft, pressed into her, her wetness hot suddenly on his fingers. He knelt behind her, shuffling closer, bent forward, encircling her waist tightly with one arm while she squirmed back against him. Breathless with anticipation they lunged and missed. He gasped in pain, 'Christ!' Her hand reached immediately back between her legs, guiding him urgently into her with her fingers. She pushed back harder onto him, again he thrust, desperate and panicked. His hand pushed her lower, fingers prising her apart, then suddenly her back arched, her head came up and she let out a stifled sob as he slid full length, plunging deeply into the heat with a groan.

Bending almost double over her, clasping her body against him with one arm, he jerked violently into her, the other hand buried, fingers spread, into the thick hair at the back of her head. His face was turned sideways on her back like a swimmer, mouth wide, gasping for air. Beneath him, knees splayed, one arm gripping the grass, the other circling the rough trunk of the tree, she pushed back onto him, panting to the rapidly accelerating rhythm of their frenzy, her head back, her teeth gritted and her eyes closed.

'You're absolutely determined about this thing, aren't you?' he murmured, glancing at the electric clock on the cooker. They were in the kitchen, drinking tea, it was half past two.

She nodded slowly. 'Do you know, tonight, all those people? Always the same questions, the same blank stares, but you know, they have absolutely no idea. It's not their fault but they just have no conception of what it's really like, what it's all about.'

'I know,' he said. 'I felt it too.'

'You see, Jack, I just can't give up, not yet,' she went on softly. 'And the longer it goes on, the more I feel we should at least try everything. For Frankie and for Ben.'

He picked up a table-mat. 'Yes, but where does it stop? Where do we draw the line? I just worry that – that it will be so much worse for them, both of them, for all of us, if America turns out badly, turns out to be a – a bad decision.'

They fell quiet, lost in thought. Susie Corning, dead in her chair, her rolling eyes still, her dancing arms limp.

'Yes,' she said eventually. 'So do I.'

'Are you sure, really sure,' he went on gently, 'that sending Frankie to this clinic represents the best thing we can do for her and for Ben?'

Her head fell. 'No. I can't say that. I can only say that doing it the other way round, letting her go without trying everything first, I can't do it, I couldn't live with that.'

He sat back, eyes on the motionless black silhouette of the cherry tree beyond the window.

'Jack, will you just talk to her? Dr Chase. Please. Just see what she says.'

'Yes but Ali, just how objective can she be?' He spread his hands. 'I mean, it's her living, treating patients like Frankie. She's bound to want us.'

'Not necessarily. Remember the Cornings? They said she wouldn't take Susie at first. And Winstanley, he said she often refuses patients. She might not take Frankie, even if we wanted her to. If she believes there's no point, no hope, or if she thinks it isn't right, for Frankie or Ben, I'm sure she'll tell us.'

'Hmm.' He pursed his lips doubtfully.

'And if she doesn't recommend it, I won't argue with that. I promise.'

'Oh yes?' He smiled wryly.

'Just talk to her. Please.'

He blew out. 'Okay.'

'Tomorrow? She's there all day, I checked.'

'Jesus, Alison, all right, tomorrow.'

'Promise?'

'Yes, I promise!' He raised a finger at her. 'But then we decide, together, based on what she says and what all the others have said. We look at the whole thing and make a common decision together. Agreed?'

'Agreed.'

But in the end the decision was made for them.

Chapter 9

THE SPEAKERPHONE SAT IN THE CENTRE OF THE KITCHEN table, plugged into a telephone extension wire leading from the phone on the wall. Jack pulled up a chair opposite Alison. 'Ready?'

She nodded. 'Ready.'

He glanced at his watch. 'It's lunch-time over there, sure she'll be in?'

'She said she'd be in all day, Jack, just press the buttons.'

He reached forward, the kitchen door opened, Janet appeared, laden with shopping. 'Good evening, you two – oh hello, what's that?' she said brightly, looking at the table. She shuffled heavily into the room.

Alison sighed. 'It's a conference telephone, so we can both talk and listen at the same time. Jack brought it back from the office. We were just about to call the clinic.'

'Oh good. Mind if I listen?' Alison glanced at Jack, who shrugged. 'I won't make any noise, promise.' She dumped the shopping and tiptoed ludicrously across the floor. Jack reached forward once more to dial. 'Where's Ben?' Janet interrupted, sitting down at the window.

'Watching a video.'

'Shouldn't he be here too?'

Alison turned to her. 'Mother, Jack and I have talked about

it, at great length. We both feel we would like an initial conversation, to gain an impression of the place, assess our feelings and get some information and advice. We thought, on balance, we'd be best doing this on our own at first.' She paused for effect. 'Completely on our own.'

'Just as you wish.' Janet remained seated, studying the back of her hand.

They were put through straight away. 'This is Elizabeth Chase.' Jack detected an educated east-coast accent.

Alison spoke towards the box. 'Oh, hello, Doctor, it's Alison Heywood here, from Cambridge, England? I'm here with my husband, Jack.'

'Hello Alison, hello Jack, it's nice to meet you at last.'

Janet was flapping a hand at her from the window. 'Um, yes, and my mother, Janet Catchpole.'

'Hello, Mrs Catchpole, nice to meet you too. Is Ben there?'

'Er, no, he's next door. We thought maybe at first just a quiet chat, er, on our own.'

'Sure, but if I may suggest, please do make certain he feels included in any decision-making process. How is he, by the way?'

'Well, we're very worried about him. He doesn't seem to be getting any better and it seems that this lack of improvement may be connected with Frankie's condition in some way.'

'It probably is, believe me,' Elizabeth said, glancing again at the pages of notes Alison had faxed her. 'The information you sent me, it's helpful, thanks for that. But there's very little here about the accident itself.'

'Ah,' said Alison. 'No. Is it important?'

'It could be. Very. What can you tell me about it?'

Jack cleared his throat. 'Well, not a great deal, I'm afraid. Apart from the eye-witness accounts, which are rather confused, the only person who probably really knows what happened is Ben.'

'And Frankie,' Elizabeth corrected. 'Has he spoken about it?'

'Not at all.'

'But he was there, he saw it happen.'

'Yes, we believe so.'

'Close up.'

Jack and Alison exchanged glances, Janet leant forward attentively on the window-seat. 'Probably, yes.'

'Can I speak to him?'

Janet immediately got to her feet, heading for the door. 'Er, yes, of course,' said Jack. 'We'll fetch him but, er, don't you want to ask anything more about Frankie?'

Elizabeth's lunch, chicken salad in a plastic box, lay untouched beside her. 'No, not just now. Maybe later.' Her door opened, Lewis waving a sheaf of papers at her in the doorway. She beckoned him in. 'Heywoods,' she mouthed, covering the mouthpiece. He rolled his eyes, rubbing his thumb and fore-finger together at her as he dropped into a chair next to her desk. She pressed the speaker button and replaced the handset. The line hissed then a woman's voice came on, older, cultured, very English.

'Hello? Hello, yes, this is Ben's grandmother speaking. He's here now, right here, aren't you darling?'

Lewis stifled a grin. 'It's only the goddamn Queen,' he muttered. Elizabeth ignored him, staring at the phone.

'Ben darling, would you like to say hello to the American doctor?'

There was some clunking on the line, the scrape of a chair, adult mutterings of encouragement. Elizabeth leant right forward to the phone, straining to listen. Silence, then perhaps the faintest ghost of a murmur, a child's whispered hello drifting over the ether like a sigh on the breeze.

'Ben, hi there,' she said lightly. 'My name's Lizzie. Can you hear me okay?'

Another pause then another murmur; 'Yes,' clearer this time.

'I'm talking to you from a place called Virginia, in the United States. Have you heard of that?'

'Um, yes. They grow tobacco.' He was standing by the table, staring at the speakerphone, Alison's hand resting on his shoulder. She noticed that her mother had joined them at the table.

'They sure do. In fact, there's a tobacco plantation not so far from here.' She paused, eyes closing in concentration, searching for words. 'We have a place here, where I work, Ben. It's kind of modern, but nice, set in some great countryside. It's called the Perlman Institute, maybe your mom and dad told you a little about it?'

'Um, I, no, I don't know . . .' Elizabeth winced.

Alison leant forward. 'We didn't want to say too much, you know, before . . .'

'It's okay, it's okay,' Elizabeth said quickly. Across the desk, Lewis watched her impassively. She was rolling the knuckles of a tightly bunched fist backwards and forwards across her forehead, eyes squeezed shut. 'No problem. So anyway, Ben, it's named after a friend of ours called Gary Perlman. Gary took a bad knock on the head in an auto accident and went unconscious for quite a while, just like your little sister Frankie. We helped him and now he's fine. Since then we've helped lots of young people like that. That's what we do here, do you follow me?'

Another pause, then, 'Yes.'

'Because you see, Ben, I believe that when something like that happens, there's a place we can go, sometimes, a quiet place to wait and rest.'

'You mean like the garden, and after.'

Elizabeth's eyes popped open, wide, drilling sightlessly into Lewis's. 'The garden, uh-huh.' She struggled to keep her voice level. 'And I guess you may know a little about that, of course.'

The line fell silent, a background tapestry of clicks and hisses growing up like an emerging landscape between them. 'Anyway, that's what we do here. We help young people like Gary and Frankie come back.'

'You can't come back.' His distant voice floated faintly across an ocean of white noise. 'It's not allowed.'

Elizabeth left mid-afternoon, drove the Jeep to Norfolk airport, took an early-evening flight to La Guardia then hired a Ford at the airport for the drive out to Connecticut. She missed the worst of the New York rush hour but it was still nose to tail much of the way. By the time she pulled into the driveway it was gone nine.

She waited, hands resting on the steering wheel, listening to the ticking of the engine as it cooled and the soft rustle of the breeze through the trees framing the porch. They'd grown much taller than she recalled, yet the house seemed smaller, less imposing than the one of her memory. The front door opened, Elliot hurried down the steps to greet her.

He cooked out for them, on the back porch, barbecuing salmon steaks and shrimp like he used to on holiday in Vermont. She sat at the same old wooden picnic table of her childhood, drinking beer from the bottle and studying him while the memories flooded back. He, too, looked smaller and less imposing, the brown hair a little thinner, shot through with grey, the wrinkles etched deeper around the eyes and mouth. But the years had been kind: he was trim and lean, relaxed in open-necked shirt and pale cotton slacks beneath the apron. Padding smoothly to and from the kitchen in his loafers, bringing freshly tossed salad, mixing a potato mayonnaise, turning the fish and uncorking wine, everything a practised and unhurried study in economy of movement, like an endlessly rehearsed ritual. As he worked they talked, gently quizzing each other about old friends, relatives and acquaintances, both grateful for the natural occupational distraction food preparation and consumption provided for that first crucial hour.

'How's Mom?' she said later, wiping fingers on a paper napkin. 'I haven't spoken to her for a while. Do you see her at all?'

'From time to time. She's fine, I believe, just fine. Happy to be in the city I think. Got a great little apartment somewhere down near the Village. You should get over and see her if you get the chance, she's quite the Bohemian these days. Writing a lot of poetry, done a couple of readings, there's talk even of the possibility of a publishing deal.'

'Still with, you know, what's his name, the dancer?'

'Anthony.' He sipped some wine. 'Choreographer. Yes, he's still very much in the frame, so I understand. He's good for her, makes her very happy, it's great.'

'And you?'

'Anthony? No, terrific legs apparently but not really my type.' He winked, taking her plate.

'I meant, have you got anyone?' she enunciated slowly.

He carried their plates through the sliding door to the kitchen. 'Nah,' he called, wrinkling his nose at her through the glass. 'I've got everything I need. The practice is busy and interesting, I have a great social life, meet plenty of people up at the tennis club, get quality time by myself, it's a perfectly good mix, good balance.'

She grinned. 'What about sex?'

'Elizabeth!' He carefully lowered a glass bowl of fruit salad onto the table.

'"Sexuality is an important part of our cornerstone need for self-expression,"' she quoted. 'You were always telling your patients that.'

'My patients are all neurotic. Anyway who needs sex when you've got the New York Giants?' He glanced at her briefly: her eyes were in shadow, it was growing dark. 'And you?'

She shook her head, thinking suddenly of Boyd. He'd been back twice since the first visit. The first time, reasonably enough, to ask her some follow-up questions, the second, definitely trumped up, to hunt for missing car keys. 'No time, the clinic's flat out and I'm perpetually exhausted.'

'So how's it going?' he asked quietly.

They took their coffee into the front room. He drew the curtains, lit the fire, slotted a Schubert CD into the hi-fi. The string quintet, one of her favourites. She sat on the rug at his feet, staring into the flames and mentally scanning along the shelves at the familiar rows of books and ornaments. All her mother's things, she noted, completing a rapid inventory, were gone.

'Do you miss her?' she asked.

'Yes.' He reflected. 'Of course. But events happen and things change. They have to, and so do people. You can't fight that.' He paused. 'But, yes, I miss her. I miss you all.'

She looked up at him, her eyes searching his. 'But it's okay.' He smiled, nodding gently. 'Really.'

She held his gaze a moment longer, then turned back to the fire. 'I'm on the edge of something, Daddy,' she began, drawing a deep breath. 'It's important, but it's scary, and I don't know what to do.' Suddenly she felt his hand on her, lightly caressing the hair at the back of her head, cupping it, the way he used to. She leant back against the chair, closing her eyes.

'Tell me,' he said.

She told him. For the first time she really told him everything. She told him about Gary Perlman and Dana Konakowski and Brooke Mills and all the successes. She told him about the clinic, its growth, its achievements, its developments. She told him about her co-directors Lewis and Nathan, her affection and respect for them and all the other staff. She told him about the gifted young doctors, nurses and medical students, the graduate technicians, software analysts and engineers who passed through their hands. About the complementary-medicine practitioners who came to them, training her people, working with the patients, developing new ideas and techniques. She told him of her lecture tours and seminars, of the interest her work generated in medical circles, in scientific circles, in academic circles, and in the wider public and media circles beyond.

'It hardly seems possible,' she said. 'So much has happened in five years, so much achieved, so much learnt, and gained.'

'I'm so proud of you,' Elliot said, softly shaking her shoulder. He waited patiently, disciplined by decades of practice.

Then, slowly, hesitantly, she began to tell him of the problems. Of patients who regressed, slipping back into unconsciousness months, sometimes years after being successfully recovered. Of those like Robert Willis who suffered dangerous, even lethal physical trauma whenever attempts were made to revive them. Of those like Susie Corning who emerged reluctantly from the twilight into a sort of barely definable catatonic consciousness, of this world but not of this world.

'And it's recent, within the last year or so,' she said. 'And only with the kids who are the most deeply under. It's as if, as our own techniques and methods have evolved, become more sophisticated, more powerful, and we reach in further and deeper than before, the risk to them gets higher.'

'I suppose that might be expected,' he said. 'Compare it to conventional surgery. The bigger, the more invasive the operation, the greater the risk to the patient.'

'Yes, but it's worse than that,' she responded. 'It's as though there's a point beyond which we can't go. That though we can reach in that far, maybe even establish contact with them, we can't bring them out.'

'Then don't,' he said simply. 'Not until you are able to do so safely.'

She looked up at him again. 'What? You mean stop?'

He smiled. 'It's a basic rule of medicine, you know that, and common sense. You're pushing back frontiers, Lizzie. From what you've told me, and from what I've heard and read, you've already pushed them back way further than anyone else in this field. Occasionally, though, you're sure to fetch up against one that slows you down, maybe requires you to pause and think before pressing on again.'

She turned forward. 'I suppose so but . . .'

'Ultimately,' he went on, 'you're going to reach one that stops you altogether. A barrier, of some sort. You do know that, don't you? You may already have reached it.'

'It's possible.' She fell quiet, head lowered. 'But it's more than that,' she said at length. She heard him breathing out behind her.

'Lizzie, I . . .'

'There's resistance. Some of them are definitely resisting. It's not physical, it's not a bodily thing, we've checked and checked, it's something else, something within.'

'Lizzie, I really think you've got to stop and look at what it is you're doing.' There was growing tension in his voice.

'There's something else.' She pushed on doggedly. 'Do you know? We ran a series of comparative tests. Two of them, running the same paired sequences on two patients simultaneously to compare parallel response data. It didn't work. We immediately ran up against all kinds of problems, overloads on the systems, spurious data, meaningless, undecipherable readings. Then we finally figured it. Do you know what it was?'

'No.'

'The two of them were using the monitoring equipment, overloading it, in fact, to establish some sort of incredibly high-speed binary synaptic exchange mechanism. Do you know what that means?'

He got to his feet. 'No.' He walked towards the porch door, slid it shut with a bang.

'They were communicating, Daddy.' Her eyes followed him as he moved around the room, picking up ornaments, putting them down, straightening furniture, not looking at her, his jaw set. 'They must have been. I couldn't reach them, the equipment wasn't making contact, they did it themselves. For that to happen, it means that there has to be a common connection point.'

'Lizzie, stop.'

'A joint plane of awareness, a mutual environment, a kind of half-way house between–'

'Elizabeth, for Christ's sake!'

'– between perceived reality and unperceived reality. In other words, a place, as real, sensorily real, to them as the environment we perceive as our own.'

He stopped suddenly, swung towards her, eyes blazing. 'When are you going to realize it, fucking with this stuff is not going to bring him back!'

She flinched, instinctively drawing her legs up beneath her. 'Daddy.'

'This is wrong, all wrong,' he muttered furiously, resuming his pacing. 'It's immoral. You knew right from the start I was profoundly against it, this – this obsession.'

'I just wanted your help,' she said, her eyes filling. 'Your advice. Your professional advice, even, if that was all you could give.'

He stopped again, glaring down at her from the fireplace, flickering shadows curling around his back. 'My advice? You want my professional advice? Fine, here it is. Don't mess with things you don't understand and are not properly trained in. The subconscious is not some amusing little theme-park playground for you and your long-haired freak friends to go tramping around in. Back up, pack up and pull out. That's my advice.'

Her head was on her knees, arms hugging her legs, shoulders shaking. 'It's there, Daddy,' she cried quietly, her voice a muffled sob. 'It's there, I know it. I've seen it.'

Dear Mr and Mrs Heywood.

Please excuse me faxing this to your office, but I felt I had to get in touch quickly following our talk.

It is my strong belief that it would be in everyone's interests to bring both Ben and Frankie here to Virginia.

I must point out right away that I am not yet able to say to what extent we might be able to help Frankie. But it would be an honour to try, and please be assured that if I felt at this stage there was little to be gained by doing so, I would not hesitate to say so now.

As with all our admissions, we would need to carry out a detailed examination and a series of preliminary tests to gain a proper understanding of Frankie's state and suitability for treatment. Many patients are not suitable, I must warn you, and regrettably the Perlman Institute must turn away those we feel we cannot help, or that it would be inadvisable to try to help. In this respect, therefore, there is a risk that your journey, should you decide to make it, might be wasted.

Furthermore you should not be misled into thinking that Frankie will necessarily regain all her faculties, be one hundred percent restored, if her treatment goes ahead and is successful. Sometimes the young people we treat do make full and complete recoveries, sometimes recovery is partial, sometimes limited. Sometimes there is no recovery. You must understand that.

Also, I should point out, the therapies and treatments they undergo are physically strenuous, placing high demands on their bodies' metabolisms and systems. As with any medical procedure, therefore, there is a risk to the patient's health. We do all we can to minimize this risk, but you should remain aware of it.

Finally I would like to add that in everything we do here we strive to ensure that the welfare of the young girls and boys sent to us remains our uppermost consideration at all times. For me it is a gesture of great faith to be entrusted with their care, as well as a privilege to work with them and their families.

There is one other point. The ethos of the Perlman Institute is based on the simple premise of innocent until

proved guilty. We have found that the medical establish-
ment often looks upon people like Frankie as persistently
and irretrievably unconscious unless the patients them-
selves prove otherwise. The view from the wrong end of
the telescope, in my opinion. We prefer to turn the tele-
scope around and look as hard as we can from the other
perspective, assuming in other words, that these young
people can be restored unless it is proved to us that they
cannot. Innocent until proved guilty. It is a philosophy
that tends to polarize opinion and, I should warn you,
has brought us into conflict with established medical and
other thinking, particularly of late. I felt I should be
honest with you about that at the outset.

My co-director Lewis Kern will be faxing you a copy
of our business terms and conditions for admission, no
doubt you will also want to study these carefully before
you reach your decision. It was a great pleasure talking
to you all, I do so hope we may meet in person.

With best wishes to you both, Ben and Frankie,
Elizabeth Chase MD
P.S. Please pass my good wishes also to Mrs Catchpole.

'What a charming girl,' said Janet, handing the fax back to
Alison. 'Wonderfully polite.' She took off her spectacles. 'What
on earth does it mean?'

Alison stared down at the crinkled pages in her hands. She
glanced up at Frankie. The corner of her mouth was curling,
one bony shoulder lifting and falling irregularly as though
tweaked on an invisible string. After a while she fell still again.
Beneath the bed the ventilator clicked, sucked and blew as
always, relentlessly driving air into the tissues of her lungs
while the musculature surrounding them wasted steadily away
from disuse. Alison had grown to loathe its uncompromising
presence, an hypnotically repetitive mechanical reminder of
hopelessness. It was wearing her down, grinding away her

reserves of stamina and determination, steadily advancing inch by inch across the battlefield in their unending war of attrition.

She spent less time with Frankie, these days, she acknow-ledged guiltily. She still visited, every day, mostly, whenever she could. But the earlier razor-sharp compulsion to spend every passing minute at her side was dulling as the months slid by. Her religious adherence to routine often slipped, the indefatig-able bedside chatter lapsing into brooding pensive silences. Her long-nurtured optimism was being steadily edged out, she realized, like an egg from the nest, by the greedy cuckoo chick of resentment.

'It means it's risky and that there are no guarantees, no guarantees at all,' she said wearily. 'It could all be a total waste of time.'

'And money,' added her mother. 'What about all that tele-scope business and stuff about established medical opinion? Does that mean they don't have the support of the medical establishment in America? Not sure I like the sound of that.'

'I don't know.' Alison studied the fax again. 'It's strange. On the one hand she says she believes she can do something for Frankie, then she spends the rest of the letter trying to put us off. It's as if she doubts herself, wants us to come but then doesn't.'

'Maybe she's just trying to be as open as possible.'

'And why does she always talk about Ben and Frankie together? Yesterday was the same, on the phone, she didn't seem really that focused on Frankie. It was Ben she wanted to know about, wanted to talk to.'

'Well, she feels there's a connection, she said so. I can under-stand that, I agree with her.'

Alison looked up at her mother. She was in the chair by the window, gazing down beyond the glass at the slowly circulating traffic below, one arm resting along the window-sill. She was wearing a tweed skirt, twinset and brown walking shoes, a white silk scarf with a racehorse motif about her shoulders. Tidy, well turned-out, as solid and dependable as ever. For as long as Alison could remember. 'What do you think we should do?'

'Oh, good gracious, that's not for me to say,' Janet scoffed, lifting her chin to peer down into the car park. She could see Jack's car, Jack and Ben standing beside it.

'Mum, I'd like to know, really. You've been with us right through this thing. I value your opinion.'

'Have you spoken to Rosemary?'

'Of course.' Alison shrugged. 'But she says that not having children of her own makes it impossible to, you know, imagine. She says that whatever we decide, she'll support us.'

Beyond the door a tea trolley was clattering noisily along the corridor. Further away a telephone buzzed at the nurses' station.

'I had a little sister once – did I ever tell you?' Janet began after a while. Alison shook her head. 'Stella. She died when she was three, pneumonia. I suppose I must have been six or seven at the time. I remember my parents, they were saddened, of course, but utterly pragmatic. It was part of the culture of their upbringing, you see. You lost children from time to time, everybody did, but it was not something you could fight, not something unnatural, it was part of raising a family. My father explained to the rest of us that it was the will of God and that Stella had been called to go and live with Jesus in heaven. We all accepted it, laid her to rest in the graveyard and life went on exactly as before. It was nature, he said. My father. Nature running its natural course. We seem to have lost that. The simple acceptance that death is a natural part of life.'

'Are you saying we should allow Frankie to die?'

Janet turned into the room. 'Losing a child from a simple germ like that would be unthinkable, these days. Antibiotics would have saved her. Easily, I imagine. But they weren't available, therefore there was no question of choice. Two days ago if you'd asked me that question I would have said we should be concentrating our efforts on Ben, that we should be putting the needs of the living before the nccds of the de ' She stopped herself, glanced at Frankie and lowered her voice. 'Before the needs of others. I've always believed that. But when I listened to that girl talking on the telephone from America yesterday, then read her letter, I wondered if we really have the right, or have the right to choose. All the technology and all the wonderful drugs and miraculous operations that we have today mean that perhaps we don't have a choice. Just as my parents and poor little Stella had no choice. Innocent until proved guilty, isn't that what she said?'

Jack leant back against the car, his eyes idly scanning the hospital's flat concrete façade. Automatically he counted up five storeys then along four windows until he found it, recognizing it by the tissue-paper sunflower stuck onto one of the panes. Ben stood beside him, leafing through a comic. They'd been to the hospital shop, been for a stroll round the car park, been to the drinks machine, been to the toilets. He glanced at his watch.

But he couldn't remember the last time Ben had been to see Frankie. He was happy enough to come as far as the hospital, knew it well, wandering its corridors at will while he or Alison paid their visit. He'd even go up to the fifth floor, sit at the nurses' station being fed biscuits and fussed over by the girls. But that was as far as he normally went of his own volition. Occasionally, earlier on, Jack and Alison would insist, steering him reluctantly through her door by the shoulder. But he would just sit or stand in the corner, head down, mute and guarded. After a few minutes he would ask if he could leave. Recently they'd more or less given up.

A gusting breeze funnelled around the side of the building, bending the silver birch saplings dotting the car park, whisking spirals of newly fallen leaves into the air, only to discard them elsewhere as the gust quickly waned. An advancing wall of harsh brightness was gliding silently across the cars towards them, he squinted up in time to catch the sun bursting into the clear from behind a scudding shower line. He checked his watch again, patting his jacket for sunglasses. 'Do you want a mint?' he said, pulling a tube from his pocket. He passed it to Ben, and ducked into the car. 'Have you seen my sunglasses?' He knelt across the seat, fumbling on the floor.

'That doctor,' Ben said quietly.

'Hmm?' He backed out, slamming the door. 'What doctor?'

'The one on the telephone, in America.'

He put on the glasses, the sun vanishing instantly behind the next shower cloud. 'Yes, what about her?'

Ben's head was down, staring at the unopened packet of mints, turning it slowly over and over in his hand.

'Frankie should go there.'

'They're coming, thought you might like to know.'

'Really?' Elizabeth turned from the mirror, her appearance instantly forgotten. 'That's, good,' she said, carrying the phone to the window. 'Yes, it is, it's good. Are they all coming?'

'Er, doesn't say, just says thanks for the stuff we sent through, given it a great deal of consideration, obviously major decision, blah blah, decided to go ahead right away, will be in contact again soon as they've made the arrangements.' Lewis paused. 'Financial arrangements I sincerely trust that means.'

Below, the Chevrolet was crawling along the street towards her apartment. She could see him craning his neck through the windshield looking for building numbers. 'Thanks, Lewis, thanks for letting me know.'

'You're welcome, have a pleasant evening.'

'Nice apartment,' Boyd said a few minutes later, looking around the bare walls. On the floor, cardboard boxes of pictures and ornaments were heaped into corners, teetering stacks of books crawled precariously up the walls, a battered suitcase stood by the front door amid an untidy litter of unopened junk mail. 'Just moved in?'

'Two years.' She folded her arms nervously. She'd put on a

dress, having searched frantically for something suitable, eventually locating it stuffed into the back of a drawer in the bedroom. Cotton, green, patterned with tiny flowers, she'd had to iron it twice to get the creases out. Brushing her hair down in the mirror, she'd realized at the last minute that the broad white of her bra straps stood out ridiculously beneath the string-thin shoulder ribbons of the dress. Glancing at the clock with a curse, she reached back quickly, unhooked the bra, pulled it off and tossed it into a corner. Immediately she began to worry that her breasts stood out beneath the cotton, or hung too low, or moved too much when she walked. 'For God's sake, this is absurd!' she swore desperately into the mirror. Then Lewis had phoned.

'Shall we go?'

'Great,' she said, a fine sweat breaking on her upper lip. It was a close, sultry evening. 'I think I'll just get a jacket.'

He drove her into Paxton, pulling up outside a large timber-framed seafood restaurant called the Marina. The restaurant was built onto the river's edge, overlooking pontoons of gently rocking pleasure yachts. Further out, fishing boats lay at anchor, upstream a road bridge crossed over into the main part of town on the far bank.

'Oh, John, this is really nice,' she said excitedly, looking around wide-eyed as their waiter seated them on the terrace, introduced himself as Gordon, lit their candle, handed them menus and explained that the night's special was marlin steaks grilled on mesquite.

'You ought to get out more.' Boyd smiled at her.

'So that's more or less all,' he said an hour later, leaning over to refill her glass. Her jacket was off, draped over the back of the chair, her cheeks glowing pink. 'And absolutely all about me. Your turn, what about you. Ever married?' She shook her head. 'Ever get close?'

'Not really.' Her eyes dropped to her plate. 'No, not at all, in fact. Dated a few of the guys at Stanford, had a disaster with a biochemistry professor, went out twice with a casualty intern at Boston, that's about it. Then all this started up and since then there really hasn't been time.'

'Time?'

'The clinic. It, well, it takes up everything, it *is* everything.'

'Hello, but didn't I just hear the sound of convenient excuses?' he teased, one hand cupped to his ear.

She grimaced. 'Well, all right then, time and will.' She looked away. 'I never really got into the dating thing. You know, at school. I think it's almost like an acquired habit, a skill. If you don't get established into the routine quite young, develop a knack, pick up a few ground-rules, then it's quite easy to – to kind of give it up, manage without.' She looked at him shyly. 'A bit like dropping a class you don't need.'

'It's a class we all need, Lizzie,' he said quietly. She said nothing, staring at her glass.

'And what about your partner?' He sat back suddenly. 'The smooth-talking Kern.'

'Lewis?' Her face brightened, eyes gleaming in the candle-light. 'Lewis has an ongoing and deeply meaningful love affair with the dollar sign. The only thing that ever gets close to his heart is his wallet.'

'You think so?' He gazed at her steadily. 'I wouldn't be so sure.' A soft blush had spread from the cleft of her neck down between the smooth swell of her breasts where they disappeared into her dress. She picked up her glass to cover her shyness. Gordon reappeared, laden with plates of cheesecake and Black Forest gâteau. They waited patiently while he fussed over them, refilling their glasses and chatting on about how Chef had been in a frightful stir all evening.

'What was she like?' she said, after he'd gone. 'Your wife.'

'Pretty, brunette, kind of petite. We met in law school, dated for about a year, then we got engaged and moved into a place out on Virginia Beach. Got married the following spring.' He looked out across the river; a faint rhythmic pump of rock music drifted across the water towards them from one of the bars on the far bank. 'It was great, you know, that first-flush thing. Pretty soon we settled down, I got a job in a law firm in Norfolk, she did legal representative work in the county prosecutor's office. After a couple of years we could afford a bigger apartment so we moved into town.'

'What happened?'

'She got hit by a truck. It was the damn stupidest thing. She's standing on the sidewalk one day down by the harbour shopping mall. There's four or five other people waiting to cross. Light goes green for them, they set off and a sixteen-wheeler ploughs into them. Three dead.'

'God, that's awful.'

He kept his eyes on the river. Out in the centre a timber barge was pushing its way slowly upstream, red navigation beacon mirrored on the water. 'Yes.'

'Did you ever find out what happened?'

'Driver statement said he was coming down the slope towards the lights, touched the brakes and nothing happened. No time to do anything, not even sound the horn. Problem was eventually traced to a mechanical fault in the brake system.'

'But wasn't somebody liable? The truck company?'

'You might think so. But it was a leased truck. The lessors claimed that the leasing company was responsible for maintenance. Maintenance on the whole fleet was subcontracted to yet another company, out of state, of course. Their insurers claimed that maintenance was correctly carried out but that it was a manufacturing fault. Manufacturer, in a third state, denies liability, citing an unapproved component was fitted. Component supplier passes the buck onto the component manufacturer, in a fourth state, and suddenly we're into at least seven different companies spread across half the continent, plus their various insurers, it's six years later and absolutely nothing has happened.' He smiled wryly. 'In my view it never will.'

'But what about compensation?'

'I wasn't after compensation. I would have settled for justice.'

She picked wax from the candlestick, her face thoughtful. 'Is that why you gave up the law firm to work for the District Attorney?'

'Uh-oh!' He laughed, holding up both hands. 'I hope we're not getting into analysis here, Doctor, I can't afford your city prices.'

She grinned mischievously, resting her chin on her hands. 'Is it?' she insisted.

He shrugged. 'Partly, maybe. I guess I just found working in a place where they set about trying to uphold the law more interesting than working in a place where they spend all day just trying to get around it.'

They stayed late, drinking coffee at the table while the restaurant emptied steadily around them, the bar across the river fell silent and the moon rose over the falling tide. Eventually Gordon began to wander in and out of their background line of vision, yawning and looking at his watch. They got up, Boyd gave him a twenty-dollar tip, and they left.

'Do you know something?' he said, guiding the Chevrolet down narrow back roads, its headlights sliding along impenetrable walls of dense forest. 'The guy driving the truck. Turns out he knew there was a fault on the brakes. Another driver on the fleet said that particular truck was well known for it, all the drivers knew it.'

'But that's dreadful,' she said, turning towards him. 'Couldn't they get him to you know, admit it, come forward or something?'

He snorted, staring through the windshield. 'Somehow I doubt it,' he replied, his face set. They were passing a sign for Everdene. 'Hey, we nailed Stamitz by the way. Our creepy friend, the mass murderer?'

'Oh, yes?'

'Brought him in two days ago. Arraignment in three weeks.'

'Congratulations, John, you must be pleased.' They fell quiet again.

'Lizzie?' He glanced across at her. Her head was down, hands clasped in her lap. 'Are you all right?'

She looked at him, her eyes round. 'John. The clinic. It *is* everything. To me. I'd like it not to be that way sometimes. Often, in fact. And I'd like to be able to do something about changing that, really I would. But I don't know if it's possible, I don't know if I can.' Her eyes fell again. 'I thought it only fair that you should know that.'

He reached out, touched her hand in the darkness. 'I do know that.'

Chapter 10

THE NEXT MORNING AT NINE HE TELEPHONED HER AT THE
clinic.

'John, hi,' she said, her face breaking into a smile. 'Thanks
for last night, I had a great time.'

'Elizabeth, the DA's going to request that you halt operations
at the Perlman.'

'What?'

'Just for the moment, you're going to have to stop the work
with the kids.'

'My God, but why?'

'Lizzie, it's standard procedure. When charges, serious
charges like these, have been filed against a company, it's quite
normal to request that all operations are suspended while the
charges are investigated.'

'But we can't, it's unthinkable! How long for?'

'I can't say. Weeks, could be months.'

She lowered the handset slowly, covering her face with one
hand. After a pause, she said, 'Is this a result of – of your
report? The report you wrote on us.'

'Partly, I guess. I don't know. But he's looking at everything,
the whole dossier, not just my report.'

'I can't believe it,' she groaned. 'It's not possible. Not now.'

'I'm very sorry.' The line was silent. 'Lizzie?'

'You knew about this last night, didn't you?' she said.

He sighed. 'I knew it was a possibility. I didn't know for certain until I got in this morning. I didn't want to worry you bef–'

There was a click, the phone went dead in his hand.

Two minutes later she burst into Lewis's office. They were already there, Nathan against the window, Lewis at his desk, hands clasped behind his head. 'Lewis, you're the lawyer.' Her eyes were wide with panic. 'What does it mean?'

He picked up a fax from his desk. 'It means precisely what Boyd says it means. It means that we must shut down operations.'

'But it's not possible,' she moaned, shaking her head. 'I just can't believe it.'

'Believe it, Lizzie, I've seen an injunction before.' He handed her the fax.

'But what about the research work?' She studied the fax, her face ashen. 'Maybe we could carry on–'

'Lizzie.' Lewis sat forward. 'We can't just go stepping around this thing like it's a turd on the sidewalk. This injunction means exactly what it says. They expect us to stop doing what we do. *Everything* we do.'

'I can't. I won't, we're too close.'

'Too close to what, for fuck's sake?'

She glanced at Nathan. He was still at the window, arms folded, face impassive. 'Lewis,' she began quietly, lowering herself into the chair in front of his desk, 'there are some things going on, some developments, some of our recent findings. I believe we're very close, possibly, to establishing the existence of a new pathway into the subconscious and maybe whole different planes of subliminal awareness.'

'Nathan, what the hell's she talking about, man?'

'Two of the kids appeared to set up some sort of brief common awareness field with each other via the control room array.'

'So?'

'It wasn't us. They bypassed us, just hijacked the gear for their own use. And there's been some other stuff lately, which may be pointing in a similar direction.'

'What direction for Christ's sake?'

Nathan shrugged. 'Who knows, man, it's too soon to tell.'

Lewis threw up his hands in exasperation. 'Common, subliminal, goddamn awareness fields,' he stammered. 'It's a crock! I mean, what exactly are we talking about here? Transferring thoughts down a wire? Some kind of computerized goddamn intelligence? Huh? What?'

'Lew.' Elizabeth leant across the desk towards him. 'We just don't know yet. But we are getting close to knowing. That's the point, that's why we can't stop. Not now.'

Lewis pushed back his chair. 'Look, folks, this is all very fascinating and I'm sorry to rain on anyone's parade but let me just point out a couple of tiny truths. Major scientific breakthroughs notwithstanding, we three are the executive directors of this cosy little party. That means that it's our necks on the line. Personally on the line. As far as I'm concerned, if the Dalmatia County DA says stop, we stop. All of it. Together. If you guys want to carry on chasing neurons down telephone lines that's fine. But I'm out.' He plucked his jacket from the back of his chair, picked up his briefcase and made for the door.

'Peter, hi, Jack Heywood at Heywood-Knight. Fine, fine thanks. Listen, I need a price please, quick as you can. It's an air-ambulance job. Cambridge to Norfolk. No, that's Norfolk Virginia, Peter, in the USA? Yep, it's a long hop so we're probably going to need a Lear or Citation or something. Right, the routing is to position empty to Cambridge, pick up the patient and entourage there, then fly direct to Norfolk . . . What? Walking wounded? No, definitely not, patient will be boarding on a stretcher, plus a lot of gear, so perhaps a Lear is too small. What about a Gulfstream? Okay. Right, total souls on board will probably be five plus aircrew, the patient, the usual two medical staff and two, or maybe three others, relatives. Huh? No, coming back empty. Oh, yes, departure date, hang on.' He covered the mouthpiece, blowing up at the ceiling. 'Christ knows,' he murmured. Carol appeared at his door, carrying a mug of coffee. He waved her in. 'Peter, not sure exactly but it could be within the next few days or so. Can you just phone around, see what's available and get me some prices at this stage? Thanks, appreciate it.'

'So, she's going?' said Carol, placing his coffee on the desk.

'Looks that way.' He nodded, glancing up at her. 'Sit down a moment, Carol.' As she sat, he got up, walking to the window. 'That job,' he began, staring at the carpet. 'The one Myriad offered you, is it still open?'

She lifted her shoulders. 'Don't know. I suppose so.'

'They're basically a good outfit, you know. Sharp as knives but financially sound. Gateskill runs a very tight ship, he's a good businessman.'

'Jack, what are you saying?'

'I'm saying talk to him, sound him out, see what he's offering and give it serious consideration.'

'You're going too,' she said quietly. 'Aren't you. To America.'

'I don't know.'

'You are.' She looked around the room. 'You're giving it up, all of it, everything you've worked for, fought so hard for. You're going, just as it was all starting to come good.'

'Carol, I don't know,' he repeated. 'Not for sure.' He sighed. 'But I do know that I need to raise huge amounts of cash, quickly, and that . . .' He trailed off, lifting his head. Outside a steady drizzle fell, enveloping the airport in a silent grey shroud. 'It is my family,' he went on quietly. 'It's in a mess, and it's my fault, my responsibility. And even though we don't know what's going to happen in America, and we don't even know if we're doing the right thing, we have made the decision. It's what we want. All of us, Ben too. And having made that decision, together, it's now up to me to find a way to make it happen. That's the way it should be, can you see that?' He turned to look at her. She had her back to him, head bowed.

After she left he returned slowly to his desk and pulled out the chair. Stretching his legs out ahead of him, his chin resting on his fingers, he looked around at the walls, the pictures, the model aeroplanes, the furniture, the bookcase, the filing cabinet. War memorabilia, he mused. Relics of a bruising, gruelling six-year campaign. Of hard-fought gains and bitter losses. Of advancing, falling back, regrouping, counter-attacking. Of struggling and of surviving. Without help, without respite and without quarter. And he'd won. And he'd lost. His eyes fell to the desk, the fold-out photographs of the three of them, beaming calmly back at him, innocent, confident, trusting.

He picked up the phone. 'Myriad? Yes, David Gateskill please.'

'If you could just sign there, please, at the bottom, and there, over the page here, and once more over here on the back, yes there, thank you.' Alison hastily scrawled signatures wherever the hospital administrator indicated, vaguely aware that she had little idea what she was signing. 'Fine, that's fine,' said the administrator, a dour, humourless man with a turned-down mouth and dry skin. 'That's the disclaimers all done. Now for the transportation requests, discharge papers and release forms.' He produced another folder and opened it. Alison hunched over the pages, following his scaly finger back and forth, signing obediently wherever it paused.

Finally it was finished. He gathered up his folder and departed for the lift with a curt 'Good morning.' Nobody, it seemed, approved of them taking Frankie away. She got up from the empty nurses' station and walked around the corner to their rest room. It was coffee-time, she could hear the subdued murmur of voices. As she walked in they fell quiet, staring into their cups, faces blank. It was as though, by removing Frankie, she was accusing them all of failure.

'I wanted to just say, something,' she began, searching for words. She hadn't prepared anything, never imagined she'd be making speeches, but suddenly it was important. 'First, I owe you, we all do, an enormous thank-you. These past months have been, emotionally, very trying, very charged for us as a family. I know you understand that. I also know that sometimes it has been difficult.' She smiled at them shyly. 'Okay, *I* have been difficult, and often, no doubt, unhelpful probably, to you and your work.' The door opened quietly, Matron slipped in, taking up station against the wall. 'But perhaps if I tell you that all the time, when I was being difficult, being a bossy, nagging pain in the arse, in fact,' she saw stifled smiles being exchanged, 'it was simply because I was just, so, scared. Terrified actually. All the time. And I suppose being pushy and aggressive like that was the only way I could find to – to manage that fear–' She broke off. 'Oh dear, I'm not really explaining myself very well, am I?'

She looked around the room: there were one or two polite but uncomprehending smiles, others looked blankly at the floor. One nurse glanced at her watch. Matron, hands behind her back, tight-lipped and expressionless at the wall. Suddenly she saw it, saw what it was. Frankie had always been like this to them. They knew no other version. She was their little Sleeping Beauty, or the patient they had to turn, or whose bags they had to change, or whose readings they had to take every hour. The vegetative case in room four, fifth floor. That was all. They had never known her before, none of them had. Not one person in the entire hospital had ever seen her, ever met her, ever known her in any other state than the one she arrived in. She had no former substance, no known personality. She wasn't a person. Frankie, her Frankie, didn't exist.

She stooped to her shoulder-bag quickly, riffled through the contents until she found it, stuffed into a side pocket. Pulling it out she smoothed it flat with her hand. 'This was taken last year,' she said, straightening crumpled edges. She handed it to the nearest nurse. 'Florida, we all went to Disney World on holiday.' Ben and Frankie, playing on the beach, grinning hugely, close-up into Jack's camera. They were kneeling at the water's edge constructing an enormous sandcastle. Frankie's hair was wet and stringy from the sea, strands of it plastered to one cheek. Wet sand stuck to her arms and knees, and down the front of her little orange bikini. One hand was held up, a paper flag on a stick in her triumphantly clenched fist, the other, fingers stretched, burrowed ecstatically into the soft sand. Her skin glowed, her eyes sparkled with happiness. Her salt-flecked lips were widely parted, sand-tipped tongue protruding, laughing with joy.

Immediately there were sighs of delight, heads crowding to the picture. Suddenly they were talking to her, asking about her, about Frankie the little girl, Frankie the baby, Frankie the schoolgirl, Frankie the living, breathing person.

'What will they be doing?' one of them asked a few minutes later. 'At this clinic?'

'They'll be trying to wake her up, simply that. That's what they do there.' There were raised eyebrows of surprise, she noted, as if the very idea was unimaginable.

'When are you leaving?' someone else said. The photograph reached Matron. She studied it for a few seconds, holding it at arm's length, face impassive. A moment later she passed it on.

'We're trying to make the travel arrangements as quickly as possible. Within the next few days, perhaps a week.'

After a time they drifted away back to their duties. She stayed for a few minutes, drinking her coffee and staring at the photograph. Then she got up and walked slowly back towards the lift. On the way she passed the nurses' station again. Two of them were there; they smiled at her. 'Good luck.'

'Thank you.' Tucking the photograph back into her bag,

she walked to the lift and thumbed the button.

'Mrs Heywood? Just a moment.' It was Matron, her rubber-soled shoes squeaking as she strode up the corridor towards her.

'I just wanted to say,' she began, grey eyes searching Alison's, 'these are good people.' She nodded up the hall. 'Forgive them if they appear not to understand. If someone removes a sick patient from their care, they can only conclude it's because their care wasn't good enough.'

'Oh, but it's not true,' Alison pleaded. 'I tried to explain, I really hope they believe that.'

Matron smiled minutely. 'Perhaps, I hope so too. Goodness knows, it's already hard enough maintaining morale these days.' Her eyes flickered. 'I don't know whether I approve of what you're doing. In any case it's not my place to say. But I do wish you luck, with all my heart, and I hope you find what you're searching for.' She stepped forward suddenly and pecked Alison on the cheek. 'God bless.' She turned quickly and squeaked back down the corridor.

The phone rang again, Jack snatched it up. 'Heywood.'

'Gateskill here. Myriad Air Services.'

Jack sat back. Christ, that was quick. But then he realized it was also utterly predictable. David Gateskill was a master of the get-in-before-anyone-else school of business management.

'I've had a quick look through your proposal,' Gateskill went on disdainfully. 'It has a lot of problems.'

'Thought it might,' said Jack flatly.

'I'm going to have to look at the numbers again very hard before I can really give it serious consideration.'

God, the bastard was enjoying this, Jack fumed. 'No doubt.'

'They'll have to be revised,' he continued pompously. 'Downwards considerably, if it's going to be remotely workable, but even then I'm not really sure it's for us.'

'Then why on earth bother ringing!' Jack exploded.

'I heard you needed a G4.'

'Pardon?'

'A Gulfstream. For an air-ambulance charter to the States. Peter Baker at London Air Charter was phoning round everywhere for quotes this morning. It wasn't until later that I realized it was for Heywood-Knight.'

'Yes.' Jack sighed, reaching for his notepad. The price had come back an hour earlier. It was astronomical, nearly nine thousand pounds.

'Costly, I should imagine.'

'Uh-huh.'

'Take ours.'

Jack froze. 'I'm sorry?'

'Take it.' There was a pause. 'It's for your daughter, isn't it?'

'Yes, well yes it is, we're sending her to a special . . . How did you know about that?'

Gateskill chuckled. 'Goodness, Jack, this is an airport. Rumours circulate faster than cucumber sandwiches at a royal garden party.'

Jack was astonished. 'Well, that's true yes, but how much? The costs will–'

'Take it. Don't worry about the costs, bloody Kuwaiti owners never do. Only thing is, you'll have to move fast if you want it. The aircraft is in Rome now, then it goes out to the Middle East for three weeks at the weekend. So it'll have to be tomorrow. I'll tell the owners we flew over to the factory for a thousand-hour check, it's nearly due anyway. We'll stop here on the way, then drop you at Norfolk before carrying on to Savannah, nobody the wiser.'

'Yes, but that's, incredibly generous.' It was also incredibly risky. If the owners ever found out they'd tear up Myriad's management contract in an instant. 'Thank you, David, I appreciate it.'

'Jack, we both know the nature of this business. Dog eats dog or dog starves to death. If I can ease out a competitor or pick up a contract via the back door or generally stuff the other bloke up, I won't ever hesitate to do so. But I'd like to think that even I would stop short at making personal gain out of another man's family misfortune. I'll have the aeroplane on the tarmac outside your office at six tomorrow evening. Try to be ready, the timing's pretty tight.'

'Yes, okay. Right, David, thanks. Thank you very much.'

'You're welcome, Jack, and good luck with your daughter.'

Jack backed through the kitchen door with a crash. Alison and Ben were there, having tea. 'How soon can we be ready to go?' he said breathlessly, dropping his briefcase and a large cardboard box onto the floor.

'What's all that?' asked Alison from the door of the refrigerator.

'Stuff from the office. How soon?'

'Well, I don't know. Frankie's ready, the hospital knows, I went through all the paperwork with them today. But I haven't begun packing or anything, and the house—'

'Passports?' He grabbed a biscuit from the table, gripping it in his teeth as he shrugged off his jacket.

'Fine, still good from last year, but—'

'Good. We go tomorrow.'

'What?' Alison gawped at him. 'Tomorrow?' Ben looked up, knife and fork in hand. 'But, my God . . .' She began to look around her in mounting panic. Janet came into the kitchen carrying an empty teacup. 'But it'll never be—' Alison stopped suddenly, staring at him. 'Why? What's happened?'

'There's a Gulfstream picking us up here at the airport at six tomorrow evening, flying us direct to Virginia.'

'Us?'

'I'm coming.' They all stared at him.

'But what about the business?'

'Sold it this afternoon to Myriad. David Gateskill. And he's laying on the Gulfstream. Free.'

'What? Gateskill?'

'Yes, that's what I thought. Mind-boggling, isn't it?'

'But Jack, the business. Your business.' She sat down next to Ben in bewilderment. 'You sold Heywood-Knight. Just like that. Are you sure?'

He looked at her. 'It's okay. Really, I feel fine about it. In fact, I feel great about it.' She was gaping at him, mouth open, eyes wide with shock and disbelief, the colour draining from her cheeks. He went round the table, dropping to a squat between them. 'Alison, I want to do this,' he went on softly, resting an arm carefully across her shoulder. He winked at Ben. 'But I want us to do it together, all of us. Dumping the business was the only way. It was also the only way to raise the money.'

'I'd like to help out in that department,' said Janet, pouring herself another cup of tea. They looked at her. 'If you'll let me.'

'Mum, that's terribly kind, but your savings – you can't, we won't let you.'

She waved her hand. 'I'm not talking about savings,' she scoffed. 'Couple of thousand in the bloody building society isn't going to make a jot of difference.' She sipped her tea. 'Mortgaged my cottage.'

'What!' Alison cried, burying her face in her hands. 'I don't believe I'm hearing this. Mum, your house, for God's sake, you can't!'

'Why not? It's my house isn't it? Did a wonderful deal at the bank. Fifty per cent mortgage. They get it back after I croak, nice lump tucked safely away to take care of the interest, I get the rest to put in the pot towards Frankie. What could be simpler?'

Alison groaned, her face still in her hands, head shaking.

Jack got up, went to Janet and kissed her forehead. 'Wonderful. It's a wonderful, wonderful gesture. But Alison's right, I don't think we can allow it.'

'Nonsense. Think of it as a reserve then, a fall-back.'

'Well, all right, we'll see. Thank you.' He looked around the room. 'So,' he went on, 'it's all settled then. We go tomorrow.' He rubbed his hands together. 'Right. I'm going upstairs to sort out some papers.' He turned for the door.

'I should like to come too,' Janet said quietly. Alison's head came up.

'Well, as you wish, I'm only going to the spare room,' Jack grinned.

'To America,' said Janet. 'If you'll allow me, I'd like to come with you, see it through with you.'

She sat in the darkened room, head bowed, hands between her knees, staring sightlessly at the green message light blinking up at her from the phone at her feet.

Much later she heard footsteps on the stairs outside, then a knock on her door. 'Lizzie?' he called softly, knocking again. 'Lizzie, will you let me in, please. I know you're there, your car's outside.' She said nothing. 'Okay,' he said. 'I can wait.' A moment later she heard a soft scraping sound as his back slid slowly down the door.

'Come in.' She sighed. 'It's not locked.'

'Not locked is not smart, Elizabeth,' Boyd said, closing the door behind him. He walked across the darkened floor towards her chair.

She shrugged. 'I could always call in the law. If they weren't too busy shutting down hospitals.'

'They're not shutting it down,' he said, dropping to one knee beside her. He looked up at the curtainless window. The faded paintwork swinging red through green in the reflected glare of a suspended traffic light outside. 'It's just procedure. Maybe it'll come to nothing and you'll be able to carry on.'

'No, that'll never happen. They want to kill it. This is just the beginning.'

'They're just being cautious. They've got to be.'

'It's not caution, John,' she said, getting to her feet abruptly. She paced barefoot, hugging her shoulders. 'It's plain ignorance. And it's fear. They're scared of it. Scared because they don't understand. Scared because their so-called experts don't understand either. Scared of politicians like Willis, scared of the media, scared of the insurance companies and the government institutions, scared to death because to move forward, to push on that little bit further, means taking a step into the unknown, reaching into the darkness a little bit. It means taking a risk.'

'It's procedure. Surely that's to be expected?'

'No, it's fear. They kill what they fear and they fear what they don't understand. It's as simple as that.'

The room was silent. After a while he straightened from the floor and went to the window, stood beside her, hands in pockets.

'Lizzie,' he began, 'that night at the clinic, you know, with that young girl, Annie, was it?' She nodded fractionally. 'Well, what happened, what you did with her, it was, one of the most extraordinary, most moving, most wonderful things I have ever witnessed.'

'Thank you.' Her voice was barely a whisper.

'But it was also one of the most terrifying,' he went on gently. 'Your work with these kids, what you do, it's astonishing. But it's also controversial and risky and so people need to be re-assured that proper precautions, proper safeguards are in place. Surely that's good sense.'

She nodded reluctantly. 'Yes, I know. But something's happening, John, something vital. Breaking off now, it's just, so awful, unthinkable.'

'But why?'

'I don't know why, I can't explain it. But it's to do with what I am, who I am–' she broke off.

He turned back to the window. 'So what will you do?'

'I don't know, I really don't. Go abroad if I have to, I've had offers.'

'America's loss.'

'America,' she repeated wryly. 'The land of limitless opportunity for the individual, yet run for the benefit and protection of corporations.'

'I'm aware of that,' he said quietly. 'It failed me too.'

'John.' She faced him quickly, eyes pained. 'I'm so sorry, that was unforgivable.' She reached out tentatively, rested a hand on his shoulder. 'And, yet you still have faith in it?' she went on softly.

'I must. What else is there if not? I must believe that, ultimately, American law will protect American people.'

She breathed out, leaning her head against his arm. They stood quietly for a while. 'Why didn't you tell me?' she asked eventually. 'Last night. When you knew.'

He paused. 'You're the first person I've asked out in six years. Since Cheryl. It was quite a big deal for me, I guess. I was just selfish. I suppose I just didn't want anything to spoil it.'

'It wasn't selfish.' She took his arm, staring through the grime-stained glass at the gently swinging traffic light, the steady changing colours reflecting in her eyes.

The next day passed in a frenzied and bottomless blur of hastily packed suitcases and last-minute shopping, rushed phone calls and dashed-off letters, overflowing cardboard boxes and forgotten farewells. Denied sleep from well before dawn, Jack threw back the covers early, descending quietly to the kitchen. There he found Alison stuffing handfuls of laundry into the washing-machine from an enormous pile in the centre of the floor.

'What on earth are you doing?' he whispered blearily.

'Pruning the roses. What does it look like I'm doing?'

'Ali, they have washing-machines in America. I believe they invented them.'

She wiped a fistful of laundry across her forehead. 'We'll never make it.' She sighed, staring around her.

He looked down at her, crouched on the floor like a nervous cat. 'How long have you been up?'

'Since four,' she muttered.

He made her tea, retrieved her from the floor. 'Come on,' he said firmly, steering her to the table. 'We'll make a list.'

'We'll never make it,' he said thirty minutes later, all pretence at calm evaporating like the dawn mist. Five lists were spread on the table before them. One contained all the tasks Jack had to complete at the office before he could hand the keys to Heywood-Knight over to David Gateskill. Another was a long list of arrangements, actions and equipment required to get Frankie from the hospital to the airport at Cambridge and from the airport at the other end in Virginia to the Perlman Institute. A third listed material on Frankie requested by the Perlman: medical records, school reports, photographs, any home-video footage, favourite story books, toys, games and CDs. A fourth concentrated on everything that needed to be done to close up the house, divert bills and mail, stop the milk, the phone, electricity, gas . . .

'How long are we going for?' she asked at one point.

'Christ knows,' he answered grimly.

The final list, three sub-lists in fact, contained those personal items needed for themselves and Ben.

'I'll stay,' he said eventually, staring at the sheets. He looked at her. 'Just for a day or two. Close up the house properly, make sure everything's settled at the office then fly out on scheduled airlines.'

'Are you sure?' she said, searching his eyes.

'Absolutely. It's probably better, in fact. Now that your mum's coming she'll be able to help you at the American end, and I can make sure everything is battened down here. And if you forget anything I can bring it.'

'It does make sense. Okay.' She pushed back the chair. 'Thanks, Jack. I'd better make a start upstairs.'

At nine he went into the office.

'Yes, I know,' Carol said simply, pulling stacks of files from a cabinet.

'You do?' he said incredulously. 'How?' She threw him an amused glance, slamming shut the filing cabinet. 'Okay, this is an airport, I know,' he went on, following her to her desk. 'Carol. I wanted to thank you. Myriad, the Gulfstream, that was your doing, wasn't it?'

'Sorry, Jack, can't take the credit for that one at all. David's idea completely.'

He shook his head. 'Not sure I completely believe you, but thanks anyway.' He paused. 'Will you take it? The job.'

'I don't know. Told him I'd think about it.'

'You're due some money,' he went on. 'Technically this is a redundancy situation, we'll look into–'

'Jack.' She stopped him. 'You don't owe me anything, not a single penny. I came into this thing five years ago with nothing but rose-tinted glasses, a shorthand-typing diploma and the half-baked notion that executive air charter was something to do with upmarket package tours to the Costa Brava. You and Bill taught me a trade, a whole new set of skills and the importance of self-reliance and living life with your eyes open. On the way, and under extreme pressure, you and I found ourselves making a brief detour up a blind alley, but we backed out again and now it's over.' Her eyes softened. She reached up, flicking a tiny shard of polystyrene packaging from his jacket. 'Completely over,' she went on gently. 'I'm going to take a break for a couple of weeks and think things over.' She grinned. 'Upmarket package tour to the Costa Brava. It's going to be pretty chaotic here and you've got a million things to do, so, well,' she kissed his cheek, 'here's wishing you luck. You and your family. All the luck in the world.'

He worked through the morning, calling clients, explaining developments, writing letters, rattling off faxes, speaking to the banks, the suppliers, the creditors, the airport management. At one point Carol put a plate of sandwiches in front of him. He managed one between calls, the rest went untouched. During the afternoon Alison phoned to say the hospital was more or less ready but making a fuss about the ambulance for Frankie. 'They won't guarantee to have one available when we need it,' she said, her voice edged with desperation. 'Said that emergency calls take priority.'

'Christ.' Jack sat back, rasping a hand across his unshaven chin. He'd already rerun the calculations himself. The aircraft arrived from Rome at five. It had to be airborne again within the hour, otherwise the flight crew would end up running out of duty hours and so be flying illegally. Then there was the ambulance at the other end. All arranged for nineteen hundred hours Eastern Standard Time. But how long would it wait if the Gulfstream was delayed? He surveyed the wreckage of boxes and packing cases strewn around the floor of his office. And the aircraft could only stay on the ground a short time in Norfolk: it had to get aloft again quickly if it was to make it down to Savannah. Suddenly he had a nightmare vision: Alison, Janet and Ben standing alone on a windswept and deserted tarmac, Frankie lying on her stretcher beside them, no one to meet them and nowhere to go. It was insanity. He wondered about calling it off.

'Jack?' Alison was still holding. 'Are you all right?'

'Yes, yes, I'm fine,' he said, rubbing his eyes.

'Don't worry,' she said encouragingly. 'I'll take care of those ambulance boys. We'll be there, I'll make damn sure of it.'

'Hello, everyone,' Elizabeth began nervously, surveying the twenty faces ranged before her. 'I've called us all together to try to explain a couple of things.' They were all there, the entire staffing complement grouped loosely around the lobby, waiting patiently for her, willing her to deny rumours they'd been hearing for days. All her people. The medical students, the nursing staff, the technicians, Nathan's assistants, the accounts clerk, maintenance man, even the duty receptionist, hovering in the doorway of her office, one ear to the phones. Only Lewis was missing, his absence more keenly sensed than she would have ever imagined possible. Not a word. Just when she needed him most.

She took off her spectacles, pinched the bridge of her nose. 'I expect many of you have seen the newspapers. Some of you have met and spoken to Investigator Boyd from the District Attorney's office. No doubt you've also heard some of the rumours,' she went on. 'Rumours are bad for everyone, so these are the facts. Pending the outcome of an investigation into various, um, allegations and charges, a temporary restraining order has been served on us which, in effect, prevents us from carrying on our business.' A murmur washed across the lobby. 'Yes I know, I'm sorry. The injunction is not very specific about what it does and does not include, but we must assume it is intended to cover all the work with our young people upstairs.' She glanced at the ceiling.

'Now, I just don't know what this means for the future of the Institute,' she went on hesitantly. 'I can't tell you how long this will go on for, I don't even know if we will ever be able to resume where we left off. I don't know how to advise you.' Her eyes fell. 'In fact, I don't really know what to say to you.'

'But why?' somebody asked eventually. It was one of the students. 'Why is this happening?'

'Well, ours is, unusual work. Perhaps even controversial. And hand in hand with controversy goes suspicion. Some people have always been suspicious of what we do. And some of those people have the power to influence those in authority.'

'Are you going to do it?' somebody else said, his voice edged with defiance. 'Are you really going to stop everything?'

'That would seem to be the implication of the injunction.' She looked around at them, the mute expressions, the anxious eyes. 'But the thing is this,' she continued, drawing a breath, 'you must all now, as individuals, look to yourselves. Your main concern at this time must be your own careers, your livelihoods and your futures.'

'But what will happen to them? The patients, all the kids?'

'I don't know.' She sighed. 'Some may remain here, some will probably leave – it's up to their families. I shall be getting in contact with all of them to explain. And we cannot take any further new admissions. That much seems to be clear.'

'But what about the English girl? Heywood.' It was the receptionist, her head poking through the sliding glass partition to her office.

'I'll be speaking to her parents,' said Elizabeth. 'They aren't due in until next week.'

'Yes, they are,' the receptionist said. 'There was a fax. Yesterday. To Mr Kern. I put it on his desk.'

For a second Elizabeth stared at her, then she strode quickly to Lewis's door, the receptionist following in her wake. Outside in the lobby the others lingered, murmuring to each other or standing quietly alone, lost in thought.

> *Dear Mr Kern,*
> *Further to my last, just to let you know that an opportunity has arisen for us to bring our plans forward a few days. Therefore we will be departing UK tomorrow the 16th at 1700 hrs GMT, arriving Norfolk airport approx 1900 hrs EST. I have made road transportation arrangements from Norfolk and expect therefore that we shall be arriving with you at around 2200 hrs your time. I will assume if I hear nothing that these arrangements are acceptable to you. In any case I will telephone again tomorrow to confirm exact departure and estimated arrival times.*
> *With best wishes,*
> *Jack Heywood.*
> *PS. Dr Chase's letter last week greatly helped us to come to a decision. Her refreshing candour, as well as a*

passionate commitment to her work, were obvious. Please tell her we very much look forward to turning the tele-scope around together.

Jack turned up the collar of his jacket, wiped rainwater off the face of his wristwatch and glanced for the twentieth time towards the gaping perimeter gate, fifty yards behind him. Nothing. Just inside it, Ben and Janet sat waiting impassively behind the misted-up windscreen of his car, their suitcases ready in the boot behind them. The gate, opened by special arrangement for their benefit, stood wide, an elderly security guard beside it, head hunched into the shoulders of his jacket, a little plastic cover stretched over the top of his cap. He tapped pointedly at his wrist, spreading his hands at Jack in an exaggerated shrug. Jack ignored him, turning forward again to a crescendo of jet turbine noise as the Gulfstream pilot nudged one throttle up, easing the sleek nose of the aircraft into a slow turn. He stretched both arms skywards, the pilot acknowledging with a single flash of the landing light as he taxied the aeroplane ponderously across the apron towards him, its nose-wheel spreading miniature bow-waves through deepening puddles on the tarmac. A minute later Jack signalled crossed fists at the pilot, the nose dipped, brakes were applied, and the engine whine died as the cut-offs were pulled. He glanced at his watch again. Twenty-five minutes behind schedule.

Ducking beneath the wings, he kicked wheel chocks into place then ran towards the cabin door and up the airstair the moment it was down.

The pilots were still in their seats, completing the shutdown checks. He waited while they finished the list, glancing through the cabin's oval windows at the empty security gate. 'Jack Heywood.' He held out a wet hand. 'This is unbelievably kind of you.'

They introduced themselves. 'We absolutely cannot hang around long,' said the co-pilot, a fresh-faced youth in an immaculate uniform. He was filling in a duty hours sheet on a clipboard, his expression a barely disguised scowl of disapproval.

'Gateskill tells me you flew seven-threes with Britannia?' his captain, a fair-haired, round-faced man of about Jack's age, said pleasantly. He was half turned in his seat to face him, one arm resting on the control yoke, his headphones loosely about his neck.

'Um, yes, that's right. Got seconded after flying college,' Jack replied, bobbing his head anxiously to the window again.

'Perth?'

'Hamble.'

'Oh, yes?' the captain said interestedly. They might have been discussing the cricket score. 'What year? I was at Hamble.'

Jack looked at him, his nerves stretched to screaming point. Above his head the steady murmur of rain on the curved roof of the fuselage; through the window, fretful gusts blew ripples across the rain-soaked apron, rocking the aircraft gently on its wheels. They were more than thirty-five minutes behind schedule now, he hadn't heard anything from Alison in over an hour. Something must have gone wrong. 'Um, 'eighty-one to 'eighty-two, -three I mean.'

The co-pilot looked at his watch, jotting a final note onto his sheet. 'Sorry, Donald,' he said quietly to his captain, offering him the clipboard. 'Really think we're getting into a difficult situation here.'

The captain glanced at it then handed it back. 'Tell you what, young Simon,' he said pleasantly, 'why don't you bugger off back into the cabin? There's a good chap. Double check everything is ready for our guests, make sure the toilets are clean and tidy while you're at it, then see if you can rustle up a cup of coffee for me and Captain Heywood here.' He winked at Jack. 'Because we aren't going anywhere without them. Is that quite clear?'

Twenty minutes later Jack dropped to a squat beside Ben,

checking his seat-belt. 'You're a lucky boy,' he said. 'This aeroplane is owned by a prince.'

'I know,' he replied eagerly. 'The captain told me.'

He ruffled his son's hair. 'Be good, won't you. Do as Mummy says and look after Granny, okay?'

He nodded. 'When are you coming?'

'Soon as I can.'

'Shit or bust?'

'Shit or bust.' Tears stung his eyes. He pulled the child's head forward suddenly, kissed him hard on the forehead. He held him tightly, then turned quickly to the stretcher behind. Two nurses were seated next to it. 'She's fine,' one of them said, smiling. 'Don't worry, we'll take care of her.'

He bent to the stretcher, brushing the back of his hand lightly down Frankie's cheek. 'Goodbye, my darling girl,' he murmured into her ear. 'See you soon.'

He embraced Janet, the whine of spooling turbines starting up beyond her window. 'Is there a bar?' she asked.

'On an Arab aeroplane?' He grinned, patting her knee. 'Don't worry, you'll be well looked after.'

Then he went forward. She was at the top of the airstair, checking through her bag. Rain fell sideways through the glare of the open doorway behind her, beyond that, an oval of heavy grey scud rolled by against the gathering darkness.

'Got everything?'

'Christ knows.' She forced a grin. 'Think so.'

'Call me at Norfolk if you get a chance.'

She nodded. 'Will you phone the clinic, let them know we got off okay?' A second whine was starting as the starboard engine spun up.

'Soon as you're airborne, everything's arranged.'

'Right then.'

Suddenly they were hugging, his arms enveloping her, squeezing her tightly against him. She buried her face in his neck. 'Don't be too long,' she whispered. 'We need you.'

'Be there before you know it.' He closed his eyes, clinging to her doggedly. 'I love you.'

She kissed his neck. 'I know.'

He stood on the empty apron and watched them taxi out to the holding point, the rain beating on his bare head and trickling unnoticed down his neck. It was almost completely dark, the distant anti-collision beacon flashing steadily atop the aircraft's tail. After a minute, the white wing-tip strobes came on, the Gulfstream turned onto the runway and there was a rumble of thunder as the throttles went forward to the stops. A moment later the brakes were released and the aeroplane rolled swiftly forward.

He watched it as it climbed steeply out, banked gently towards the lighter horizon to the west then vanished into the bottom of the overcast. Then he turned his back to the rain and walked slowly across the puddle-strewn tarmac towards the office.

C h a p t e r 1 1

'THANKS, DICK, YES I'M STANDING HERE OUTSIDE THE entrance of the Perlman Institute, a former private abortion clinic and site of this morning's demonstration organized by the local human-rights action group Unheard Voice. As you can see, they are protesting against experiments allegedly being conducted inside the Institute, which specializes in the treatment of young coma victims.'

The camera pulled back from the deeply tanned face of the fair-haired reporter talking into the microphone. Behind him, a small group of about six people, holding placards, walked in a silent circle at the foot of the main entrance steps.

Janet sat forward on the edge of the bed. 'Alison,' she called, fumbling for her glasses. 'Alison, quick! It's the Institute, they're on television.' Alison appeared from the shower room wearing a bath robe. 'What's happening?' she said, rubbing her hair on a towel. She sat down on the bed between Janet and Ben.

'There's Dr Chase,' said Ben, pointing at the screen.

She was standing to one side of the reporter, head lowered, eyes hidden behind her spectacles, staring at the ground ahead of her, face set. On the other side of the reporter a tall, dark-haired woman wearing a lemon trouser suit was half turned to watch the demonstrators.

'And with me is the Institute's founder and clinical director, Dr Elizabeth Chase, and Mrs Floyd Beamon of Unheard Voice. Er, Mrs Beamon, if I could come to you first, could you perhaps tell us, what is the purpose of today's demonstration?'

The woman leant eagerly towards the microphone. 'Yes, Bob. We're here once again to speak on behalf of the young people suffering unimaginable pain and indignity inside this shameful building,' she said, her voice strident. 'Behind these doors, unconscious children are being subjected to obscene, immoral and unregulated experiments involving among other things, electric shocks, hallucinogenic drugs and hypnosis. We are here as concerned right-to-life Christian parents to draw attention to the human-rights abuses going on within this house of shame and plead once again for the lives of its voice-less victims.'

'Dr Chase, human-rights abuses?'

'But, we believe in right to life,' Elizabeth said, her voice small. She flinched as the reporter thrust the microphone closer, half obscuring her face. 'That's the whole point of everything we do. We try to revive unconscious people who might otherwise be condemned to spend the rest of their lives imprisoned within themselves, or, or worse still, waiting help-lessly to have their life support terminated—'

'Ask her about the Willis kid,' interrupted the other woman.

'Er, yes, indeed.'

'— aware, perhaps, of their surroundings and the outside world but quite unable to reach it or communicate with it . . .' Elizabeth trailed off helplessly.

'Poor thing,' said Janet. As they watched the screen, a car pulled up in a cloud of dust in the background. 'And as for that other woman, frightful, just look at those shoes.' Alison sat forward on the bed gnawing her lip thoughtfully.

'Republican Congressman John Willis is pressing the District Attorney to bring homicide charges . . .'

'There's Dad!'

'. . . following the tragic death of his son Robert while undergoing treatment.'

'. . . electrocuted to death in an obscene night-time ritual we heard.'

'. . . tragic heart-attack. Everything we ever do is exhaustively tested on us first.'

'Dad. Look, it's Dad, getting out of that car!'

'. . . our responsibility once again to put a stop to this immorality and close this despicable house of shame, once and for all.'

'What on earth is he doing there? He was supposed to come to the hotel.' As they watched, the car driver dropped bags at Jack's feet, climbed back into the cab and sped off. Alison reached for the phone.

Jack brushed dirt from the lapel of his jacket and peered around through a haze of settling dust. There seemed to be people everywhere. Beside him a group of placard-bearing demonstrators were walking in circles in front of the main steps. Further off, a television crew was conducting interviews near a massive outside broadcast lorry with a tall telescopic transmitter mast. Long coils of electrical cable snaked from the lorry across the drive and up the steps into the building. All around, there were camera operators, sound engineers, harassed-looking girls bearing clipboards and sun reflectors, demonstrators, spectators and hangers-on. White-coated technicians stood or squatted to watch from the top of the steps. More people peered through the glass entrance doors and windows. Dazed and bleary, Jack wondered if he was at the right place: it was as though he had blundered onto a film set. To one side a man leant against an old green Chevrolet, watching quietly, arms folded. He glanced towards Jack briefly. Jack stared around: there was a small brass plaque beside the main door. Stepping cautiously over the television cables, he picked up his bags and wearily began climbing the steps.

Half-way up, the doors opened and a woman appeared.

'Mr Heywood? Mr Jack Heywood?'

He looked up at her. 'That's right.'

She hurried down the steps towards him. 'I'm so sorry, we weren't expecting you until later.' She relieved him of one of his bags. 'Your wife's on the telephone.'

Bewildered, he followed her through the doors, the lobby cool and quiet suddenly after the heat and confusion outside. The woman led him to a phone. 'Hello, Alison?'

'Jack, you made it! Are you okay? We saw you on TV.'

'Yes, I'm fine, bit tired, hell of a week, and the flights were all cocked up, but I'm okay. What's going on?'

'God knows. Probably best if Lizzie explains. Is she there?'

'Lizzie?'

'Dr Chase. Listen, Jack, I'm at the hotel. Wait there and I'll come right over and pick you up.'

'What about Frankie's session? That's why I came straight here. Have I missed it?'

'No, we've put it off until later in the day. We wouldn't have gone ahead without you.'

'Oh, good. I'll wait for you here then.' He gazed around the lobby. 'See you in a while?'

'Quick as I can. Jack?'

'Hmm?'

'I'm very glad you're here.'

The receptionist showed him to the washroom, made him a coffee and sat him in a reception armchair. A few minutes later a slight, blonde-haired young woman with spectacles hurried through the doors. She was wearing crumpled cotton trousers and a plaid blouse beneath a white lab coat. Jack watched as she spoke into the receptionist's window then turned immediately towards him.

'Mr Heywood?' She held out a hand, folding her spectacles into a pocket with the other. She smiled warmly but her eyes were tired and apprehensive, searching his anxiously. 'I'm

Lizzie Chase. I'm so sorry about all this. Please come on up, you'll want to see Frankie.'

She began to lead him across the lobby towards the staircase. 'What's it all about?' he asked, gesturing back towards the entrance.

'We seem to be attracting some negative publicity, just at the moment. I don't fully understand it. Normally my partner, Lewis, takes care of the media and things like that, I'm not very good . . .' She hesitated.

'Oh yes, Mr Kern. I have some papers for him and there are one or two other business matters I'll need to discuss with him when we get the chance. Is he here?'

'Um, not right now.' She stopped suddenly on the stairs, a hand at her mouth, her face to the wall.

'Dr Chase?' he said uncertainly.

She said nothing, head bowed. Then she nodded. 'Sorry,' she whispered. After a moment, her hands fell. She turned to him, her face pale and drawn, eyes round with fatigue. 'I'm so sorry,' she repeated. 'I'm just a bit, tired I guess.'

'Know how you feel,' said Jack. 'Um, is there anything I can do? Glass of water or something?'

She shook her head. 'Thanks, I'm fine. Really. It's just, in the last week or so, things have kind of come to a head. There have been some developments, I'll explain, everything, as soon as I can.' She looked at him suddenly, eyes wide with concern. 'Please don't be anxious about Frankie's well-being. We're taking very good care of her.'

'Okay,' he said simply. 'You're the doctor.'

'I'm so sorry about all the trouble outside.' She looked towards the entrance doors. 'It's not what I would have wanted for you, it's not the way we do things.'

Jack felt a stir of uneasiness. Chase a nervous wreck, no sign of the other partner, demonstrations and TV cameras outside. An awful premonition took root. The whole journey, the arrangements, the taking of Frankie from hospital, closing up the house, the selling of Heywood-Knight, all of it might have been a dreadful mistake. He swallowed. 'No problem.'

'Thanks.' She smiled wanly, then held out her hand to him once more. 'Please call me Lizzie.'

'Jack.'

They shook hands again. 'Would you like to see her now?'

'Very much.' He followed her up to the first-floor landing and along a corridor towards a pair of double doors.

'Jack, this is probably going to seem a little strange to you,' she said, one hand on the door. 'But please don't be alarmed, we're taking the very best care of her.'

Frankie was flat out on the operations-room bed. It had been raised to about four feet so that the two technicians methodically attaching the neural net to her body could work around it at a comfortable height without stooping. As Jack entered they were patiently affixing bouquets of electrodes to the shaved dome of her skull.

'We're in the process of prepping Frankie for this evening's session,' Elizabeth went on. 'As you can imagine, it's quite a long process to get everything attached and tested.' Jack nodded blankly. His daughter looked so tiny, her little white body fragile against the stark black upholstery of the bed. With her head shaved she looked even younger, exactly as she had as a baby. He followed Elizabeth towards the bed. The technicians smiled as he was introduced, shook hands politely then continued with their work. In the background, pop music played over two wall-mounted speakers. Jack thought he recognized one of Frankie's tapes.

'During the last week we've been studying her, carrying out progressively more detailed and thorough examinations to try to establish as accurately as possible a complete physical profile as well as gain an insight into the dimensions of her unconsciousness.'

'Dimensions?' Jack asked, struggling to concentrate, his mouth drying while they leant over her with their clips and wires and tubes of adhesive. He scraped a hand over two days' growth of stubble on his chin, rubbed sleeplessness from his eyes. It was like a bizarre dream, a week of frantic meetings, phone calls, bank managers, accountants and solicitors. Twelve hours of overcrowded airports, striking ground staff, delayed aeroplanes and bone-jarring Atlantic turbulence. Another hour queueing for a taxi outside Norfolk airport in unusually muggy autumn heat. Two nightmare hours in the company of a non-English-speaking, navigationally challenged and suicidally inattentive cab driver from Puerto Rico named Erno. Finally emerging, bruised and shaken, to find himself in the middle of civil disorder and televised mayhem. Seconds later, he was standing, exhausted, grimy and sweat-stained, in a clean, quiet, environmentally controlled room watching total strangers plaster electrodes all over the bare body of his daughter.

'That's right, encephalographics programs we have developed allow us to look much closer, with much greater clarity and detail, than conventional scans and EEGs. They enable us to construct a very accurate three-dimensional real-time model of Frankie's brain.' She was walking slowly around the bed, studying Frankie, reaching out occasionally to touch her arm, or squeeze her foot. 'She's done real well.'

'Ah, good.' He licked his lips, looking away. 'Humans Not Guinea-pigs', one demonstrator's placard had read. He glanced around the room. There was one small window, sealed shut, and a large dark glass panel set into one wall. He could see faint shadows moving beyond it. 'So what happens next?'

'Well, now we're ready to begin,' she said. 'Calling and listening, reaching out and reaching in.' She brushed a fingertip lightly down Frankie's cheek. The technicians paused in their work, standing back patiently. 'She's perfect,' Elizabeth said softly. 'Really lovely. You must be very proud of her, hanging in so well like this.'

He cleared his throat. 'Yes, well yes we are . . .'

There was a knock on the door. A man appeared. The one

who had been leaning against the Chevrolet. 'Reception desk sent us up,' he said lightly, his eyes shooting to the bed. 'I hope that's okay.' Elizabeth nodded uncertainly. The man smiled at Jack. 'You must be Mr Heywood. Visitor for you.' The door opened wider, and a moment later she was in his arms.

'Thank God you're here,' Alison whispered, hugging him to her.

'Can hardly believe I am,' he joked, kissing her forehead. 'Are you all right?'

She nodded, standing back to look at him. 'You?'

'Better now.' He smiled.

Boyd coughed lightly. 'Have you got a moment?' he said to Elizabeth.

'Sure. Um, John, this is Jack Heywood, from England, and his wife Alison. This is their daughter, Frankie.' She looked on awkwardly as they shook hands. 'John, er, works at the District Attorney's office.'

'Nice to meet you both,' Boyd said politely, then turned to Elizabeth. 'Downstairs perhaps?' he said, his eyes boring into hers.

'What in God's name do you think you are doing?' he said. They were in her office. Outside, the TV crew was packing up, the demonstrators long since departed, dropping their placards into the back of a pick-up and driving off with practised precision as soon as the cameras stopped rolling.

'I'm going to treat her, John,' she said, her eyes on the floor. 'If they want me to, that is.'

'Then why did you tell me she was just here for tests?'

'I don't know. In case the restraining order got lifted. In case she turned out to be unsuitable for treatment. To buy time, to – to . . .'

'To get me off your back.' He was standing in the middle of the floor, head cocked. 'I can't let you do it, you do know that, don't you?'

'You can't stop me,' she said, defiantly. 'It's not your juris-
diction any more.'

'What?'

She was backed against the desk, hands gripping its edge.
'Americans, remember? American law protecting American
people, you said. It made me think.' Still she didn't look at him.
'They're foreigners. It's different. A whole lot more complicated now. I checked.'

'That's nonsense, Lizzie, you must know that, a technicality.'

'Also, I'm not going to charge them anything for the treatment.'

'They're just technicalities,' he repeated. 'Delaying tactics. It
won't wash. They'll stop you eventually. They can lock you out
of the building – they could even put you in prison. They'll do
whatever it takes. They'll have to enforce it.'

'Who will?'

He looked away from her. 'We will.'

'I know,' she said softly. 'But it'll buy me more time.'

'Time for what?' he pleaded. 'What is it that's so damn
important?'

Finally she looked up at him. 'Do you ever think about
dying?'

'What?'

'About what it's like, what actually happens. Not the physical part, but what happens to us as individuals, what happens to
our consciousness, our spirit, if you like, our self-awareness. Do
you ever think about that?'

He shook his head slowly.

'I do. It's where I work, where I have been working for
the last five years, right there in a dark place somewhere on the
frontier between unconscious existence and oblivion. Ever had
a general anaesthetic, John?'

'Sure, um back-molars extraction, at the dentist.'

'What do you remember?'

'Nothing, nothing at all.'

'Indeed, but you weren't dead were you? Ever dream at night?'

He blew out. 'Not much, occasionally.'

'Sure you do, we all do, a lot. But the amount we remember just varies enormously, that's all. Ever been knocked unconscious?' She pushed forward from the desk, began pacing the floor.

'Er, yes, once, for about ten minutes. Collided with a two-hundred-pound quarterback in a college football match.'

'What do you remember?'

'Nothing. Well, bits and pieces, kind of mixed with periods of nothing. Lizzie, I–'

'That's good. Ever had a near-death experience?'

'Sure, every day, driving in on the State Parkway.' He smiled sheepishly, she stood still, her eyes burning into his like blue coals. 'I guess not.'

She pointed at the ceiling. 'Frankie Heywood has. She's having one right now. Every single one of the kids I've ever treated has had one. Ever daydreamed?'

He swallowed, eyes following her as she resumed pacing back and forth before him. 'Of course.' On the desk her telephone warbled, she ignored it.

'Of course, we all do, and that's the whole point. Unconsciousness, it's like a moving staircase. The top end of the staircase, let's say, is daydreaming, a genuine form of unconsciousness, but the lightest kind, a brief waking reverie. Next comes a nap, very light sleep, we're aware of it, part consciously part subconsciously. Next comes classic REM dreaming sleep, the sort we all have most nights but often fail to remember, we are that much further down the escalator. After that comes the kind of in and out unconsciousness you suffered playing football, then profound sleep, then the deeper unconsciousness of the sort induced by a general anaesthetic or more serious injury, then the very deep kind that these kids upstairs are experiencing.'

'Okay,' he said patiently. 'So there are different levels of unconsciousness, so what?'

'I can plumb the deepest of them, seek out that tiny flicker of awareness that we call our "selves", isolate it, and create an artificial environment that will allow it to exist independently. And maybe even allow us to interact with it.'

He was becoming confused. 'Sorry, what?'

'Well, nearly.' She paused, lost in thought, the window buzzing as outside the last of the television trucks rumbled down the driveway. 'All the time,' she went on, 'when we day-dream, or sleep or have an anaesthetic or suffer serious injury, we travel down that moving staircase. The further we go down, the more isolated we become and the harder it is to come back up. I've spent five years developing ever more powerful tech-niques to help people move back up the staircase from ever further down it. Maybe there's a point beyond which we cannot come back, but that doesn't mean we stop existing, we're just–' She groped for the words. 'Moving off into a totally different plane of self-awareness.'

'Lizzie, I'm sorry but you're losing me. Now, I appreciate –'

'John,' she came to him quickly, rested her hands on his shoulders, her face inches from his, 'John, the subconscious, the spirit, the soul, call it what you will, it goes on, it continues, it exists, unconstrained, unfettered but on a totally different plane from anything we have experienced or can relate to. It may even co-exist with others, I'm not sure. I'm so close, so very close to making contact with that plane, that field of awareness. Can't you see how important that is?'

Jack's head sank back against the neck-rest, his eyes closed. 'What on earth is going on?' he murmured wearily.

Alison glanced at him from the driver's seat, easing the Ford to a halt. In front of them a pair of automatic level-crossing gates were descending to the horizontal, warning bells sounding. A moment later a mournful blare and an enormous goods train began clanking slowly past, filling her line of vision in both directions. 'I'm not sure. I got the impression something was up, some of the staff seem, I don't know, edgy, and there were one or two other things. But it wasn't until we saw the television this morning that I realized something serious is going on.'

Jack opened his eyes, turning his head to look out of the open window. It was stiflingly close, the air heavy and solid. He could see the train extending right back along the track, wobbling unsteadily out of the shimmering heat haze half a mile down the line. 'What about whatsisname, Kern, is everything okay with the money end?'

'Haven't seen him. Not once. And another thing, nobody's mentioned money at all since we got here.'

Jack shrugged. 'Don't push it, we're in no hurry if they aren't.'

'In fact, now I come to think of it, we haven't even been asked to sign an admission form, or an agreement or anything. It's strange.'

The tail of the train emerged at last from the distant bend. 'What do you think?' Jack asked eventually.

'I just don't know. It's not what I expected at all. Yet they've been doing the most amazing tests and things on Frankie. Jack, you should see it, they're incredibly kind of focused on her. But at the same time gentle, compassionate. Especially Lizzie. She's extraordinary.'

The barriers came up, Alison eased the car forward, bumped across the tracks then turned onto a wide main street. 'Hmm,' said Jack, non-committally. 'How's Ben?'

'Well, do you know I really think he's coming on,' she replied. 'Lizzie's fantastic with him, they all are. He seems really involved, really interested in what's going on.' She hesitated. 'She wants to hypnotize him.'

Jack lifted his head. 'What?'

'Psychoanalysis. Get to the bottom of whatever it is that's

blocking him. She says it might also be very valuable in planning their treatments for Frankie. You know, if she can find out from Ben what happened in the accident, what she said just before, what they did, that kind of thing.' She glanced at him. He was staring ahead through the windscreen, face pensive.

'Christ, I don't know, it's all so bloody sudden.' He turned to her. 'What does Ben think?'

'He's absolutely all for it, quite relaxed, wants to do it.'

Jack exhaled slowly. 'I think I need a drink.'

'He's dying to see you.'

A smile crossed his lips. 'Me too.'

'And there's another thing.'

'Hmm?'

She was smiling back at him.

'Surprise,' she said, pulling into the motel car park. 'You'll see.'

He saw. As she pulled up, a door opened on the first-floor balcony and Ben came clattering down the steps to greet him, dressed in blue shorts and a huge white T-shirt with the Perlman logo emblazoned across it.

'Dad! We saw you on television. Grandma said it couldn't be and it was too fat to be you but it was you.' Jack stooped, Ben ran into his arms. 'I'm so glad you're here,' he went on, hugging Jack's neck.

'Me too,' he said, kissing Ben's head. Then he froze. There was a darkening: it was unmistakable, just a millimetre or two but there was no doubt. The roots were darkening. Jack stared up at Alison. She was smiling at him, eyebrows raised, hands on hips. 'When?' he mouthed.

'Two days,' she breathed. And there was another surprise. 'Come on,' she said, picking up his bag. 'I'll show you to our room.'

They made love as soon as they could, her arms circling his neck, her lips searching for his as he backed the door closed behind him. She led him to the bed, pulling the shirt from his back and the shoes from his feet as he sank onto the mattress. 'Ali, I'm absolutely filthy,' he protested as her tongue went to his chest. She shook her head, her mouth sliding down into the hairs of his stomach, her fingers to his trousers, tugging him free. Immediately her lips encircled him, tongue working, one hand pumping steadily until his hardness was complete and he felt the pressure rising dangerously inside him, like fire. Stepping back quickly she slipped her pants from beneath her dress then returned to kneel astride him, reaching between her legs, closing her eyes and leaning forward to seal her mouth over his as she guided him swiftly into her.

They showered, then returned to the bed to make love again. Slowly, tenderly, exploring again long-lost pleasures, re-discovering forgotten secret delights. She lay on her back, her eyes closed, sighing softly as he caressed her lightly with his hands, teased the firm skin of her nipples with his lips, lifted her knees to taste the pungent moist warmth between her thighs. Then she curled behind him, her hands reaching for-ward to explore his chest and body, her mouth biting softly at his back and shoulders and neck, one leg crooked across his thigh, her pelvis thrusting gently at him until he could bear no more and turned to her, sinking deeply into her with a gasp.

Afterwards he fell into a deep sleep and she slipped silently from their bed. Later she returned, waking him gently. 'Jack,' she kissed his lips, 'we have to get up now. It's time.'

'Well now, good evening, everyone, and can we all see and hear okay?' Elizabeth stood by the bed and looked around the room, one hand resting on Frankie's arm. She was wearing simple short-sleeved surgical greens and flat-heeled canvas shoes. Jack peered through the glass partition from the darkened control room, shuffling his chair in closer. Ben was beside him, expertly adjusting a pair of headphones over his ears; next to him sat Nathan, chewing thoughtfully, his brown eyes reflect-ing green off his screen. Through the glass, Jack could see Janet seated beside the life-signs monitor, talking earnestly to the young pony-tailed technician he'd seen earlier. Alison was sitting at the foot of Frankie's bed, her face expressionless, a nurse standing beside her. He raised his hand to wave but she ignored him.

'She can't see you, Dad,' said Ben, reaching up to fit headphones over Jack's head. 'It's one-way glass.'

'Oh, right.' He swung the microphone in front of his mouth. 'What's that on Frankie's head?'

'Virtual-reality headset. Nathan's programmed all Frankie's photos and videos and music and some special graphics stuff into it so that they can play it to her and see if they get a response, isn't that right Nathan?'

'My man,' Nathan murmured, his eyes on the screen.

'Can you hear me, Jack?' called Elizabeth, looking up at the glass.

'Loud and clear.'

'Nathan and Ben?'

'Check,' replied Ben instantly.

'Life signs?' She swivelled to Janet and Gardner. Gardner nodded, Janet held up one thumb.

'Christ, now everyone's a bloody rocket scientist,' muttered Jack nervously. Through the glass everyone was smiling. Alison grinned at him, wagging her finger.

'Yes, and we can hear you loud and clear too, Jack.' Elizabeth smiled. 'Well now,' she went on immediately, turning back to the bed, 'we all know Frankie, of course. She's been working real hard for the last week or so, helping us run tests and telling us all about herself and giving us a pretty good idea just how she's feeling. This afternoon we fitted her net and elevated her metabolism a little, so tonight for the first time, we're going to run some preliminary sequenced configurations and do some very broad baseline scanning for spikes.'

Jack covered his microphone and turned to Nathan. 'What was that?'

'Gonna drop a few pebbles and listen for a plop.'

'But before that Frankie's got something to show you.' Straight away she reached a hand carefully beneath the wiring at Frankie's chest and with a deft half twist disconnected the breathing tube at her throat. Jack froze, Frankie lay motionless, a deathly white corpse encased in a wiring shroud. Seconds ticked by. Agonized, he looked at Elizabeth. She was standing back from the bed, watching thoughtfully, one hand at her chin. He glanced at Alison: her eyes were wide, the colour draining from her cheeks, she looked anxiously up at the glass then back to the bed. Suddenly her hand went to her mouth.

'It works a little like a heart pacemaker,' Elizabeth went on, as they stared at the steady rise and fall. 'With just a little help from Gardner here and the life-systems net, we provide a tiny electrical back-up to the muscles controlling her breathing. But be in no doubt, it's her muscles, she's doing it.' Jack squeezed Ben's shoulder. Through the glass Alison beamed at him, fists clenched triumphantly. Over by the life-signs monitor, Janet was alternately dabbing her eyes with a handkerchief and hugging a bemused Gardner. Elizabeth was watching Frankie, her face set, hands on hips. 'So, at fifteen thirty-five this afternoon, and for the first time in twenty-seven weeks, little Frankie Heywood here showed us she can breathe without mechanical help.'

'Smart kid, your sister,' Nathan murmured to Ben.

'Okay, Nate,' Elizabeth went on, 'let's make a start.'

At the end it was warm. And dark. And silent. There was no movement, no sound, no touch, no smell. No near, no far, no up, no down. There was no sensation at all, just a deep, comfortable, weightless black void enfolding all like an impenetrable blanket.

Aeons passed in an eternity of textureless looping instants. The void travelled on, turning slowly over and over, plunging deeper and deeper into the endless black. Motion without movement, distance without dimension, passage without time.

After a long while there opened a fleeting window of realignment, a fragmentary awareness of spatial aspect, a minute and barely discernible adjustment of orientation like the brief stirring of a sleeping leviathan. Then the moment closed once more and the void flew silently on.

And then, much later, there appeared an evanescent implication of hue in the far distance. Gradually it grew nearer, a single tiny glimmer punctuating the unfathomable black like a softly spoken word in silence. Slowly the distant cloud grew, a suspended dwarf swirl of purples and blues and greens, taking form, gaining substance and dimension. Tendrils of incandescence spread out across the void like arms, floating, swaying, turning slowly in a ceaseless spiralling ballet of colour and shape.

Soon the cloud was all-enveloping, a dazzling silent fanfare of light and movement. Then at last, imperceptibly, it began to contract. The arms coiling back, the colours solidifying, the light shrinking but intensifying until gradually the whole presence coalesced into a solitary glowing unity. Ephemeral, flickering but brilliant. Floating silently in the firmament like the beginning of a newborn star.

Chapter 1 2

'GET SET, *GO!*' JACK SHADED HIS EYES WITH HIS HAND, WATCH-
ing idly as Ben dived untidily into the pool once more and set off
in an ecstasy of thrashing towards the far end. Beside him, her
hair encased in a pink rubber swimming hat with little yellow
flowers on it, Janet cruised demurely down the pool, her head
up, her neat strokes barely ruffling the water's surface. 'His
swimming's coming on really well,' Jack remarked, sinking back
onto the lounger.

Beside him, Alison reached out to touch his arm. 'I seem to
remember his father was up to some pretty heroic swims when
the need arose.'

'God, don't remind me,' he groaned. 'Without doubt the
worst moment of my life.'

She lifted her head from the cushion and turned to him, her
eyes hidden behind sunglasses. She was wearing a white one-
piece swimsuit, her body tingling with warmth and freshly
applied sun oil. 'Tell me,' she said. 'We never really discussed
it.'

He thought back. The mad sprint down the shingle, the
mind-numbing shock of cold as the water hit him, the casting
around in desperate kicking panic before the flare burst. 'It
wasn't so much the swimming out to get him,' he said pensively. 'It was, just reaching him, finding him, just paddling out

to sea like that. A few minutes more, a few minutes later . . .'

'I know,' she said softly. 'It's unbearable. Why did he do it? Do you think it might have been connected to the visit to Susie Corning in some way?'

'Possibly. Who knows? Therapist seemed to think that something significant must have happened to trigger a response like that. But he's never opened up about it. Or even acknowledged it.' His eyes were on Ben. 'As far as he's concerned it never happened.'

'Lizzie's here,' sang Janet, from the water.

She was walking around the pool towards them, pausing to watch Ben dive in again before pulling up a plastic sun chair beside them. The motel poolside was quiet, just two other families passing through in Winnebagos, a sales representative with a laptop taking an early lunch, an elderly couple asleep under a parasol. There was a faint smell of diesel fumes above the chlorine and sun oil, the background rumble of passing traffic over the splashing laughter of children at play.

'I do hope you're all right here,' Elizabeth said, looking around. 'I'm afraid the Tropicana Motel is about the best Dalmatia's got to offer.'

'It's fine, absolutely fine thanks,' said Alison. 'How is she?'

'Good, resting well. I came to tell you that we've finished a preliminary analysis of last night's session.'

'Did we get a plop?' asked Jack. She was wearing the same clothes as yesterday, tiredly rubbing a finger up and down beside one eye. Frankie's session had finished well after midnight. He suspected she'd continued working on the results all night.

'Ah, Nathan's pebbles.' She smiled. 'Well, not so much a plop as perhaps the echo of a plop.' She leant forward on the chair, resting her elbows on her knees. 'The point is, the reason I came to talk to you is, that although it's early days, two things came out of yesterday's session. First thing is that the resonances, the sort of spiking we got indicates that she's still in there. I'm absolutely sure of it.' Jack felt Alison's hand slipping into his. 'That's the good news.' She hesitated. 'The not so good news is that I suspect she's in very deep. Now, I've left Nathan's team to go over the figures once more and there are two or three sections of the sequence I want to run again, but I thought you ought to know right away.'

'Does that mean that you might not be able to – to get to her?' Alison asked.

'Maybe.' Elizabeth's eyes fell to her shoes. 'In truth, it means I don't know, I just don't know.' There was a sudden schoolgirl shriek from Janet in the pool as Ben duck-dived between her legs. Over the fence the rumble of heavy diesel and a puff of exhaust plumed skywards as a truck throttled up at the lights. 'Get to her, yes, possibly. But get her out?' She raised her head to them, her eyes anxious. 'It seems that the deeper we go, the more difficult, the more dangerous it becomes to recover these children. There's been . . . quite a lot of problems recently, particularly with the very deep ones. I've – I've lost some, trying, and others have had difficulties afterwards, you did know that?' She squinted out over the water, lost in thought, reflected shards of sunlight glancing from its undulating surface onto the pale skin of her face. 'I believe you met Susie Corning,' she said quietly.

'Yes. We were just talking about her.'

'Such a lovely girl. So beautiful. I was just so sorry to hear she'd died. We couldn't believe it.'

'Do you know – I mean, have you any idea what happened?' Jack asked tentatively.

'Nothing really specific. Nothing I can explain.' She paused. 'Tell me, again, how was Ben when you went to visit her? How was he – how did he react with Susie?'

They looked at each other. 'Quiet,' Alison answered. 'I was watching him. He seemed to be studying her, you know, watching her, her bodily movements, but we only stayed a short while and he didn't mention her after we left.'

'And that was the only occasion they met?'

They nodded.

'I can't figure it.' She shook her head. 'Maybe I was wrong to take her on. She was one of the deepest.' She looked at them. 'Frankie may be in that far. She may be in further.'

Jack looked around the poolside. The man with the laptop was packing up to leave, the elderly couple stirring sleepily under their parasol. He sat forward suddenly on the lounger. 'Listen,' he began, glancing at Alison, 'we knew before we came here that there was a risk attached to this. Nobody has tried to hide that from us, least of all you. But we had a choice. A choice between letting Frankie go on indefinitely as she was, or terminating her life support and allowing her to die, or bringing her here for you to try to revive. We decided to bring her here and we made that decision based on what we thought was best not only for Frankie but also on what we thought was best for Ben.' He jerked his head towards the pool. 'Almost the moment that decision was made he began to take a turn for the better and every day he gets stronger. Not only that, more progress has been made in one week with Frankie, what with all the testing and her breathing without the ventilator yesterday and the session last night, than in six months in England. If you feel it's worth going on,' he turned and looked at Alison, 'then so do we.'

Her eyes studied them, switching from one to the other. 'I do,' she said quietly. 'I do.'

Alison touched her arm. 'We know you can only do your best,' she said softly, 'and we're so grateful to you for explaining everything, what's happening, what you're trying to do. The risks. It helps us enormously, really it does.'

Elizabeth looked away. 'There's one more thing you should know.'

'Yes?'

'Our licence to practise has been suspended, my business partner has walked out, there are homicide charges pending against me and human-rights activists are trying to close us down.' She shrugged, her face a tired smile.

'Yes, but apart from that . . .' They turned to the pool. Janet was leaning against the edge, her chin resting on her arms, her rubber hat askew, Ben grinning breathlessly beside her. 'Apart from that there's nothing really to stop us. Is there?'

Elizabeth wondered about dropping in at the apartment for a shower and a change of clothes and maybe even a sleep, but, in the end, she drove slowly back to the clinic. Stepping out of the car she found Gardner and the maintenance man scrubbing sprayed red graffiti from the brickwork beside the front doors. 'What did it say?'

'Have a nice day,' joked Gardner. 'Nothing, really, Lizzie,' he went on, seeing her face. 'Just gibberish, kids probably.' She stared at the wall, mouth set. 'Guess who's back in town.' He nodded towards the doors.

'Lewis?' She burst into his office. 'My God, Lewis, it *is* you! Thank God you're back.' He rose from his desk to meet her, smiling broadly as she hurried to hug him. 'God, I've missed you, it's been a total nightmare.'

'Well, for goodness sake, put me down, Doctor, you'll have the neighbours talking.' He laughed, easing apart from her. He flicked his eyes towards the window. She turned. There were two of them, cleanshaven, clean-cut, mid-forties, dark suits, leather briefcases. They could have been brothers, twins even. To one side of them Nathan lounged in jeans and T-shirt, picking rubber from the soles of his trainers. 'This is Dean Caldwell,' introduced Lewis, as the two men rose politely to shake her hand, 'and Larry Chambers. They're from the Defense Department.'

Forty-five minutes later she pulled off her spectacles, wearily dabbing her forehead with the back of one hand. 'Let me see if I understand this correctly,' she said, her head buzzing. The five of them were still sitting in Lewis's office, the men had removed their jackets, a litter of half-empty coffee cups and papers scattered across the floor between them. 'You're saying that the Defense Department is willing to underwrite a continued line of funding for the research work in return for which we sign over the intellectual property rights.'

'That's right,' said Caldwell, loosening his tie. 'And don't forget the up-front capital payment for the existing technology and research rights.'

'Yes, yes, I see,' Elizabeth said thoughtfully. 'It's very generous. But, in effect, we'd be working for you, is that right?'

'In a manner of speaking,' said Chambers. 'But only in the loosest sense. You'd be free to carry on with your work unhindered but with the protection and resources of the Department and without having to worry how to finance it.'

She looked at Lewis. He raised his eyebrows, spreading his hands. 'It's a wonderful opportunity, Lizzie. Think what more could be achieved with proper funding. Plus you wouldn't have to work under public licence. You'd be licensed directly by government.' He paused, smiling. 'Nor would you have to put up with any more grief from Channel Three news and the placard-waving pinkoes.'

'That would be nice,' she said, her face pensive. 'But the work. Who'd manage it? Who'd direct it? Who'd decide which direction it went?'

Chambers sat back, glanced at his partner. 'Well, in the broad sense there would be an element of involvement at Department level, of course,' he replied. 'A steering committee would be set up to oversee the work, follow up on it, offer some, uh, guidance as to those areas that are of particular interest to the Department and its objectives.'

'Guidance?' She caught Nathan's eye.

'Uh-huh, but you'd be the boss of your own team, you'd be in charge of the actual project work, there'd be no interference, you have our word on that.'

'And do you have any idea, yet, which areas of our research

you feel might be of particular interest to the Department and its, um, objectives?'

Caldwell scratched his shoulder, watching Lewis. 'Let me emphasize again that we don't have any pre-agendas, Dr Chase. We'd like you to feel free to continue all or any areas of your research that you choose to, within certain obvious budgetry and practical limitations, of course.' He cleared his throat. 'However, Lewis here has obviously told us a little of your and Mr Greenwater's work on the peripheries of the artificial intelligence field.'

Silence fell. Suddenly Elizabeth got to her feet, gathering up her notes. 'Well, it's a very interesting proposition, gentlemen, very interesting indeed,' she said, extending her hand towards them. 'What I'd like to do, if it's okay with you, is think it over, talk it through with my co-directors here and get back to you in a little while.' They glanced at each other in bemusement, rising slowly to shake her hand. 'Thank you both so much for coming down here,' she smiled warmly, 'and I hope you have a good trip back to Washington.'

She left the room and went straight to her office. She dropped her notes in the wastebin, picked up the telephone and punched numbers from memory. As she waited for the ringtone she heard an unfamiliar electronic click on the line. A moment later the phone was answered.

'Dr Chase please,' she said.

'I'm sorry, Dr Chase is not available right now. He's with a patient. Could I ask him to call you back or would you care to leave a message?'

'No, that's okay, I'll call back.' She hung up, lifted the receiver again and dialled once more. Again the click. 'Mr and Mrs Heywood's room please.' As she waited to be put through, a call-waiting light began to flash on the phone. 'Alison, hi, it's Lizzie. Look, if it's okay with you I'd like to bring the session with Ben forward to this afternoon, make a start right away.' A second call-waiting light came on. 'About four? Great, see you then.' She hung up, clicked the first waiting button. 'Elizabeth Chase.'

'Listen to me, you sick, cold-hearted, murdering fucking bitch, we're going to put a stop to you and your fucking freak friends once and for—'

She crashed the phone down, biting her lip. 'Dear heaven,' she whispered. She leant back in the chair, breathing deeply. After a few seconds she reached out for the phone once more, lifted it slowly, eyes wide with apprehension as she fingered the second call-waiting button.

'Lizzie, it's John, I need to speak to you.'

'Oh, yes, John, hello. Um, me too, but I can't talk now. Can I catch you later?'

'Sure, any time.' He hesitated. 'What is it? Something up?'

'Nothing. Another threat call.'

'Oh, I'm sorry. Bad?'

'Is there any other kind?' She paused. 'Are you tapping the phones, John?'

'What?'

'There's a click every time I pick up the receiver. It wasn't there yesterday.'

'Are you sure?'

'Of course I'm sure!'

'Okay, okay, I believe you.' He thought for a moment. 'But it isn't the DA's office, couldn't be. Leave it with me, I'll look into it.' He could hear her breathing. 'Lizzie? Are you all right?'

She rubbed her neck. 'Yes, yes, I'm fine. Just tired, I guess, a little under pressure.' She turned to the wall, her eyes falling on the framed Christmas photograph. 'John, I've got to go now. I'll talk to you later.'

For a few minutes she did nothing, staring reflectively at the neat clutter of her desk. Then there was a tap on the door. She jerked forward, snatching up her phone. Lewis appeared. 'Hi, Lewis.' She smiled, covering the mouthpiece. 'Look, I'm right in the middle of something just now, can I catch up with you later?' He raised his hand, the door closed behind him. Breathing out slowly, Elizabeth began to dial.

He answered right away. She closed her eyes, picturing him in his chair, in front of his desk or next to the window, surrounded by all his equipment, his finger pads and neck-operated pressure switches, his music and voice synthesizers, his CD-ROM library, his batteries of electronic gadgetry, reaching out across the world via his phone lines, computer screens and modems.

'Hello, Gary,' she said softly. 'How's business?'

'Dow Jones is taking a pasting Alaskan Oil has come up dry again and IBM has dropped three points in the last hour and a half otherwise just another fine day on Wall Street.' The voice was a synthetic electronic monotone, devoid of expression or punctuation.

'So how much have you made today?' She could hear rock music playing in the background.

'So far three thousand seven hundred eighty how are you Elizabeth.'

'Tired, Gary, very tired.'

'Not surprised I'm getting calls from the media every ten minutes the net is hotter than hell and the web site has had more visitors in the last two weeks than the previous eleven months.'

They talked for a while. She asked after his grandparents, they were fine, he said, planning a vacation to Europe just as soon as Rose had had her hip replacement. Gary was gearing up to go with them: he had a lot of friends and business contacts over there and had been invited to address a neurology convention in Geneva.

'How's Lana?' she asked, after a while.

'Great she's at work did we tell you she is pregnant.'

'What?' Elizabeth laughed. 'Really?'

'Really sixteen weeks how about that.'

'Gary, that's absolutely fantastic, congratulations, I'm so pleased for you both.'

'We just did the amniocentesis it's a little girl guess the name.'

Suddenly she felt her chest tightening, her eyes pricking with tears. She swallowed, lips compressed, fighting for control. Down the phone line she heard the music grow quieter.

'Elizabeth are you okay.'

'Fine, I'll be fine.' Her forehead was resting in one hand. 'Gary, there's something I wanted to ask you, something personal.'

'Shoot.'

'It's kind of difficult. It's something we never really talked about.'

'What do I remember.'

She lifted her head. 'Pardon?'

'You want to know if I remember anything during the period I was unconscious.'

'Yes, well yes I do.'

'No nothing.'

'Nothing at all?'

'Dad lost control of the car it was raining like crazy and pitch dark suddenly there were all these flashing lights up ahead and I knew we were going to hit.' He paused, cutting the music, the line instantly quiet. 'Mom turned to me right before we hit she smiled took my hand and just said don't be afraid Gary the next thing I know is waking up in Boston two years later.'

'Nothing else?'

'Nothing sorry.'

Elizabeth breathed out slowly. Outside a warm autumn wind was plucking yellow leaves from the little trees lining the driveway, bowling them along the ground playfully.

'But there was the dream afterwards.'

Stopping at the kerbside, Ben looked both ways, checked behind him and across to the far side, as he had been told. But nobody was there, just as he had expected. So he waited for a gap in the silent, coloured blur, stepped into it off the pavement and passed easily to the other side.

Carrying on down the grassy slope he turned left into the park near the swings, his thumbs tucked into the shoulder-straps of his rucksack, which rode easily on his back as he walked. Soon he was among the trim lawns and neatly tended flower-beds, passing the trickling fountain and the quiet corners with the rosebeds and little wooden benches. As he moved down, he looked neither left nor right, following the winding paths with familiar ease. Even though he knew he should go back to the kerbside, search again among the fast-moving colours, he kept walking, moving steadily deeper down the gardens, for there was no point in going back.

At last he reached the tall wall of the privet hedge, following it until he found the archway, turned immediately beneath it into the wide expanse of the beech tree avenue. There was less light than on the other times, and no breeze, the rustling leaves silent and motionless, the tunnel of overhanging boughs tightly interwoven, brooding and watchful.

Entering the avenue, he felt a damp chill penetrating the wool of his pullover, his jeans and boots quickly becoming wet from dense tangles of brambles and nettles. He kept walking, anxious but determined, his eyes fixed on the slowly growing circle of light at the far end, his nostrils filled with the smell of cool dankness and leaf mould. He glanced behind him: there in the distance the cars and lorries passed each other in an endless circling procession like a distant fairground roundabout. He should go back, he knew, keep searching there, it was what they wanted. But there was nothing, no point, he must go on.

He pushed forward, tramping a path through the thickening undergrowth with his wellingtons. Gradually the end of the avenue grew nearer, the far-off semicircle of sky milky and pallid. Beneath it the grey-green meadow lay like a gently rolling ocean. She was there, he could see, moving slowly towards him, arms held upward and outward above the waist-high grass. Spreading the white of her shirt like sailcloth, surging across the undulating surface towards him, like a sailing ship across the sea.

But the brambles were growing thicker, rising up around him, plucking at his jumper and snagging his jeans. He picked up a heavy beech bough and began swinging it from side to side before him, hacking a swathe through the undergrowth, forging a path down towards her. Soon he grew tired, stopping breathlessly to peer around at the tangle surrounding him. In an instant he realized he could no longer see her, the sallow green glow of the meadow ocean vanishing behind dense curtains of thickly twisted vegetation. Behind him, far in the distance, the sound of fairground music. Glancing back in panic, he saw the fading lights of the merry-go-round, the brightly painted cars and lorries and buses frozen, trapped in wildly spinning arcs of harsh blue light, the clamour of bells and the wails of sirens drowning the brash grinding of organ music. He should go back, they wanted him to.

Then he heard her. She was calling him, just ahead through the green, calling his name, calling for him to come. He glanced round once more: behind him the merry-go-round was fading. He turned his back on it once and for all, picked up his stick, raised it high and thrashed forward again. Instantly the light began to brighten around him, the vegetation thinning slightly as her voice grew nearer, clearer, encouraging him, entreating him. Head down, he hacked urgently ahead, turning this way and that with the sound until her voice was all around him, filling his head. He struggled on, shouldering his way into an impenetrable mass of thickly tangled undergrowth that dragged at his clothes, tearing the skin of his hands and forearms as he slashed at it furiously, the stick like a machete.

Finally it stopped him. Gasping for breath, his hands and arms torn and bloody, he bent forward, leaning on the stick, his heart pounding, a waterfall of thunder in his ears. 'Come on!' she called once more, her voice now soft, sensually compelling.

'Please hurry.' He straightened slowly, licked blood from his arm, plucking the heavy stick from the ground, two-handed like an axe. Raising it in his fists he lifted it high above his head, his feet planted, and with a last desperate shout swung it forward and downward with all his strength. It scythed through the curtain, effortlessly disintegrating the tangled stems into a vaporizing green mist. Suddenly unbalanced, he reeled uncontrollably into the light, an unspoken cry of alarm in his throat, his eyes wide with surprise. At the same instant he glimpsed her, right in front of him, her hair like corn, her green eyes smiling, his name on her lips. He pitched forward, the stick flying in his hands, soaring unstoppably downwards. As he fell he watched it smash into the gate, which jumped and exploded into a million shimmering fragments, hanging in the air like a dissolving memory then falling as dust to the ground.

He lay, sprawled in the gap, gasping and swallowing, his eyes closed, the thunder receding, relishing the sudden caress of warm sunshine on his back. A moment later he heard rustling in the grass and then she was kneeling beside him, her hand on his shoulder. He opened his eyes, her knees were close by his face, her legs slightly parted. He could smell the warmth of her body, her skin pale and soft. Blinking in the harsh light, he turned his head with an effort, slowly lifting it until his face rested on the skin of her legs. She was stroking his head and back, her hair lightly brushing his cheeks, hanging in a gossamer golden veil about her face.

'You did it.' She smiled, bending to kiss him. He turned his face into the soft warmth of her legs. Parting his lips, he pressed his tongue against her skin and closed his eyes once more. 'You did it,' she said again. 'I'm so proud of you.'

Then there was a sharp stab of pain in his arm, moments later an explosion of light and noise, a sudden piercing scream that drilled through his body, convulsing it like electricity. 'Come on, Ben!' The shouting grew, it was all around him, deafening him. He reeled from it, his hands at his ears, desperately scrabbling up onto his knees to escape it. But it grabbed him, flung him back, driving the air from his chest, crushing him to the ground.

'Come on, that's enough!'

'No!' he screamed, struggling desperately, but there were hands on him, pressing him back, pinioning him down. And more voices, shouting, all around, shouting for him to stop.

'Ben! Come on, it's okay, stop now.'

'Come on, Ben, easy now, you're safe, it's okay.'

With a whooping gasp he opened his eyes, his head switching from side to side as a mask was looped over his nose. Hands gripped his shoulders, his legs were heavy and numb, his fingers and toes tingling, he drew deeply from the mask. Gradually the pounding in his chest eased, the roaring in his ears subsiding as his breathing steadied.

Finally he was quiet, the mask was removed, a moist towel cooling his cheeks and forehead. Fingers brushed damp hair from his face. 'Mum,' he croaked. He felt weak and sleepy.

'Yes, darling, I'm here, we all are.' He looked up: her face was strange, pale and anxious. 'Lizzie's here and Granny and Dad. We're very proud of you, you've done so well.' She forced a wan smile. 'Rest now, darling, it's all over.'

He turned his head to one side, his chest heaving once more. 'No,' he cried softly, the tears flowing unchecked, 'it isn't, it can't be.'

'I can't be sure but I suspect it's an FBI tap,' Boyd said quietly down the phone.

'Great.' Elizabeth's head sank back on her shoulders. The glow from the traffic light changed steadily from red to green and back again, throwing the pattern of cracks across the ceiling into gaudy relief. Exactly like a scale map of the Nile delta, she reflected disinterestedly. It was growing dark; outside, the wind was still fitful and gusty. Country music from the bar across the street wafted through the open window, together with the raucous clatter of an empty beer can blowing along the sidewalk.

'Why?' she asked doggedly. 'Why on earth would the FBI want to bug the phones?'

'God knows,' he replied. 'But you do seem to be attracting a lot of attention these days.'

He tried to keep his tone light, but her voice was flat and demoralized. 'It seems to be coming at me from every direction,' she said tiredly, picking threads from the carpet. She was sitting cross-legged on the floor. Around her a circle of textbooks and medical papers lay open, their white pages ghostly pale in the gathering gloom.

'It may not be as bad as you think. The FBI are generally only really interested in internal security. I suspect they're probably just keeping tabs on those so-called human-rights groups that keep harassing you.'

'Really?' she replied, half-heartedly.

'It's possible. You did report the abusive calls, didn't you?'

'Uh-huh.'

'Well, that's probably it.'

She paused again, slipping off her spectacles to rub her eyes. 'Lewis wants us to sell out to the Defense Department.'

'What?'

'He's set up this deal, they buy us out for a big lump sum then pay us to continue the research work under their "guid-ance".' She emphasized the word distastefully.

'Wow,' he said. 'And what do you think?'

She sighed. 'I think I would really just like to get right away from all this.' She glanced at the books around her. 'But I can't, not just yet.'

'Would you like me to come over?'

'Are you going to give me a hard time?'

'You bet.'

She hung up with a smile. A moment later she picked up the phone and dialled again.

'Hello, sweetheart,' Elliot answered, straight away. 'How's things in the war zone?'

She snorted. 'So you've heard.'

'Word gets around,' he said gently. 'Even in the psychiatry profession eventually. Are you all right?'

'I guess so, a little battle weary maybe.' She hesitated. 'Daddy, I really need to talk to you.'

'Of course.'

'But it – it follows on from the other thing, though.'

She heard him breathe out. 'Now why doesn't that surprise me?'

'I'm just so, deep into this now, I have to see it through. But I so need your help, your advice.'

'Professional or paternal?'

'Both, Daddy. Both would be just wonderful.'

She told him about the session with Ben. How she'd set it up in her office, arranging the furniture so all the family could be present and comfortable, the lighting calm and subdued, the do–not–disturb sign on her door, the phone disconnected. How they'd all sat in a circle, drinking tea and talking quietly about nothing in particular, the weather, their motel, Ben's favourite sports and interests. 'It was fine,' she explained. 'A wonderful atmosphere, warm and supportive, just as it should be.'

'Uh-huh.' She could hear he was jotting notes. 'What about your, er, colleagues, and the technical equipment, the wiring thing – what do you call it? The neural net?'

'Nothing. No people, no wires, no computers, nothing at all. Simply a mild sedative to help him relax and then straight-forward induced hypnosis.'

'Okay, so far so good. What happened?'

'God, Daddy, he practically dived in. Straight away, no hesitation, no resistance at all. I've never seen anything like it. It was as though he had been waiting, dying to get on with it.'

'Well, that's fine. It just shows you set it up well, that he was very relaxed with you, keen to help, subconsciously eager to begin externalizing. Where did you start?'

'Scene of the accident, just before. He went straight there, very quick, totally lucid, completely co-operative.'

'Sounds great. I wish all my patients were that easy.'

'But I couldn't control him. Right from the start. I'd put him into situations, I was particularly trying to get him to focus on the scene of the accident, for instance, but he was off on his own.'

'Off?'

'Yes, I kept dragging him back and he just kept heading off again.'

'At random?'

'No, not at all, always the same, always the same place.' He heard the catch in her throat.

'Where?'

'Landscape, mainly,' she said, struggling to keep her voice even. 'You know, a lot about trees and fields and paths. Ever come across that before?'

He ignored her. 'Did you let him go?'

'I couldn't stop him, Daddy, he was so single-minded, so determined.'

'Was he animated? Did he talk much, move around?'

'Yes, both, a lot, although much of the talking became in-decipherable, and towards the end he really struggled, we had to restrain him, physically hold him down.'

'This is the boy who witnessed his little sister knocked down.' His voice was subdued. 'Feels he may have been responsible in some way, is that right?'

'Yes.' Suddenly there were tears in her eyes, her whole body tense and shaking.

'And he saw the accident, watched it happen?'

'Yes.' The receiver shook in her hand, slippery with sweat. 'Have you come across it before?'

There was a long silence. Through the window the sounds of laughter and country music grew louder then subsided again as the bar door opened and closed with a bang. Eventually she heard the ghost of a sigh down the line. 'Once.' His voice was very quiet. 'Was there a barrier of some sort, a bridge, a wall?'

'Yes.' She closed her eyes, crushing tears onto her cheek. 'A gate. Daddy, you knew about that, how . . .'

'But he didn't breach it. The barrier, the gate. Lizzie, did he go across it?'

She was crying freely. 'Daddy, please tell me, please, please, tell me.'

'Elizabeth, listen to me. You must not let him cross that barrier.'

'But why?'

'Because I don't believe you'll ever get him back.'

Boyd let himself in through the unlocked door. She was still on the floor, hugging her legs, her head on her knees, crying softly. He went to her, lowering himself onto the carpet behind her, his body close up against her back, his arms wrapped around her, enclosing her within him like a shield.

For a while he held her quietly, feeling the soft shaking of her shoulders, listening to the whine of the wind through the window. Finally the spasms subsided and she fell still.

'Help me,' she whispered.

He rested his head against hers. 'I wish you'd let me.'

'I'd like that.' She sniffed. 'Very much. But I'm afraid.'

'I know.' He patted his pocket, produced a handkerchief. 'Here.'

She dried her eyes and then blew, noisily like a trumpet. He laughed softly in her ear, squeezing her tighter with his arms. 'Not just a beautiful and talented physician, but a gifted musician too, apparently,' he teased. She swatted his arm with the handkerchief. 'Tell me,' he went on quietly.

He felt her draw a deep faltering breath. 'John, can I ask you something very personal?'

'Of course.'

'How did you feel – I mean, what did you feel . . . when Cheryl died?'

'Awful,' he replied simply. 'A terrible kind of numbness. Shock, disbelief, pain. Guilt.'

'Guilt?'

'Sure, guilt. Loads of it. What if I'd only done this or that, left the office five minutes earlier, or offered to pick her up as I knew she wanted me to. What if I'd done the shopping myself as she'd tactfully suggested that morning, What if, what if, you never stop.' Her hand found his. 'But after a while, and with the proper help, I got to accept that guilt is just one more symptom of the whole grief thing.' He shrugged. 'You learn to deal with it, manage it. And then, gradually, you start getting over it.'

'Do you get over it?'

'Sure. Eventually. It's a big hurdle, a mountain, and you just have to climb it. At first you think you'll never be able to. But little by little you discover you're slowly covering the ground, putting it all behind you, moving on. The difficult thing, I found, was making the start, making the decision to set out. Finding the will to confront the thing. It's like a big scary bear. In the end, you just have to face him down.'

They sat together in silence. Eventually she shifted awkwardly on the floor before him, turning her face to his. 'Thank you,' she whispered, kissing him tenderly on the lips, her eyes misted in shadow.

'You're welcome.' He smiled, and kissed her back. 'Does it help?'

'Yes. Yes, it does. Perhaps more than you'll ever know.'

Chapter 1 3

THEY WERE INSIDE A MOUNTAIN, FOLLOWING A STEEP CAVE-
path that narrowed as it ascended, twisting sinuously upwards
through the lichen-stained rockface. It was dark and oppressive, the air hot and foetid. There were others with them,
strangers, murmuring quietly, apprehension etched onto faces
pallid in the dim light. As they climbed, a rumble emanated
from far below, deep within the mountain, a moment later, a
blast of hot air struck them, the ground shuddering beneath
their feet. A quiver of unease passed through the throng; there
was the smell of sweat and fear.

Then they were being herded onto a small train, fastened
into cramped open carriages with hard seats and unyielding
restraints that dug into their shoulders and thighs. Around
them the sense of unease heightened into anxiety, a small child
began to sob, pleading for release. His father bent to soothe
him, his face a mask of false reassurance.

For there was to be no release. Suddenly they were thrust
back in their seats and the train leapt forward, plunging without warning into the mouth of a gaping tunnel to drop with a
stomach-turning lurch into a spiralling black void. There was
a deafening crescendo of thunder, screams of terror whipped
away on a howling rush of wind that buffeted their bodies and
tore the breath from their lips.

Moments later they were ejected abruptly from the mountainside, shooting into the open only to be plunged instantly into a dense dark forest. Hurtling uncontrollably through a mesmerizing blur of greens and browns, twisting beneath overhanging arches of giant hanging creeper, thrusting skywards into the bright canopy, a fragmentary glimpse of blue, then spiralling down again towards the forest floor.

Then, without warning, they were blasting straight upwards, exploding into the clear, decelerating to apogee, slowing until they were hanging high above the ground, suspended in space, floating and motionless, the earth a distant inverted patchwork of colours and shapes. Seconds passed, the nightmare silence stretching on until slowly, sickeningly, they stall-turned and began to tumble earthwards, the rush of wind building into a thunderous screaming storm as they dropped like a rock to the ground.

'Good God in heaven!' muttered Janet, tottering off the ramp.

'Again!' cried Ben, tugging at her arm.

'Not on your bloody life! I need a drink. You go, I'll wait for you over there at that table with Mummy and Daddy.' She straightened her skirt with a wrench and strode purposefully towards the bar.

'I don't believe it,' said Jack incredulously, pulling out a chair for her. 'He's not going again?' They were sitting outside a mock-Tudor English tavern called Ye Olde King Harrye. It had a brightly coloured half-timbered glassfibre façade, a gaudily painted, squeaking pub sign, which swung back and forth electrically, and serving wenches in long dresses and white aprons bearing trays of imported English beer at four pounds a pint.

'That boy's not right,' said Janet, draining her Budweiser. She flapped her hand at a passing wench. 'Once more unto the breach, Moll Flanders,' she said, pointing at the bottle.

'That's the fifth time,' said Alison, as Ben joined the queue entering the mountain. He turned to them, waving. They waved back dutifully. 'He doesn't want to do anything else, see anything else, won't even stop for an ice-cream.' They watched from their table as he disappeared into the entrance, streams of tourists eddying about them.

'Fine by me,' said Janet, withdrawing a powder compact from her handbag. She turned her head critically from side to side in the mirror. 'Me and my hardened arteries can well manage without any more of that.'

'He used to hate those rides,' mused Alison. A cool breeze bowled fallen leaves and dropped litter along the pathway. She pulled her cardigan closer about her shoulders. 'Remember Disney, last year, we barely got him on the roundabout.' Jack nodded, gazing into the dregs of his beer.

'So. How did it go this morning?' Janet enquired innocently, dabbing powder on her nose. She stole sideways glances at them past the mirror: their eyes were cast down, faces set. Then she snapped the compact and dropped it into her handbag. 'Come on, for goodness sake, it wasn't that bad. Look at him!' She gestured towards the mountain. 'He's fine, absolutely raring.'

'About the only one who is,' said Alison morosely.

It was two days since the analysis session with Ben. After it was over and a form of breathless calm had descended on Elizabeth's office once more, there was tacit agreement not to discuss it right away but to rest for a day before regrouping. Later that evening Elizabeth had telephoned the motel to check on Ben and say she was doing some research into what had happened and would get back to them as soon as she could. Late last night she had called again and asked to see them, alone.

Jack drank the last of his beer. 'Frankly I think she was as stunned as we were. In fact, she said so.' He looked at Alison: he knew she had been badly shaken by the experience, staring wordlessly through the car window on the way back to the motel afterwards, sitting pensively by the pool all day yesterday. He, too, had been shocked by Ben's reaction under hypnosis. His complete and immediate immersion, his instant acceptance of the simulation, his fervour and forcefulness. Then there was the writhing and struggling, the grunting and high-speed talking, and the sudden, violent, copulatory thrusting. Finally the terrifying ordeal of the ending, the screaming and fighting, like a wild animal, as Elizabeth dragged him back to wakefulness. 'She wants to consult further, says she's never encountered a reaction quite like it.' He put down his glass. 'She doesn't know if it's safe to continue.'

'Me neither,' Alison put in. 'I don't think I could go through that again, it was like watching him have some awful kind of fit or something. I thought . . . at the end I thought he wasn't going to snap out of it.'

'Yes, but he did though, didn't he?' Janet persisted. 'And just look at him now. He slept like a baby that night, I can tell you – I'm in the same room, remember? He's eating like a horse, full of energy and fun, stronger every day.' She looked from one to the other. Jack was gazing at the mountain, rubbing a hand absently across his chin. Alison was watching a pigeon strut hopefully about at their feet.

'Listen, nobody said this was going to be a picnic,' Janet went on encouragingly. She squeezed Alison's hand. 'What he went through, that day of the accident, it's unimaginable, too awful for words. But it has got to come out, somehow, and that's bound to be traumatic. For him and for you. But maybe it has to be that way for the therapy to work. Maybe he must be allowed to confront it in his own way.'

'But he isn't confronting it,' Alison protested, 'he's avoiding it, running away from it. You saw him, you heard him, he refused, point blank refused to confront it.'

Janet sighed. 'I don't pretend to understand any of this hocus-pocus, and frankly I'm not sure I want to.' Her beer arrived, she poured it carefully into her glass. 'But I am a believer in God, the power of prayer and the body's own powers of self-restoration, and that goes for the mind too. Possibly, just possibly, Ben is showing us the way through this, the way out of it. Maybe we've just got to let him take us to wherever it is he needs to go, to confront it and deal with it. Maybe we shouldn't be stopping him, but helping him. Maybe we should be going there with him.'

Silence fell, she picked up her glass, held it critically to the light.

'Do you know?' Alison said. She and Jack were both looking at her mother. 'That's exactly what Lizzie said this morning.'

Elizabeth closed the door of her office and walked into the lobby. Half-way to the stairs she was stopped by a call from the reception desk. 'Package for you, Lizzie.' The receptionist was scribbling a signature onto a delivery-man's clipboard.

'Oh, uh, could you just leave it on my desk? I'll pick it up later.' She climbed the stairs to the first floor, turned left onto the landing and opened the door of the watchroom. Sally was there, drinking coffee with one of the young technicians. 'Hi there.' Elizabeth smiled. 'Everything quiet?'

'Fine.' Sally glanced up at the wall. Along its length was mounted a double row of monitor screens, a carefully hand-written name-tape stuck along the bottom of each. The screens displayed life-signs readouts and a video image of each patient relayed from their rooms. There were twelve monitors. All but four were switched off, their name-tapes removed, their blank screens identical flat grey reflections. 'Not many left now,' she added quietly.

'No,' said Elizabeth, scanning the monitors.

'I see our friends from Unheard Voice are back,' Sally continued, breaking the silence.

'Yes, I'm afraid so.'

'Where do they all come from?'

'Goodness knows,' said Elizabeth. The demonstrators had

already been there when she arrived at the clinic that morning. A small bus-load this time, mostly women; some had brought children with them. They'd also brought a dummy on a stretcher. It was covered in wires and wore a Hallowe'en Frankenstein mask. A sign around its neck read: 'Less rights than a laboratory rat.' Her eyes remained on the monitors a moment longer then she turned to face them. 'And what about you two?' she said brightly. 'Any plans?'

They glanced at each other. 'Well, um, Fulton's still got a place open back at MIT,' Sally began.

'Oh, yes? Well, that's great,' Elizabeth said.

'Research post,' he mumbled shyly. 'Immunology.'

'Immunology's good work, Fulton, you should take it.'

'And I can always get back into regular nursing,' Sally went on. 'If I wanted to, that is. Although I've been thinking lately I might take some classes. Geriatric care. Working here with the kids has kind of made me think about old people more.' She laughed nervously. 'I can't think why.'

'I can,' Elizabeth said softly. 'Sally, it's a wonderful idea, you'd be a natural.' Her eyes lingered on Frankie's monitor.

'What will happen to her?' Sally asked.

'I don't know. She's just so far in. I'm beginning to wonder if I was wrong to take her, particularly now, with all this happening.' She waved towards the window. 'And I'm also beginning to wonder whose interests I'm really serving by trying to treat her.'

'Hers, Lizzie. You always do what's best for the children, always.'

'Maybe,' she said, staring at the screen. 'And maybe this time it's different.'

After a few minutes she left them, wandered along the quiet corridor, pausing to glance into some of the rooms, the empty as well as the occupied. She looked in on Frankie, sat down at her bedside, lightly stroked the soft skin of her cheek with the back of her fingers.

At the end of the corridor were the double doors through to the operations centre. She pushed them open. Nathan, his back to her, was leaning through the gaping hole in the wall to the control room, the glass partition at his feet, waterfalls of wiring tumbling past him to the floor.

'Hi there, cute buns,' she said quietly, looking around the room. Normally a buzz of activity, today it was deserted.

'Best buns in the business, babe.' He backed out awkwardly through the hole, a bunch of connectors clutched in one hand and a wiring diagram in the other.

'I see we're reduced to doing our own maintenance now, are we?' She winced.

'Keen young electrical-engineering assistants with long patience and firm bodies?' He grinned. 'Who needs them?'

'All gone?'

'Yep, thank the Lord. All 'cept Gardner. Damn good thing too. Nothing but trouble.' He picked up a screwdriver, gripped it between his teeth and leant forward into the hole once more.

'Nate?'

'Uh-huh.'

'Thanks. For everything.' She swung open the door.

'Hey, scattybitch!' His voice was muffled.

'What.'

'Remember Boston?'

'Sure, what about it?'

His chuckle floated back through the hole. 'Good times.'

She went to the last door and opened it quietly. 'Annie,' she called softly, walking towards the bed. 'Come on now, it's time to wake up.' Annie sighed deeply, her face contorting into a grimace of distaste. Moments later her features slowly relaxed and her eyelids fluttered open. 'Hello, sweetpea,' Elizabeth said softly. Annie smiled, blinking sleepily, then immediately sat up, wrapping her arms round Elizabeth, pressing her face against her chest.

'Ho, well, come on now, what's all this?' Elizabeth stroked her head.

'Don't want to go.' Annie hugged her tighter, her voice small.

'Don't want to . . . but sweetheart, Mom's coming today. You're going to ride in an ambulance to the airport, then you're going home.'

'Don't want to.'

'Sure you do. Just imagine, back home with Mom and Dad again, all your own things, your own room, your friends. Just a few more weeks and you'll be ready for school again. Much better than lying about here with a lot of crackpots like us.' Elizabeth held her for a while longer, rocking gently, then eased her back onto the bed. 'Come on, let's have a good look at you. You've got a big day today.' She slipped on her spectacles, lifted the stethoscope from her neck and moved it about Annie's chest. 'Sounds great,' she said encouragingly.

'What's that noise?' Annie asked. Outside, the sound of chanting was growing more strident.

Elizabeth moved the girl forward to listen at her back, then lowered the stethoscope. She felt Annie's neck and throat. 'It's some people outside, sweetpea, protestors. Nothing to worry about, they won't hurt you.'

'What are they protesting about?'

'Well,' she produced a pen flashlight from the pocket of her lab coat and peered forward, watching closely as she angled the beam onto each pupil in turn, 'the thing is, some people think that what we're doing here is wrong.'

'Why?'

'Lots of different reasons.' She lifted Annie's nightgown, pressing her fingers gently along her abdomen and sides. 'Some of them just seem to hate the building, somehow confusing what we do here now with what went on here before.'

'That's crazy.'

'You bet. And some of them believe that if someone gets sick then it's God's will and people shouldn't interfere with that,

God will make them better in His own time if He chooses to. Others are saying that because we use a lot of high technology and unusual methods here, then that is wrong. And some of them are saying that we just use people like you to try out things, for scientific reasons, not medical ones.'

'But it isn't true.'

Elizabeth replaced the nightgown and sat back. 'I know that, Annie, but they're scared, I guess. They say that because you're not able to talk to us, we might hurt you and you'd be unable to tell us, or do anything to stop us. Or that we might be hurting you but you might not even remember it afterwards.' She paused. 'I can understand their concern.'

'But it didn't hurt.'

'Hmm?'

'It didn't hurt, I remember.'

Elizabeth looked at her. 'What do you remember?'

Annie stared down at her hands, her face a fierce frown of concentration. 'I remember going on a very long walk. There was me and the tall, dark-skinned boy with curly black hair. I was asleep, he woke me up, told me that we had to start heading back now, and so we began to walk together.'

'What was it like?' Elizabeth strove to keep her voice even. 'Your walk.'

'Kind of long, hard at first. I wanted to stop and rest a lot but the boy just kept talking to me and saying we had to keep moving, and so we did.' She grinned sheepishly. 'He held my hand.' She raised her left hand from the bed. 'And so anyway we just kept walking. It was tiring, but it didn't hurt, not a bit.'

'Then what happened?'

'Well, then, after quite a while . . .' She bit her lip.

Elizabeth took her hand. 'What?'

'Well, then things began to get dark, kind of confused. And there was a noise, like wind. I was scared because then I was alone.'

'What happened to the dark-skinned boy?'

'I don't know. He was right there, walking with me. Then he wasn't, and I was scared, a bit. But then in a while I began to hear your voice, calling me, calling my name. So I walked on a bit further by myself, then I remembered suddenly it was you holding my hand and telling me you needed my help and that I had to wake up.' She shrugged. 'That's it, I guess.'

Elizabeth stayed a few minutes longer, sitting on the bed beside Annie. After a while she rose to leave. 'I'll come and see you later, when it's time to go.'

Annie nodded. 'The dark-skinned boy.' She held up her left hand again. 'Do you think he was an angel?'

Lewis locked his car and strode purposefully towards the steps. Immediately the demonstrators' hitherto lacklustre chanting became more spirited, and at the same time they moved across in a solid phalanx to cut him off from the entrance. In a moment they were barring his path.

'Look, it's him.'

'Who?'

'I don't know. Shift along, I can't see.'

'Shame, shame on you.'

'Shame on who? Who is it?'

'Him, the business director. Isn't it?'

'The money man.'

'Money man! Purveyor of shame!'

'Trader in torture!'

'Shame! Shame! Shame!'

Lewis calmly lowered his briefcase to the ground between his feet, hitched up his trousers and buttoned the jacket of his double-breasted suit. 'Listen to me,' he said levelly, peeling off dark glasses. Out of the corner of his eye he could see a radio reporter hurrying across the gravel drive towards them, microphone in hand, tape-recorder bouncing at his hip. 'You are without doubt the saddest bunch of dried-up bitches I ever saw. Why don't you all just piss off back to your tepees in the woods or wherever it is you crawled from and stop hindering respectable citizens from going about their work.' There was an instant of stunned silence. He glanced towards the approaching reporter and lowered his voice. 'And while you're at it, do everyone a favour and take a goddamn bath!'

There was immediate uproar. Lewis ducked beneath a mass of waving arms, thrown leaflets and flying placards. The radio reporter arrived to find himself at the perimeter of a seething, impenetrable mass. Elbowing his way laboriously through the throng, he eventually arrived breathlessly at the centre to find Lewis surrounded by a cordon of furious-faced demonstrators, his briefcase held protectively in front of his chest.

'Don Riley, WKWV Radio!' he shouted above the tumult. Immediately the noise began to subside, punctured by instantly aroused curiosity and ingrained media awe. The reporter thrust a microphone in front of Lewis. 'What happened?' he asked, adjusting his levels.

'Mob rule is what happened, Don,' said Lewis, lowering his briefcase and straightening his jacket indignantly. 'I arrived at my legitimate place of work. I was prevented from entering my place of work. I asked these people to please let me pass and you see the result. And this in a supposedly free and democratic society.'

'He called us dried-up bitches!'

'I did no such thing, madam, I will contest that most vigorously, and I would also thank you to moderate your language. This is a children's hospital.'

'No, it isn't.' A tall, dark-haired woman was elbowing her way forward. 'This is a house of shameful and barbaric perversions against young people.'

The reporter swung the microphone towards her. 'I'm sorry, and you are?'

'Linda Beamon, lead spokesperson for Unheard Voice.'

Lewis reached out and swung the microphone back. 'Ah, yes, that will be Linda Beamon, wife of Mr Floyd Beamon who, as your listeners may or may not be aware, Don, chairs a county sub-committee which, among other things, processes planning applications for land use in this area.'

'Er, no, I er, didn't know. Mrs Beamon?'

'That's got absolutely nothing to do with the atrocities being carried on behind these walls. We're here–'

'The same sub-committee that both issued and then subsequently revoked the operating permit held by the previous leaseholders of this property under pressure from local so-called human-rights activists. The same sub-committee that issued the operating permit for the Perlman Institute and is now also under pressure to withdraw it. The same sub-committee, Don, that is, by pure coincidence, processing at least three other proposals for the use of this land right as of this moment.'

'Is that so? I–' The reporter swung from one to the other. The crowd was falling quiet.

'That's a complete irrelevance, the point at issue here is the systematic abuse of children.'

'One from a supermarket chain, another from a consortium proposing a small industrial park. And a third, most interestingly, from a realty development group, one of whose directors just happens to be the aforementioned Floyd Beamon. Now, wouldn't you say that's just the tiniest tad curious, Don?' He bent to pick up his briefcase, glancing at his watch.

'Well yes, indeed. Mrs Beamon, do you have any comment to make?'

'You're damn right I have.'

Lewis pushed forward onto the steps, his hand reaching for the microphone boom one final time, the other pointing skywards. 'So you see, what we have here, Don, is vested interests masquerading as human interests, commercial opportunism cowering behind rights-abuse placards and the sort of bigoted witch-hunt mentality and cynical media exploitation which, I put to you all, is at the root of society's problems, is unconstitutional, undemocratic and downright unAmerican.' There was a ripple of desultory applause from the back of the crowd abruptly cut off by a chorus of angry shushing. Lewis nodded to the crowd, turned and swung through the entrance. A moment later he pushed open the door of his office.

'Lew, that was absolutely marvellous.' Elizabeth looked up at him from his filing cabinet. 'I heard it all through the window. How on earth did you find out all about the supermarket chain and Beamon and the planning sub-committee?'

'Know your enemy,' he said, glancing towards the cabinet. She was flicking through some of the patient files. He threw off his jacket and walked to the coffee machine, wrenching the top button of his shirt loose. 'First lesson at Harvard Law. Er, can I help you with anything?'

'I was looking for the file on Raoul Hernandez.'

'Second drawer down.'

'I wanted to check what date he left, see if Annie Dean ever met him. After she woke up, that is.'

'Oh, yes?' He poured a cup of coffee. 'And did she?'

'I don't think so.'

'Is that good?'

'I'm not sure. Lewis, I found this.' She held up a letter. It had a Defense Department seal on it. Immediately his shoulders slumped, his eyes falling to the floor, lips pursed.

'It's eleven months old, Lewis. You've been negotiating with them for nearly a year, and yet the first I heard of it was three days ago.'

> *My dearest Elizabeth,*
> *You were right, I do know a little of what you are encountering with your young English boy. (Ben, is it?) I came across it myself, or something very like it, with a patient of mine more than fifteen years ago. She too was young and deeply traumatized by the death of a sibling,*

witnessed very close at hand. A death for which she held herself responsible.

The physician in me instinctively knows that there are some areas of the human psyche that we are just not ready to deal with — both as doctors and ordinary people — just as there are still many areas of human physiology that we must learn more about before we can begin to operate on them or treat their ills. But the scientist in me knows that, in time, all these areas will be explored and, as in all pioneering work, risks will need to be taken if breakthroughs are to be achieved. Somebody has to be first, just as somebody had to perform the first heart transplant or first tonsillectomy or first Caesarian.

You will remember very little of these sessions, I was careful about that. They are, however, forever etched deep in my memory. My purpose was to help you efface your completely unjustified sense of personal guilt over Daniel's death and at the same time encourage an acceptance of it that would ultimately allow your life to pass on over it. I was only partially successful. Yes, your life moved on, but completely so, out of reach, right away from us. And in trying to help you confront your guilt, what I encountered instead was an unexpected loophole into something else, your famous 'alternative plane of awareness', if you wish. Like the fool I rushed in, you were completely uncontrollable, it scared me to hell, and I withdrew from it.

Some, like you, are born to pioneer. The rest of us merely follow in your wake, profiting from the risks pioneers undertake. Don't judge me too harshly for that. But do, my dearest girl, tread like an angel.
With all my love
Dad

Night had fallen, a sharp autumn chill descending with it, misting windows and coating the ground with a carpet of glistening dew. A brilliant luminescent half-moon slipped slowly in and out of a ragged veil of thin, high cloud. Through the open window a fitful cold breeze fidgeted at the blind, fluttering the letter lying on the desk.

'I knew the ice was going to break,' a young girl said. Her voice was barely recognizable, muffled, with long pauses between each phrase, slow and heavy as though recorded at half speed. 'I just knew it. He'd been skating the same patch for nearly two days. Cutting into it. The same pattern, more than fifty times. I wrote it down. I could have stopped it, just moved the goalposts a bit, that's all.'

Elizabeth sat motionless, headphones covering her ears, staring at the steadily winding capstans of the cassette player, a single tear escaping the corner of one eye. A while later the capstans stopped and the cassette player clicked off. She swallowed, sat in silence for a moment, then reached forward, ejected the cassette and inserted the next.

Hours later Lewis knocked softly on the door. Hearing nothing he came in. The room was dim and cold but he could see the pale outline of her sitting at her desk. 'Elizabeth?' he ventured. 'Can we talk?'

'Sure, Lew,' she said softly, from the darkness. 'Come on in.'

'Are you okay?' he said, rubbing his hands. He looked around the room. 'Jesus, it's cold in here. Lizzie, are you sure you're okay? You're white as a sheet.'

She nodded slowly, eyes on the small stack of cassettes on her desk. 'Yes, I'm okay, just kind of tired.'

'Please, please believe me,' he went on, a little while later. He'd closed the window, his jacket was draped over her shoulders, her desk lamp was on. 'There was never any deliberate intention to deceive you, Lizzie, you must understand that. But there were problems cropping up everywhere, lawsuits, bad press, money problems. I wanted to protect you from all that, it was my job, after all. But at the same time I felt I had a responsibility to protect our future, begin sounding out other possible formats, other ways of structuring the business. The Defense Department package was just one of many possible options.'

'But you went ahead with it, without telling me and Nate.'

'I know.' He sighed. 'But I also knew you'd be against it, and then, what with the injunction hanging over our heads, I just panicked.'

'So you went to Washington and firmed up a deal.'

He was watching her eyes. 'Yes. No, worse than that. I signed one. Well, a memorandum of understanding but it comes to the same thing. In principle, at least, they think they already have access to the technology.'

'What?' Elizabeth stared at him, aghast.

'It's the main reason they came down here. To have a look at Nathan's box of tricks upstairs.'

'Lewis, I can't believe I'm hearing this. How could you?'

'I'm sorry. But I did it in our best interests. And it's a wonderful package, Lizzie, enormous potential, just think of it.'

She pushed back her chair, rose to her feet. 'I can't, Lewis, I just can't. What on earth do they want it for? It's unimaginable.'

Lewis said nothing, studying the floor. She walked slowly to the wall, hugging herself, gazing at the picture. 'Anyway,' she said eventually, 'perhaps it doesn't matter any more.'

'What do you mean?'

She turned to him. 'Can you keep them off our backs, just a while longer?'

'Christ, Lizzie, I don't know, it's starting to get ugly. They're on the damn phone non-stop, they're planning to come down again in the next couple of days, tomorrow maybe, God knows . . .'

'Stall them, please, just a little longer.' She swept the cassettes into a drawer and handed him his jacket. 'You owe me that. I have to go out now but I'll speak to you in the morning.'

His face fell. Suddenly she bent to him, kissed his cheek. 'I trusted you, Lewis, I always did, ever since that first terrible coffee in the hospital in Philadelphia. I knew that you had what I lacked to make this dream happen and that I could trust you to do it.' She picked up her car keys and walked to the door. 'Now I need you to help me see it through. Hold them off, just a while longer. This is just too important.'

The door closed, and he shook his head slowly. 'Better believe it.'

Jack opened the door. 'Goodness, well, hello there, come on in. Alison, look it's Lizzie,' he called. He clutched the bathrobe clumsily to his midriff with one hand. 'Has something happened?' he asked quickly. Her face was set like stone.

Alison appeared from the bathroom, her forehead smeared with cream. 'Is Frankie all right?'

'I'm sorry, it's terribly late,' Elizabeth said, standing awkwardly at the door. 'Please don't worry, Frankie's fine, absolutely fine.'

'Oh, well, good, do come in, please.' Alison hastily gathered clothes into a bundle from the bed, dropped them into a drawer. 'Sorry it's such a mess in here, we've been out all day. Look, here, sit on the bed, I'll get a chair.'

'It's kind of you but I won't stay long. I just came to explain things properly, kind of put my cards on the table, after our talk this morning.'

'Ah,' said Jack. He squeezed past her to a table by the window and began to remove plastic motel glasses from cellophane wrappers. 'In that case I think maybe we'll be needing a Scotch. We were just about to have a nightcap.' He glanced at her. 'You look as if you could do with one.'

'Thanks.' She smiled wryly. 'Maybe I could. It's about Ben and it's about Frankie.'

'Have you come to a decision?' asked Alison.

'That's why I'm here,' Elizabeth said. 'I wanted us to do that together.'

Jack glanced at Alison, she nodded, he reached out, rapping softly on the wall with his knuckle. Within moments a door opened to an adjoining room and Janet bustled in, clad in dressing-gown and slippers, her rollered curls tightly secured beneath a hair-net. 'Did I hear someone mention a Scotch?'

They talked at length. Lizzie explained about the difficulties at the Institute, her fears for its future, the dwindling staff, the steady exodus of patients, the financial problems. She explained about the growing pressure from the protestors, the graffiti, the phone calls and threats, and her increasing anxiety for the welfare of her remaining patients. She told them about the lawsuits, the surveillance, the phone taps, the mounting chorus of disapproval from the medical establishment, their lack of insight, their jealousies and suspicions. She told them about the Defense Department and its efforts to secure access to her research work.

She told them about her personal fears and doubts concerning the moral validity of certain aspects of her work. How she could see the protestors' point of view, how recent events had undermined her belief in herself and her right to conduct the work. How deeply her failures affected her and how she was thinking increasingly of abandoning the programme altogether.

And then she told them about herself, describing her childhood, and Daniel and the way he'd died. How her father had tried to help her through the crisis in much the same way as she was now trying with Ben. 'I blamed myself, I felt I was responsible, just as Ben does. I was supposed to be looking after him, after all.'

The room was silent. 'Dreadful,' Janet said at length. 'It must have been simply dreadful for you. All of you.'

'Yes, it was,' she said quietly. 'And yet the whole episode, the whole trauma, was removed from me, completely wiped from my subconscious. So in a way I never really knew. I have no memory of the therapy sessions, none at all. I never even knew they took place. Not until I received the tapes from my father today.'

'So, then, it was successful for you, the treatment,' said Alison. 'You got over the trauma, managed it, got on with your life.'

'Yes, I did, but not the same life. A completely different one. I cut myself off from everything to do with my former life, deleting it as though it had never existed.'

'Are you saying that this will be Ben's way of managing it too, if we continue?'

'Perhaps. He's already functioning subconsciously in a different world. If we erase it, together with the trauma, as my father did with me, he may emerge a completely changed person, a stranger to you, as you would be to him.'

The window shuddered suddenly as a truck thundered past outside. Jack reached for the bottle and tilted it to their cups. 'And what about Frankie?' Alison asked.

Elizabeth exhaled. 'I told you we were rerunning all the numbers after her session and the tests we made in the first week.' Their faces were mute and attentive. 'Well, they're bad. I still believe she's there, I've always felt it. But she is so very deeply under. Getting to her, trying to get her back, going in that hard, that far, it's a terrible risk and just right now . . .'

'Are you saying it can't be done? That she can't be reached?'

Her eyes dropped. 'No. I'm just saying I don't think I can do it. I'm sorry.'

'I can.'

They turned. He was framed in the doorway, the light from the room behind throwing his slight body into silhouette beneath his pyjamas, his silver hair tousled from sleep.

'I can get her, I know I can. Please let me.'

C h a p t e r   1 4

WITH A DRY WIND AT THEIR BACKS PLOUGHING FURROWS through the tall grass with a hiss like rolling breakers, they set off across the plain towards the far horizon. Retreating patches of shadow mottled the panorama as slow-moving clouds wandered leisurely across the clear azure like grazing sheep. There was no sound, save the sigh of the wind, the swishing of their legs and the steady rhythm of their breathing.

They walked for most of the day, pausing occasionally to share chocolate or drink from the water bottle in his rucksack. Eventually, with the sun sinking slowly towards the horizon far ahead of them, the meadowland began to thin. Patches of bare, rock-strewn earth appeared, the grass shorter, stiffer, tufted into clumps. Small bushes and short, twisted trees like olives drew near, the ground beneath them hard and uneven. After a while it began to slope gently downhill. Linking hands, they crested a low ridge to the sound of running water, breaking suddenly into a giggling, skittering slide down a deep shale bank towards a boulder-scattered stream.

'It's just so beautiful,' she cried breathlessly, her green eyes alight. The stream was wide and shallow, its busy winding passage filling the air with a reverberating gurgling tinkling sound. Limpid water eddied around sandy pools at their feet. Further out, it splashed around lichen-stained rocks and stones. Beyond, mid-stream, heavier, deeper waters rolled silently over unseen obstacles on the uneven stream-bed. 'Shall we stay here the night?'

He swung the rucksack from his back, dropped to a crouch at the water's edge, cupped his hand into the icy crystal. Immediately his fingers melted into a brown blur, the murmur of trickling water deepening to a muffled hum. He looked up: the light around them had sickened into a thick yellow mist. 'What's happening?' he heard her cry in alarm.

'Christ knows! It's all tripping out again, just like before.' Nathan swung around sideways on to his console with a curse, repeatedly flicking reset switches and pulling popped circuit breakers with one hand while the other pounded across his keyboard, redirecting sequencer signals and cancelling alarms to bring the telemetry back on line. Beside him Jack watched in mesmerized apprehension. Turning to the glass his eyes met Alison's: she was staring blindly towards him, face drawn. In front of her, Frankie lay encased within her wire mesh. On the bed beside her Ben's body twitched in spasm, a cranial net attached to his head.

'Life signs, Sally!' Elizabeth raised her voice above the persistent clamour of an alarm, moving swiftly around Ben's bed.

'Frankie's fine, absolutely no change, slightly elevated but steady and stable.'

'Okay, and Ben?'

'Hopping all over the place. Heart eighty, breathing fast and shallow but he's not hypoxic and he's not stressed, he's just . . .' Sally studied the screen, Janet rigid beside her, '. . . incredibly busy.'

'Right, Nate, what have you got?'

'Fourth of goddamn July. Everything going off at once. I'm having to bring the whole monitoring array off-line until I can figure a way to stop it overloading all the damn time.' He paused. The last alarm stopped.

'Right. And in the meantime?' Her voice was firm and clear in the sudden silence.

Nathan shrugged. 'Meantime, he's on his own.'

She pursed her lips, studying Ben, her fingers feeling the pulse at his neck. 'How long was it, in total?'

'Altogether? Uh, seventy-five seconds.'

Jack straightened his microphone, cleared his throat. 'Um, Lizzie.'

She looked up at him. 'It's okay, Jack, they're in good shape, both of them. Sally, can you just watch things for a couple of minutes while Nathan gets straightened out and I have a word with Jack and Alison? We'll be right along the corridor in the watchroom. Hit the button if anything happens, anything at all.' She made for the door, Alison in tow.

'Right, as I said they're both fine,' she repeated a moment later, handing Alison a cup of water. She glanced up at the wall monitors. Janet had risen from her chair and was bending over Ben, apparently holding his hand.

'But what happened?' asked Jack. 'It was all so incredibly fast.'

'We don't know for sure, but on one level it appears that there is a massive data exchange of some sort going on.'

'What, between the two of them?'

'The three of them: Frankie's net, the control centre and Ben. The system is still sending and receiving data to Frankie, and at the same time we got an immediate burst of very intensive activity from Ben. But the problem is, trying to keep track of it is just overloading the telemetry.'

'Is it dangerous?' Jack asked anxiously.

'Not dangerous in itself, but it does mean we're having trouble keeping track,' Elizabeth answered.

'But Ben, he's so, agitated.' Alison's eyes were round with worry.

'His life signs are all still right on line and telling us he's in good shape. Frankie, too. Believe me, if they weren't we'd have stopped already.' She nudged her spectacles up her nose, staring at the monitors pensively. 'No, the problem we have at the moment is the telemetry, trying to keep up with the data exchange, following what's happening.'

Jack sat forward. 'And, um, what is happening?' he asked. 'In your view.'

She looked from one to the other. 'I don't know for sure, nobody does. But what we believe may be happening is that Ben, in some way, is reaching out, perhaps using the master command console and neural networks as kind of stepping stones.' She sat down, glancing at one of the blank monitors. 'There was a girl here, Annie Dean. She went home yesterday. She woke up a few weeks ago, a little while after a similar episode where we matched a phased program with another boy called Raoul. Yesterday she told me that she remembers meeting Raoul, they walked together, he talked to her, told her that she had to wake up.'

'But, was she really experiencing these things, or could she just have dreamed it?'

'Perhaps both.' Her eyes were thoughtful. 'And yet she described his appearance, very accurately. And they never met.'

'So you think they might have been communicating in some way?'

'Maybe, although perhaps communing might be a better word. And that's another curious thing.' She drained her cup and got up. 'Annie remembers Raoul talking to her. A lot, non-stop. But he's Peruvian. He doesn't speak English.'

'Guaranteed Mutual and Medical? Yes, this is Lewis Kern of the Perlman Institute, returning the call of a Mr, uh, Hixby.' Lewis waited, fingertips drumming on the desktop, straining in his seat to peer out of his window as yet another car ground up the drive. 'Mr Hixby? Yes, Lewis Kern, you asked me to call. Sorry I've been a while getting back to you . . . Your letter? Oh, yes.' He scrabbled through the mountain of papers on his desk. 'Uh, I don't quite seem to have it immediately to hand, perhaps you could just remind . . .' He listened at length, the phone tucked under his chin as he rummaged through his overflowing in-box. Gradually his hands slowed. 'Yes, I understand that, Mr Hixby,' he said quietly, 'but it does seem just a tad drastic, wouldn't you say? Yes, but you must also appreciate that if you suspend our indemnity insurance coverage we will be quite unable to continue to function . . . Yes, I know it's only a temporary suspension pending the outcome of the FDA investigation, but it is still a very serious blow. Couldn't you just continue coverage for the moment until . . .' A commotion was starting up outside in the lobby: he could hear the sound of feet, raised voices. 'Aah, yes, we must indeed think of our other clients, of course. No, we wouldn't want them to feel compromised, heaven forbid. Well, must go now, Hixby, got sick children to attend to, have a nice day.' He banged the phone down. 'FDA investigation?' he murmured thoughtfully. There was a sudden crescendo of noise outside. He pushed back his chair with a curse and yanked open the door.

'What the hell is going on out here?' he roared. There were four demonstrators just inside the entrance, Linda Beamon at their head. The receptionist was standing nervously in front of them, hands raised to prevent them entering further. She turned as Lewis approached, her face strained and anxious.

'Oh, Mr Kern, thank goodness. I tried to stop them, but they insisted.'

'Christ,' he muttered, striding across the floor. He glanced across to the waiting area. Two technicians from the Defense Department laboratories were lounging in easy chairs, flicking through magazines. They'd arrived three-quarters of an hour earlier, sent down from Washington for a technical briefing with Nathan. Mr Greenwater was very busy, Lewis had told them politely, likely to be tied up all day. That was okay, they'd replied. They could wait.

'All right, Judy, I'll see to this. Well, well, Mrs Beamon,' he went on. 'This is an unexpected pleasure. Under normal circumstances it'd be a rare delight to stand around and shoot the breeze with you, but we're all just slightly busy today and so, if you don't mind, I'll keep it short. By entering this building uninvited, unfortunately you and your friends here have just crossed the line between legitimate peaceable protest and a wilful act of trespass. This,' he pointed to the floor, 'is private property and you are illegally trespassing on it. I'll give you just five seconds to turn right on about and remove yourselves from the premises, or I will call the police and have you forcibly removed. I will then happily sue your sorry ass to Talahassee and back.'

'Go ahead, big shot,' she said calmly. 'They're right outside.'

'What?' He looked over their heads: a squad car was parked in the drive. 'Well, fine, saves me a call.' He pushed past towards the doors. Behind the demonstrators a small balding man in a grey suit was standing, briefcase in hand. He was waiting, his entrance blocked, half in half out of the building. 'Excuse me?' he said uncertainly.

'Just a moment.' Lewis brushed past him and doubled down the steps towards the squad car. Two uniformed policemen were with it, one sitting behind the wheel, the other lounging against the door. Nearby, more demonstrators were standing in a loose knot or sitting on the ground, squinting at him in the weak afternoon sunshine. 'Officer, there is an unlawful entry in progress within this building. I have just asked four trespassers to leave and they have refused. Could you please come and eject them?'

The officer unfolded his arms, scraping a leisurely arc in the gravel with the toe of his boot. 'Well, now, let's just take things one step at a time, shall we?' he drawled, producing a notebook. 'Name?'

'Kern, Lewis, administrative director. Look, Officer, there is a crime taking place right now not thirty yards from where we're standing–'

'Is that C–U–R–N?'

'No K-E –' He broke off. The policeman waited, eyebrows raised, pencil poised. Lewis pursed his lips and gazed slowly around the site, his hands on his hips. 'You're not going to do anything, are you?' he said quietly, nodding at the car's gold County Police Department crest. He glanced up at the main entrance: Linda Beamon was watching through the glass. 'Of course not,' he breathed, almost to himself. 'This is your county, your people, your home. Why the hell should you?'

'We're here just to make sure there's no trouble, Mr Lewis.' The policeman smiled. But Lewis was already on his way back towards the entrance.

'Er, excuse me,' said the man with the briefcase again, as he pushed through the doors.

'Hold on for just one more moment, please.'

'So?' Mrs Beamon smirked.

'Oh yes, I met the brother-in-law, or is it your cousin? Doesn't really matter. All the same cosy little gene pool, isn't it?' Lewis leant towards her. 'Mrs Beamon,' he went on confidentially, 'what exactly is it that you are doing here?'

'We're holding a vigil.'

'A what?'

'A vigil. For the souls of your victims. A peaceable visitation for the purposes of holding a religious service of remembrance. I think you'll find it's quite legal.'

'I see,' he said. 'And what is it that you hope to achieve with this peaceable visitation?'

'We're going to shut you down.'

He sighed. 'Why? Why is it so important to you to do that?'

'Why?' She looked at him in bafflement. 'Because we just don't want your kind here.'

The short man with the briefcase had elbowed his way through into the lobby. 'I'm looking for Mr Kern,' he said, producing a card.

Lewis looked at him. 'Aren't you with them?'

The man glanced at Mrs Beamon. 'Er, no. I'm Grey.' He handed the card to Lewis. 'State Hospital Administration.'

He awoke at dawn, the sound of chuckling water filling his head as it had his dreams. The air was chill and grey, he was alone. Dressing quickly, he sat on the riverbank and ate a raisin bar from his rucksack. He drank from the stream, filling his water bottle for the day's travel then, rolling his sleeping bag and shoes into the rucksack and tying his jeans around his neck, he stepped carefully into the stream.

Half-way across, the icy water had risen to his waist, pulling solidly at his legs and thighs, unsteadying his footing on the slippery rocks beneath his feet. Gasping with the cold, he waded on, thrusting the heavy rucksack into the air above his head, teeth gritted, eyes fixed on the gnarled and twisted limbs of an ancient acacia tree on the far bank. A moment later the tree vanished into a chaotic gurgling blur as his toes reached falteringly forward into nothingness and he plunged beneath the surface.

He sank deep, the freezing water gripping vice-like at his head, pounding in his ears, stunning the air from his lungs. Thrashing wildly he twisted and turned, his body tumbling through the charging stream, spreadeagled in freefall. Foaming white turned to deep, running black, tendrils of weed slipped between his fingers, his leg struck rock, then his shoulder, his head glancing from the gritty bottom, the torrent bowling him relentlessly downwards, over and over like a falling puppet.

After an eternity there was a perceptible slowing in the chaos, the thunder diminishing in his ears, a browning of the blur and a fleeting caress across his skin as the rushing chill emptied into a wider, gentler warmth. With the waters slowing, his battered body relaxed from struggle. He opened his eyes, blinking up through a brown opaqueness at a distant quivering yellow orb, warm pressure building in his ears to the pulsating rhythm of his own heart and the distant, muffled thud of a slowly tolling bell.

Suddenly his body convulsed, doubling him in two. His feet found mud, legs firing him like coiled springs for the light. A moment later he burst clear, gasping and retching, arms thrashing blindly at the smooth undulating surface.

Gradually his wild flailings slowed, his panic receded, his lungs gulping greedily at dense warm air. He smelt woodsmoke, the sound of hammering and children's laughter drifting across the river, punctuated by the dull clang of the church bell. He stared around him, treading water breathlessly, his body drifting across the slackening current like flotsam. Nearby he could see his rucksack, spinning lazily, floating low in the water. Beyond it the river slid onwards, wide and brown, its banks lush and green, heavy with vegetation and tall, overhanging trees. He was just twenty yards from the nearer bank. Further downstream stood a small village, ramshackle wooden houses clustered at the shore, a lopsided wooden jetty jutting into the sluggish stream. Coughing and spitting, he struck out for the shore.

Five minutes later he dragged the sodden rucksack from the mud, hoisting it onto his back with a heavy grunt. Rising slowly upright he paused, head shaking as a wave of dizziness swept over and past him like a passing cloud. Then he pulled on his soaking jeans, pushed his feet into his shoes and set out unsteadily for the village.

Drawing near he could see people working on boats at the water's edge, repairing nets or cleaning fish. Men were sawing and hammering at piles of fresh planking for the jetty; others tended a driftwood fire or just stood by and watched. Suddenly there was a chorus of ecstatic squealing and a dozen small children emerged from behind the jetty, charging along the bank towards him like escaping piglets. In an instant he was engulfed in a sea of excited chattering and grinning faces. Thin brown arms stretched towards him, reaching out to touch his face and hands. Small fingers plucked at the logo of his T-shirt, slipped into the sodden pockets of his jeans, and fumbled at the buckles of his rucksack.

'Stop!' He laughed nervously, wading heavily through the throng. 'Okay, okay, stop.' He looked up, apprehension mounting. Another child, a boy, was walking slowly along the riverbank towards him. He was much older than the others, taller, his naked body lithe and supple, moving easily, relaxed yet watchful, like a young puma. Some of the younger ones broke off and ran back towards him, shouting and waving, taking his hands, urging him similarly onward.

At five yards they stopped, facing each other. His skin was a deep warm mahogany, smooth and hairless, naked save for a small black medallion at his neck, the muscles of his chest and stomach taut and lean. The children fell quiet. Ben sniffed, wiping an arm across his nose self-consciously. Their eyes met, the boy's gaze level, calm, a study of suppressed curiosity. Then, after a brief hesitation, they stepped forward across the divide.

They walked through the village together, the children crowding at their heels. Occasionally the boy stopped to show Ben to a relative, or pay his respects to a toothless village elder, or point out the more important huts, the school, the meeting hall, the church. As they passed along the single dusty street, people emerged, hurrying forward with packages of food. Dried strips of meat, dates, sultanas and nuts. Ben accepted them with a polite duck of the head, tucking them into the pockets of his rucksack.

At last they reached the village outskirts, a lone dirt track pointing straight out across the scrub like a finger towards a distant horizon of miniature silver clouds. The smaller children fell back silently, their arms crooked across their eyes, watching Ben and the boy move forward into the glare.

'That way?'

The boy nodded, pointed, walked on a little further then

stopped. Lifting the leather thong from his neck, he lowered it over Ben's head. Ben peered down, a medallion disc of polished ebony hung from the thong, a patterned arc of tiny white dots descending across its face above a single jagged line. 'Thanks,' he said, fingering it. Then he turned and set out along the track.

After a couple of hours he slowed to an exhausted halt in the centre of the track. His shoulders were aching and chafed, his bare head burned and his feet were tired and sore. He shrugged the pack from his back and slumped wearily to the ground beside it, tugging the trainers from his feet with a gasp. Undoing his jeans, he eased the coarse denim carefully to his knees. The skin between his thighs was rubbed red raw and bleeding. He pulled out the bottle, trickled some water, teeth gritted, onto his thighs and then, squinting into the glare, upended it to his lips. Then he ate, chewing slowly on a handful of dried fruit, staring back along the track from where he had come.

Munching steadily, he turned forward again. The view was exactly the same. In both directions. An identical mirror image. An arrow-straight track bisecting a wide plain of featureless yellow scrub, both ends vanishing into a shimmering blur in the middle distance.

He swallowed, anxiety rising, his head swinging first in one direction then the other. He scrambled to his feet, swivelling this way and that, then looked straight up again, craning his neck to the sun, a hand cupped to his eyes. It was perfectly vertical, directly overhead, his shadow a small dark puddle at his feet. In an instant he had lost orientation, as uncertain of the direction he had been walking as he was certain that whichever way he chose to go on would be wrong.

He stared around in panic, his breath coming in rapid shallow pants, the landscape about him an unsteady shimmer, the ground shifting uncertainly beneath his bare feet. Suddenly his hand flew to his neck. The thong. It was still there, the medallion at his chest. He ground his eyes shut, breathing deeply, turning it over and over in his fingers, its smooth hardness solid and reassuring. The river, the village, the boy, they had not been a dream. Gradually the fugue passed, the crisis receding like a passing squall, his breathing steadying, the pounding melting slowly from his chest.

He pulled the still damp sleeping bag from his pack and tied it about his shoulders like a cloak. He peeled the jeans from his chapped legs and stuffed them into the pack. He lifted the neck of his T-shirt to his forehead and pulled it inside out so that it fell back across his sunburned head like an ancient Egyptian headdress. Finally he hoisted the rucksack onto his back, wriggled his feet back into his trainers and set out along the road once more. By nightfall he had walked out from the plain, had emerged from its uncompromising flat harshness into a slowly transforming landscape of green fields, gently rising pastures and cool, scented woodland. As he made camp, sinking wearily into his sleeping bag within a leaf-strewn glade near a small brook, he peered up, his face lit by the blood orange glow of the sun sinking slowly behind the approaching foothills.

He awoke to the tinkling of bells. Hauling himself reluctantly from the clinging vestiges of deep sleep, he stretched aching limbs inside the sleeping bag, yawned sleepily and opened his eyes. Soft shafts of early-morning sunlight slanted through the trees surrounding the glade. Beyond the trees he detected movement on the track, shapes and colours, greys and browns passing in a misted haze slowly across his line of vision. Together with the metallic clink of the bells, he heard a damp, trumpeting snort and the sound of heavy animal breathing.

He sat up. Somebody was coming. A moment later a girl appeared through the trees. She was wearing heavy cotton trousers and a kind of long-sleeved fleece jerkin. She carried a long crook and a bag slung over one shoulder. Behind her, plodding through the trees led by a rope around its neck, its udders swollen and heavy, followed a large brown cow.

She led the beast right up to him, clucking and grunting while she leant against it, turning it sideways then bringing it to a halt beside his sleeping bag. Twin clouds of hot vapour plumed from its nostrils, wisps of steam rising from its back like morning mist. As soon as it stopped, its head dipped and it tore at the lush grass at his feet. The girl watched it, cooing softly and patting its flank, then she released the tether, and squatted down beside him. She had a wide, light brown face dotted with darker freckles and olive-coloured eyes, which slanted slightly upwards at their edges. Her dark brown hair was braided into neat, tight plaits that merged into a single gleaming twist at her neck. She smelt of leather and sandalwood. She studied him slowly, her expression a mixture of concern and amusement, then she took his arm and tried to tug him from his sleeping bag.

Ben watched her. He sat up further then hesitated, pulling down his T-shirt , clasping the bag around his middle, ashamed suddenly of his nakedness beneath. But she just gave a fierce grin and wrenched the bag to his ankles, gripped his arm tightly and led him from his bed, steering him firmly beneath the beast with more grunts and clicks of the tongue, as though herding a calf to its mother. Crouched on all fours he waited under the animal, smelling the rank sweetness of its hide, sensing the raw power of its twitching flesh, feeling the heat of its distended udder close by his cheek. Then the girl was crouching next to him, her face inches from his. Reaching up she smoothed the heel of her hand down the udder's side, her fingers plucking deftly at one teat. He felt her other hand at his neck as, without taking her eyes from the teat, she eased him forward towards it. He closed his eyes. A moment later there was an explosion of hot wetness at his face, the sound of a girl's laughter, the stamp of a hoof and the teat was at his lips. He opened his mouth to receive it and then he was swallowing thick warm sweetness, desperately, as fast as he could, guttural grunts at his throat while he gulped furiously to stem the flood, hot milk cascading from his mouth, down his cheeks and neck, her fingers brushing his lips with each pumping stroke.

They sat in the glade together preparing for his departure, the cow grazing contentedly to one side. While he rolled up his sleeping bag and refilled his water bottle at the brook, she produced apples, bread and cured ham from her bag, then tucked them into the pockets of his rucksack. She unwrapped a small linen cloth bundle revealing a thick, pale yellow paste. Digging into it with her finger she raised it to his lips with a grin, the white cotton of her shirt hanging loose about her shoulders. It smelt sweet and pungent on her finger; he opened his mouth, the rich cheese instantly coating his throat and tongue with a sensuous, heavy oiliness. Still smiling, she dug her finger once more then reached forward slowly, lightly smearing it onto the chapped skin of his thighs. He closed his eyes, teeth gritted, her ministering fingertips an ecstasy of torment.

Finally he was ready. She stood before him, inspecting him critically as he tucked his T-shirt into his jeans and stooped to retie the lace of one trainer, the rucksack packed ready at his feet. As he straightened up she reached forward and draped her heavy fleece jerkin about his shoulders. He stared at her in surprise, but she just grimaced, indicating the distant hills beyond the treeline. She leant towards him, feeling at his neck, pulling the ebony medallion free. She studied it, her eyes wide and soft, her fingers gently rubbing its hardness. Then she released it, stood back suddenly, picked up the cow's trailing tether, pointed once more up the track, turned and left the glade. Ben watched her go, a momentary pang of loneliness gripping him. Then she disappeared.

Swinging the rucksack to his shoulders he set out along the path. Almost immediately he was aware of the ground rising beneath his feet, the weight of the pack heavier on the stretched muscles of his legs and back. Within minutes he was breathless and sweating. He stopped to remove the jerkin from his shoulders, rolling it into the straps atop the pack before setting off once more, plodding steadily, eyes fixed on the path ahead, which meandered gently upwards, slowly winding through quiet, leafy woodland then breaking into bright sunshine and open pasture again.

By early in the afternoon he had fallen into a weary, trance-like rhythm. He was trudging heavily up the side of a steep hill, his head down, a roughly hewn staff hacked from a willow branch with his penknife in one hand. Suddenly he stumbled, the ground rearing steeply beneath him, loose rocks skittering away beneath his feet. He looked up in alarm, instinctively falling forward onto all fours as he slithered downwards, scrabbling for purchase.

Gasping and panicked, he clawed at the crumbling stone, feet pedalling frantically for grip. Then abruptly the slide stopped, the reverberating clatter of falling rocks a diminishing echo all around him. Finally all was still. He clung to the hillside, arms shaking, sobbing for breath. His chin was grazed and stinging, one knee of his jeans ripped, a rivulet of warm wetness trickling down his shin. 'Dad,' he whimpered fearfully, rigid with terror. Slowly he turned his head upwards, blinking up at the harsh skyline near vertically above him. He was just below the wide craggy ridge of the hill's summit. Below him the ground dropped dizzily away. He swallowed tearfully, staring at the blurred and bloodied fingertips tightly gripping the rock-face before him. Then slowly, gingerly, his tongue darting nervously across parched lips, he cocked one leg up, crab-like, beneath him. Then he unprised the fingers of one hand from the stone, reached up tentatively and with a soft grunt levered himself slowly upward once more.

Five minutes later he breasted the ridge, heaved himself forward with a final desperate sob, and flopped exhausted to the ground. He lay there, flat out, the rucksack shaking on his back, his face buried in his arm. High above him a solitary eagle soared effortlessly along the ridgetop, its head switching mechanically from side to side as it hunted, wingtips stretched wide into the warm, lifting thermals.

Eventually the storm subsided, the pounding in his ears fading as his breathing steadied. Slowly he lifted his head. Immediately ahead and below him the ground plunged giddily away, sweeping around a vast, mile-wide crater-shaped depression. The insides of the crater dropped sheer, rocky and precipitous. Lower down they began to flatten, became tinged with green, dotted with tiny trees and bushes. The base of the crater, far below him, was a solid, leaden expanse of ink-blue water. He hauled himself to his feet, wiping an arm across his face and tilting the bottle to his mouth, eyes following the sharp outline of the ridge around the lip of the giant crater. Away in front of him, beyond the far rim, the earth dropped away, then rose once more, the soft yellows and browns mottled by patchworks of darker green woodlands. Beyond them, sunlight glinting silently from their snow-capped peaks, the mountains rose like monstrous brooding giants.

By nightfall he was into the mountains, climbing steadily. The sun had sunk swiftly into the jagged horizon, flinging long fingers of shadow across the barren landscape. He was ascending a wide glacier bed, the frozen waters aeons since departed leaving a flat, arid, rock-strewn valley. It was featureless, vegetationless and desolate, like pictures he'd seen of the surface of Mars. At the end of the valley, engulfed in shadow, stood the sheer and uncompromising granite face of the mountain.

As he climbed, it grew colder, a strengthening wind descending with the failing light. At dusk he paused one last time. Chewing a stick of dried meat he pulled on his jersey, then unrolled the fleece jerkin the girl had given him, shrugging it heavily onto his back, sniffing vaguely at the faint tang of sandalwood. It was too big for him, reaching down almost to his knees, but it was warm and comfortable with a deep, fur-lined collar. He secured it about his waist, then upended the rucksack, emptied the contents onto the ground and began to repack.

Suddenly he was overcome with fatigue, a dizzying, bone-wearying tiredness that drained and disoriented him, deflecting his awareness, stunning him into immobility. He stared down at his fingers, frozen at the buckles of the rucksack, overwhelmed by uncertainty, unsure what they were doing, what he was doing. Waves of lethargy dragged at his consciousness, sucking at his equilibrium like a deadly destabilizing undertow. He ached to lie down, to curl up and sleep, for just a short while. And yet he knew that he could not, instinctively aware that sleep, this sleep, meant failure. He squeezed his eyes shut, grinding the heels of his palms into their sockets, head spinning.

'If it wasnae for your wellies, where wud ye be?' he sang slowly, teeth gritted. He looked up: the first star had appeared, burning in the milky firmament like a beacon. 'Inside a hospital or infirmaree.' He stamped his feet in time to the song, the words a distant unconnected echo of memory. 'You'd catch yersel' the death of a cold or even pleurisee.' The park, a wet and windy November afternoon, racing scud tearing at violently swaying treetops, ripping clouds of leaves from writhing branches. His mother, walking at his side, holding his hand while he tottered unsteadily forward, barely weeks after his first steps. His father holding his other hand, bending to him, singing happily. He, mesmerized by the stimuli, sensing anxiety in the elements yet security between the firm grip of their hands, faltering unsteadily forward, head down, his eyes fixed on the stark glossy redness of his new boots. 'If it wasnae for your good old wel-lies.'

With the echoing clatter of his feet and staff on the loose rocks mingling with the low moan of the wind sighing down the valley, he continued on his way up the glacier bed.

Two hours later it was pitch dark and the wind had risen to an icy howl. He had left the dry glacier valley at its head and had begun to work his way up through a giant confusion of fallen rocks and boulders. There was no path to follow. He zigzagged his way upwards by feel and instinct, clambering over smaller obstacles, squeezing through narrow cracks between others, ducking under arches where, in another millennium, blocks of granite the size of houses had tumbled on top of one another.

By midnight he had cleared the rock field and was slogging slowly up a narrow ridge line with steep drop-offs to either side. It was completely exposed and bitterly cold, the freezing wind buffeting at his body and legs, nudging him off balance, sucking the warmth from him. By now he climbed by rote, without thought or reason, hunched forward, planting one foot in front of the other only because he had always done so, and to stop meant change and the sleep of failure. Twice since the glacier valley he had felt its will-sapping onslaught. Twice he had repelled it, head flung back, screaming wildly into the wind until the spasm eased.

Gradually he moved up the ridge, his progress slowing to breast a short incline. As he cleared it the path ahead levelled for a short while then vanished into towering columns of black rock that thrust skywards towards the summit like a petrified forest. He leant on his staff, his breath coming in quick rasping gasps, wincing as tiny shards of wind-driven ice pricked at his eyes above the T-shirt wrapped around his face.

Soon the towers engulfed him, the wind dying to a low moan that drifted through the columns like murmured chants through cloisters. There was no path: he pushed forward into the darkness at random, his way lit by the dull glow of reflected moonlight from the gleaming black walls. He wandered deeper, the columns closing, sheer and smooth, soaring skywards to curve across the diminishing night sky in giant leaping arches. Gradually they sealed above him, the arches lowering and co-agulating, interfusing to form a solidifying canopy of rock. Soon the murmur of the wind was dying to a whisper; there was no other sound save the hoarse rasp of his breathing and the click of his staff on the rock floor, the gaping cavern closing lower around him with every faltering step. It began to grow warm: he tugged the T-shirt from his face, then undid the fastenings of the jerkin. In an instant he was engulfed with fatigue, the cavern walls melting into a shimmering haze as his legs buckled. He dropped to his knees, the ground shifting, dis-integrating beneath him. Brightly coloured lights danced before his eyes, he could hear voices, far-off shouting and a persistent growing clamour like the wail of a distant siren. He slumped forward, squeezing his eyes shut, hands clamped to his ears against the rising tumult. They were shouting, he could hear them screaming his name, their voices anguished and beseeching. He hunched lower, rocking backwards and for-wards on his knees. 'If it wasnae for your wellies!' he screamed, his arms enveloping his head, his voice a disembodied shriek. Something was floating, hanging in the air in front of him. 'If it wasnae for your wellies!' Something black and gleaming, floating, drifting from side to side through the veil of tears before him. He sat back, gasping with effort, forcing his eyes to slits. It was the medallion. The one the river boy had given him, swinging on its thong around his neck. His fist flew to it, grasped it tightly, the cave immediately steadying, consolidat-ing, the cacophony receding in his head like a routed army. Slowly he looked up, the cave still and solid around him, the medallion warm, hard and smooth in his fist. Ahead, at the far end of the cavern, he could see light, a soft shaft of velvet moonlight slanting down through the solid air of the cave. At its base a small figure lay, curled into a tight sleeping ball on a cushion of straw. At the top of the light, through a jagged chink in the cavern roof, an arc of tiny stars curved down towards it.

'Nathan?'
   'In and in deep.'
   'Sally?'
   'Okay, steadying down again now. Respiration falling back,

heart dropping through eighty, BP one-thirty over seventy.'

'He's gone,' Alison whispered. In the control room, Jack dropped his headphones to the desk and pushed back his chair. 'Hasn't he? He's gone.' Alison's voice quavered, her eyes wide with panic.

'No.' Elizabeth brushed damp hair from her forehead, bending quickly to the monitor.

'Then why didn't he wake up? Why? He's gone!'

'Shush, darling.' Janet stood up and put her arm around Alison's shoulder. 'We don't know that. He may just be, resting.'

'Resting, m-my God!' she stammered, her voice shrill with fear, her hands at her head. 'Jesus, Mother, you saw him, you heard him, he won't wake up, it's – it's killing him!' She lunged forward grabbing his hand from the bed. 'Ben! It's Mummy. Please, please, you must wake up!' The hand lay limp and damp in hers. 'Ben, please!' A moment later she felt Jack's arms around her.

'Ali, it's okay, it's okay, give them a minute.' He drew her back from the bed. Elizabeth went swiftly from the monitor to Ben's side, reaching to his neck for a pulse, rolling one eyelid back with her thumb. 'Nate?' She began moving the stethoscope across his chest.

'Same, residual spiking, nothing else.'

'Uh-huh. And Frankie?'

'As before. Maybe some faint background resonances but nothing specific.'

Slowly Elizabeth straightened up from Ben's bed, staring down at him pensively.

'What is it?' Alison demanded. 'What's happened?'

Elizabeth looked from one to the other, her face drawn. 'Janet's right,' she said quietly. 'According to all the readings, he's asleep.'

'What, you mean not unconscious?' Jack asked.

'Yes, unconscious, still in a deep post-hypnotic trance, in

fact, but, physically, metabolically speaking, his body's sleeping.' She glanced at her watch. 'I'm not surprised, it's been more than five hours.'

They all looked at him, his skin pale and damp with sweat, his head hanging to one side, lips pursed.

'Lizzie, couldn't we try again?' Alison pleaded. 'Give him another injection, and the – the shocks?'

'We will but not now. He's physically exhausted, completely drained. We'll let them both rest for a few hours, then we'll try again.'

'But will he wake up again?'

'From sleep, yes, yes he will.'

'And from the unconsciousness, the trance?' Jack strove to keep his voice even.

She looked down again, licking her lips, heart thudding. 'He must.'

He sat down on the ground beside her and gazed up at the light.

'You've come,' she said sleepily.

'I know.' He grinned, plucking a straw stem from her pigtails. 'Did you think I wouldn't?'

'I had the dream,' she murmured. 'The one about the dancing stars.'

He nodded. 'We've got to go back now.'

'We can't, it's too far.'

'I know that, but maybe we can try.'

They fell quiet, staring up at the night sky through the rent in the cave roof.

'Come on,' he said later. He licked his thumb, wiping a smear of green from her chin. 'We've got to go.'

Chapter 1 5

THEY RETURNED TO THE CLINIC AT MIDNIGHT, AS ARRANGED. They'd gone back to the motel, showered and changed. Alison had refused food, Jack nevertheless insisting that she lie down for an hour. He and Janet had picked at broiled tuna steak in the motel grill, Janet returning to her room to wait alone, sitting in darkness on Ben's empty bed sipping slowly at a large gin and tonic.

'What a lot of cars,' she observed, as Jack parked. 'I wonder what's going on.'

They climbed the steps and pushed through the swing doors. The lobby was milling with people, some sitting, some standing, alone or in groups. On one side a circle of female demonstrators were cross-legged on the floor, eyes closed, hands linked, their faces lit by the flickering glow of candles. Near the stairs a harassed-looking Lewis Kern was talking earnestly to a group of four men in suits. Close to him was a blue-uniformed security guard, another was standing by the service elevator, a third just inside the front entrance. Two policemen lounged beside the reception desk chatting with a strained-faced night receptionist. Journalists scurried to and fro brandishing cameras, notebooks and microphones. In the middle of the floor the night-time cleaning lady looked on in bewilderment, mop in hand. A short, balding man in grey was sitting in one of the easy chairs, talking into a mobile telephone, a laptop computer on his knee. Opposite him slumped two more men, a pile of large metallic suitcases at their feet, arms folded, heads back, apparently sleeping.

Jack took Alison's arm, guiding her through the mêlée, Janet following closely in their lee. Suddenly a photographer stepped in front of them firing a staccato burst of blinding light straight into their eyes. 'Mr and Mrs Heywood, Mr and Mrs Heywood!' A reporter appeared at their side, notepad in hand. 'Could you give us a reaction to the news?' Jack brushed them aside, blinking back floating orbs of white, steering Alison quickly to the stairs.

A minute later they entered the ordered calm of the operations room. 'What's going on?' he asked immediately.

Elizabeth looked up at them, a tired smile on her lips. 'They're fine,' she said quietly. 'Resting well.' Instinctively he realized that she hadn't been downstairs, hadn't left the children's sides, not for one minute. Alison went straight to Ben, bent to him and took his hand softly between hers. Janet stepped smoothly around the beds and over trailing wiring looms to her station next to Sally at the monitor. She slipped the cardigan from her shoulders onto the chairback and produced glasses and notebook from her handbag, her eyes already on the screen. Jack returned to the corridor, pausing to glance back along it. There was a crescendo of commotion drifting up from the lobby.

'Hi, man.' Nathan greeted him from the darkness as he entered the control room.

'Did you get a break?' Jack asked, pulling on his headphones.

'Later.'

Jack glanced at him: Nathan's eyes were inches from the screen, hooded with fatigue. 'Anything happening?'

'Uh-uh. We just ran through the session code while they napped.'

'Find anything?'

'Hard to say.' He blew out. 'Frankie, maybe.'

Elizabeth looked round at them. 'Welcome back, everyone.' She glanced at her watch. 'It is now midnight seventeen on the twenty-ninth.' Suddenly the door burst open. An instant later a security guard stepped swiftly inside and stood to one side of the door. He was followed immediately by Lewis Kern and a tall elderly man in a brown hat with a drooping white moustache carrying a battered leather briefcase. An instant later a photographer dashed through at the crouch, flashgun popping. One of the policemen came next, his hand resting on his gunbelt. Finally John Boyd stepped through to one side, his face expressionless.

'Get him out,' growled the old man with the moustache. The security guard seized the photographer by the arm. The policeman stood gaping at the wired-up bodies of Ben and Frankie on the beds. Elizabeth was moving swiftly around them, quickly placing herself between the children and the group at the door.

'Just what on earth do you think you are doing in here?' she said coldly, staring at Boyd.

'I'm sorry, Elizabeth,' he replied quietly. 'There's nothing more I can do.' In the control room Nathan stared in disbelief through the glass; Jack stood up, turning for the door.

'Lewis?' Elizabeth swung to him, eyes wide.

'Sorry, Lizzie.' He shook his head. 'I did my best, but it's over.'

'Are you Chase?' interrupted the older man gruffly. She nodded. 'Right. I am William Warner,' he announced, lifting his briefcase to his chest. 'District Attorney.' He withdrew a single sheet of paper then glanced around the room.

'By the authority vested in me by the State of Virginia, I hereby serve immediate notice of closure on the Perlman Institute of Dalmatia County, Virginia, under the Protection of Minors Act.' He looked up. 'Said order to be served with immediate and enforceable effect.'

Behind the glass Jack threw open the control-room door. Immediately outside stood a burly security guard, a rifle held diagonally against his chest. 'Would you remain in there where you are please, sir?' the guard said firmly. Behind him two men pushed past into the control room.

'You have no right to do this.' Elizabeth was addressing Warner directly, eyes blazing. 'Please leave, now.'

'I have every right, young lady. Kindly button your lip before you find yourself in even deeper trouble.' She glanced at Boyd, whose eyes were beseeching her to silence, spread hands pushing discreetly for calm. 'Now then, I want you all to listen very carefully to what I have to say,' Warner went on. He gestured to the door. The security man pulled it open, two uniformed nurses squeezed past followed by a middle-aged man in a white lab coat. 'This is Dr Fellows. Following application by the District Attorney's Office, the Court has today approved his appointment as acting senior physician of this institution, effective midnight tonight. I am therefore placing all patients remaining within this establishment into his care as of now.'

'Don't touch them!' Elizabeth stepped in front of the nurses.

'I've already warned you!' Warner pointed at her menacingly. 'This is a Court order and you are in contempt. One more word and I swear I'll have you locked up. Now step aside.' She did not move. 'Right now!'

Suddenly her eyes were filling. 'John,' she whispered uncomprehendingly.

'Do it, Lizzie,' he said gently. 'You have to.'

Slowly her head dropped, shoulders slumping in defeat. Immediately the nurses moved to the beds, staring uncertainly at the mass of wiring. The doctor followed. 'Don't touch the nets,' Elizabeth implored him, grabbing his arm. 'It's all they've got, don't remove them.' He looked at her blankly then pushed past her to the beds.

'Right, now I want this room cleared.' Warner was saying. 'In fact, I want the whole damn building cleared.' He looked at

Alison. 'Are you the mother?' She nodded, face white with shock. 'Is your husband here?' She nodded again, raising an arm towards the glass.

'Fine. Now, I need to speak to you both, alone. Please be re-assured that your children are in safe, capable hands. This injunction was obtained for their protection. If you would be kind enough to accompany me downstairs everything will be explained momentarily. Investigator Boyd?'

Boyd stepped forward. 'It's all right,' he said gently, resting a hand on Alison's arm.

'But, the children . . . I should . . .'

'They're in excellent hands, really, it's okay, everything will be fine. Come on downstairs for a few minutes, and District Attorney Warner will explain.'

The door flew open once more, there was a shriek of horror from the corridor. 'Dear Jesus! Dear sweet Jesus, what have you done?' Linda Beamon lunged into the room towards the beds, her hands at her face. Kern jumped forward, grabbing her arm. 'Stay away from them.'

'What the—' Warner started in shock. 'Get her the hell out!' he roared furiously. 'Get them all out, everybody, right now!'

The policeman jerked into life. 'Okay, okay, you heard the District Attorney!' he called, moving swiftly towards Lewis. 'Everybody out!' He nodded to the security man, and they began to herd people towards the door. Warner was already outside, muttering angrily, 'Goddamn disgrace.' He strode down the corridor. 'Clear the whole damn building right now! I want some order here.'

Twenty minutes later the lobby was deserted, a litter of dropped placards, paper cups and abandoned food cartons strewn across the floor. Even the cleaning lady had been ushered out, her bucket hastily propped against the wall next to a solitary fluttering candle. One of the security guards was standing, feet astride, just inside the main entrance, his hands clasped behind his back. Near him the reception desk sat empty, alternating patterns of steadily blinking lights illuminating the abandoned switchboard.

In the seating area, Elizabeth sat hunched in an easy chair, a handkerchief twisted between her fingers, Boyd crouching beside her.

'Come on, Lizzie,' he said gently, 'we've got to get you out of here.'

'They'll kill them,' she said tearfully. 'You do realize that, don't you? They'll disconnect them and they'll be gone for ever. Both of them.'

'I thought you said the boy was just under hypnosis?'

'He is! But he can't come out without us, without the net, it's our only link, our only means. I–' She looked around in bewilderment. 'I've got to get back up there,' she said suddenly, starting to rise. Boyd grabbed her arm.

'Lizzie!' he hissed. The security guard was wandering towards them. 'There is absolutely no way they're going to let you anywhere near them. Warner's not kidding, he'll put you in prison if you try.' He rose to his feet, his arm gripping hers. 'They'll be all right, Fellows knows what he's doing.'

'Sorry, Mr Boyd,' said the security man. 'She really has got to leave the premises now.'

'Thank you, we were just going.' He began to walk Elizabeth slowly towards the doors, the security man following close behind, a string of keys jangling in his hand.

In her office District Attorney Warner was reading out loud from a typed sheet of notes. 'The final emergency application to the Court was, in fact, made via the DA's office following notification by an inspector of the State Hospital Administration this afternoon, a Mr, ah, James Grey.' He read quickly, his hat in front of him on Elizabeth's desk. Across from him Jack listened closely, Alison staring sightlessly at a group photograph on the wall, hugging her shoulders. 'In his view there was a significant risk that patient welfare was being compromised. Earlier in the day we had already received notification that the Institute's insurance coverage had been suspended, plus we were in receipt of information from law-enforcement agencies that political activists had actually entered and occupied the premises, thus further compromising patient safety. We had also discovered that the Institute's clinical director had for some time deliberately been in breach of a temporary restraining order. There was also a notification via the Defense Department that the clinic's business director was obstructing government agency representatives who were being denied legitimate and contractually agreed access to the clinic and its facilities.' He paused for breath. Jack was shaking his head.

'There were also other, communications via, ah, diplomatic channels.' He flicked a glance at them, then read on quickly, as though addressing a court. 'Following discussions with the State Hospital inspector during the afternoon and early evening therefore, it was unanimously agreed that the directors were acting irresponsibly, in fact illegally, and were negligently placing patients at risk. It was therefore decided at four o'clock that in the interests of the patients there was no alternative but to remove the directors and apply for an immediate closure order.' He looked at his watch. 'This was granted at nine twenty-five and served at twenty past midnight tonight.' He dropped the sheet onto the desk and looked up at them, lacing his fingers. 'Now I'm real sorry that you and your family have gotten caught up in all this. But, do you see, it had to be done and done now. It's for their protection, in fact.'

Jack swallowed. 'Um, we shall be needing legal advice, right away.'

'Of course,' Warner agreed. 'We'll get right onto it. I would also urge you to contact your embassy in Washington as soon as you can. I believe they are waiting to hear from you.'

'When can I see my children?' Alison murmured.

'Real soon, ma'am. What we're going to do, if it's okay with you, is allow Dr Fellows and his staff a few hours in peace and quiet to, er, tend to the needs of the patients, and get everything kind of straightened out up there. And then, perhaps, in the morning . . .'

Alison stiffened. 'No, I want to see them now.'

'Ma'am, it's for their own good. God knows what's been going . . .' He checked himself, breathing out slowly. 'We must allow Dr Fellows proper time to carry out a thorough examination, and allow the patients time to rest. After all, all hospitals have visiting hours, it's for the good of the patients. Now first thing in the morning we'll see–'

'No, now, dammit! They are my children.'

'Ali.' Jack took her arm. She stared at him, her gaze searching his face. There was a tap on the door. One of the security guards appeared.

Warner looked up. 'Ah, Stein, everything buttoned up?'

'Yes sir, building's cleared and secured.'

'Very good. Everybody out that should be out?'

'Yes sir, just the replacement medical staff and security here, and the, um, family and–'

'And?'

'Well, perhaps you'd better come, sir.'

Warner glanced at the Heywoods, then pushed back the chair. 'Would you wait here just a moment, please?' He made for the door, flicking an eye at the security guard as he passed. 'Mr Stein here will stay with you.' A minute later he was upstairs in the operations room. Dr Fellows was standing between the beds, his arms folded, the two nurses looking on uneasily. 'Well?' He raised his eyes at the doctor.

Fellows tilted his head, stepping to one side. 'The patients' grandmother.'

She was sitting behind the life-signs monitor, one stockinged leg resting elegantly across the other, hands folded neatly in her lap. Her glasses rested on the white wool of her cardigan, suspended from her neck by a string, below a single-strand necklace of creamy white pearls. Her skirt was deep green tartan, her shoes brown and stout.

'How do you do,' she effused, eyebrows raised expectantly. 'Janet Catchpole.'

Warner swallowed. 'How do you . . . Ma'am, I'm sorry but I must ask you to leave. Right away.'

'I'm terribly sorry, really I am, but I can't do that.'

'I beg your pardon?' He gaped at her.

'Well, you see, I'm British, so are these children, foreign visitors to your country. They are also juveniles – what do you call it? Minors. And, unfortunately, quite unable to speak for themselves. Now then, up until about half an hour ago these two minors were in the care, the sole care as authorized by their parents, of Dr Chase and the Perlman Institute. But un-fortunately the Perlman Institute has been officially closed and Dr Chase removed from her position, so now they are no longer being cared for by the only person authorized by their family to do so. Not only that, their parents are temporarily absent and, as far as I know, have not yet authorized transfer of their care to a third party. Therefore, until such time as I receive confirm-ation from them to the contrary, responsibility for these children, it would seem logical, reverts to their nearest next-of-kin here present, which would appear to be, for the moment at least, me.'

'We've got to get them out.' Elizabeth was pacing across the carpet. In one corner Jack crouched on the floor jotting notes, the telephone clamped under his chin. Alison stood by the window, watching the ebb and flow of early-morning traffic beneath the gently swaying lights. As she watched, a white Jeep appeared at the far end of the street and sped up the road towards the apartment. A minute later there was a knock on the door and Lewis strode in, dressed in jeans and sweatshirt. Elizabeth stopped pacing. 'Lew, what's happening?'

'Complete lockout,' he said breathlessly, slumping into a

chair. 'Nobody in, nobody out without clearance. Guards on the door, names on clipboards, security passes, the works.'

Jack looked up from the phone. 'Did they let you in?'

'No chance. Wouldn't let me further than the bottom of the steps.'

'Did you see anybody?' said Elizabeth, chewing a thumbnail. 'Was anyone coming and going?'

'Some. Recognized a couple of the Defense Department geeks arriving, there was a change of nursing staff at nine, but new faces, nobody we know. An older guy rolled up in a rental car but they turned him away, and–' He stopped.

'Who else?' said Elizabeth.

'Your good friend Boyd of the DA's office is in there.'

'Did he say anything?'

Lewis shrugged. 'Said he'd find out what he could, then drop in here later. Very accommodating of him, I'd say,' he added caustically.

'Nobody else? Gardner, Sally?'

'No, that was it.' Elizabeth turned away, resumed pacing.

'What about Janet?' asked Alison, from the window. 'My mother.'

Lewis shook his head. 'Couldn't tell you. Sorry.'

Jack put down the phone and stood up.

'What did they say?' asked Alison.

'They're sending somebody,' he said. 'From the embassy. They'll be here this evening.'

'Yes, but what did they say?'

'Well, apparently they already knew about it.' He checked his notes. 'They were notified last night and say they have been kept fully informed since. They say they're quite satisfied that the decision to, close the clinic,' he glanced at Elizabeth, 'was taken solely in the interests of the children and that all correct procedures have been followed.'

'Correct procedures? But they won't let us see them!'

'Yes, they knew about that, too.' He fiddled with his papers.

'But they said that allowing the new staff the night to carry out full examinations, check the facility and ensure that the premises were properly, um, fit, was not unreasonable, under the circumstances.'

Elizabeth stopped again. 'Fit?'

'Sterile, was the word they used.'

'That's absolutely goddamn absurd!' scoffed Lewis. 'They're stalling, it's just delaying tactics.'

'Maybe.' Jack's eyes were on his wife. 'They want us to wait here and not try to see the children until the embassy representative gets here.'

'But why, for God's sake? Why do we have to wait?'

His lips were compressed. 'Ali, Cambridgeshire Social Services. The embassy received notification that they've been granted a care order, on Frankie.'

'What?' The colour drained from her face.

'They applied to take her into care. Compulsorily. To stop us going ahead with the treatment.'

Alison covered her face. 'My God.' She looked at Jack. 'Stanhope.'

Suddenly the front door banged open and Nathan barged in, carrying a small leather case and paper bags of doughnuts and bagels. 'Breakfast,' he announced, dropping the bags on the floor. Nobody moved. 'What?' He looked around at them. 'What happened?'

Jack cleared his throat. 'I'm sorry, but I think, it is possible, that all this, closing down the clinic, getting locked out and everything, might be our fault. Some sort of, diplomatic pressure or something.' The room fell quiet; beyond the window, lowering clouds were crowding the sky, the light flat and dull.

Lewis sat forward suddenly. 'Nah,' he said, rising to his feet. He pulled a bagel from a bag. 'Can't be, too much other stuff going on. Everybody just wanted to fuck us up, that's all.'

Alison walked to Jack, her eyes beseeching. 'Can it really be true?' He put an arm around her shoulders. 'They're going to take her?' Her head fell slowly to his chest.

'God knows,' he said helplessly.

'So, what else is new?' Nathan said briskly, picking up the leather case.

'We can't get in,' said Elizabeth. 'Nobody can.'

'Is that so?' He gripped a bagel between his teeth, unzipped the case and pulled out a laptop computer. 'Jack, Alison, come on man, grab a doughnut, got something to show you.'

Ten minutes later he paused at the keypad, studying the screen of the laptop. After a moment it went blank. 'Ah,' he said. He was sitting on the only armchair, a wire running from the computer to the phone socket in the wall. Elizabeth was leaning on one arm of the chair, Jack and Alison crowding in behind. Lewis was on the far side of the room, talking into his mobile telephone.

'What is it?' said Alison.

Nathan licked his teeth, reaching into his shirt pocket for gum. A moment later the screen lit up and he jerked forward. His fingers danced across the keys. 'That's my girl.' A few seconds later he stopped, sat back and turned the screen towards Alison. 'Say hello to Frankie.'

'She's still hooked up!' exclaimed Elizabeth.

'Damn right.' Nathan scrolled up the screen rapidly. 'And just take a look at her.'

'What's the matter?' asked Alison. Seconds ticked by while they studied the screen. 'What is it?'

Elizabeth straightened. 'She seems to be fine,' she said thoughtfully. 'In fact, there's quite a bit of activity, baseline, non-specific and very low level, but it's there all the same.'

'But that's good, isn't it?'

'Yes.' Her face was set. 'Yes, it is quite good. Or, at least, it might be if we were there with her. With them both.'

'What about Ben?' asked Jack.

She looked at him. 'I don't know. He's not there.'

*

'They've already unhooked him,' said Boyd. Nathan handed him a coffee cup then returned to his laptop on the easy chair. It was mid-afternoon, dull and humid. A fine rain had begun to fall. In the apartment the air was close and oppressive; there was a strong smell of coffee and stale food. 'They did it this morning. They're doing the same with Frankie this afternoon. Then they're going to move them both to Norfolk General. Probably tonight or tomorrow morning.'

Alison sat propped against the wall next to Jack. 'But when can we see them?'

'I can't say. You've spoken to your embassy?'

'Yes,' said Jack. 'We know.'

'I'm very sorry. I gather it's unlikely you'll be able to see them without a representative present.'

Jack exhaled slowly. 'How was Ben? Was he awake?'

Boyd shook his head. 'I don't know, I don't think so. I only saw him for a moment, he looked tired, you know, kind of pale. And, well, sort of staring. One of the nurses said something about trauma-induced catatonia.'

'That's just nonsense,' said Elizabeth, from the window, her back to the room. 'They have absolutely no idea what they're doing.'

'I can't bear it,' Alison groaned. Jack pulled her close to him.

'Well, good work I'd say, Investigator Boyd.' Lewis scowled up from the only other chair, his briefcase open at his feet. 'You must be very proud.'

Boyd looked around the room. 'I'm sorry. I never imagined it would come to this. It was just a temporary injunction, while we looked into the Willis charges.' He glanced towards Elizabeth. 'But it just, kind of blew up.'

'Well, isn't that a pity?' said Lewis sarcastically. 'Still, should get you a pat on the back from the big man – who knows, maybe even a promotion?'

'Back off, Lewis,' muttered Nathan from the easy chair. 'Isn't his fault.' He tapped repeatedly at the laptop, then sat back, folding it shut with a snap. 'That's it folks, they just pulled the plug on us.'

Suddenly Alison stiffened. 'Jack, I can't just sit here, we've got to get in to see them, got to do something.'

Boyd held up his hand. 'Alison, I promise they will not let you into the building, no chance. It's much better that you stay here where we can contact you, then come on in as soon as the embassy official arrives.' He forced a wry smile. 'In any case your mother is with them, she's doing a grand job.'

'How is she?' asked Jack. Alison's head sank down onto her arms.

'She's, well she's quite a character, isn't she?' he said encouragingly. 'The DA's going crazy. I think he finally met his match. She didn't move from their side all night. Not once, never even closed her eyes. Then this morning she had everyone running around in circles, English tea and toast, then hot water and towels, insisting everybody clear the room while she, you know, washed.' Nathan shot a glance at Elizabeth's back: her head lifted fractionally from the grime-stained window. 'Then the newspapers, then something to write on.' He patted his pocket, withdrew a folded note. He handed it to Jack. 'She asked me to give you this and to tell you she's fine.'

'Can we call her?' he asked, opening the note. 'Speak to her on the telephone?'

'Sorry, I doubt it,' Boyd said. 'But I'll be going back later, I can take a message and anything she needs.' He gestured at the note. Jack scanned the list. A change of clothes, some toiletries, a toothbrush. He snorted. 'She wants her duty-free gin sent over.'

'And her ginseng and primrose-oil tablets,' added Alison, her forehead on her arms.

'Um, yes, those too.' He paused. 'Who's Stella?'

'Hmm?'

'She asks for her letter-writing kit, then adds we mustn't forget Stella.'

Alison's head came up slowly. She took the note from him. 'Innocent until proved guilty.'

Elizabeth turned from the window, her face set. 'We have to take them back. Now. Today.'

'You got that right,' said Nathan flatly, his arms folded.

Lewis looked up from his briefcase. 'I beg your pardon?'

'Elizabeth, don't be ridiculous, it's impossible.' Boyd was staring at her in astonishment.

'No, it isn't, it's essential. We have to get them back and then we have to finish what we started.'

'Um, excuse me, but what's with all this "we" business?'

'Lewis, I'm going to need you, badly. For once in your life you're going to have to do something simply because it's important and the right thing to do, not because there's a fat pay cheque waiting at the end of it.'

'Lizzie stop, now, just hold on one minute and listen.' Boyd had his hands held up.

'No, John, I can't, it's too late for that. I brought these children over here. I have a responsibility to them. We have to get them back, it's their only chance.'

'Only chance? Lizzie, what the hell are you talking about?'

'Tell them Nate.'

Nathan sat forward, looking directly at Jack and Alison, fingers linked. 'Little Frankie,' he began, his face a frown of concentration, 'there's just no way she's ever gonna wake up on her own – doctors in England told you that and they got it right. She needs a hell of a lot of help. Now, with the neural net, the equipment arrays, the programmed sequences, Lizzie here, and with Ben hooked in, everybody and everything working flat out together on this thing, then maybe there's a chance we can pull her back.' He tapped his laptop. 'In fact, the signs are, were, that she was just getting a little bit spiky, that maybe we were starting to get through.' He paused, looking around the room. 'Lizzie and me, we're finished here. They're shutting us down good and tight, we won't be able to set up again, anywhere, not for a long time, and our equipment is probably being packed up and trucked off to Washington as we speak. Frankie gets unhooked, goes to Norfolk General, or back to England, then she's gone. There ain't anyone in the world can help her.' He looked back at the Heywoods. 'Sorry, but that's just the way it is.'

'And, what about Ben?' said Alison.

Elizabeth breathed in. 'Ben's in trouble, too. The whole point was that we should be with him every step of the way. Helping him along, watching his metabolism, monitoring him for signs of stress or difficulty, bringing him out if he got in a mess. But he's all alone now, stranded. And God knows what he's going through. He's in real danger.'

'Elizabeth, listen to me, please.' Boyd spoke quietly, his face lost in shadow. Outside the light was dying, heavier rain falling onto the glistening sidewalk in a steady hiss from thickening dark clouds. 'I understand why you want to do this, truly I do. But we're talking about the law here, the simple basic principle that decent, intelligent, law-abiding citizens are just that. They abide by the law and the law abides with them. If they don't, if they just cast it aside, or take it into their own hands, even when they feel they're justified, then there's nothing, only chaos.'

'And Cheryl?' she asked, her eyes on his. 'Did the law abide with her?' His face fell. 'John,' she went on gently, 'I'm sorry, but I can't stand by and do nothing while the system fails these two young people. Surely you can see that, better than anyone.'

'You'd never get in, never get near them.'

'Maybe not, but you could.'

'No,' he said softly. 'I'm sorry, I could not.'

No one spoke. Outside they could hear a car approaching slowly, sploshing along the kerbside towards the apartment.

'So, no fat pay-cheque, huh?' Lewis was riffling through his briefcase. A moment later he pulled out a sheet. 'Gotcha.'

Alison was clasping Jack's hand tightly. 'They're going to take them away from us,' she said, her eyes filling, 'when all we ever did, all we ever tried to do, right from the beginning, was help them, and do the right thing.'

'There is no right thing,' he said stonily. 'There is no right, and no wrong. There's only responsibility, and obligation, and doing the best you can.'

'And choice,' said Elizabeth.

'And love,' said her father. 'A parent's love for the child it created.' He was standing in the open doorway, his body in shadow, the shoulders of his jacket dark with rain. Elizabeth's hands went to her face. Nobody else moved.

Elliot glanced around the room. 'Somebody order pizza to go?'

He telephoned her at eight. 'It's me,' he said quietly.

'John, where are you?'

'I'm at the clinic. Sitting at your desk, in fact.'

'Are you all right?'

'I guess. Just tidying up a few loose ends, I'll be heading off home in a few minutes.' He hesitated. 'Are you really going ahead with this thing?'

'Yes, John, I must.'

She heard him sigh. 'I can't help you, you do understand that. It's not the act itself, not what you're doing, I know you believe it's the right thing to do. But the principle . . .' He sounded very down, as though he was trying to convince himself.

'I know,' she said gently. 'It's okay, I understand.' The line hissed quietly. 'I like a man of principle, you know,' she teased. 'In fact, I'm in love with one.'

He sat back in her chair, fingertips lightly stroking the top of her desk. 'You really are something special, Elizabeth Chase, did you know that?' He waited, she said nothing. 'Do you have a plan?'

'More or less.'

'Is it a good one?'

She smiled. 'I don't know, we can only do our best.'

'Where will you go?'

'It'll have to be back here. It's not ideal but there's nowhere else – Lewis's apartment is too busy, smack in the middle of town, and Nathan's is up four flights of stairs.'

'Lizzie, you are crazy, they'll find you in hours, it's the first place they'll look.'

'Maybe not. Hardly anybody knows about it, I never really properly moved in, my official address has always been the clinic.'

'No. It won't do.' She heard him breathe out again. 'Listen, go to the Stamitz place. In Everdene, remember?'

'Yes. Yes I remember but, John–'

'It's completely empty, been sealed up for weeks. Miles from anywhere, and nobody will think to look there in a million years. Do it, Lizzie. Your apartment is a dead loss, believe me.'

'But–'

'And, for what it's worth, there's one security guard on duty here at the main entrance plus a pair of nurses upstairs with Janet and the kids. That's it. There are no other patients left. Fellows goes off duty at nine but he'll probably be coming back later if Ben and Frankie get moved tonight.'

'John,' she said simply. 'Thank you.'

'Be careful.'

'I will.'

'Elizabeth.'

'Yes.'

'I love you.'

C h a p t e r 1 6

LEWIS PARKED HIS CAR NEXT TO A LARGE, PLAIN-SIDED VAN and cut the motor, the rain outside instantly louder, drumming an insistent tattoo on the roof. Straightening his tie in the rear-view mirror, he pushed open the door, stepped quickly into the deluge and hurried up the steps. He rapped his knuckles on the glass. A uniformed security guard appeared, eyeing him suspiciously. 'What is it?' the guard called through the doors, his chin lifted in query.

Lewis withdrew a folded sheet from his breast pocket. 'I'm Kern. Got to authorize the Defense Department audit,' he called, his voice floating indistinctly through the glass.

The guard winced. 'Got to do what?' He peered at the paper pressed up against the door, the words indeterminate in the weak light, smudged with rain. It had a Department of Defense seal on it, addressed to Mr L. Kern, something about agreed joint authority for audit and inspection of the Institute's facilities and equipment.

'I've got to sign off the equipment,' Lewis yelled, tugging his collar up against the rain. He glanced behind him anxiously, the driveway was empty. 'Before they can take it to DC. They're waiting for me . . . Look, open the goddamn door and just read the authorization, could you? I'm drowning out here.'

The security man eyed him doubtfully, then reached to his

belt for a ring of keys. Seconds later Lewis was inside. 'Thanks,' he puffed noisily, shaking rainwater from his jacket. 'Hell of a night to be out signing shopping lists.' He pulled out the sodden letter again, glancing at the guard's name badge as he smoothed it onto the desk. 'Right. Officer Stein, isn't it? Okay, here we go. There's two guys here from the Defense Department, packing up equipment on the first floor, right?'

'Uh-uh, wrong.' The guard shook his head, scrutinizing the letter. 'They're already all finished up, they left.' He looked up at Lewis.

'They what?'

'It's all loaded in that truck.' He nodded towards the van parked outside. 'They went off to get something to eat before setting back for Washington.'

'Right,' said Lewis. 'Precisely. That's the point, they can't leave until I sign off this authorization. They phoned to say they were ready, said they were going to grab a bite and could I come in and complete the equipment audit.'

'The what?'

'The inventory audit. It's basically a shopping list. Look, all I have to do is take a quick poke around the truck, make sure their list of stuff ties up with my list of stuff, sign off the damn authorization and we're all out of here.' He licked his lips. 'Sooner the better as far as I'm concerned – shitty night to be out counting boxes of paperclips.'

The guard pursed his lips, studying the letter. 'Doesn't say anything about any damn shopping list,' he muttered doggedly. Behind him a rotating flashing light appeared at the far end of the driveway.

Upstairs on the first floor, Janet turned slowly from the rain-streaked window, one hand rubbing the back of her neck. She looked up and smiled wanly at the nurse sitting on the other side of the room. Between them the children lay on regular hospital beds, tucked beneath sheets and blankets. They were completely free of their neural nets, all the electrical equipment gone from the room, the wiring looms, the computer monitors, the visors, the lights, speakers and microphones. Frankie lay in a raised lying position, a drip feed in either arm, her head to one side, the ventilator clicking beneath the bed. On the bed next to her, Ben lay hunched on his side. His mouth was open, his body jerked occasionally, eyes moving ceaselessly beneath thinly slitted lids. The nurse rose and bent to him again, one hand to his forehead.

'How is he?' asked Janet weakly.

'He's quite heavily sedated,' she replied. 'I'll be glad when they get him to Norfolk. It'll be much better for him there.' She looked up at Janet. 'Mrs Catchpole? Janet? Are you all right? You look awful.'

'I'm okay, dear, a bit achy in the chest, perhaps a little cold.' Her hand slid to her shoulder, her face grimacing with pain. 'I wonder, Darlene, perhaps a glass of water.' She started to rise from the chair then slumped forward to the floor.

'Mrs Catchpole!' The nurse skidded round the beds to her. 'Jackie! Jackie, get in here quick. Janet's collapsed!'

In the lobby, the security guard looked up from the letter. An ambulance was pulling up outside, beacons flashing, backing slowly up to the bottom of the steps. 'Now what?' he complained. He put the letter on the reception desk and went to the doors. 'Would you just wait right there, please, Mr Kern.'

'Expecting another admission?' Lewis asked lightly.

'Yes, no, maybe an ambulance coming to collect later, hell, I don't know, nobody tells me shit.' He unlocked the doors. Two paramedics were doubling up the steps, heads down against the downpour.

'This the Perlman place?' asked one. A buzzer sounded suddenly on the switchboard, call-light flashing. Lewis glanced through the glass partition. On the desk next to the switch-board lay a clipboard and a set of truck keys.

'Yes, it is. You here from Norfolk General for the British

kids?' The security man glanced at the switchboard. It was a call from upstairs.

'Look, would you like me to get that?' Lewis volunteered. 'You're obviously tied up.'

'You stay right there!' The guard shot Lewis a warning glance, finger pointing. The paramedics were looking at each other. 'What kids?' one said to him.

'The English kids, Hayforth, or something like that – hell, I can't remember,' he flustered. 'You mean, you're not here to pick them up and take them to Norfolk?'

They looked at each other again, hands on hips. 'No. We're from Paxton, got a nine-eleven telling us to attend a heart-attack, female senior citizen, the Perlman Institute outside of Dalmatia, a, uh, Dr Fleming attending.' Another car was speeding up the drive towards them, headlights on full.

'Look, could you just wait right there one minute? All of you.' The guard held his hands up, swivelling between Lewis and the paramedics. Then he pushed open the door of the reception office and reached for the phone. A middle-aged man with grey hair, carrying a medical bag, had got out of the car and was running up towards the doors. One of the paramedics pulled them open for him. 'Wait!' the guard yelped in alarm, one hand on the phone. 'Ah, shit, let him the hell on in. Why not, everybody else is. Hello, Jackie, is that you? Okay, it's Walt on the door here what the–'

'Walter, it's Darlene. Mrs Catchpole collapsed, we think it could be a heart-attack, we're gonna need back-up and–'

'Heart-attack?' The guard glanced through the doorway. The paramedics looked at each other.

The grey-haired man leant in through the reception door. 'I'm Dr Hugo Fleming,' Elliot Chase said. 'You have a heart-attack victim here, I understand, a Mrs Catchpole?'

'I, uh, hold on, Jackie, are you there?'

'Walter, it's Darlene for Christ's sake–'

'Darlene, Jesus, right sorry look, did you call a doctor,

um . . .' He looked desperately at Elliot.

'Fleming,' he enunciated slowly. 'F-L-E-M . . .'

'Fleming, right! Listen, Jackie–'

'We've got her on a bed in the next room but Dr Fellows is off until later and there's precious little medical equipment left so get them here as quick as you can.'

'Well, okay Jackie, if you say so but–'

'For fuck's sake Walter, it's Darlene! Now can you please just get on it!' The phone went dead.

'Look, um, Walter, maybe this is a bad time.' Lewis shrugged. 'Perhaps if I came back later . . .'

'You stay right there.' The guard snatched up Lewis's letter from the desk, brandishing it at him like a cudgel. 'I'll be right back. The rest of you follow me.'

A minute later Lewis was sprinting across the deserted lobby, around the stairwell and along the corridor towards the rear of the building. 'We lucked out!' he hissed, holding open the fire door. Jack ducked through beneath his arm, closely followed by Nathan, an empty canvas tote bag slung over one shoulder. 'All the stuff's already loaded up. It's in a van around the front.' He held up the keys. 'Like taking candy from a baby.'

'Well, all right Lewis.' Nathan grinned.

Elizabeth appeared in the doorway. 'Got this from the ambulance,' she whispered breathlessly, clutching a small air cylinder and mask. 'Okay, listen,' she wiped wet hair from her face with one arm, 'Nathan, you go ahead and do the dispensary, you've got the list, take as much as you can. Lew, you help Alison in the ambulance. Get anything at all, but the most important things are the resuscitation kit and portable ventilator. Then get on over to Everdene with Nathan and the equipment truck. We'll meet you there.' Lewis tugged up his jacket collar and ducked out into the rain. Nathan disappeared soundlessly along the corridor. Jack followed Elizabeth towards the fire stairs, his heart pounding in his throat.

On the first floor Janet lay on the bed in the room three doors from the children, her eyes closed, her breathing laboured. The nurses were bent over her. 'Janet! Mrs Catchpole, can you hear me?' One held her wrist, feeling for her pulse. The other undid the buttons of Janet's blouse, stooping to press one ear to her chest. 'I can't hear a damn thing,' she muttered. Along the corridor there was the sound of elevator doors opening followed by rapidly approaching footsteps. 'In here!' one of them called.

A minute later Elliot leant forward, his stethoscope moving slowly across the bare skin of Janet's chest, his eyes shut with concentration. At the foot of the bed, ranged in a semicircle, the others looked on.

'That was damn quick,' muttered one of the nurses.

'I wonder, would you mind closing the door?' Elliot glanced up briefly, his fingers probing Janet's neck.

'Uh, I should be getting back downstairs,' said the security guard hesitantly. 'If you don't . . .'

Elliot straightened. 'Could you just wait one moment, please? I may need you here.' He looked at the nurses, his mouth dry. 'You were quite right, it is her heart.' His mind raced. 'Um, could you tell me exactly what happened, please?'

The nurses glanced at each other. 'Yes, well, she didn't look too good all evening,' one said. 'After Mr Boyd came back with her things. Kept saying she felt cold and was kind of rubbing her shoulder a lot. Jackie thought it was exhaustion, she was up all night apparently, and didn't have a whole lot to eat during the day.'

'Shall we fetch the stretcher?' asked one of the paramedics.

'Ah, no. Just hold on for a second. It may be better to, um, stabilize her here before we try moving her.'

'Look, I really have to get back downstairs. There's this guy waiting in the lobby.' On the bed Janet gasped suddenly, shoulders stiffening in spasm.

Three doors away Elizabeth slipped the mask over Frankie's nose and mouth and cracked open the cylinder, a grey rubber air bladder inflating slowly on Frankie's chest below the mask. She looked at Jack and made a gentle squeezing motion with one hand. He nodded, reaching for the bag, the murmur of low voices drifting towards them along the corridor. Elizabeth quickly disconnected the breathing tube from Frankie's throat and ducked beneath the bed to the ventilator. A moment later she reappeared, eyes searching the room. Jack watched her anxiously, his face questioning.

'Plug,' she mouthed, pointing at the tracheotomy opening in Frankie's neck. It was nowhere to be seen. They froze as a door opened along the passageway. There were voices. A man's, close, speaking from the open doorway, then a woman, younger, quieter, from further within the room, the words muffled and indistinct. Jack and Elizabeth stared at each other, eyes locked across the bed. Finally, a different man spoke, his tone lower, authoritative. A second later the squeak of a hinge and the door closed again with a clunk.

Jack jerked his head towards a tray of instruments and cotton bandaging. Within a minute Elizabeth had secured a swab over the tracheotomy vent with surgical tape. Then, carefully sliding her arms beneath Frankie's knees and shoulders, she lifted her cleanly from the bed with a grunt. Jack placed the air cylinder on Frankie's stomach and slipped the rubber bladder into Elizabeth's outstretched fingers. Then he unhooked the two drip bags from their stand, and placed them on Frankie's chest. Elizabeth tilted her head towards Ben. Within seconds he was gathered up in his father's arms, wrapped in a blanket.

They paused at the door, listening. Jack stooped, groping for the handle. Then they were in the corridor, moving swiftly towards the fire stairs. He pulled the heavy door wide for her, jamming it open with one foot, she swung through sideways and started down. At the bottom she waited, peering anxiously up the well, fingers squeezing the air bag every few seconds. Jack held his back against the fire door until it closed behind him with a dull thump, then descended the stairs, Ben's limp body clasped awkwardly to his chest. At the foot of the well they repeated the process, he turning his back to push open the fire door, holding it while she passed through into the corridor, then swinging through to follow her.

'Well, you can both just hold it right there.'

'No!' Elizabeth gasped involuntarily. They looked up in alarm.

He was at the end of the passage, the light from the lobby behind throwing his shadow up the floor towards them, his legs spread, his arms raised, hands outstretched, fingers folded around the handle of his gun.

'Right. Now just come right on up here where I can see you, nice and easy.' They glanced at each other. Elizabeth closed her eyes, lowering her head to brush Frankie's cheek with her lips. 'I'm so sorry,' she whispered.

They moved along the passage and into the strip-lit glare of the lobby, the security guard moving backwards ahead of them, arms raised and pointing. 'You, you're Chase, aren't you?' he said, as she emerged into the light. She nodded. He stared at Frankie, clutched in her arms, the oxygen cylinder and drip-bags draped across her chest, the air bladder. 'Just what, in God's name, do you think you're doing?' He gaped, gun arm drooping fractionally. Then he saw Jack. 'And who the hell are you?'

'I'm their father,' he said quietly. 'You can put the gun down, we're not going to hurt anybody.'

'Right, okay, yes that's right, we met last night,' the guard said quickly. 'But I'm sorry, if you don't mind we'll just keep things as they are right now while I call in some help.' He backed towards the reception desk. A moment later the elevator opened behind them and one of the paramedics emerged.

'Hold it!' the guard yelled in alarm, the gun swinging wildly.

The paramedic looked at him in astonishment. 'What the hell is going on?'

'I said stop!'

'But I just came for the stretcher, for God's sake! What is this?'

'I don't know but nothing and no one seems to be what they say they are, so you just hold on right there while I find out what in hell is happening. There's some damn strange shit going on here.' He stared around him. 'And where's Kern for Christ's sake, and—' He swung towards the doors, eyes wild with confusion. 'Jesus Christ, the goddamn truck's gone!'

'Walter, put down the gun.' Boyd closed the door of Elizabeth's office and walked slowly into the lobby.

'Mr Boyd, thank Christ! Look, these two were trying to abduct the kids, an ambulance rolls up when nobody here called it, there's a guy upstairs says he's a doctor and – and I think that little shit Kern has stolen the Defense Department guys' truck—'

'Put it down,' Boyd repeated quietly. 'They're leaving now and we're not going to stop them.' He stood in front of the guard, smiling gently.

'Not going . . . But, Mr Boyd, I can't just let them walk out of here with those kids like that.'

'Yes, you can, Walter. I want you to, I'll take the responsibility.'

The lobby was silent, save for the spatter of rain on the steps beyond the doors and a rhythmic hiss as Elizabeth squeezed air into Frankie's lungs. Beside her Jack hefted Ben in his arms; to one side the paramedic waited, arms folded.

'But . . .' The guard's face fell, the gun dropping slowly to his side. Boyd stepped forward and put an arm around his shoulder. 'It's all right, Walter. These are good people. They're just doing what they need to do.' He turned him gently towards the corridor, glanced back at Jack and Elizabeth, his eyes jerking towards the entrance doors. 'Come in here, have a cup of coffee, and I'll explain everything.' He led him slowly across the floor and into Elizabeth's office.

*

Two hours later he slowed the Chevrolet to a crawl, peering ahead through labouring windscreen wipers. Checking behind once again he made sure the road was empty then accelerated quickly, wrenching the car off the road and onto the track. The vehicle lurched heavily, ploughing through a series of deep, water-filled ruts. Half-way up he cut the headlights, feeling his way the last quarter-mile until at last the jagged darker outline of the house emerged against the heavy grey of the rain-laden night-sky. A single dull glimmer of light showed in an upstairs window.

He eased open the front door to be met by Janet, bearing blankets and a lit candle, floating silently across the darkened hallway like a wraith. She saw him and started. 'John, oh, goodness, you frightened the life out of me!'

'And you me.' He grinned. 'Glad to see you made it.'

'It was easy. After you sent the ambulance away, the gallant Dr Fleming and I just walked out through the front door while you were talking to the nurses and security man in Lizzie's office.'

'Is everything okay here?'

'Well, I think so. It's certainly clean and spacious and seems to have everything, although there appears to be a problem with the plumbing and there's no electricity, hence the candles.' She looked at him. 'Everyone's upstairs, first door on the right.'

He collected a candle from the hall table and started up the stairs. The bedroom door was wide, the room lit by flickering candlelight. On the far side of the room beneath a tall, blanket-covered window, Elliot Chase was stooped over an iron bedstead, carefully inserting a drip into Ben's arm, his face a shadowed frown of concentration. Elizabeth was bending over a second bed in the centre of the floor, her back to the door. Across from her Alison held a flashlight over the bed. She looked up as he entered. 'Lizzie,' she whispered.

She swung round, a stainless-steel instrument dish clutched in one hand, her face a half-mask of startled relief. He came to her, hugging her to him with one arm.

'Thank you,' she mumbled. 'Thank you for coming, thank you for tonight at the clinic, thank you for everything.'

He kissed her. 'What about the kids?'

She stood back. 'We're just trying to get them stable and comfortable, then we need to get life-signs monitors up and running and see how they are, bloods, sugars, fluids, electrolytes. Frankie seems to be fine, but Ben . . .' They looked across at him: he was hunched on his side, flushed and shaking. 'He seems to be running a fever and he's badly dehydrated. Dad's taking care of him.'

Lewis appeared through a doorway in the wall between the two beds, wet hair plastered back across his head, shirt dark with rain. 'Well now, look who's here,' he said, with a grin. He wiped the damp from his hand. 'I hear you did good tonight.'

'I hear you did pretty well yourself. Illegal entry, fraud and grand larceny. You've obviously got a flair for it.'

Nathan's distorted voice floated through the doorway. 'Kern, can you just quit gassing for five minutes and get the rest of the stuff in, man. We don't have all night.' Boyd peered through the doorway. Nathan was crouched on the floor, studying a wiring plan by the narrow glow of a penlight clamped in his teeth. All around him were stacked growing piles of gleaming metal cases and writhing heaps of heavy black cabling.

'Need any help?' Boyd ventured.

Suddenly the overhead light-bulb came on, flickered, dulled to an orange glow, then went out again. Nathan glanced up at it. 'Jack's in the basement,' he said, taking the penlight from his mouth. His voice dropped. 'If we don't have power, we don't have shit.'

Boyd left the bedroom and returned to the stairs. Half-way down he met Janet coming up bearing another of Nathan's boxes.

'On holiday, are they?' she said, squeezing past him. A gust of wind flung rain against a large window beside them on the stairs.

'I'm sorry?'

'Your friends. The ones who lent you this house. Gone away for a bit?'

'Oh, um, yes. In a manner of speaking.'

He crossed the hall and found the entrance to the basement. Stooping beneath low beams he descended carefully, his candle guttering in a sudden cold draught from below. As he neared the bottom he caught sight of Jack on the far side of a large basement area littered with boxes and crates. He was hunched forward on a packing case in front of a large diesel generator, a hurricane lamp hanging from a beam above his head. His feet rested in two inches of ink-black rainwater, there was an over-powering reek of kerosene, the incessant crashing of rain outside and the gurgle of blocked drains.

'Jesus.' Boyd stepped gingerly onto the concrete floor. It was completely awash, and instantly he felt freezing water soaking through his shoes. Jack had his back to him, as he crossed the floor Boyd could see his head was down, his face in his hands. He hesitated, then backed quietly away.

'Ho, Jack!' he called loudly from the foot of the stairs. The head came up, a sleeve wiped hastily across the face. 'How's things in the engine room?' He sloshed noisily across the floor. 'Holy Mother, did we hit an iceberg or something?' Ten minutes later they were both seated side by side in front of the generator. Boyd's toolbox, retrieved from the trunk of the Chevrolet, lay open beside them.

'Water,' said Jack, frowning at the engine. He sniffed loudly, spitting fuel into the drifting litter at his feet. His hands were black and oily, blood trickling from a skinned knuckle, his eyes were red-rimmed and heavy, his forehead smeared with grease. 'Everywhere. It's in the tank, in the fuel lines, in the injectors and it's probably in the cylinders.'

'But she did kind of fire up briefly when you cranked her over?' Boyd hung a motoring flashlight from a fuel line and rolled up his sleeves. Jack nodded. 'Okay, then we'll work backwards. Start with the injectors and clean out all the way back to the tank. But first,' he reached into his pocket and pulled out a half-bottle of Jack Daniel's, 'jump start. Courtesy of our generous and accommodating host.' He unscrewed the cap and handed Jack the bottle.

Jack upended it to his lips, eyes fluttering shut. 'Do you know?' He gulped, the alcohol searing his throat. 'This time last year I had it all. A wife, two great kids, a house, a business of my own doing something I love. The whole package.' He stared at the generator. 'We used to be a team, a unit, a self-sustaining system, something strong and alive that existed independently of anything else, ran itself like a – like a little engine.'

'Yeah, I know what you mean,' Boyd said quietly.

'But then, at some point, somewhere, it all began to fall apart, to break down.' He drank again. 'Bad maintenance, I suppose.'

'Yes, but bad maintenance can be fixed.'

He narrowed his eyes. 'Or maybe a defective component,' Jack went on softly, as though he hadn't heard. 'Then came Frankie's accident and then Ben's problems started, and pretty soon everything was just coming to pieces. But it was only then, when things were at their absolute worst, that I began to realize I just wanted it back, wanted it back together, working again, like before. More than anything. It was the only thing that mattered.' He contemplated the flooded basement. 'And now . . .' his gaze fell on the oily sodden leather of his shoes '. . . what the fuck have I done?'

'Jack, you did what you thought was right,' Boyd said quietly. 'What you believed you had to do. Jack?'

'Hmm.'

'I really believe it will be all right.'

'Why did you come?'

'Parental instinct, I guess. The more isolated you were

becoming, the more hemmed in, the more I wanted to be with you.'

'Really?'

'Sure. It's a normal human reflex, you know. Nothing wrong with that is there?'

'Nothing at all. It's wonderful. I'm so glad you're here. Really. Is that also why you sent the tapes?'

'Hmm, partly, maybe. No not really. I sent those because, well, they belong to you and because they were relevant to where your work seemed to be leading you.'

Janet awoke slowly, her neck sore and stiff. Her back was numb and her legs cold. She sat still for a while, eyes closed, listening to the gentle murmur of voices across the room. Then, shifting painfully in the chair, she passed her tongue across parched lips and blearily opened her eyes.

It was light, a heavy dull grey suffusing the room from the partially uncovered window. In front of it Elliot and Elizabeth sat next to each other at the bottom of Ben's bed, talking quietly. Elliot was holding one of her hands, smiling as he spoke. Nearby, Alison was lying on a mattress at the foot of Frankie's bed, still fully clothed, face down, fast asleep. Through the doorway into the next room Janet could see a pair of denim-covered legs on another mattress: one foot wore a white sock, the other still bore its scuffed trainer. She sat forward, peering into the room, her blanket an untidy heap at her feet. It was Nathan, flat out on the floor, his head resting in the crook of his arm. Lewis was half sitting, half lying on a cushion, propped against the far wall. His head was lolling sideways, snoring steadily.

'Good morning.' Elizabeth smiled at her. Janet raised a hand in silent greeting. From the landing, the heavy thump of slowly approaching feet echoed on the stairs. Alison stirred at the sound, sighing deeply. She raised her head, blinking up at the doorway. Boyd and Jack clumped wearily through the door then stopped, silently surveying the wreckage. They were both completely black, shirts untucked, filthy and oil-stained, faces smeared with grime, hair rust-flaked and dishevelled. They looked as if they'd emerged from a coal mine. They raised their hands, black, greasy and bloodstained, into the air.

'Many hands . . .' began Jack. He reached out with one finger and flicked on the light switch. The bulb glowed bright and steady.

'. . . make light work,' finished Boyd, grinning at Elizabeth. In the next room an electronic chime sounded and one of the computers flickered to life, a groggy 'All right!' coming from the direction of Nathan's mattress. Jack sank to his knees next to Alison. She reached up with one hand, pulling his head down to kiss him. Elizabeth came quickly around the beds, arms outstretched to Boyd. 'Whoa, Doctor!' He smiled, holding up his hands again, and she stopped. 'Not until I've cleaned up a bit. You've got patients to attend to.'

'Well done.' She beamed.

'It's Jack here did it. I just kept shovelling the coal. Anyway, the pump's now priming the main tank, you should have water again in about half an hour, hot and cold. Bathrooms are working fine and the kitchen seems to be on line.'

'In that case,' Janet hoisted herself unsteadily to her feet, 'coffee.'

It took most of the day. In the morning Jack and Boyd slept in an adjacent room while Lewis and Nathan resumed assembly of the computer equipment. By noon everything was reconnected and running and Nathan was embarked on the laborious task of testing and aligning each unit and reconfiguring the software. Meanwhile Alison and Elizabeth removed all unwanted furniture from the bedroom, scrubbed down the walls and floor, wiped the bedframes, door handles and windows with sterile solution, and remade the beds with plastic barrier undersheeting and fresh linen. A little while later Lewis wheeled in the life-signs monitor on a squeaking kitchen trolley and positioned it between the beds, a thick bunch of electrode wires clasped in his fist like a wilting bouquet. 'Yours, I believe,' he said disdainfully, handing them to Elizabeth.

'Come on,' she told Alison. 'Pull up a chair, we'll start with Ben.'

Janet and Elliot, selected as the least known or conspicuous, took Elliot's hire car into Everdene and spent an hour pushing overladen trolleys around a shopping mall.

'Was I really a convincing heart-attack victim?' she asked again, as they offloaded into the car.

'Absolutely,' he reassured her. 'Had me completely fooled.'

'Have you seen many?'

He straightened up, lips pursed thoughtfully. 'No. None at all.'

'Well,' she sniffed proudly, a six-pack of kitchen rolls tucked under one arm, 'it certainly felt like the real thing, I've never been so terrified in my life.' She handed him the pack. 'And, I must say, you were very convincing as the heart specialist, although it did seem to me, if I may say so, that you kept that stethoscope moving around in my underclothes rather a long time.'

'Yes.' He laughed coyly. 'Sorry about that. Couldn't for the life of me think what else to do.'

'It's quite all right,' she said, eyebrows arched. Suddenly she froze, staring into the gaping trunk of the car. Her hand flew to her mouth.

'Janet?'

She nodded mutely, pulling a small handkerchief from her sleeve. Elliot rested an arm about her shoulder, glancing around the car park. 'Try not to worry,' he said softly. 'Lizzie, she'll do everything, whatever it takes, believe me.'

'I know.' She dabbed at the corners of her eyes. 'So stupid of me.' She blew her nose neatly. 'Sorry. Won't happen again.'

'Don't be ridiculous. Are you sure you're all right?'

'Absolutely. Thank you. Sorry. Where next?'

'Hardware store, then pharmacy.'

By the time they returned to the house, Ben's life-signs monitor was on line. 'How is he?' asked Janet, fumbling for her glasses. She stooped to the trolley, eyes scanning the screen.

'Blood pressure's down and he's still running a temperature,' said Elizabeth, from beside Frankie's bed. 'Fluids and sugars are all out, we're working on stabilizing those now. They really hit him with the sedatives yesterday. He's very weak.'

'What's the priority?' asked Elliot, leaning to the screen.

'Priority's got to be to get him out,' she said simply, wiping an arm across her forehead. Beside her, Alison bent forward, carefully attaching an electrode to the skin above Frankie's ear. 'As soon as Frankie's done we're starting on his neural net. Then when he's hooked up and Nathan's ready, we'll back up the sequence and try to pick him up exactly where we left off, then bring him on out from there.'

Suddenly there was a heavy vibration beneath their feet followed by a raucous clattering overhead. They all looked up. A helicopter swooped low over the house, banking steeply. Boyd appeared in the doorway, moved to the window, crouching down beside it to peer skywards. 'Vehicles all in the garage?' he asked.

Elliot swallowed. 'All except the hire car. We haven't finished unloading the shopping.' The clatter receded then turned back in a wide circle and slowed to a stationary hover. 'He's a quarter of a mile over to the west,' observed Boyd.

'Has he seen us?' Elizabeth asked anxiously.

Boyd said nothing, watching as the helicopter executed a slow three-hundred-and-sixty-degree turn, the window reverberating beneath his fingers. Then it paused, the treetops swaying wildly thirty feet beneath its spinning rotor, kicked up its tail and rattled off northwards. He watched it go. As the noise faded to a hum, he turned back into the room. 'I don't know,' he said. Elizabeth stared at him, face pale, eyes wide and darkly ringed. 'But the sooner we get this over with, the better.'

Late in the afternoon he returned to the bedroom carrying a tray of hot soup and bread. She was alone, sitting next to Ben's bed, head down, gazing trance-like at a wire filament in her fingers. Ben's electrode net was almost fully attached, the wiring cascading from his body to the floor and through the door to the next room like a fast-flowing stream. 'Lizzie?' he whispered. She didn't move. He touched her shoulder. She started, swivelling to him quickly, eyes confused, a bewildered smile on her lips. 'By my calculations,' he said, placing the tray beside her, 'you haven't slept at all in the last two nights. Why don't you break off for an hour or so, then start again afresh? We'll keep an eye on them, promise.'

She laid a hand on his arm. 'Thanks, but I can't.' She looked down at Ben. 'You're in a great deal of trouble, aren't you, John?' she said quietly.

'Probably. But nothing I can't handle. Warner's a pussycat, really. He'll come round, he needs me.'

'What will you do?'

'Take a vacation, that's for sure. There'll be a suspension while this all gets sorted out. Thought I might drive down to the Keys. Drink a few sundowners and get my feet wet.' He glanced at her. 'Sound good?'

'Sounds great.' She smiled, her eyes searching his. 'He's all alone there, John, it's burning him up, exhausting him. I got him there and I must get him out. Quickly. No matter what it takes.'

'What do you mean?'

She kissed him softly. 'Nothing.'

In the adjacent room Nathan sat on an upturned packing case, watching the master console scroll through thousands of hours of code. He patted his pockets, pulling out a pack of gum. Behind him Lewis lay on his back on the mattress, hands linked behind his head, eyes closed.

'Hey, Lew.' Nathan lobbed the gum pack onto the mattress.

'What,' he replied sleepily.

'What you going to do man?'

'What do you mean?'

'After this. What you gonna do?'

'After this?' Lewis sighed deeply, opened his eyes and reached for the gum. 'Something like around five years, I should imagine.'

Jack and Alison were sitting at the bottom of the stairs, soup bowls on their knees. Jack looked around the dimly lit hallway, grey-painted walls adorned with garish supermarket pictures of wide-eyed children, mountain streams and kittens. Furniture draped in sheets, a threadbare rug on oak-stained floorboarding. He put down his bowl and laced his grime-stained fingers. 'Was just thinking,' he said quietly, 'the day he was born. Remember?'

'Oh, yes.' Her head sank to his shoulder. 'Like it was yesterday.'

'Best day of my life.'

'Hmm.' He felt her nodding. 'It was wonderful.' She was quiet, remembering. 'Wonderful. But do you know? I don't think it was for me the best day, not the most important day.' She lifted her head. 'It was fantastic, of course, a new baby and everything, exciting, terrifying as well. But at the same time, I knew we weren't yet complete, what we were, what we were making, it wasn't, you know, finished, accomplished yet.'

The lines of his face were dark and deeply etched, eyes round with worry, dulled with defeat. As though he'd aged ten years in as many months. She stroked his neck. 'Jack.'

'What we were,' he echoed softly. He looked around the hallway again. 'Who'd have thought . . .'

She shifted on the step, one hand reaching to her pocket. A moment later she pulled it out, the photograph of Ben and Frankie on the beach. It was badly dog-eared now, criss-crossed with white crease-marks and torn along one corner. But the warmth still blazed through like a beacon, the energy, the vigour, the life. They clung to it, heads together, arms entwined, staring down into it, the laughter, the happiness, the vibrant blues and yellows and pinks melting into a bright warm blur before their eyes.

Chapter 17

HE WOKE UP SLOWLY AND ROLLED ONTO HIS BACK. THE oblique slant and warm tone of the thick wedge of sunlight angling across the ceiling told him it was early afternoon. He stretched sleepily, listening to a pealing shriek of seagulls wheeling high in the sky above him. Further off, the crash and suck of waves toppling lazily onto the sandy beach wafted through the little window, borne on a soft summer breeze that plucked at the thin cotton curtain, throwing stippled yellow patterns across the wedge.

He watched for a while, waiting patiently, while the familiar warm waves drifted over him and his eyelids began to sink once more, the solid outline of the wedge melting to a blur, rippling across the ceiling like a floating yellow veil. Sighing deeply, he turned onto his side and closed his eyes once more.

But this time there was a bell. Slow, distant, hypnotically persistent. A dull off-key clang, which dropped into his consciousness every few seconds like a stone into a well. It was the bell from the church, the little wooden church in the village with the ramshackle jetty down by the river. Reluctantly he opened his eyes again, an uneasy resentment growing in his stomach. His gaze fell on the chair by the door. His clothes lay on it in a forgotten heap, the discarded rucksack on the floor beside it. Hanging on a nail in the door was the fleece jerkin the girl with the cow had given him. In the corner his staff stood propped against the wall, the black medallion hanging by its leather thong in the smooth Y of its crook. He hunched over to face the other wall. Tugging the sleeping bag higher he squeezed his eyes shut, his knees drawn to his stomach, head buried in his arm.

She was far along the beach, crouching beside a seaweed-fringed rockpool, a little wooden shrimp net in one hand, the other submerged in the shell-strewn pool, watching her fingers open and close slowly like an anemone. Then her hand vanished, a heavy shadow settling over the pool, darkening the crystal surface of the water. She looked up, squinting at the bulky dark outline standing over her, her mouth open, eyes wide and questioning.

'Come on,' he said morosely. 'We've got to go.'

They walked along the water's edge in silence, following the wide curve of the beach, their shoes printing smooth dents in the damp sand. At the far end of the beach a steep green headland jutted onto the shore, a jumbled confusion of giant boulders cascading from its base into the sea beyond the breakers. Soon they were clambering among tumbled jagged outcrops, their hands grasping at sharply encrusted barnacles, feet slithering precipitously on trailing fronds of greasy sea grass.

After a while he stopped, sniffing at the heady tang of salt and drying seaweed. He looked back. Her head was down, bobbing in and out of view as she clambered through the rocks. Beyond her, the sandy beach had vanished behind the curve of the headland. Turning forward he could see that the boulders ahead rose in steeper confusion as the cliff-side edged steadily nearer to the sea. He gazed up, cupping a hand to his eyes, studying the steep outline of the headland, following the irregular zigzag of a narrow path that wound up its sheer grassy face. Behind him a series of breathless half-sobs as she approached slowly through the rocks towards him.

'Don't like this,' she grumbled a minute later, flopping onto a boulder.

'Tell you what,' he said, licking his lips, 'let's go up there.' He hesitated, watching as her eyes followed his arm up the cliff-face, her bottom lip wobbling.

'There?' she wailed querulously. 'I can't, it's too high.'

'Yes, you can.' He picked up his stick. 'I'll help you. We'll imagine we're mountain goats.'

Half an hour later they crested the ridge of the headland onto gently undulating moorland, the air filled with the sound of larksong and the scent of drying grass. Behind and far below them the glittering sea stretched away silently to melt in a blue haze on the horizon. Gasping, he stared around him, shrugging the pack to the ground. Suddenly his knees buckled, a wave of giddy fatigue sweeping over him, dark spots of grey swirling before his eyes, ears pounding. He dropped to his knees, hands pressed to his head as the spasm swept across him.

'What are you doing?'

'It's okay,' he said, shaking his head dizzily. 'It's okay. Let's have a drink and then go on a bit.'

'Can't we stay here and rest?'

'No, we'll have a rest later.'

With the sun sinking at their backs, they set off across the moorland plain. Soon the sandy beach, the clamber through the rocks and the headlong scramble up the cliff-side were a distant memory as they traversed a series of wide grassy downs beneath advancing lines of grey, flat-bottomed clouds. They spoke little, pausing occasionally to drink from the water bottle or eat biscuits. Twice during the afternoon Ben folded onto the ground, racked by fatigue attacks. Every so often Frankie complained that she, too, was tired and wanted to go back. By dusk the moorland had grown coarser, the ground peaty, boggy and tussocked, laced with hidden, twisting ditches and muddy black pools. Overhead the clouds had merged into a solid heavy overcast. In failing light and falling temperatures Ben searched for somewhere to spend the night, Frankie, floundering and fractious at his side. By the time they stumbled upon the derelict shepherd's shelter an hour later it was dark and raining.

He gave her the last of the biscuits to eat while he unrolled the sleeping bag against the rough stone wall of the shelter. The roof had long since collapsed, but working by the weak glow of his torch he managed to rig up partial cover using a rusted sheet of corrugated iron supported by his stick and a rotten roof timber. A short while later, exhausted and hungry, he pulled off his shoes and crawled into the sleeping bag beside her.

'All right?' he asked, jabbing at the rolled-up jerkin beneath their heads. The ground was lumpy and unyielding, her body felt slight and cold, smelling of sea salt and damp wool. The rain drummed noisily on the metal above their heads, and somewhere lower down he could feel a steady tapping on the sleeping bag where water leaked onto them.

'Yes,' she whimpered tearfully, slipping a thumb into her mouth. She shivered against him, his woollen jumper pulled down low over her summer shirt and beach shorts. He snuggled up behind her, slipping an arm beneath her chest and pulling her close, stroking her head and rubbing her side for heat. Eventually a meagre moist warmth began to suffuse the bag. A while later he felt her breathing deepen.

He awoke shortly before dawn, watery, pallid light showing dimly above the roofless walls of the hut. The rain had stopped but the sky was damp and still overcast, a thick, low-lying mist drifting across the soggy landscape. Rubbing his eyes blearily, he crawled, shivering, from the bag and began to pack up. Soon he woke Frankie but she refused to leave the warmth of their bed, lying curled into a ball deeply within it as he made ready around her.

'Well, I'm off then,' he said eventually, hoisting the rucksack to his shoulders. 'See you around. Just keep heading east and you should find your way.' He made heavy tramping footsteps noises towards the rubble strewn doorway.

There was movement at the bottom of the bag. 'Which way's east?' she asked, her muffled voice anxious.

'East is the direction we came yesterday. It's easy, but just watch out for the quicksand and the wolves, that's all.'

They walked all morning, the grey cloud enfolded about them like a wet shroud. It was bitterly cold, a stiff wind at their faces, which penetrated the damp fabric of their clothing and deposited fine mist droplets in their hair. Before long he stopped to unpack the cowherd's jerkin for her.

'It's too big,' she protested. She waddled in circles, flapping the empty sleeves like a distressed penguin. It was much too long, reaching well below her knees, the thick leather heavy with damp. But she was protected: the fleece inside was dry, and with the collar turned up her face and head were well shielded from the wind. 'And it's too heavy.'

'Here, take this too,' he said, blinking giddily. He rolled up one of her sleeves. 'It's very special.'

'Gosh, thanks,' she said, fingering his staff admiringly, her cold and hunger forgotten.

Around noon they were tramping across a boggy field, the ground descending gently beneath their feet. Ben looked up, startled by the coarse screech of a crow. Immediately ahead there was a darkening in the mist, a tall rising line of shadow stretching directly across their path as far as they could see. He stopped, panting heavy clouds of vapour into the damp air above his head. 'What is it?' she called, hurrying awkwardly up from behind. 'Is it cliffs again?'

'No, not cliffs.' He shifted the pack on his back, gazing up at the endless grey. 'It's a forest.'

Her eyes dropped to the ground. 'I can't go there,' she said quietly, standing motionless beside him.

'Yes, you can. Maybe we'll find some food, nuts, fruit and things.' He could feel the distant thunder growing in his head, advancing waves of tiredness sweeping over him. 'We can't stop. Not here.'

'No, but you don't understand. I just can't.'

He looked at her, her slight body engulfed within the cowherd's jerkin, her head down, eyes averted.

'We have to go on a bit, Frankie,' he said softly. 'The thing is, Mummy's waiting. And Daddy.' He nodded towards the forest. 'It – it wouldn't do for us to stop here. We must go on a bit.'

'I'm afraid,' she whispered, tears rolling unchecked down the pale skin of her cheeks. 'We'll get lost. For ever.'

He knelt to her, his hand reaching into his shirt. 'No, we won't.' He pulled out the medallion, ducking his head to lift it from his neck. 'We've got this. It – it tells us where to go.' She raised her eyes slowly, staring at the smooth black glint of ebony in his hand. 'It's our most precious thing, Frankie, and you can wear it.'

The forest was dank and still, the air heavy with the pungent scent of wood mould and decaying vegetation. Only weak light penetrated the dense canopy, dull shadows falling among boundless ranks of towering, brooding trees, thick with moss and tightly entwining creepers. They walked on, enveloped in silence save for the snap of twigs beneath their feet and the coarse rasp of his breathing. Soon she began to fall behind. He'd stop, aware suddenly that the uneven rhythm of her foot-fall had dropped back, or jerked from his reverie by her cry of alarm. Then he'd wait, bent double, hands on knees while she hurried to catch up, the jerkin flapping awkwardly at her knees, one hand grasping the unwieldy stick, the other clutching the medallion. But always, the moment he stopped, the tiredness began to overcome him again, dragging him downwards like a treacherous unseen undercurrent.

Finally he halted, and turned to see that she was slumped on the ground twenty yards behind him, her face pale and slack.

'What's the matter?' he panted, walking back to her.

'I can't.' Her mouth was set. 'I just can't. Leave me here.'

He glanced up towards the forest roof, heart pounding. The light was failing, it would be getting dark soon. 'You know I'm not going to do that, Frankie. But you see, the thing is, we just can't stop now, not here. And we can't go back. So we must go on. Together. We must.'

'I'm sorry I'm sorry!' she wailed, her face anguished. She lifted her arm, covering her eyes, her mouth turned down in defeat. 'I tried, but I can't do it. It's too hard, just too hard!'

'Look,' he began, sinking to his knees beside her, his legs like lead. He stared around at the forest. It looked exactly the same as it had when they entered it, the trees spreading concentrically from them as though they were perpetually at the centre of some dark preternatural maze. 'What if . . .' He swallowed drily, sliding an arm across his forehead. 'What if I carry you?'

He carried her. Piggy-back, hoisted awkwardly onto his hips, the cumbersome rucksack swinging across his stomach. She kept her arms wrapped tightly about his neck, her forehead pressing against his back, eyes securely closed. With his arms linked together beneath her legs, he staggered on, hunched forward, his breathing a hoarse rasp, moving in a heavy trance-like rhythm, his head down, his eyes sightlessly following the worn point of his stick across the forest floor.

With the coming of darkness, soon the very substance of the forest began to shift and change around him, melting into a continuous, cold oppressiveness, a formless, dank singularity that closed around him like drifting fog. Tall shadows slid slowly through the peripheries of his vision as he trudged steadily onward, sometimes passing far away to one side, sometimes gliding silently overhead, or huge and close, crossing the path directly in front of him. He ignored them, looking neither left nor right, focusing his eyes straight down and his will on his load, the solid and unmoving deadweight across his back, his leaden legs moving by rote across the shifting grey blur.

But then, suddenly, he stopped. He raised his head. A solid line of darker fog stood before him, melting away into the distance like a towering wall, a misty black ocean or a cloud-filled chasm. He moved forward towards the brink, the stick gripped tightly in his fist, the darkness stretching upwards, ahead and down, infinite. There was no far horizon, there was no visible bottom, just a floating grey frontier stretching away in either direction from his feet. And there were the shapes. Some small and near, flitting quickly past him with a noise like passing sighs of wind. Further out across the abyss larger shapes moved, left and right, in the distance great mountains of barely discernible shadow drifted slowly by with a deep, pulsing rumble.

Legs buckling, he dropped to his knees, the familiar pounding growing in his ears, the floating spots dancing before his eyes, advancing waves of fatigue washing over him, pressing in on his temples like a vice. He sank forward onto his hands, lowering his head, his eyes squeezed shut, the weight pressing down on him, forcing him to the ground. Lower, hunching down into a kneeling crouch, his body gripped by convulsions of shuddering, numbness spreading through his limbs like setting cement. Baring his teeth with effort, he raised his head once more, staring out into the abyss. She was there, alone, standing far out in the middle, the shapes flowing swiftly around her, the noises rising and fading like passing sighs. As he slid flat out to the ground, the tiredness like a giant hand at his back, crushing him prone, dragging him into unconsciousness, he heard her calling him, her voice a tiny distant mewl on the sighing wind.

'Don't do this,' said Elliot, following her to the dressing table. 'Please, Lizzie, I'm begging you, don't do this.'

She threw a handful of connectors onto the floor beside her and sat down in front of the mirror, peeling off her spectacles. 'We're losing him, Daddy, and it's my fault, I can't just stand back and watch. I won't.' She picked up a tube of adhesive cream and the first connector. 'Nathan?' she called, leaning to the mirror.

Behind her, Nathan was plugging multi-core cabling into the

back of the master console. 'Uh yes, okay, maybe. But it'll be a very basic patch in, and there's a big risk of overload, probably end up smoking the whole damn array.'

'Fine, whatever you can manage, but don't let it blow.' She picked up the next connector, carefully trailing the filament back over her shoulder. 'I'm going to need your help,' she said quietly, glancing up at Elliot's reflection in the mirror.

He shook his head. 'This is insanity.'

'No, it isn't, it's his only chance, *their* only chance now. You and I, we can help them, together. We must.'

'But Lizzie, for God's sake, you heard the tapes, you've seen it yourself with Ben. There's no control, no escape route, no safety net, it's, it's–' His shoulders slumped.

'Daddy,' she smiled, 'this is what it was all for, can't you see that? What everything has been leading to, since the very beginning. This has nothing to do with pushing back frontiers of knowledge, or, or, pioneering breakthroughs. This is about people, families, parents and their children, brothers and sisters. Love, Daddy. You said it. A parent's love for the child it created.' She craned her neck, glancing past the open door. 'That's why they're here. That's why we're all here.'

'Headlights on the driveway!' An urgent shout from the stairs, Lewis's voice, high and tense.

A shadow passed quickly across the doorway. 'How many?' called Boyd, heading for the window.

'Two so far. No, Jesus, three.' Lewis paused. 'They – they've stopped. Shit, look at that! They're just sitting there.'

An alarm went off on the master console. Immediately Elizabeth swivelled towards Nathan, fingers pressed to her forehead.

'He's tachycardic,' said Nathan, bending to the screen. 'It's – it's okay, I think, just very irregular. Christ, I don't know, every-thing's just way down. He's in real trouble.'

'Daddy, go to him, quickly. I'll be through in a minute.'

He hesitated, his face drawn and pale. 'What do you want me to do?'

'Take me back,' she said. 'Like you did before. Back to the lake. Nathan will do the rest.'

'Jesus Christ, Lizzie,' he pleaded, his voice anguished, 'please, please don't do this.'

Boyd reappeared in the doorway. 'They're waiting for back-up is my guess.' he said. 'Or Warner, or the embassy people. We may have a few minutes yet.' He looked at her. 'What are you doing?'

'John, can you hold them off? You and Lewis, go out and talk to them or something. Tell them we need an ambulance, a medical team – anything. Just keep them away for as long as possible.'

Glancing at Elliot he knelt down beside her. 'What are you doing?'

'It's time,' she said softly, carefully attaching the next electrode. 'Your big scary bear, remember? Well, it's time to face him down.'

'Lizzie!' It was Alison's voice. 'Elliot, he's struggling again. I – I think it's another convulsion.'

She looked up at Elliot in the mirror. He was shaking his head slowly, eyes tear-filled. 'Go on, Daddy,' she whispered. 'Go to him now.'

Boyd leant forward and kissed her cheek. 'Be careful.'

She smiled. 'Can you hold them off?'

'I'll think of something.' He rose to his feet. 'Lewis! You're with me, let's go.'

Elliot looked at her once more, closed his eyes and turned for the bedroom.

Running. Sprinting flat out across the broad white plain of the lake, knees pumping rhythmically, arms like pistons, flying towards a milky silver disc suspended far ahead between a pale sky and a horizon of gleaming steel. It was icy cold, the clear air dry and brittle, lancing into her lungs, prickling the skin of her cheeks like tiny needles.

Then, as she ran, the ground began to soften under her, lifting and sinking slowly beneath her feet. She ran on, faltered, lost pace and direction, hand darting instinctively sideways, unbalanced by the undulant footing and tilting horizon. She recovered quickly, powered on, a solitary dot of black appearing ahead on the heaving white. She strove towards it, eyes locked, face set, driving through the cloying softness as though through deepening sand, her legs like rubber, feet like lead.

Gradually the dot grew nearer, took shape and form, rising from the pitching white like a black slit in silk. Then a crack like a rifle shot and the ground heaved beneath her, pitching her sideways. She skidded, staggered, crashed down with a stunned gasp, icy wet shocking her skin. Dazed and winded she rolled quickly onto her knees, head reeling, hands scrabbling urgently at the ground about her. Then she was clambering up once more, dragging mired feet from the cloying slush, striving for the black gash.

She charged forward, the fissure widening, spreading before her, a bottomless black void on a heaving plateau of frosted grey. As she drew near she felt a familiar pressure growing around her, a noise like far-off thunder rising in her ears, the air thick and heavy, pulling at her, dragging her back. She wrenched free, resolute and unstoppable, fighting onwards. Then, with a final, guttural shout, she flung herself forward, diving headlong into the gaping black void before her.

Instantly there was a hurricane blast of white hot wind, the ground lurched under Ben's body and the air erupted with noise. Above a dissonant percussive roar that reverberated deep within his stomach, vibrating the earth beneath his prone body, his head was filled with a rising scream of wind and unbroken detonations of air-shattering thunder. He recoiled, gasping at the assault, his knees jerking instinctively up against his chest, arms tight-wrapped over his head.

Hunching into a ball on the ground, he squeezed his eyes shut, sobbing soundlessly, while chaos raged around him like a storm. Then he heard it again. A snatched fragment of sound tossed up to him on the wind like wreckage in a gale. A thin, highly pitched wail that rose imperceptibly from deep within the tumult, soaring high over the storm towards him like a flung lance. It was her voice, Frankie's, she was calling him, calling for him to come, calling his name.

Summoning himself, he raised his head, cupped his hands to his face against the onslaught and slitted his eyes. Lightning filled a pale, grey-orange sky pulsating with heat and noise. Violent arcs of whirling incandescence wheeled through the air. Below, darker, heavier shapes like hard-coloured shadow flashed by in a spinning kaleidoscope of motion.

She was standing in the centre of the maelstrom, facing him, her mouth working soundlessly, her screams snatched from her lips on the wind, hair and clothes flying chaotically. He tried to move, struggled to raise himself, force himself towards her. But the numbing fatigue overwhelmed him, the deadness of his arms and legs dragging at him, pinning him down like a blanket of lead. Grunting with effort he turned onto his side, reaching an arm forward into the swirling abyss, fingers outstretched. Through the howling fog he caught sight of her again, turning about in panic and confusion, searching for him, calling his name. Then the suffocating tiredness overcame him again and his head sank to the ground once more.

'Ben, come on, let's go.' Lizzie's voice, a murmur, suspended close by his ear, soft and warm in his head above the shriek of the tumult. He felt her hand at his neck, an arm sliding under his shoulders. 'Ben, you can't stay here. I need you to get up now, I'll help you.' He raised his head again, drawing lifeless legs reluctantly beneath him, the hands at his chest, lifting beneath his arms until he was on his knees. 'Good boy, that's it, up you come.'

He opened his eyes, searching for Frankie again. She was still there, standing in the eye of the storm. But smaller, further away, with hard, gleaming shapes circling dangerously close all around her like giant wheeling gannets. The arm was at his waist, lifting him, pulling him up, all the while the voice encouraging, cajoling in his head. He rose to his feet, wavering unsteadily. 'That's it! Well done.' He licked his lips, head reeling. 'Now, come on, let's go.' Pushing his swaying body forward against the buffeting gale, he reached out unsteadily, planted his staff and stepped into the flying darkness.

Instantly the storm engulfed him, the circling lights and shapes spinning in a dazzling confusion of noise and colour. His head filled with an explosion of sound, shrieking wind, sky-splitting peals of thunder, above it the sudden violent blatter of a nearby horn blast, shouting, sirens, and a succession of dull, splintering crashes that reverberated away into the distance like receding gunfire. He staggered forward, head down, the arm tightly gripping his waist, the voice at his ear a mesmerizing, non-stop murmur of encouragement.

Lifting his head he squinted forward, searching through the swirling fog and dazzling flashes. Frankie. She was drawing closer, he could see her clearly now. But she was struggling, fighting, her body ducking and bending as though pulled, dragged backwards. She turned her head to him and screamed, her feet planted, arms flailing, body bent almost double, thrashing desperately. 'Ben!' He raised a leaden arm, opened his mouth to shout, but a brilliant flash of lightning burst before his eyes, a blast of hot, thunderous wind and a giant wall of fiery light plunged between them like an express train.

He flinched reflexively, jerking his arm back. 'For Christ's sake!' An anguished shout of alarm floated above the thunder. Then a discordant blare of a truck horn, somewhere far behind him the incongruous tinkling of a shop bell, breathless pounding of running feet, a gasp of horror, 'Sweet Jesus!' and all the while the arm, tightly encircling his chest, the voice, a liquid warm murmur deep within his head. 'It's okay, Ben, let's keep going, you're doing fine.' The wall flashed by, suddenly it was gone. He gritted his teeth, picked up one foot and faltered forward once more.

The thunder was changing, more voices filling the air, more sounds. The tortured screech of machinery, the protesting squeal of tyres, a concussive metallic crashing. 'Ben, Ben can you hear me?' A man's voice, far off. Close by an anguished shout of fright. 'For God's sake, get off the road!' The thunder was receding, the wind dying to a howl, the wheeling flashes slowing. 'That's real good, sweetheart, come on, keep going.' The voice softer, fainter, the grip at his waist growing slacker.

'And don't dilly-dally on the way.' His grandmother, singing.

'Keep going Ben, you're doing so well.' He moved onwards, he was near her now. He could see her clearly, waiting for him, the zigzag parting, the white shirt, the badly knotted tie, her arms outstretched, eyes wide with fear. 'Help me.' A huge wall of shadow was approaching behind her.

'Go to her Ben, quickly now.' The voice a dying whisper, the arm slipping from his waist.

'Mary, Mother of Jesus, just little girls!'

'Ben. Ben! It's Mummy.' Somebody else was counting. The man, he was counting slowly backwards from ten.

'Go on Ben. Go to her, she's waiting.'

'Don't leave.' The arm vanished from him, the voice fading, dropping further and further behind. 'Go on now, you can do it, you're doing just great.' He lifted his feet heavily, stepped forward, wobbling unsteadily onward like a baby. 'Nine, eight, seven . . .'

He glanced behind him, they were thirty yards behind, arms linked, heads together. 'You stay there,' his voice called. They waved cheerily. 'I'll be right back.'

'Six, five, four . . .' He kept lifting his legs, putting them down, moving forward in time with the counting, closing the distance between them. 'Wasnae for your wellies where wud you be!' Her hands were outstretched to him, mouth beseeching wordlessly, behind her the wall of darkness surged towards her.

'It's okay,' he heard his voice saying, mouth moving in slow motion. He held her gaze, stretched out his hand, the darkness rushing towards her, rearing up behind her like a giant tidal wave.

'Three, two . . . ' He raised his arm unsteadily towards her, feet plodding endlessly forward. She stretched out her fingers, the darkness enveloping her, the knotted wood of his roughly hewn staff solid, hard and smooth in her tightly closing palm.

C h a p t e r   1 8

JACK AWOKE WITH A START, WRENCHED FROM A FITFUL, CHAOT-
ically dream-filled sleep by the sound of a large vehicle
manoeuvring close by. He licked sweat from his lip, breathing
deeply while the dreams receded, his throat dry, his head like
wool. Blinking blearily he rolled onto his back, fumbling for his
watch. Outside it was light, the sky clear, liquid early-morning
sunlight slanting across the ceiling above the curtained window,
the busy twitter of birdsong shrill above the raucous throttling
of the vehicle's engine.

Quickly he slipped from the disordered sheets and moved
soundlessly to the window. He reached out and inched the
curtain aside, craning his neck to peer through the narrow slit.

'What is it?' Alison mumbled, her eyes following him from
the bed.

'Removal van. Two doors down.' He watched for a moment
longer then dropped the curtain and turned back into the room.
Her arm was outstretched towards him from beneath the
covers. He padded to her, sat down on the bed, took her hand
in his.

'How are you doing?' she asked softly.

'Okay.' He forced a smile. He lifted her hand, brushed it to
his lips. 'Fine. And you? How did you sleep?'

She settled deeper into the pillow. 'Not bad. You?'

He grimaced. 'So, so.'

She looked up at him anxiously. 'Did you try the pills again?'

'Hate the damn things, take hours to start working, then you spend the whole of the next day blundering about like a bloody zombie.' He patted her hand. 'Don't worry, it'll sort itself out. Cup of tea?'

She smiled sleepily. 'Lovely.'

He pulled on a dressing gown and went out onto the landing, closing the door quietly behind him. He paused outside Frankie's room, then pushed open the door. It stood empty, spotlessly clean, flooded with light, curtains hanging wide. Next door Ben's room was the same. Clean, tidy but unoccupied, the bed neatly made, toys and books incongruously well ordered along the shelves, clothes folded away into drawers. He stared at the empty bed, fragments of nightmare haunting him like distant echoes. Then he closed the door and descended to the kitchen. A while later he heard Alison on the stairs.

'You're not going to believe this.' He nodded towards a pile of mail on the table, as he poured carefully from the teapot. 'Letter from David Gateskill at Myriad.'

'Oh yes,' she said suspiciously. 'And what does he want?'

'Says he's got some outline ideas for establishing a couple of scheduled passenger services into Brussels and Rotterdam.'

'Sounds ambitious.' She accepted the teacup. 'And?'

He picked up the letter. 'And he wants to know if I'd care to have lunch, and a chat "to explore possible areas of mutual interest", whatever that means.'

'But that's wonderful, Jack. It means that he probably wants your help setting it up.'

'My help? Gateskill? I doubt it. The man's a complete shark, hunts alone.' He studied the letter. 'Still, free lunch and all that.' He looked up at her. 'Carol works there now, you know.'

She shrugged. 'Somehow it doesn't seem to bother me. Should it?'

He leant forward, kissed her softly, her mouth warm and wet

with tea. 'My God, you are incredible,' he murmured.

'You're not doing so badly yourself.' She reached up, smoothing his eyebrow with her thumb. 'Are you really all right, Jack?'

'Fine.' He smiled. 'Better every day.' He brightened suddenly, nodding towards the heap of mail. 'There's one there from the USA, Connecticut postmark.' Suddenly a car horn sounded right outside the window. Alison jerked to her feet. 'Good God, it's them!' she said, aghast.

Jack stood up, peering past the heavily green-budded foliage of the cherry tree. 'It *is* them.' He looked at her uncomprehendingly. 'They're hours early.'

'Something must have happened,' she said, moving quickly for the door. A moment later they were hurrying around to the side of the house.

Janet was getting out from the driver's seat. 'Coo-ee, surprise!' She waved cheerily.

Jack breathed out, rolling his eyes at Alison as he held open the gate for her. 'Hello, Mother. Everything all right?'

'Terrific, absolutely super,' she sang lightly, her eyes ringed with tiredness. 'Everyone to bed just ever so slightly late and then up again wonderfully early this morning. Big cry for breakfast at the burger place and we just thought what a terrible shame for Mummy and Daddy to lie in bed all morning and miss out on the fun.' She smiled mischievously. 'What about you two? Good night?'

'Fine, thanks.' The back door of the car popped open and Ben dropped quickly to the pavement. 'Hi Mum, hi Dad. Forgot my roller-blades.' He trotted around towards the boot of the car. Jack stooped to the open door. 'Hello sweetheart, did you have a nice night at Granny's?'

She swivelled her head towards him, grinning lopsidedly. 'Ah-ah.'

*

Dear Jack, Alison, Janet, Ben and Frankie,

Many thanks for your last. Sorry I've been so long getting back to you, it hardly seems possible that it's six months since you guys invaded our shores. Thanks for the package of letters and photos, very good to hear you're all well and that your social services people are seeing sense at last. By the looks of her writing and drawings Frankie is obviously making excellent progress, which is just great news. Thank you, Ben, for all the stuff on classic Chevrolets, although sadly I shall probably be changing the old Impala soon for one of those modern people-mover things which will better suit our needs.

The main news here is that we're looking to move into a place of our own, soon as we can. Elliot's house here in Connecticut is really fine and he's a wonderful host – always doing the cooking and shopping and helping out. But we can't go on abusing his hospitality for ever and in any case the house isn't really ideal. I've been scouting about up north for a little single-storey place that I can fix up just for us. New Hampshire, Maine, Vermont, maybe. Elliot told me how much Lizzie used to love the country up there. Money is something of a problem over the short term, but Elliot keeps picking up the tab for everything and the Perlman family have been incredibly generous. The redoubtable Rose has flown down here from Boston on two or three occasions and leaves embarrassingly big checks every time she does – I'm beginning to get anxious, being a kept man is not quite my style! Once we're properly settled somewhere I'm hoping to set up an office at home and maybe earn a crust doing some freelance legal work.

What else? Oh, yes. Everything went through more or less okay at the DA's office. As predicted, I got suspended pending the outcome of the investigation, but in any case I handed my resignation, there's nothing for me there any more. It's not clear yet what charges if any are going to be pressed over the incident, but I just have a feeling that, with an election year looming, old Bill Warner's mind is on other things and the whole matter is probably going to slide into the deep outfield and get quietly forgotten. Here's hoping.

We put a call through to Nathan Greenwater last week. He's fine, although being pursued hard by the Defense Department. He says it may have something to do with their not being able to get any of the Perlman computer equipment to perform. Apparently when they finally unpacked it all, they found that the hard disks had somehow mysteriously got wiped! Less than pleased, evidently, started out by bombarding Nathan with threats but have since moved on to tempting him with offers of highly paid research posts at their skunk works outside of Washington.

I asked him if he had any news of Lewis. As you may recall, he dropped right out of sight that morning we came down out of the Stamitz place and nobody seems to have seen hide nor hair since. Nathan said he heard nothing for months but then received a newspaper clipping through the mail out of the blue. It was something about a civil liberties organization called Unheard Voice hiring a hotshot lawyer (no names mentioned but guess who) to launch a legal test case against the Department of Defense. Violation of civil rights by unlawful phone tapping or something. I guess that boy's just not cut out for the quiet life.

We're all fine. Lizzie continues to be really well, fit and healthy. She has made wonderful progress over the past few months. It's hard to say for sure whether she is fully aware of herself, and us, all the time or not, but somehow I sense she is and that she is at peace, even when she seems to withdraw for a while. I spend a lot of time just watching her and wondering about that. Right now she's quiet, although her eyes are always on the move. Checking up on us, Elliot says. He is indefatigable in his researches into her condition and confident that her motor and cognitive functions are improving all the time. One day she'll be restored to us, of that I'm certain, but it is going to take time, we have to accept that. For myself I'm quietly hopeful, and happy to just have her here with me. Now that spring has arrived, I spend a lot of time driving her around out in the countryside or down along the coast. She loves it, I know. Me too, just being together and close, that sweet-running little family engine thing we were talking about, remember Jack?

I send you all our very best wishes. As soon as we get settled into the new place I'll pass you our address and then you must come and visit. Janet too, Elliot specifically asked me to pass on his best personal regards to her . . .

God bless.

Love

John

Alison folded the letter carefully into its envelope then sat back on the park bench. 'We must go,' she said pensively.

'Already?' Jack teased, watching idly as a group of youths played football. 'We only just got here.'

She nudged him in the ribs. 'No. The States. To see Lizzie and John, and Elliot, we must go.'

'I know. We will, definitely, soon as we can organize it.' He hesitated. 'I only wish there was something more . . .'

They glanced up, the urgent calls of the footballers and the chatter of birdsong drowned by the diminishing whine of jet turbines. Overhead a small commuter plane was descending towards the airport.

'Are you really all right?' she asked quietly, moving closer.

'Yeah,' he said, pulling a face. He slipped an arm around her shoulder. 'Sleepless, jobless, penniless and twitchier than a turkey at Christmas time. But apart from that, things couldn't be better.'

'Yes they could,' she said. 'And they will be, you'll see.'

They fell silent, surveying the ranks of neatly tended flower-beds across from them. 'The thing is,' he whispered, rubbing her shoulder thoughtfully, 'the one inescapable fact is, that you were right. Right to hold out. Right to insist we try everything, right to explore every last hope. You were right and I was wrong. There's no getting away from that.'

'Jack.' She squeezed his arm. 'That's hindsight nonsense and you know it. There is no right and there is no wrong, you said that, remember? There is only doing the best we can. And you did that. We both did, as a team. And I couldn't have done it without you. I simply wouldn't have been able to. Believe me.' Her eyes searched his. 'Do you? Believe me?'

He pulled her to him, kissed her forehead. 'I believe you.'

'Good.' She settled her head against his chest. A young couple was approaching slowly along the path towards them, pushing a double buggy. 'Look at that,' she said. She was nudging him in the ribs again.

'What?' He glanced up. 'Oh, no,' he said firmly, raising his finger. 'No, no, no way and no.'

'Spoilsport.' She nuzzled his neck, eyes on the approaching buggy. 'It would be great, though. Couldn't you just imagine it? Then we'd be really complete.'

'Give me a break,' he said good-naturedly. He sat back again, turning his face up to the crisp spring sky. The afternoon sun was warm on their backs at last, the air filled with the scent of cut grass and moist flower-beds. Next to the bench sparrows pecked hopefully around a litter bin. A moment later, the young couple with the buggy passed them, identical twins aboard, heads folded together in sleep. 'Yes, well,' he went on, stroking her hair, 'let's just watch how things pan out on the job front, and the money front, and the house front for a bit, shall we?

Then perhaps we'll see.' She snuggled nearer, eyes closed. 'Anyway, we've plenty on our hands right now just keeping tabs on those two.'

She opened her eyes. They were down by the swings. Frankie was sitting in her little electric wheelchair. Ben was balanced precariously on the front of it, arms braced, his feet rolling along backwards on his skates, one hand manipulating the control stick while his sister yelped garbled instructions at him bossily. 'Good grief.' He snorted. 'They look like a mobile motorway pile-up.'

An elderly couple walked slowly past, heads down, heavily muffled in overcoats and hats, arms linked, a small terrier scurrying excitedly from side to side between them on its leash.

'Do you think she's all right?' she said, after a while. 'Lizzie.'

He pulled her closer to him. They gazed at their children. Ben had climbed onto a swing, Frankie's head was up, switching unsteadily from side to side, watching as he soared in ever-widening arcs high into the sky above her. Suddenly she turned towards them and grinned, one arm lifting ponderously in a little sideways wave.

They waved back.